abduction

abduction

Wanda L. Dyson

BARBOUR
PUBLISHING

dedication

Marlene Bagnull, who caught the vision and believed.
Pastor Christi Horowitz of *Rehoboth Ministries,*
an inspiration and mentor of untold value.

And most of all, this book is dedicated to
Danielle van Dam, Samantha Runnion,
and to all the children—treasured on earth, adored in heaven—
you are not forgotten, though you are greatly missed.

prologue

The day he chose to kill her, a warm breeze and bright skies seemed to promise that summer was going to show up on schedule. It was the kind of day kids love. Wish for. Dream of. The kind of day when anything seemed possible and fantasies were ripe for the making. Big, fat, fluffy clouds begged for someone to come and discover the rabbits and the horses and the castles. Parks waited for someone to notice how pleasant it would be to stroll across the lush green grass or stretch out under the branches of a shady oak. Playgrounds anticipated skipping feet, and toys grew anxious for curious hands.

It was the kind of day when little girls giggled and little boys tried not to notice how silly they were when they did.

A perfect day for murder.

He watched them from the top of the bleachers as they skipped out of the gray brick school building with a group of other ten-year-old girls. They wore matching sandals and pink shorts and T-shirts and carried identical yellow and pink book bags. The two girls began walking across the softball field in the direction of their home, talking, giggling, oblivious to anyone who might be watching.

But he was watching.

He had been watching the twins for some time. He knew everything about them—had made it his business to know. They were ten, with identical curly blond hair, smoky green eyes, and bright smiles full of teeth and gums. One tended to be outgoing, making big gestures and laughing boisterously loud. But it was the other one who caught his attention. The shy one. While her sister was looking to be the center of attention, not so Amy. Sweet, quiet little Amy.

They lived on Grafton Street with their mother. Their father had left two months earlier. The mother now worked part-time at Raffe's Department Store in the children's department and wouldn't be home for another hour.

Once home, the girls would go in and stay there until their mother arrived home to make dinner. They had been instructed in all the right things to do—lock the doors, don't open the door to strangers, and if anything happens, call the police.

They didn't know he'd already cut the phone line. The older one would try to call for help but would be at a loss as to what to do. No one had told her about a backup plan in case the phone lines were down—which he greatly appreciated. By the time the mother arrived home, he'd have an hour's head start.

And Amy would be his.

Forever.

Slowly he descended the bleachers, his sneakers making no sound, keeping one eye on the girls. Not that he needed to at this point. He knew from watching them every day exactly which way they went home. And exactly where they crossed the street at Blocker. And exactly where he planned to be when they went past the alley.

Amy.

Sweet little Amy. With the shy smile and the wary looks. He knew she sensed him. He could read it in her eyes. The way she was always looking around for him but never seeing him. It was a game he enjoyed. Watching her grow wary. . .nervous. . .fearful. She knew he was coming for her.

It only made the game more fun.

She would be so frightened. Too frightened to speak. . .to scream. . .to try to run. Oh, yes, she would be an excellent player in the game. She would be so afraid of the pain. So afraid of dying.

So afraid of him.

Anticipation mounted, growing restless deep within him. It was time. All the planning and the watching had led to this day.

This moment.

And now. . .it was time to start the game.

chapter 1

Twenty years later

"Ted? Mr. O'Connell wanted to see you as soon as you got back from lunch." The receptionist, a young woman in her early twenties, handed him three phone messages and then turned her attention back to the ringing phones. "King, Marlow, and Winters. How may I help you?"

"Thanks," Ted murmured as he strolled down the hallway back to the accounting department. Winding his way through the maze of gray cubicles, he nodded to the few faithful souls who had returned early from lunch or had skipped going out to eat altogether. He used to be one of them—foolish enough to think that his talent and intelligence were actually going to be appreciated. It hadn't taken him long to figure it out; production was all that mattered to keep your job; being connected was all you needed to advance.

He pushed through a pair of glass doors and strolled through another maze of cubicles until he reached his own. It was the standard size—small—but tucked along the outside wall, which meant that he at least had a window. As one of four senior accountants, he had a coveted view of the park. But the goal was that corner office that boasted three times the square footage, a view of the park *and* the lake, and a bonus package that made the accompanying salary irrelevant. Of course, unless you were related to someone on the board, or at least a college buddy, you didn't have a chance.

Ignoring the light flashing on his phone, he tossed the messages down on his desk, straightened his tie, and headed for the office of the controller.

O'Connell was as wide as he was tall, with oversized tortoise-rim glasses framing his round face and bald head. Most company employees made the mistake of thinking that either his girth, his ridiculous glasses, or his constant blinking and fidgeting was an indication that he wasn't all that bright. Ted knew better. O'Connell was no idiot. But when it came to numbers, Ted could run circles around the man. Ted's brilliant mind still couldn't trump the fact that O'Connell had a brother on the board. O'Connell surrounded himself with men like Ted to make himself look good.

O'Connell was sitting at his desk staring intently at an open file as Ted rapped gently on the open door. O'Connell looked up, blinked, and waved Ted in.

"Shut the door and have a seat, Ted."

Ted eased the door shut. "You wanted to see me?" He crossed the room, keeping his eyes on O'Connell as he sank in the leather chair in front of the desk. "Anything wrong?"

"Yes." O'Connell closed the file and leaned back, his chair groaning in protest. "How well do you know Maryanne Bubeck?"

Ted shrugged as he relaxed in his chair. "Not well. She's been with us about two years, keeps to herself, seems to do her work with minimum fuss."

"Know anything about her personal life?"

"Not really. I don't think she's married, but I don't know if she ever has been or not. Can't say I know much more than that."

O'Connell pushed his glasses back up his nose and blinked

rapidly a few times as he sighed. "Have you noticed her acting strange lately?"

"Strange?" Ted shook his head again. "Can't say that I have, but her desk is way in the back, so I don't see her that much. Has she done something?"

"We're not sure." O'Connell blinked again as he began tapping his forefinger mindlessly on the arm of his chair. "I don't want to accuse someone without absolute proof."

"Accuse someone of what?"

"Embezzlement."

It was Ted's turn to blink as his mouth dropped. "You're kidding! Bubeck is embezzling from us?"

"We're not sure. Security has already cleared you. That's why I wanted to see you."

Ted jerked back. *"Cleared* me?"

"Until we eliminate suspects, everyone has to be cleared. I hope you understand our position."

"It's just strange to be hearing that I might have been a suspect in something like this."

"This person's been using everyone's access and passwords, but one of the times the system was accessed using your password, you were in Chicago at a conference."

"So how much money has been taken?"

"None. What our suspect doesn't realize is that we have a safeguard on the system. Any time someone tries to transfer funds without using a special access code, it alerts security. Right now our suspect thinks he's moved about a hundred and twenty-five thousand, but he hasn't. The Feds have already been called in."

"The Feds?" Ted blew out a heavy breath. "This is big stuff."

"This is a major crime."

"Well, I'm glad I'm no longer a suspect." Ted's laugh lacked any real amusement. It stung to think that he'd been a suspect in the first place. The years he'd put in. . .the long hours.

"I'm sorry, Ted. It couldn't be helped. Anyway, security has narrowed this down to Miss Bubeck. I'd like you to keep an eye on her and let me know if you notice anything suspicious."

Nodding, Ted rose to his feet. "I'll watch her. Is there anyone else who might be a suspect?"

O'Connell shrugged. "They don't tell me everything they're thinking. For now, they say they're watching Bubeck, so we watch Bubeck."

"Gotcha."

Ted walked slowly back to his desk, his thoughts swimming with money transfers and federal agents. He glanced toward Mary-anne Bubeck's desk, but she wasn't there. Probably not back from lunch. He sank down in his chair, scooted up to his desk, and stared at the phone messages still waiting to be handled.

Why was he being asked to watch Bubeck? Sure, he was the senior accountant in the department, but rarely did that earn him the right to be privy to the inner workings of the department. Did they think he was involved? Were they just setting him up? Were they monitoring his every move? Watching whom he talked to? Listening in on his phone calls?

Convinced he was being watched, Ted stood up, slipped off his coat, hung it up, rolled up his sleeves, and sat back down at his desk. He picked up the phone and returned the first message. Might as well let them see just how boring his day really was.

By five, Ted had a splitting headache. He tossed the budget reports he was working on into his briefcase and drove home. He needed a handful of aspirin and some peace and quiet, but the idea of peace and quiet was shattered the minute he opened his front door and stepped in.

Jessica was screaming at the top of her lungs.

Ted tossed his coat over the back of a sofa chair, pulled his tie loose, and started working on the top button of his shirt as he entered the kitchen. His wife had her head buried in the freezer.

Karen was a petite woman with large, round eyes that hinted of brown, gold, and green. Since having the baby, she was carrying about twenty extra pounds that stubbornly refused to melt away, so she'd taken to wearing baggy clothes that hid her figure. He noted with distaste that she was wearing the same black shorts as the day before. Of course, quite a few things had started to slide since Jessica had been born. The house wasn't quite so spotless, meals ran late most of the time, clothes kept piling up in the laundry room for several days before being washed.

"Ted! I didn't hear you come in." She pulled a small plastic teething ring from the freezer, slipped it into Jessica's mouth, and sighed as the screaming stopped. "I'll be glad when she stops teething." Karen reached up and kissed Ted lightly on the lips. "Dinner will be ready in about half an hour."

Ted leaned down and rubbed noses with his baby daughter. "And how is my precious today? Suffering, huh? I can relate, sweetheart." He pulled out a kitchen chair and sank in it. "Did you call the dealership about the car?"

Karen paled as she turned in his direction, dropping her eyes. "I forgot. I'm sorry."

"You forgot? It's the only thing I asked you to take care of today."

"I know," she mumbled. "I'm sorry."

"Get me some aspirin. I have a raging headache."

Karen set her knife down. "They're in the bathroom."

As she started out of the kitchen, Jessica dropped her teething ring and began to whimper. Karen stopped, turned, and reached for the ring.

Ted glared at her. "Is it too much to ask that you get the aspirin before my head explodes?"

Karen yanked her hand back, dropping the teething ring. "I'm. . .I just thought. . .her screaming. . .your headache." She whirled and ran out of the room, returning quickly to hand him the bottle of aspirin. He poured two into his hand while she rushed over and grabbed a glass, filled it with water, and held it out to him.

As he tossed the aspirin into his mouth, Karen picked up the teething ring and gave it back to Jessica, who clamped down on it. "Bad day at work?" Karen sidled back over to the counter and picked up her knife.

"Tense." Ted set down the glass and stood to his feet. "I'm going to take a shower. What time is your dad supposed to be here?"

Karen glanced up at the clock as she tossed the salad. "You've got about half an hour."

"Plenty of time." He turned at the doorway. "And, Karen, I'm sorry for snapping at you. I just have a lot on my mind."

Karen smiled up at him, her eyes glistening with unshed tears. "No, it's my fault. I should have made a note to myself or something. I'll make sure I do it tomorrow. Go take your shower. It'll help you feel better."

What would help him feel better was if his wife had bothered to dress, clean the house, and maybe even make a simple phone call between soap operas and afternoon talk shows. Karen had always been a little flighty, but ever since the birth of the baby, she seemed constantly overwhelmed by the simplest things. Frankly, Ted wondered if she was starting to lose her grip on reality.

Thirty-five minutes later, Karen wiped her hands on a kitchen towel and then opened the front door. "Hi, Daddy." Smiling, she leaned forward to kiss his cheek.

Walter Timms accepted the kiss as if it were his due and strode through the door, shoulders squared, with a stiff bearing that hinted of the military. His gray hair was trimmed in a severe crew cut that only seemed to emphasize his heavy jowls and thick neck. Tonight he wore neatly pressed dark slacks and a white shirt, no tie, and a gray sports coat. As always, his black shoes were spit-shined and gleaming as he marched toward the kitchen. She trotted behind, nearly running into him when he stepped into the kitchen and stopped. She scooted around him and headed for the stove.

"Ted will be out in a minute," she told him as she opened the oven and checked the roasting chicken. It was golden brown and the little plastic timer had popped. Grabbing the potholders, she reached in and pulled it out, the warm fragrance nearly making her sigh. "He had a rough day at work."

"Men usually do," her father said sharply, all the while inspecting the food and the table and then finally resting those piercing eyes on his granddaughter. "Isn't it a little late for that child to still be awake?"

Karen set the roasting pan on the stove, tossed the potholders on the counter, and rushed forward, lifting little Jessica from her chair. "I was just waiting for you before I put her down. I thought you might want to see her."

"It's important to keep kids on a strict schedule. You should know that."

"I know. I'm sorry. I'll be right back."

Karen passed Ted in the hall. He had changed into neatly pressed jeans and a short-sleeved V-necked pullover. He filled the hall with the scent of English Leather and Irish Spring soap. "Daddy's in the kitchen."

"Did you offer him a drink yet?"

She shook her head, trying to swallow back the feeling of being overwhelmed. "Not yet. I have to get Jess down."

"You should have done that already, Karen. Never mind. I'll get him something. Just don't take too long. I'm really hungry and I'm sure your father is, too."

"I won't be long." Karen slipped into the nursery, fighting back tears. No matter how hard she tried, she couldn't get organized. She couldn't remember the simplest things. She was forever disappointing people, letting them down. *You can't count on Karen.* How many times had she heard that over the years? And how true it was.

"Okay, my precious. Time for bed." Karen tucked Jess under the quilt, taking the time to run a finger down the baby's cheek. Jess smiled up at her, gurgling, kicking her feet in delight. "You're the only one who seems happy with everything I do. You love me, don't you, baby?"

Jess kicked her feet again, pumping her little fists in the air. Karen took that as an unqualified yes. "I love you, too, precious baby."

When she returned to the kitchen, Ted and her father were sitting at the table, tall glasses of iced tea in hand, deep in conversation. Neither man seemed to notice that she had returned as she picked up the potatoes and carried them to the table.

"Do you remember the woman we hired when Bud Griese retired a year or so back?"

"The tall redhead you told me about?" Walter moved his arm out of Karen's way as she set the potatoes down.

"That's her. Well, O'Connell called me into his office this afternoon and told me that they suspect her of embezzling funds. Can you believe that?"

"You can't be serious!" Karen spun around, her eyes wide, mouth gaping. "Embezzling?"

Ted looked up at her. "That's what they say." Then he turned back to her father. "And get this. . .*I* was under suspicion for awhile. I'm cleared now, but they actually thought I might be involved."

Karen's father shook his head. "After you've been with them for years!"

"I know. Needless to say, it unhinged me. I felt like they were staring over my shoulder the rest of the day. My head was splitting by the time I got home."

Karen returned with the chicken and set it on the table in front of Ted. He picked up the carving knife. "And to make matters worse, we're behind at work, so I had to bring some of it home."

"You have to work tonight?" Karen set the bowl of steaming peas on the table and slid into her chair.

Ted sliced a section of chicken and lifted it over to her father's plate. "Quarterly budgets are due soon. I have to work on them."

Her father turned and looked over at her, his disapproval almost palpable. "Where's the salt and pepper?"

Karen looked at the table, then jumped up. "I'm sorry. I forgot."

"She's forgetting everything these days," Ted muttered.

Her father picked up his fork. "I warned you before you married her that she's never had both feet firmly on the ground. You have to stay on her all the time."

"I know. It's just gotten worse since the baby."

Karen set the salt and pepper down in front of her father. "Jess has been teething. It's making her fussy."

"It's too much for her to handle. She's never been real strong and this has her overwhelmed. Maybe I need to hire someone to come in and help." Ted continued speaking as if he hadn't heard her.

"No! I can do this," Karen yelped. "I'm not overwhelmed." Even as she said the words, she knew neither of them would take her seriously. Even the desperate tone in her voice told them that she was indeed in over her head.

She wanted so much to be a good wife and a good mother, but experience had proven her to be a dismal failure at the former, and time threatened to prove her just as great a failure at the latter. How many times had Ted needed a particular shirt, only to find that she had forgotten to wash and iron it? How many times had he found dust on the windowsills or blinds? How many times had he come home to find her rushing to get dinner on the table, only to learn she'd fixed something he didn't care for? He'd ask her to call a doctor, a plumber, or a car mechanic and make an appointment, and she'd get caught up with bathing Jess or playing with Jess. She'd lose herself in enjoying her baby and forget everything else.

"Thought you *had* someone coming in." Karen's father eyed her with stark disapproval, and she dropped her eyes.

Ted shrugged. "Just for two or three days a week right after the baby was born, but she quit. Maybe we need someone full-time. Someone who can handle the baby and keep this place running smoothly."

"I can do it," Karen insisted.

Ted reached over and stroked her arm. "Honey, we're just looking out for you, not condemning you. We know you've never been all that stable."

Karen felt herself shrinking into her chair. "I'm fine. I know I am. It's just that Jessica has been so fussy, and I spend so much time trying to make her feel better."

"You'll never change," her father accused. "Quit making excuses and just accept the way you are."

Karen flinched as she stared at her plate, her appetite gone. Maybe if she made a list of everything she needed to do every day and stuck to it, crossing things off as she finished them. . .got organized. Other women did it; surely she could, too.

But she wasn't like other women. Even as a child, her father had regularly pointed out her weaknesses and faults. She was lazy, she was scatterbrained, she had her head in the clouds, she was irresponsible, she was stupid, she was worthless. The list was as endless as the daydreams she sank into when life got too hard.

She frequently stared at other women on the street. They seemed so smart and successful. She pictured herself just like them. Capable and admired. Someday. Someday she'd walk out of her house with a briefcase in hand, dressed in a smart gray pinstripe suit with a silk blouse with her hair neatly twisted on top of her head. Someday everyone would stop and stare and envy her. Someday everyone would look at her with respect. Someday she'd figure out how to be better at everything.

"Karen, are you listening to me?"

Karen jerked her head up and stared over at her husband, desperately trying to recall what he had been saying. The words eluded her. "I'm sorry. I wasn't listening."

"There's a news flash," her father snapped.

Ted sighed, his impatience flowing over her like a shroud. "I asked you if you made any dessert."

"Oh, yes." Karen jumped to her feet, reaching for plates. "Strawberry cake. I'm sure it will be delicious." As soon as she said it, she knew she'd made a mistake. Dread swamped her as Ted narrowed his eyes.

"When did you have time to bake a cake?"

Swallowing hard, Karen dropped her eyes. "I didn't."

"Then where did it come from?"

"Rene dropped it off," she whispered.

"I didn't hear you. And surely if I did, I didn't hear you correctly. Did you actually say that you had that woman over here today? I thought we discussed this before. I don't want you falling into that woman's clutches."

"What woman is this?" Walter asked, looking from Karen to Ted.

"She's a neighbor. And a pest. Always sticking her nose into other people's business. One of those women's libbers, too. She took one look at Karen, saw a sweet young woman, and decided to make it her life's work to convert Karen to her way of thinking."

"Oh, no," Karen insisted. "She's just really nice. And I didn't invite her over; she just dropped over with the cake and. . ."

"Like I said," Ted repeated firmly, "sticking her nose in where it isn't wanted."

"She's just out meeting people." Karen looked over at her father, hoping he would help diffuse Ted's anger. "They just moved in. Her husband is the new pastor at. . ."

"So she's trying to steal you away from your church."

"No." Karen sighed heavily, accepting defeat. "Of course not."

Ted waved his hand through the air, cutting through the conversation like a sword, a clear indication to Karen that the subject was to be dropped. For now. "Is the coffee made yet?"

She stepped back, eager to diffuse the tension. "I'll put it on right away. It won't take long."

"Oh, well." Ted frowned, pushing his chair back from the table. "We might as well wait in the living room."

Karen's father shot her a hot look as he followed Ted from the room. "You'd think she'd have learned something from her momma. Now, there was a woman who understood and appreciated what a man goes through. Always took good care of me. Had things done and ready when I needed them."

Karen tuned her father out as she measured the coffee. Her mother had explained that a man works hard all day and all a woman has to do is take care of the home and children for him. It was her job, her God-given responsibility. Karen's mother died of cancer when Karen was seventeen, and it would seem most of those lessons had died with her.

She'd just have to try harder. Make lists. Pay attention. She'd prove to Ted and her father that she could do this.

Karen cut thick slices of cake and set them carefully on plates. Strawberries and cream eased down off the cake and onto the plate. Ted's animosity toward Rene was something Karen couldn't quite understand. From the first time the woman had stepped foot in the yard, offering a smile and an introduction, Ted had shunned her. It made no sense, really. Rene had never said one unkind word about Ted, although Karen had observed unease in the woman's eyes when she'd shaken his hand. Ted had decided that he didn't like the woman and had forbidden Karen from becoming friends with her.

While Karen couldn't be rude and snub the woman the way Ted could, she tried to honor Ted's feelings and not pursue a relationship with Rene. Rene seemed to understand. Every once in awhile, Rene would drop off cookies, a pie, a cake, or some little item for Jessica, tell Karen she was praying for her, and leave.

The coffee pot choked out its last bit of brew. Inhaling deeply, Karen smiled as the aroma filled her senses. She didn't like the taste of coffee all that much, but she loved the smell.

Ted appeared suddenly in the doorway. "What are you doing?"

Karen lifted a plate and smiled as she held it out to him. "I was just getting ready to bring you and Daddy your cake."

"Jessica has been screaming for the past five minutes. Didn't you hear her? Or have you been off in one of your daydreams again?"

Karen shoved the plate into Ted's hands and ran down the hall toward the nursery. Sure enough, Jess was screaming, her face red from the effort, her eyes filled with tears. "Oh, baby, I'm so sorry. I didn't hear you. What's the matter, sweetheart?"

Karen lifted Jess into her arms and cradled her close, humming as she began to pace, trying to soothe.

"Does this happen often?"

Karen looked up at her husband standing in the doorway, coffee in hand, concern in his eyes. She shook her head. "No, of course not."

"How do you know? You didn't hear her tonight. I'm really concerned, Karen. I never thought that you'd put our child at risk, but I'm not so sure now."

"I was just caught up with. . ."

"Your mind was wandering again, honey." He sighed heavily. "You get lost in your mind and you don't hear anything going on around you. I can be talking to you. Jess can be screaming. And you're off somewhere, lost in some fantasy world."

Karen swallowed hard as she held Jess tightly. The baby squirmed.

"Karen, don't squeeze her so tight. You're hurting her."

Immediately Karen eased up on her embrace.

"She's not a toy, Karen. Do you understand that?"

"Of course I do." Karen could feel her lip quivering, her throat tightening.

Ted reached out and stroked Karen's cheek, brushing away a lone tear. "Honey, I'm just concerned, okay? I worry about you and the baby. On top of that, I have all this pressure at work. It's not a good time for you to fall apart on me."

"I'm fine. I swear, Ted. It's just been a bad day."

He stared at her, searching for something. She held his gaze, practically willing him to believe her. To trust her. She wasn't going to hurt Jess. She wasn't.

Never.

chapter 2

Monday, April 10

Karen yawned as she shuffled down the hall, tying her robe, her slippers slapping softly against her bare feet. Fatigue plagued her. Jess had been crying nearly nonstop all weekend. Ted had merely apologized for being unable to help and spent most of his time at the office.

Even as she rubbed her eyes, trying to wake up, she was looking forward to lifting Jess from her crib and hearing those soft mews of recognition. To cradling her close and smelling that incredible mix of baby powder, shampoo, and Jessica. To stroking those sweet little hands as she dressed Jessie in a day romper.

Karen pushed open the nursery door. The first gray light of the day slipped through the open curtains, making the Hundred Acre Wood mural on the wall appear far more haunted than harmless. The Winnie-the-Pooh mobile hung over the crib, eerily silent and still.

With an overwhelming sense of dread, she crossed the room, trying to understand exactly what could be so very wrong. Fear crawled up her spine.

When she reached down for the quilted pink comforter, Karen

was surprised to find her hand trembling. She lifted the comforter, but sweet little Jessica was not curled up beneath it. She looked around the nursery. No Jessica. Not on the floor. Not on the changing table. Not in the rocking chair.

It was ridiculous to think she would be. Jessie was only seven months old—far too young to have crawled out of the crib. Her absence made no sense at all.

Karen's stomach clenched.

Spinning on the heel of her slipper, she rushed from the room, down the hall, and into the living room. There was no cooing of contentment or whimpering for food. The playpen was empty, as was Jessie's swing. In the kitchen, the Tigger- and Piglet-decorated highchair sat empty.

Jessie? Where are you?

The truth taunted her without a trace of mercy. Her baby was gone! Swallowing the need to scream, Karen tried to convince herself that Ted had taken Jess to bed and she just hadn't noticed the tiny baby curled up between them.

Walking quickly and still fighting to control her hysteria, she headed back down the hall, ignoring all the pictures of Jessica on the wall.

In the master bedroom, she yanked at the covers on her bed, causing her husband to groan sleepily and roll over. Jess wasn't there either.

"Ted? Where's Jess?"

"Hmmm?" Ted blinked furiously as Karen snapped on the light. His dark curly hair was mussed, tufted at odd angles. He ran his fingers through it, but it didn't help. Until he went through his daily routine of shampoo, mousse, dryer, and styling brush, it would be out of control. The curse of curly hair, he often complained.

"Jess?" He yawned as he stretched. "Crib, of course."

"No!" Karen felt the hysteria rising now, clawing at her. "She's gone! I can't find her anywhere!"

Ted sat up, rubbing his face as he stirred from sleep. "Ridiculous. Too young to get up and walk away."

"I know that!" Karen snapped. "But I can't find her!"

With a heavy sigh, Ted rose to his feet. Tugging at his red plaid pajama pants, he strode with defined purpose across the room and out into the hall. He was confident. Assured. And prepared to prove her wrong.

Karen desperately wanted him to prove her wrong. She stood and waited, wanting him to walk back into the room with Jess cradled in his arms and laugh at her foolishness. For once, she wouldn't mind if he raised that eyebrow and smirked at her, mocking her fears.

Ted returned. Alone. "What did you do with the baby, Karen?"

"Nothing!" she screamed, clenching her fists. "She's gone!"

The bewilderment on his face gave way to a new kind of determination. "Call the police. I'll get dressed."

Karen snatched at the phone and dialed. "Someone stole my baby! Please help me!"

By the time Karen had gone through her story three times and given her address twice, Ted had returned to stand behind her, his hands resting lightly on her shoulders. She leaned back into him as she listened to the dispatcher assure her that someone was on the way.

Her hand dropped and Ted reached down to take the phone from her. "They're coming," Karen mumbled as Ted put down the phone.

"Why don't you get dressed?" Ted instructed. "I'll make coffee."

Karen swiped at her tears. "I don't understand, Ted. How could someone take our baby?"

"The police will find her." He gently pushed her forward. "Get dressed."

Karen nodded and stumbled into the bathroom. Get dressed.

Have coffee. It was all too normal. Yet nothing was normal. Nothing would be normal until Jessica was home in her arms. Who would take her? And why?

She went through the motions of brushing her teeth, combing her hair, and slipping into clothes. Her mind was whirling with thoughts of Jessie. It wasn't as if she'd been negligent and left Jess unattended somewhere in the park or in the car. Her baby had been safe and sound in her own crib.

Polly Klaas had been asleep in her bed and it hadn't been safe at all. Someone had taken her and killed her. Karen's hand flew to her mouth, choking back a sob. And little Danielle VanDam. She had been taken from her bed, too. And found dead.

Oh, God, please, not my Jessica. Don't let this be happening!

"Karen?"

Ted's voice cut through her thoughts. She turned and fled to the kitchen where he was pouring coffee into blue mugs. "Ted! What if we never get our baby back?"

Ted set down the coffeepot. "Don't go looking at worst-case scenarios before the police even arrive."

That confidence again. Optimistic, unwavering, and strong—the result of being an only child, she was sure. Ted's parents had given him every opportunity to succeed, every encouragement to overcome, every resource to believe in himself above all else. Ted didn't know *how* to lose.

Karen nestled her head against Ted's shoulder. "I want my baby home. I want Jess home safe and sound. I don't think I could stand it if I was to lose her. I'd just die."

"Don't think like that." Ted stroked her back and then pulled away. "The police will find Jessie and everything will be fine."

"What if. . ."

"Don't, Karen. Don't even think it." He stepped back, reaching for his coffee mug. "If you look for trouble, you're bound to find it. Stay positive."

She nodded and he rewarded her with a warm smile of approval. "That's my girl. Trust me, sweetheart. We'll get our baby back."

Two police officers arrived a few minutes later. They didn't offer any such assurances. After briefly interviewing Karen and Ted, they called for more help. An hour later, Karen and Ted had been pushed aside to wait in the living room while two more uniformed officers, a crime photographer, and a detective wandered through the house. "Gathering evidence," they said.

It was the detective who had Karen trembling. He was a tall man with dark hair and green eyes, but he wasn't the least bit friendly. She almost felt as though he had judged her and found her guilty of some unspeakable crime. One of the police officers told her Detective Johnson was good at his job. She reasoned that was because of his icy stare. What criminal wouldn't confess when faced with that?

Only Karen didn't have anything to confess to. She had committed no crime. But someone had, and she wanted this detective to find her baby.

Now.

Instead, he continued walking through the house, eyeing pictures on the wall with an intensity that threatened to melt the photographs. She wanted to scream at him to stop admiring Jessica's pictures in the hallway and go find her! Didn't he understand that every moment he wasted was another moment the kidnapper had to get farther away?

Wiping at the tears streaming down her face, she looked up at Ted. His hair was in wild disarray, his face pale, and his eyes rimmed with red.

"Ted?" she whispered, not realizing how raw her throat was until the word came out.

Her husband looked down at her from his perch on the arm of the sofa and squeezed her hand. "It'll be okay, honey."

"But they're not even looking for our baby!" She was ready to stand and yell at the detective when he finally sauntered over, pinning her and Ted with that cool arrogance.

"Okay, let's go over this again. You went to the nursery. . ."

Karen clenched her fists. "How many times do you have to hear this?" The detective narrowed his bottle-green eyes. A twitch developed in his cheek. "Someone broke into our house and stole my baby girl! Why aren't you doing anything! Why are you all just standing around?"

Detective Johnson flipped open his notebook, clearly deciding to ignore her, and clicked open his pen. "Why don't you tell me the events of last night? Was Jessica crying a lot? Maybe being a little too fussy?"

Suddenly Karen understood. "You think I did this? You actually think I would hurt my little Jess?"

Ted reached down, his hand patting her on the shoulder. "Honey, it's just procedure."

"No," Karen stated emphatically. "I did *not* hurt our baby. Now, go find her."

Detective Johnson sighed heavily and looked at Ted. "What time did you put the baby to bed? Was she crying? Teething, perhaps?"

"Stop it!" Karen rose to her feet, only to have Ted pull her back down.

"Calm down, Karen. They have to ask. Just answer their questions so they can get on with the investigation." Ted held her close, wrapping strong, confident arms around her.

But Karen was too angry to be comforted. Her baby was gone and no one seemed to think this was a big deal. Even Ted was calm. And that only increased her frustration.

Pushing away Ted's arms, Karen jumped to her feet. "Doesn't

anyone get it? Am I the only one here who seems to understand what's happened?" Her voice continued to climb to a near-hysterical pitch. Ted reached for her, but she swatted his hand away. "My infant daughter is missing. Now, someone had better get out there and find her and bring her home to me safe and sound! Do your job!"

"Calm down, Mrs. Matthews. You're not helping your daughter with all these hysterics." Detective Johnson leaned back in the sofa chair, tapping his pen against his knee, one eyebrow lifted.

"If *your* child had been taken, what would you be doing?" she demanded angrily.

"I'd be cooperating with the police so they could find her. Or don't you want us to find her?"

The question hit Karen like a fist in the face. She staggered back, lost her balance, and found herself sitting back on the sofa, Ted's hand on her shoulder. "That has to be the stupidest question anyone has ever asked me."

Detective Johnson raised his pen over his notebook. "Then let's get through this so we can find her."

Karen leaned back into the sofa, seeking support, shaking as the tears started again. She didn't even try to wipe them away as she stared at the detective. *Why are you doing this to me, God?*

There was no bright light from heaven to ease the pain. No angelic visitor to comfort her. No thundering voice or soft whisper with the answers to the questions that tormented her heart. The heavy silence was broken only by the sound of the clock in the living room marking the seconds, the minutes, the hours since her daughter's disappearance.

The front door burst open and Karen's father came barreling in, a police officer hard on his heels. "Sir, you can't go in there!"

"It's my daughter's house! I can go in if I bloody well feel like it!"

"Daddy!" Karen jumped to her feet. "Someone took Jess!" She

flung herself in his arms. He held her stiffly, patting her awkwardly on the back. "Now, now. Gonna be fine, girl." He looked over at Ted. "What happened?"

"Someone kidnapped Jessica."

Walter reached out and placed his hand on Ted's shoulder. "Oh, dear heavens. What can I do to help?"

Karen eased out of her father's arms and sank down on the sofa, clutching her arms around her stomach. She could hear the sound of the detective's voice as he directed questions at her father and Ted, but she turned inward, tuning them out. *Please, God. Help them find Jess.* Doubts assailed her as the pain welled up, choking her. She clenched her fists against her stomach as she began to wonder, *Oh, God, what could I have done?*

chapter 3

J J stared up at the wall where two young faces on glossy paper stared back at him. Two beautiful, helpless children. Six-year-old Gina Sarentino: black hair, brown eyes, a missing front tooth, pierced ears. Seven-month-old Jessica Matthews: light brown hair, hazel eyes, small mole or birthmark on her cheek.

Both of them gone without a trace.

Gina Sarentino had been walking home from a neighbor's shortly after four in the afternoon on April 3 when she disappeared.

Jessica Matthews had disappeared from her crib, in her home, in the middle of the night, with her parents just down the hall.

This newest case had him scratching his head.

And looking twice at the parents.

The sight of the empty crib had set his stomach churning. He knew that had caused him to be unusually rough on the parents. The baby might still be alive. This could be a simple kidnapping case. Someone might call with a ransom demand.

The Matthews' house was an unassuming ranch in an upper-middle-class neighborhood. The furnishings were simple but moderately expensive. There was no sign of forced entry. No sign of an intruder. And no sign of seven-month-old Jessica Matthews.

JJ's instincts were still screaming that nothing was the way it appeared. After eighteen years on the force, he'd learned to listen to his instincts. No one had broken into that home and stolen the baby. He'd stake his badge on that.

Had they killed the baby by accident? Shaken it to death? Dropped it? Or had it been deliberate? Tired of the crying and the diapers, had they simply smothered it and buried it?

Oh, they had been properly upset. Karen Matthews had been sitting on the edge of the sofa, her bare feet primly flat on the floor, her face buried in her hands as she sobbed uncontrollably. Academy Award material. The husband, Edward "Just Call Me Ted" Matthews, sat next to his wife, appearing visibly shaken, upset, disturbed.

He'd spent most of the previous day with them, taking reports, gathering evidence, talking to neighbors, and studying the parents. They had cried, pleaded, begged. They wanted him to find their baby.

He just couldn't get a good read on them.

JJ leaned back in his chair and frowned at the crowded room. The Monroe County Sheriff's Department was a three-story brick building right across the street from the courthouse. Built in the early 1950s, it was once a modern, state-of-the-art facility. Fifty years later, it barely kept up with safety standards.

The first floor housed the patrol officers and processing. The second floor accommodated Narcotics, Vice, the detective divisions, and the chief's office. The third floor consisted mainly of holding cells and interrogation rooms.

The elevator, installed in 1955, was a temperamental piece of machinery that broke down more often than not and managed to run just perfectly as soon as elevator repair showed up. After getting stuck in the elevator a few times, most people opted to use the stairs.

The second floor was divided into four areas. Narcotics and

Vice were arranged on the south side of the floor. Homicide and Criminal Investigations took up the north side.

When Gina Sarentino was reported missing, Chief Harris had called JJ into his office and handed him the case file. *"Vince Sarentino is a close personal friend of the mayor. We're going all out on this one. Find the girl."*

The department had formed a special task force led by JJ that included three other detectives and a couple of gophers. They took up residence in a small conference room off the main bullpen. Somehow JJ managed to fit two desks, a conference table, a computer, and a coffeemaker in the room before running out of space.

Anything you need, Johnson, just ask.

What he needed was more manpower and a larger space in which to work. He tripped over himself nearly every time he came in the room.

Marsha, one of the second floor's shared secretaries, appeared in the doorway. "Harris wants to see you."

JJ lurched out of his chair with the usual dread. Harris wasn't a bad guy. Just a pain to deal with.

"Yes, sir?" JJ asked as he stepped inside the chief's office.

Harris explained and handed JJ a slip of paper.

Stunned, he stared hard at Harris. "You can't be serious!"

"I am quite serious."

"Sir, with all due respect, have you lost your mind? This is a police station, not a carnival."

Harris glared. "You'll do it, Johnson, or you'll turn in your badge."

chapter 4

Z oe pulled her suitcase out of the car trunk. She could still hear the questions ringing in her ears now six and a half hours later.

"Tell me, Miss Shefford, how did you know the girl was dead?"

"Miss Shefford! Miss Shefford! How was she killed?"

"Miss Shefford! Can you tell us what shape she was in?"

Walking briskly to her front door, she pulled the suitcase behind her, wheels squeaking across the brick as she tried to forget the reporters, the questions, the publicity.

And that police chief! He'd all but manhandled her to stand there in front of the cameras while he went on and on about what a fantastic job she'd done.

Right.

She'd done what she always did. Refused to answer their questions, turned their attention to the police, and caught the first flight home.

Home.

Zoe wrinkled her nose as she stepped through the door of her townhouse. She had forgotten to take out the trash. After six days away, the house smelled a little ripe.

Leaving her suitcase by the door, she headed for the kitchen, opening windows as she went along. She tossed the mail on the kitchen table and immediately opened the back door, setting the trash can on the deck.

The refrigerator didn't offer much hope of a meal. She hadn't bothered to shop before leaving. Then again, she hadn't expected to rush out at 4:00 A.M. to catch a plane to Grafton, West Virginia.

The orange juice didn't look promising. A week beyond the expiration date, the milk didn't smell too fresh. And the iced tea was cloudy. Zoe did find a can of root beer behind the butter and was more than happy to settle for that.

She turned on the radio and sorted the mail. Bills in one stack, junk mail in another, and anything that looked interesting enough to open in the final stack. Junk mail went out the back door and into the trash can. She tossed bills in the basket on the counter.

When the DJ started reading the news headlines, Zoe kicked off her shoes and wiggled her toes. She was preparing to head upstairs to unpack her suitcase when she heard the kind of news she always dreaded.

The lead story reached Zoe's ears as news bites: Another missing child—an infant; no leads yet; disappeared from her crib; parents pleading for safe return; second missing-child case in less than two weeks; police form special task force.

Zoe sagged against the doorframe. Too many missing children and too many parents pleading with tear-streaked eyes and soul-wrenching sobs for a safe return. Too few parents getting their wish. Zoe knew the numbers all too well: nearly sixty thousand non-family abductions each year. More than a hundred missing children found murdered. Many more never found.

How well she understood the parents' pain.

She heard the phone ring in her head before it actually did.

Staring at it, she fought back the dread that always came with these calls—the helplessness, the hopelessness, the gut-wrenching understanding that she was their last hope.

They recalled her successes.

She recalled her failures.

Taking a deep breath, she picked up the phone. "Hello?"

"Miss Shefford? Zoe Shefford?"

"Speaking." *But far from willingly. Go ahead. Get it over with. Tell me about the baby. Tell me how sweet she was. How much she is loved. I know.*

"This is Detective Johnson from the Monroe County Sheriff's Department. I was given your number."

"I just heard about it on the radio. They said the baby was taken two days ago. What about the other child?"

A pause and a heavy sigh. "Nine days."

Zoe curled her fingers around the cord. Nine days. Too long. If they didn't have a solid lead on the child within 48 to 72 hours, the chances were slim to none of ever seeing the child alive again. "How soon do you need to talk to me?"

There was another pause on the other end of the line, and she could almost see this man scratching his head, wondering if he was doing the right thing. It forced a wistful but fleeting smile out of her.

"Uh. . .sometime today? I don't know how these things work."

She did. She took another deep breath. "I just got home from West Virginia." The memory shot through her; a little girl, seven years old with big brown eyes, brown hair, and two missing front teeth. Kathleen. Buried behind an old hunting lodge some twenty miles from nowhere in the mountains.

"Yeah. . .I heard that you found her."

"Too late," she reminded him sadly. Two days too late. She shook off the memory. "Anyway, I just need to unpack, shower, and change, and then I'll come down to the station. You know I can't promise anything?"

"Yes."

Zoe hung up the phone, dropping her forehead against the wall. *Where are you, Jessica? Talk to me, baby. Tell me where you are.*

Detective JJ Johnson stared at the phone, his brow wrinkled, his fingers drumming an erratic pattern on the desk blotter. He was up to his ears in dead ends and was not at all happy about calling Zoe Shefford. But the pressure was on from as high up as the governor. Pressure to give anything a shot. Zoe Shefford was the biggest "anything shot" he'd heard of.

A psychic?

She was the best, they said. Amazing, they said. Had found more than forty-seven children, they said.

He didn't much care what they said.

A psychic? What kind of detective used a psychic? Not him. Nope. Not JJ Johnson. He relied on his own talent, instincts, and hard work. Bringing in a psychic was like kicking him while he was down.

He didn't like it. He didn't like it at all. Calling in some voodoo queen was admitting he didn't have a clue what he was doing.

JJ imagined her slithering in with black hair, heavy black eyes, a scarf tied around her forehead, a ton of dime-store beads around her neck, and a crystal ball in her bag.

And expecting him to hang on her every word.

Not in this lifetime.

It was his job to lead this task force, and he had no intention of handing over the reins to some decked-out demagogue of deceit.

But try telling that to the boss. Harris had narrowed those

beady little eyes and handed him the psychic's phone number. *"I want these kids found and I want this guy in custody. The governor wants us to call this woman. If you can't find them, maybe she can."*

Right. And pigs fly with yellow wings.

Since the boss ordered it, he didn't have any choice but to let her do her hocus-pocus routine. Then he'd get back to what he did best. Good old-fashioned detective work. He didn't need tarot cards, crystal balls, and magic wands. His tools were ballistics, forensics, and DNA.

JJ's partner, Matt Casto, stuck his head in the office. "You call her?"

Matt was probably the closest thing to a best friend that JJ had. He had gone through the academy with JJ, and although they were never partners on patrol, they remained close friends. JJ made detective first. Matt followed a year later. Now they were both assigned to the same task force.

Tall with blond hair and gray eyes, Matt was a dedicated flirt. There wasn't a female officer worth her badge who hadn't been hit on by Matt Casto. But he was a good officer, a good friend, and a great detective. JJ was glad Harris assigned him, although JJ would never let Matt know that.

JJ nodded as he closed one of the case files. "I called her. She'll be over in a couple of hours. Anything on the fingerprints yet?"

"Nope. Walt says another couple of hours at least." Matt stepped in, closing the door behind him. He glanced around the room, frowning. "Why do you always keep this place so dark?" He strode purposefully across the room and flipped open the blinds.

"I like it dark. Helps me think." JJ exaggerated his response to the light pouring into the room, blinking furiously at Matt and shielding his eyes with his hand. "Do you have to open them all the way?"

Matt shook his head and closed them a little, subduing the light. "You are a sad man, JJ." His gaze flickered over the photos tacked on the wall but didn't linger. They narrowed in on JJ. "You think the parents killed the Matthews kid, don't you?"

JJ leaned back, making the old metal chair squeak in protest. "I just don't know. At times when I listened to Karen Matthews, I could believe everything she was saying, and other times. . .well, my instincts were screaming that they know where that kid is."

"Harris isn't buying that."

"Nope. He thinks it's related to the other kidnapping."

"We have no sign of forced entry." Matt straddled a chair and stretched out his long legs. "No muddy tracks on the nursery carpet, and the parents swear they never heard a thing."

JJ scratched the side of his head. "But there *are* tracks in the backyard going right up to the nursery window. It was raining, and there was mud under that window. If the perp had come through that window, why aren't there any tracks on the carpet?"

Matt shrugged. "Unless he took his shoes off."

JJ tilted his head, pondering. "Maybe, but it doesn't feel right. You're about to break into a house and steal a baby—are you going to take the time to take off your shoes and then have to struggle to get back into them with a baby in your arms? What if the child wakes up and starts to cry? Are you going to risk running and leaving your shoes for the police? I don't think so."

Matt played out the scenario in his mind.

When JJ looked over at Matt, Matt was peering through the door of the office.

"Isn't that Mrs. Sarentino?" he asked.

JJ nodded. "Sure is." He eyed the petite twenty-five-year-old woman with a heavy heart. Her brown hair was barely combed and pulled back in a clip. Her light brown eyes were red-rimmed and her cheeks splotchy. Her shoulders were slumped, and it wasn't because of the chubby little cherub perched on her hip. This woman was suffering, and there was little JJ could do about it.

Opening the door, JJ filled the doorway. She caught sight of him. "Detective?"

He backed up, swinging his hand in a wide sweeping motion to invite her in. Matt stood up and perched on the corner of JJ's desk so that Annamarie Sarentino could use the chair.

JJ shut the door behind them. "What can I do for you, Mrs. Sarentino?"

She gazed up at him, hopeful. "I was. . .have you heard anything at all?"

"I'm sorry, no. We're doing everything we can, but we have nothing to tell you yet." JJ wished he could give her a different answer. "Have you talked to your ex-husband?"

She nodded slowly as the tears streaked down her cheeks, and she shifted the baby in her lap. "He called me last night."

"Is he coming out here to help you?"

"He's been here. He flew in with his new wife the day after Gina. . ." She stifled a sob. "He said he's been in touch with the mayor, who assured him that you're doing everything you can. But I needed to come ask you myself." She lifted her face to his. "I'm sorry if I'm bothering you."

"You're not, Mrs. Sarentino. I'm just concerned about you. Isn't there anyone who can be with you right now? You shouldn't be going through this alone." JJ slowly eased down into his chair.

Annamarie shook her head. "I don't have any family close, and they can't afford to take off from work and fly out here or anything. I'll be okay."

The tears started flowing again. She sniffled and pressed a tissue to her nose while she looked around. When she spotted Jessica's picture on the wall, she stiffened.

"Is she. . .the other one?"

JJ glanced up. "The other missing child? Yes."

"Such a sweet-looking baby. The parents must be devastated."

He didn't bother to comment. What could he say? This woman was as different from Karen Matthews as beef was from chicken. Karen Matthews wasn't devastated. She was only pretending to be. Mrs. Sarentino, on the other hand, was struggling to cope with a recent divorce from her childhood sweetheart, a toddler, and now the disappearance of her six-year-old daughter. This woman broke his heart.

"I'm going to do everything I can, Mrs. Sarentino. I promise you that."

She nodded slowly and wearily climbed to her feet. "I know, Detective. And I appreciate everything you've done. I just miss my little girl, and I can't help wondering what. . ."

"Don't," JJ interjected quickly. "Don't give up hope yet."

"It's been nine days. And each day that goes by. . ."

"I know. But we'll find her. We won't leave a single stone unturned."

"I just never should have let her go out to play. I just didn't think something could happen right there on our own street." The baby whimpered and she tucked his head under her chin, reassuring him. "You'll call me if you find out anything?"

"I will. Immediately."

Stunned and dazed, Karen wandered from room to room picking up one thing and placing it somewhere else, oblivious to what she was doing. Her mind wouldn't stop spinning. She couldn't hold a coherent thought for more than a few seconds before it was gone. Maybe Ted was right. Maybe she was on the verge of a nervous breakdown. Maybe she was losing her mind. Maybe she had. . .

No. She couldn't have hurt Jess. Surely she'd remember that if she had. She couldn't be capable of such a thing. She just couldn't be. She loved her baby.

But Detective Johnson had made it perfectly clear that he had two suspects. She and Ted. That was it. He wasn't even considering the possibility that someone else had done this. He was going to be watching their every move. And in the meantime, the real culprit was taking Jessie farther and farther away.

Why me, God? What did I do to deserve this?

Choking back a sob, Karen made her way across the kitchen, her hand clutching at the counter. That simple act kept her from falling flat across the sun-washed floor in hysteria.

She felt invisible. Except for the eyes of Detective Johnson boring down the back of her neck. She wasn't sure she would ever feel free of his anger and his conviction. And he had convicted her. She'd been weighed and judged, declared guilty. End of story. Case closed.

Suddenly a familiar sound penetrated the misery. The phone was ringing. She nearly ran to it. Hoping. Maybe.

"Hello?"

"Karen? Why didn't you call me? I just heard the news!"

"Ray." Karen didn't know whether or not she was glad to hear her brother's voice. They had never been particularly close, and the rift between them had only widened after she married Ted.

"Are you okay?"

"No. My daughter is missing, Ray, and the police think I did it. I don't know what to do."

"Call a lawyer! Hasn't Ted done that already, or is he still running around believing he can handle everything by himself?"

Karen flinched at the sarcasm—and the truth buried in the midst of it. "No, he hasn't hired a lawyer. I don't think he realizes that the police suspect us."

"Look, Karen. It's common police procedure to look at the parents first. They'll clear you. And in the meantime, they'll still be looking for other suspects. They'll find Jessica."

Karen swiped at the tears that were marring her vision again.

"Karen?"

"I'm here." She could hear a faint clicking in the background and could almost see her older brother tapping his desk with his pen, a habit he'd never lost. He was always tapping. The table, his books, countertops, steering wheels. It had driven their father nuts. One of her strongest childhood memories was of him yelling at Ray to "stop that infernal tapping."

A faint smile curled at her pale lips as she pulled out a kitchen chair and dropped into it. "Stop that infernal tapping."

There was a quick burst of laughter from Ray. "You never change."

Karen's smile faded quickly. That was something her father said about her. And it wasn't a compliment. "No. I guess I don't."

"Hey, Karen. I'm sorry. I didn't mean it the way the old man does. I like you the way you are."

"Naive and helpless?"

"Naive, maybe. Helpless? Only because Ted makes you think you are."

The tapping started again and she realized he was getting upset thinking about Ted. "Will you come, Ray?"

The pause. The silence. It told her the truth before his words did. "You know I can't, Karen. I'd more than likely punch the guy in the mouth before I was there five minutes. I'm here for you. You need to talk, call me. But don't ask me to come."

The disappointment was keen but manageable. It wasn't as if he'd ever said yes when she'd asked for his help. He'd never been there for her, and it was time for her to stop asking him to be or expecting him to be. He had his own life in Richmond. A good job with a software firm. A pretty, intelligent wife who was a professor at the university. Two perfect little girls who were in ballet and took piano lessons.

The tapping stopped. "Karen, I have to go. Keep me informed, please? I do care."

Right. "Okay, Ray. Tell the family I said hello."

"I will. We'll be praying for you."

Praying? She hung up the phone. Since when? Her brother had never been one for church and all its rules and regulations. Forced to attend church from the time they were born, Ray had rebelled as soon as he could and never looked back. Only Karen had maintained the tradition of church every Sunday morning.

Karen leaned back against the counter and slowly collapsed to the floor. She didn't know how to handle this. She needed someone to tell her what to do.

She needed someone to tell her that God intended to bring her baby back to her.

"There is a God in heaven." Matt whistled softly. "Tell me she's guilty of something. Puh. . .leez, let me interrogate her."

JJ looked up and out the small window of his office to see what it was that had Matt primping like a schoolboy just before the prom.

She was tall and slim, with a willowy softness that seemed to make her float as she wove her way through the desks in the bullpen. Her hair was long, blond, curly—a wild halo of gold. JJ came to his feet as he realized that she was heading straight for his office. He combed his fingers through his hair and then straightened his tie. "Matt, don't you have something you need to be doing?"

"Not a chance," Matt replied, never taking his eyes off the golden image that stopped outside the office door and lifted a delicate hand to knock. He stepped over and pulled open the door. "Detective Matt Casto. May I help you?"

The smile that crossed her face was soft, whispery, fleeting. "I'm looking for Detective Johnson."

"My loss." Matt's voice was husky with regret.

"I'm Detective Johnson." JJ stepped out from behind the desk and extended his hand. "What can I do for you?"

She turned dark green eyes on him—studying him. He could feel her probing into places he didn't want anyone to go. It sent a shiver up his spine, and the fires of latent anticipation cooled. And then he knew.

He dropped his hand before she could take it and stepped back. "You must be Zoe Shefford."

The smile on her face was filled with amusement. And approval. He wasn't sure which pleased him more, and it aggravated him that it mattered.

She wasn't at all what he'd expected. There was no flash; just fluid motion. No bangles and beads and dark whispers; just long, lean lines of gold and green, pink and yellow. And that aggravated him as well.

She flipped back her gold hair and flashed those green eyes in a move that was as artless as it was enticing. "I know I'm a little early. I hope you don't mind."

Matt stepped over in the range of sight, pulling her attention away from JJ. "It's quite all right. Please, have a seat."

She eyed the chair and then sat down, her flowery skirt floating down around her legs as she crossed them. "As I said on the phone, I'm glad to do what I can, but I can never guarantee anything."

It seemed as if her attention was pulled—no, dragged—from the two men to the pictures on the wall. She set her purse on the floor and stood up, walking over slowly.

JJ watched her with skeptical interest.

Zoe studied each picture, taking her time moving from child to child. She reached out and let her fingertips trace the first picture, closing her eyes.

"Gina," she whispered softly.

JJ folded his arms across his chest. "Anyone could know that.

Her name and picture were in the paper."

Matt flashed him an impatient look.

Zoe didn't seem to hear JJ, or if she did, she didn't care. "She's skipping, happy. She was somewhere that pleased her. She doesn't see the danger coming. Unaware. It sneaks out and snaps her up." Suddenly Zoe yanked her hand back as if she'd been burned. "I'm sorry." The whisper was low, husky, filled with pain.

Visibly shaken, Zoe reached out and touched the second photograph. "This is different."

She shook her head as if to clear it and then turned to JJ. "Gina was taken by a man, but not the baby. I see a man and a woman, but I can't see their faces. It's too shadowy, but she's not like Gina. I can tell you that much."

She echoed enough of what had been moving in his own heart to make him put the walls down for a moment. He took a step closer. "Is she alive?"

"I'm not sure. I think so."

"What do you need?"

"To touch something of hers. Can we go to the parents' home? I need to see her room, touch her things. Maybe then." She looked back over at the pictures. "For Gina, too."

JJ noticed how her last words seemed to be pulled out of her. There was reluctance, hesitation. He wondered at it.

Matt flashed her a bright, sexy smile. "That was incredible!"

She tilted her head, looking at him with an amused smile. "Silly man, do you really think she'll wait forever? If you care at all, and you do, you'd better do something about it. Someone else is already trying to draw her attention away from you."

JJ watched in amusement as Matt's color paled. "I. . .I don't know what you mean."

Zoe reached down and picked up her purse. "Yes, you do. All the others—they may soothe your ego, but she soothes your soul. That will always be more important. You won't find another like her."

Matt stepped back away from her, suddenly jamming his fists into his pockets as if he were afraid she might touch him and expose his soul to the world.

JJ just smiled.

Zoe tucked her purse under her arm and turned her attention to JJ. "When will you be ready to start?"

JJ felt the question echo in his mind as if it somehow had more than one meaning, but for the life of him, he didn't know why. "Let me call Mrs. Matthews. If she's home, we can ride over now."

Zoe nodded. "I'll wait outside."

Matt waited until she was gone to drop into the chair. "How did she do that?"

JJ picked up the phone, making a face. "You don't really buy that act, do you? She could have heard someone out there talking about you and Paula."

"You don't believe she's a psychic?"

"I don't believe in psychics."

Matt pointed to the pictures. "But she saw things."

"Did she? Or did she just want us to think she did?" He flipped open the Matthews file and dialed the number. "Think about what she said, Matt. Gina is hurt, terrified, scared. Wow, what a revelation that was. Don't know why I didn't think of that myself."

"But you heard what she said about the Matthews kid!"

"I have to give the lady a shot. But trust me, if anything solves this case, it's going to be old-fashioned police work."

JJ lifted his head. "Yes, Mrs. Matthews? This is Detective Johnson. I need to come by for a few minutes."

chapter 5

Z oe stepped out of JJ's office and pulled the door closed behind her. The quiet in her mind was shattered. But it had been shattered before she heard the office clatter of phones ringing, computer keyboards tapping, people talking, a woman screeching, a man arguing, and a chair scraping across the tile floor. She took a deep breath.

The children. It always tore her up. So why did she do this to herself? Because she had to? Because she had been destined for this? Because she had the gift and had to use it? Each time she looked at one of the faces, touched their pictures, felt their terror, she would remember the one she hadn't been able to save. The most important one. And the pain would engulf her, draining her.

Experience had taught her when to focus and when to forget. Even for a little while. She shifted her thoughts to the two detectives. Matt had been easy to read. Smiling, she recalled his expression when she mentioned his relationship with his girlfriend. He was a harmless flirt, but it would cost him the love of his life if he didn't rein it in.

But the other. Johnson. *Handsome* wasn't a word she would use to describe him. His eyes were green, but they were the color of washed-out glass. His black hair was wavy but too thick to tame. He was tall—maybe a shade over six feet—with broad shoulders and a tapered waist, but the effect made him look like a brawler. His lips were full, but his mouth was hard and his nose too wide and slightly crooked. He was the kind of man who wanted to look intimidating. Forbidding. He enjoyed it, too, and that wasn't the least bit attractive.

There was something compelling about him though. Intense. He would be noticed in a crowd but considered somewhat unapproachable. Yet something simmered just below the surface—secrets and shadows and whispers. She was intrigued, and that was something she *did* find attractive.

Zoe barely heard the door open behind her but felt his touch—fleeting, reluctant. His fingertips grazed her elbow and were gone. And in that moment, she felt something shoot through her that was so unfamiliar, so foreign, she could only blink as everything in her stilled.

"Ready, Miss Shefford?"

They walked in silence, his wide stride eating up the distance. He didn't open the car door for her, and she wasn't sure she was expecting it. As he pulled the car out of the lot, she stared out the window.

It was a mild day, full of sunshine and warm breezes. The kind of day that would normally depress her, but today she barely noticed. Her thoughts were consumed by the sullen, silent man beside her.

She turned to look at him, trying not to admire the way he filled his shirt or the way his scent permeated the car. Instead, she concentrated on darker emotions that seemed to be draped over him like a well-worn coat. "You don't like me, do you?"

JJ looked over at her, his gaze cool, detached. "I don't even *know* you."

"But. . . ," she prompted.

"But I don't believe in all this stuff with spirits and tarot cards and crystal balls."

She knew the battle was far from over, but she sighed with dramatic relief. "Oh, good. I don't either."

"You're the one who claims to be a psychic," he replied pointedly, one eyebrow cocked with skepticism.

"I don't have a sign in my front yard either."

JJ shrugged as his eyes looked everywhere but at her. "Lady, as far as I'm concerned, you're here because the boss insists, not because I believe in all this spirit-world hype. You claim to be a psychic, fine. Do whatever it is you do. And I'll do what I do."

"Which is, precisely?"

He did look at her this time, and that cool gaze had the edge of frost that should have had her retreating. Instead, she smiled at him. "Oh, did I touch something tender?"

"No, lady, you did not. I'm a cop. That's what I do. Use your psychic powers to figure out what that means."

"Ouch." She laughed lightly and watched JJ frown as she did. "I did touch something tender."

"Look, you may be able to use all that mumbo jumbo to make someone as gullible as my partner think you're able to read minds or whatever it is you're supposed to do, but don't try it with me. I don't buy it."

"I see." She lifted a hand. "May I?"

"May you what?" He spotted the red light and braked.

"Touch you?"

One eyebrow lifted in amusement. "You're kidding, right?"

"Not at all." She reached over and laid one of those delicate hands on his shoulder. Closing her eyes, she shut her mind to the woodsy scent he wore, that cool expression he favored, and the muscles that tensed beneath her fingers.

Suddenly she yanked her hand back.

"What's the matter? Didn't like what you saw?" JJ laughed sarcastically. "Now, this is where you tell me that you saw something so terrible, so horrid, that you can't tell me, right? But maybe for another fifty bucks you can be persuaded."

Zoe clasped her hands in her lap and turned her head to look out the window. "Boy, you sure have me pegged, don't you?"

Her voice was calm, her expression detached, but inside she was a raging turmoil of conflicting emotions. He was cool and detached for good reason. The sarcasm and skepticism were justified. And he had grounds for keeping his distance. Worse, it broke her heart to know, and she wished she didn't.

As they turned off the highway and into a moderate but well-maintained housing development, she heard his thoughts loud and clear. She didn't look at him. "I don't do it for the publicity. In fact, I always ask that the media not be brought in at all. Sadly, my wishes are not always honored."

"I didn't say a word."

"You were thinking it." She turned her head and looked at him. His mouth twisted in a smile that was both mocking and insulting. "No, I wasn't."

"Yes, you were. I heard you."

JJ laughed harshly. "Like I said, save it for someone who actually buys your act. I really don't care why you do what you do."

"No, you don't *care* why, but you were *wondering* why. There is a difference."

He turned onto a side street, his eyes never leaving the road. "And I wasn't even thinking of you at all. I was concentrating on my driving."

"Suit yourself."

"I always do."

"I know." Now she had his attention.

"Care to explain that comment?"

"I thought you didn't buy my act."

"I don't."

"Then I shouldn't care to explain anything I say, should I?"

She saw the temper flare in his eyes, and for some reason it pleased her that she'd managed to break through that cool act of his.

"You're deliberately trying to provoke me."

"Am I? Hmmmm. Let's just say that I understand you far better than you think I do. Perhaps even more than you want me to." She deliberated for less than a second. "I know about her."

"Her, who?"

Zoe toyed with one of the rings on her finger. "Macy."

She watched the muscle in his cheek jump as he clenched down on his teeth and spoke. "Who told you about Macy?"

"You did."

"No, I did not."

"Yes, you did. That's what I saw when I touched you. I make you think of her; that's why you dislike me so much. Or resent me. Call it what you will. I make you think of things you don't want to think of."

His knuckles went white as he gripped the wheel, refusing to look at her. "I don't know where you dug up the information on Macy, but that's my private life and I don't appreciate anyone digging into my privacy."

"I didn't dig up anything on you."

"And pigs fly with pink wings."

◆　◆　◆

"Looks like all hell is breaking loose over at the Matthews' house."

Rene Taylor withdrew her hands from the dishwater and grabbed a towel. Wiping her hands, she joined her husband at the front window. "Reporters. I hope nothing else has happened. That poor woman has been through enough in her life."

"I can't even begin to imagine having a child vanish like that." Rene's husband, Jeff, draped his arm over her shoulders, gathering her close, as if that simple gesture might ward off the possibility that tragedy could strike their own lives.

Rene pressed her lips together, staring out at the hoard of reporters gathering like wolves around a fresh kill. "I should go over and see if there's anything I can do to help. It's driving me crazy to watch her go through this alone."

"I thought her husband told you to stay away from her."

"He did, but ask me if I care." She whipped the dishtowel off her shoulder and wiped her hands again. "I stay away only to protect her, not because I'm the least bit intimidated by that coward."

Jeff smiled, his arm tightening, squeezing her with affection. "I've yet to meet a man who intimidates you, my love."

Rene couldn't help herself. She smiled. "You make me sound ferocious."

"Far from it. You're just a kitten with claws. But even kittens know how to defend themselves when threatened by a dog with a bad bite."

"He's not a biter. He's a barker. And his bark doesn't bother me. I just don't want him taking out his anger on her. She isn't a strong person at all."

"Then all we can do is pray." Jeff turned from the window and dropped down in his recliner. He picked up his Bible and began paging through it. "In the meantime, I have a sermon to prepare."

Rene tossed her towel over the back of a chair. "Those reporters are going to eat her alive. I'm going over there for a few minutes. I can't stand by and do nothing."

Jeff closed his Bible, hooked a finger over the top of his glasses, and slid them down to the edge of his nose. He peered over the top of them. "Be careful."

Rene blew him a kiss. "I'll leave long before he's home. He'll never know I was there."

Pulling the front door closed behind her, Rene squared her shoulders, ready to storm through the wall of reporters. No, they didn't intimidate her. Few things did. But it hadn't always been that way. Once upon a time she had cowered in fear merely from the way her first husband looked at her, knowing that at any moment his fists would take over.

Afraid, intimidated, hurt, and wounded, it had taken years to build up the courage to go to her pastor for help. The Reverend Bennett Reed, then in his early sixties, had meant well, but he'd clearly been raised in a different era and was unprepared for the rise in domestic violence. With a pat on her hand and a warm smile, the old man had sent her home, gently admonishing her to submit to her husband's authority.

That advice may have been well intentioned, but it nearly cost her life. Her husband had found out. Enraged that she had dared tell anyone, he had beaten her so badly that a neighbor—frightened by the screams—called the police. Rick was arrested and Rene spent a week in the hospital. It was in the hospital that she'd met Margaret Elizabeth Brennan—a woman who not only had survived an abusive marriage but had gone on to open a shelter for abused women.

Margaret promised her a new life. Rene had been skeptical. Margaret promised that Rick would never find her. Rene had listened. When Rene was released from the hospital, Margaret took her to a private shelter, and slowly, as days passed into weeks and weeks into months, she began to feel safe. When Margaret helped her find a job, Rene began to feel independent. And slowly, very slowly, she began to heal.

She recognized the cowering fear in Karen Matthews' eyes, and it drove her crazy. True, she hadn't seen any evidence that Ted Matthews beat his wife, but there were more ways to abuse a woman than with fists.

Circling the house, Rene climbed the wooden stairs to Karen's kitchen door and rapped softly on the window. A few seconds later, Karen pushed back the curtain and then frowned, slipping the door open a crack. "You shouldn't be here. I'm sorry, Rene. It's just. . ."

"I know. Ted doesn't want me here. But do you?"

Rene watched as Karen chewed on her bottom lip, indecision in her eyes.

"Karen, I won't stay long, okay? I'll leave well before he comes home. I just thought you might need some help with those reporters. And maybe you could use a friend?"

JJ pulled up in the Matthews' driveway. Satellite vans lined the streets. Reporters congregated in little groups, swigging coffee or cold sodas while camera crews lingered nearby waiting to be called into action.

"Ready to run the gauntlet?"

"I've been running them for years," Zoe replied as JJ eased the car through the crowd and turned into the driveway. Reporters jumped, scrambling across the yard, yelling to the camera operators, smoothing back hair, and straightening jackets.

JJ got out first. The minute the reporters recognized him, they shoved microphones in his face and started asking questions.

"Do you have any leads?"

"Have the parents been given polygraphs yet?"

"Are the parents suspects?"

"Is this case connected to the other little girl?"

"Do you think it's the same kidnapper?"

"What can you tell us about the Matthews baby?"

JJ turned to look at the reporter, a young woman with short blond hair and big blue eyes. "Seven-month-old Jessica Matthews is missing, taken from her crib in the middle of the night. That's about it."

"What about the parents?"

"I can't comment on that at this time."

Zoe eased through the crowd as JJ diverted the reporters' attention. She was almost to the front door when one reporter stepped in front of her. "Aren't you that famous psychic?"

"No comment," Zoe replied as she tried to step around him.

"Have the police brought you in for the Matthews baby?"

"No comment," Zoe repeated firmly.

"Will you be trying to find Gina Sarentino, too?"

Suddenly JJ was at her elbow, easing the reporter out of their way. "We have no comment at this time."

When they made it up the steps to the front door, it swung open. Karen Matthews stood there, looking from JJ to Zoe. She stepped back, swinging the door open wide.

As soon as the reporters caught sight of Karen, they started screaming out questions again, but she closed the door firmly behind JJ and Zoe without reply.

Karen was older than Zoe had anticipated. Standing barely five-foot-two, she looked to be in her late thirties or early forties. She was a pretty woman with a square face and large, light brown eyes that looked more gold than brown. The wavering smile and slumped shoulders made Zoe want to reach out and comfort her.

Zoe followed Karen into the living room, declining the offer of something to drink. While JJ spoke quietly to Karen, Zoe walked around the room, looking at the baby pictures on the wall, on the end table, and on the mantle. She picked up the receiving blanket tossed across the side of the playpen and fingered it.

She had just began to feel the pull when she heard a woman ask loudly, "Who is she?"

Zoe turned in the direction of the voice and found a middle-aged woman staring at her. She was tall, maybe five-ten or five-eleven, with short, spiky brown hair and big brown eyes that seemed unusually sharp and observant. They darted everywhere, but Zoe doubted she missed a thing. And it was those eyes that held Zoe's attention.

Zoe had the distinct impression that this woman had her in the crosshairs. A shiver ran down Zoe's back.

The woman smiled, but there was a cool edge to it. "Are you with the police department?"

Karen started to make the introductions. "Rene Taylor, this is Detective Johnson and. . ."

JJ spoke up. "Miss Shefford. She's here with the department to help."

The woman took another step forward, eyeing Zoe cautiously. "You're here to help in what way?"

Zoe turned to Karen and offered a comforting smile. "I have some success finding lost children."

"I thought you looked familiar." Rene stepped around the coffee table. She reached out and slipped the blanket from Zoe's hands. "You're that psychic."

"Yes."

Rene lifted her chin. "I'm sorry. This won't do at all. Karen is a Christian."

Zoe looked over at JJ for help, but he seemed as much at a loss as she was. She was going to have to deal with this herself. "I don't understand. If I can help. . ."

The woman shook her head again as she stepped over to Karen and took her hand. "No. You can't. It's nothing personal, but Karen cannot use a psychic to find this child. As a Christian, she must depend on God, not the devil."

Zoe smiled again, speaking slowly, patiently, as if to a child. "I'm not the devil, Mrs.—"

"I know that, Miss Shefford. But I'm sorry. It's not right."

"I admit that I'm not exactly a religious person," Zoe replied softly. "But I believe in God, and I believe my gift is from Him."

"No," Rene argued firmly. "Your gift is *not* from God. And you will *not* use it on Jessica."

Rene turned to Karen. "I'm sorry, Karen. Perhaps I'm overstepping here. I know that you don't attend our church, but as a Christian, you can't use a psychic. You know that, right?"

Karen swallowed hard, looking uncomfortable and confused.

Zoe squared her shoulders for battle. "If Mrs. Matthews is a Christian, how come she didn't have a problem until you *told* her it was a problem? You're interfering with police work here. I've been called in to help find Jessica. Has it dawned on you that if you prevent me from doing my job, something terrible could happen? Could you live with that?"

Zoe turned to Karen. "Are you going to let this woman dictate what happens to your baby?"

Karen wrung her hands, looking from Zoe to Rene and back to Zoe. Confusion racked her pretty features, twisting her face into a portrait of misery. "I want my Jessica back, but. . ."

"Then let me do my job, Mrs. Matthews." Zoe's voice was soft, cajoling, gently pleading. *Come on, Karen. Don't listen to these wackos!*

"I can't," Karen whimpered.

Rene nodded with satisfaction as she turned to JJ. "I'm sorry,

Detective. I believe the matter is settled."

Zoe was all but pushed out the door. Reporters immediately surrounded her and JJ, pressing in with endless questions, camera flashes, microphones, and tape recorders. JJ shielded her as they ran the gauntlet back to the car.

"Do you have any leads on baby Jessica?"

"Have the parents been polygraphed?"

"Do you think this case is tied to the other missing girl?"

"Do we have a serial killer on the loose?"

Janice Alberry watched with a cat-like smile as JJ spun around and climbed into his car. She clicked her tape recorder off and stuck it in her pocket, thinking about the anger that had flashed in JJ's eyes when she'd asked him about a serial killer. He'd whirled on her, nearly knocking her tape recorder out of her hand, growling an emphatic "No!"

So the unflappable JJ Johnson was upset. Interesting. And the woman with him—a famous psychic. Detective Johnson was using a psychic? Even more interesting.

Pulling a small notebook out of her pocket, she jotted: *Find out about the woman.*

"Hey, Jan. Get anything good?"

Janice glanced up at Freddie King, a reporter for one of the local television stations, and closed her notebook. He was an arrogant boob, but his connections made him worth a smile. She gave him a thousand-watt grin. "Who knows. They're playing this tighter than the Green Bay Packers."

"That's because they got squat. You know it's bad when they bring in that psychic, Zoe Shefford. Not that she isn't good; she is.

Probably one of the best in the business. But bringing in a psychic is never good press, no matter how you spin it."

"Yeah, I noticed she was here. They're really reaching on this one. Good ol' JJ didn't look too happy. You think Harris brought her in?" *Zoe Shefford. Remember that name.*

"I heard it was the governor himself who wanted her called in. He'll be campaigning for reelection in a couple of months—can't have a serial killer stealing headlines."

Janice felt her fingers itching to write down these particulars, but she couldn't afford to let Freddie think she wasn't on top of all this information. *Old news. Look a little bored.* "Yeah, ain't that the truth. Have you ever seen Shefford work?"

Slipping on his sunglasses, Freddie graced her with one of those lazy, lopsided smiles that had women viewers sighing. "You want the headlines, darlin', you're going to have to work for them. I'm not giving you anything. Go do your homework."

Janice wanted to kick him in the seat of those finely pressed pants as he turned on his heel and strolled off to his air-conditioned truck, his cameraman on his heels like a lap dog.

Fuming, she yanked out her notebook and wrote. *Zoe Shefford. Psychic. Top in her field. Called in by governor. Serial killer?*

Okay, Freddie. She closed her notebook and headed for her car. *I'll do my homework. I'll find out everything there is to know about Zoe Shefford and her work. With any luck, I'll make a few headlines of my own.*

She climbed into her car and glared at the air conditioner that hadn't worked in years as she turned the key. The engine sputtered, caught, and choked as it turned over.

If she was going to get a headline, she was going to have to dig and see what she could find on Zoe Shefford. Maybe a little dirt. No one was spotless. You just had to ferret it out.

◆　　◆　　◆

"Well, what was that all about?" Zoe propped her elbow on the edge of the car door and, leaving Karen Matthews and the accusations behind, looked to JJ for answers.

"Got me."

Curling her fingers into her hair, Zoe stared blindly out the windshield. "I don't think I've ever had anyone tell me I was the devil before."

"Not to your face, maybe."

Raising both eyebrows, Zoe turned to stare at him. "You think I'm in cahoots with the devil? You can't be serious."

"I never said that." A devious smile flitted across his face. "I think my exact thoughts were 'decked-out demagogue of deceit' or some such thing."

Zoe couldn't help herself. The laugh erupted involuntarily, filling the car with the pleasant sound of amusement and wonder. "You didn't."

"I did," he admitted with a smirk.

"And now?" she asked.

"Now what?"

"Now what would you call me?"

She could almost feel his gaze taking in everything from the wild curly hair that tumbled down across her shoulders and back, nearly reaching her waist, to the soft-pink silk blouse and flowered skirt, to the dainty leather sandals on bare feet and toes tipped in bright pink polish. "Delightful-looking decked-out demagogue of deceit."

She laughed again, shaking her head. "We're making headway."

He instantly sobered. "Don't count on it. I'm not blind, but I'm not stupid, either."

The smile disappeared. "Meaning?"

"Meaning I'm not oblivious to a pretty woman, but I don't let any woman lead me around by the nose. You may be attractive, but I'm not going to get all gooey-eyed over you just because you flash that smile and bat those eyelashes."

Now she was insulted. "Excuse me, but I don't bat my eyelashes, and you can keep your backhanded compliment."

He pulled the car into the department parking lot and turned off the engine. "I wasn't trying to compliment you. I simply answered your question."

She glared at him as she shoved open her door. "Remind me not to ask you what you think anymore. It's obviously a one-way trip down a worthless road." She stepped out of the car, slammed the door, and started to stalk off.

Then she whirled around, leaned down, and glared at him through the open window. "Your father was right about you!"

Zoe saw the color drain quickly from his face, his eyes dark and bleak with something far deeper than pain. She immediately wanted to take back every word but couldn't. It was too late. She had hit him hard. He wouldn't forget or forgive easily. And because she couldn't stand knowing that she had put that look on his face, she spun around and ran to her car.

chapter 6

JJ gripped the steering wheel, desperately wanting to snap it in half, his knuckles white with the need. His mind hot with the rage. His heart heavy with the pain. Her words had ripped through him like a serrated knife, cutting, slicing, ripping, tearing at his soul.

How did she know those words could reduce him to a hulking mass of insecurity and self-doubt? How could she know? She had claws and wasn't afraid to use them. Probably took delight in using them, slicing her way through men with a certain personal pleasure.

He loosened his grip on the steering wheel. Well, if she thought she was going to put JJ Johnson under her slim little feet, she had another thing coming.

JJ climbed out of the car, the only hint of his anger revealed by a slammed door.

Matt eyed him cautiously as he barged into his office and dropped into his chair. "Offhand, I'd say it didn't go well."

"Karen Matthews and her friend heard the word *psychic* and kicked us out of the house. Starting going on about the devil and then showed us the door." He looked up at the clock. It was almost four.

"Where's Gerry and Wayne?"

"Gerry called in—he's still talking to the Matthews' neighbors—and Wayne went over to talk to that adoption attorney who said he might have some information for us."

JJ rubbed his hands over his face, trying to set aside lingering feelings left by Zoe's attack in order to concentrate on the work ahead. "What about the lab? Anything on the fingerprints?"

Matt nodded, picking up a file and tossing it across the desk to JJ. "Mr. Matthews, Mrs. Matthews, and a few smudged ones that don't match either the mother or the father but aren't clear enough to identify."

JJ flipped open the report and stared at it. "So someone else *was* there." He picked up his pen and rolled it through his fingers while thoughts tumbled through his head. "I still can't shake the feeling that they did something with that baby. Maybe they had help."

"Oh, before I forget." Matt stood up, dug into his back pocket, and pulled out a small envelope. He tossed it down in front of JJ. "My sister wanted me to let you know that you're invited to Amanda's birthday party on the twenty-ninth."

JJ picked up the envelope and ripped it open. "Is it time for that child to have another birthday?"

"It's been a year, pal."

"How old is she this year?"

"Eleven."

JJ shook his head as he tossed the birthday invitation onto the desk. "Heavens. . .I'm getting old."

Matt tilted his head, studying JJ carefully. "Nah, not much gray at all."

JJ glared. "Funny."

"I thought so."

"Tell me you-know-who won't be there."

"Pete? He probably will. He usually makes it to all the family events."

JJ growled low in his throat then coughed. "I feel the flu coming on."

Matt laughed. "He is a pain, isn't he?"

"I like most of your family. But your cousin is a jerk."

Matt threw up his hands. "I'm not saying a word."

JJ took a deep breath and picked up the Matthews file from his desk. He stared at it. "Matt, get together with Gerry. Tear the Matthews' lives apart. I want to know everything from parking tickets to anti-war protests. See if there's anything I can hang my gut instinct on."

When Ted Matthews pulled into the driveway, he was surprised to find himself facing an army of reporters overrunning his front yard.

"Mr. Matthews! Do you have anything to say to the kidnapper?"

Ted gripped his briefcase. "Yes. Return my daughter."

"Mr. Matthews! What do you think of the way the police are handling this?"

He stopped at the steps and turned around. "I think it's shameful the way they refuse to go look for the kidnapper. They have no leads, so they place the blame on the easiest targets—my wife and me!"

"Mr. Matthews! Will you sue the department for mishandling this case?"

"I have no idea. It depends on whether they get their act together and find the kidnapper."

"Mr. Matthews, do you think your daughter was taken by the same man who took Gina Sarentino?"

"I have no idea. I'm not a detective. I only know that my

daughter," he choked back a sob, "my precious Jessica, has been taken, and we want her back. This is difficult. . . . It's pushing my wife to the edge." He threw up his hands. "Please excuse me."

If he thought he'd find peace in the house, he was wrong. He set down his briefcase just inside the door. "Karen?"

"In here," he heard her call out. He stepped into the kitchen to find her sitting at the table with another reporter.

The reporter stood up and reached out to shake his hand. "Lorraine Wallace."

"Ted Matthews." He draped his suit coat over a chair, pulled it out, and sat down. "Why is the press here?" he asked.

"Because I called them," she replied, her voice trembling. "A psychic was here today with that detective. While they're busy trying to pin this on us, the real kidnapper is getting away with our daughter. If the police won't help, we'll have to find her ourselves."

"I just wished you had discussed this with me, Karen. None of this is good for you. You know you haven't been all that strong since Jess was born."

Karen swallowed hard, her eyes pleading with him to understand. "I'm fine. Really."

The reporter turned to Ted. "How are you taking this?"

"I'm numb. I just can't believe someone would do this. What kind of world do we live in when a baby isn't even safe in her own crib? In her own home?" He sighed heavily and then looked over at Karen, squeezing her hand in a show of comfort. "We were just so happy when Jessica was born. She's the light of our lives."

The reporter jotted something down, closed the notebook, turned off her recorder, and rose to her feet. Tomorrow he would read in some paper that he was numb and that Jessica was the light of his life.

He sat while Karen escorted the woman out. He assumed she

would return with another reporter and the scenario would begin again, so he was a little surprised when she returned alone. She brushed her fingers through his hair and then kissed his cheek.

"I hope you don't mind. I probably should have called you first, but I felt so helpless. I had to do something."

Ted shook his head as he pulled her down in his lap. "You need to check with me on things like this. You know how I worry about you and all this stress. Have you been taking your pills?" He watched her shift her eyes away from him and knew the answer. "You know you need them, honey." He pushed her up off his lap. "Please go take your pills now. Before you forget again."

Silently, she nodded and headed for the bathroom.

"Karen?"

She stopped and looked at him, her fingers twisting in the hem of her shirt.

"I have to ask you. Are you sure you didn't hurt Jess and just blocked it out? Like you killed the kitten?"

chapter 7

Finally, on Thursday morning—three long days after Jessica Matthews disappeared from her crib—JJ arrived at the station to find good news waiting for him in his office.

"We have a lead!" Matt jumped to his feet as the words exploded from his lips.

"On which case?" JJ asked quickly. He set down his coffee on the edge of the desk and slipped out of his jacket.

"Matthews."

"You're kidding! Talk to me." JJ pulled out his chair and sat down. He picked up his coffee and peeled off the lid.

"Gerry was interviewing neighbors. He missed one. Across the street. Lady by the name of. . ." Matt looked down at his notepad. "Ethel Marsh. Anyway, she was away. Now she's back. Gerry talked to her, and it seems Mrs. Matthews neglected to mention the fact that up until just before the baby disappeared, she had a woman coming in twice a week. Cleaning, babysitting, errands—that sort of thing. And the woman had a key to the Matthews' house."

JJ rocked back in his chair. "Did anyone contact Karen Matthews?"

"Not yet. Gerry just called five, maybe ten minutes ago. He is on his way."

JJ picked up the phone. "Let's find out about this cleaning woman."

Karen Matthews answered the phone on the third ring. "Mrs. Matthews? Detective Johnson. Did you have a housekeeper or cleaning woman coming in a couple times a week? One that you might have forgotten to mention to us?"

There was a slight pause before Karen answered. "Oh. You mean Alice Denton? Why is that important?"

JJ picked up a pencil and rolled it between his fingers, trying to keep his frustration from breaking loose. "Did she have a key to your house? Was she familiar with your routine? With the baby?"

"Oh. She quit working for us before Jessica disappeared. I just didn't think. . ."

JJ snapped the pencil between his fingers and tossed the pieces down angrily. "You didn't think? The woman had a key to your house and you didn't think?"

"She gave the key back!" Karen said abruptly. "And I can't believe Alice would have taken Jessica! She has children of her own to worry about!"

Just then, Gerry opened the door and stepped in. Seeing JJ on the phone, he quietly shut the door behind him and grabbed a chair.

"Just give me the woman's name and address, Mrs. Matthews."

JJ snatched a piece of broken pencil, realized what he'd done, and tossed it to the floor. Then he reached for the pen Matt set in front of him.

When he finished writing down the information, he pushed the pad toward Matt. Matt picked it up and, with Gerry leaning over his shoulder, read what JJ had written. Immediately Gerry took the pad and went over to the computer terminal in the corner and began typing away.

"If you think of anyone else, Mrs. Matthews, I'd appreciate you letting us know." He slammed the receiver down. *"I didn't think,"* he snarled in a high-pitched voice, mocking Karen Matthews. "No kidding."

Gerry looked around in his chair. "There is no Alice Denton at this address. The house is owned by a Mr. Harold Harrison."

JJ stood up and grabbed his jacket. "Let's get over to that house. We need to talk to this Alice Denton woman."

The house was a small rambler in an older section of town. The neighborhood was still neat and clean, the border between lower middle class and middle class. No built-in swimming pools in this neighborhood, though you might find a few aboveground K-mart specials.

The house, like most of its neighbors, had a postage-stamp front yard with neatly trimmed shrubs that had probably been planted back in the sixties. No fancy berms and dusty miller here. Daffodils and tulips were the flower of choice.

JJ climbed out of the car and looked around. A woman knelt in a flower bed next door, pulling weeds. He couldn't tell her age. Her hair and face were buried under a big straw hat.

When the car door slammed, she looked up, shielding her eyes from the morning sun with her hands. "No one lives there," she yelled out, slowly standing to her feet.

JJ walked across her lawn. "Did someone live there up until recently?"

Up close, he could see that she was in her late fifties—maybe early sixties—with clear green eyes and a soft, clear skin. She took care of herself and would make no apologies for it.

"Mary Deere. Moved last Monday."

The day Jessica Matthews disappeared. Maybe he'd been wrong about the parents after all.

JJ pulled out his badge. "Detective Johnson. Do you have any idea where she moved to?"

She shook her head. "No. She was a strange one. Kept to herself. Didn't have much to do with the neighbors. Rarely had anyone over."

Suddenly the name hit JJ between the eyes. "Wait. Did you say Mary? Not Alice?"

"Mary. Mary Deere. Leastways that's the name she gave me. Nervous thing, she was. And rude. I called to her one afternoon and she just ignored me. Went right on in the house like I didn't say a word to her."

Or because she didn't recognize the name. "Could you tell me what she looked like?"

The woman started pulling off her garden gloves. "Red hair. Not like Irish red or anything. More dark brown with a lot of red in it. Don't know if it was natural or not. Didn't look it. Tall, real thin. Skinny almost. Like she didn't half eat at all. All bones and angles."

"How old would you say she was?"

The woman shrugged. "Mid to late thirties maybe."

"What about a husband? Boyfriend? Children?"

She shook her head. "Nope. Saw one man come and go from time to time, but nothing steady. No kids. Don't know that she was ever married. If she was, she didn't want anyone to know."

"Why do you say that?"

"Got all uptight when I asked her if she was married. Nervous-like. Snapped at me that her past was none of my business."

"Did you ever see her with a child? Maybe an infant?"

The woman paused as she twisted the gloves in her hands. "No. Can't say that I ever did. Wait. The day before she left, I saw her putting an infant car seat in her car. But never saw an infant."

"What about the man who owns this house? Do you know him?"

"Oh," she waved one hand airily. "Harry? Sure I know him. He rents it now that he lives with his daughter and her husband."

"Do you know where that is? I'd like to talk to him."

"Sure. Let me get that number for you."

JJ left Gerry to collect the information while he and Matt strolled around the house. Looking through the window, it appeared as if she'd left in a hurry. Good old Harry would have to clean up the mess she left behind.

Gerry met up with JJ and Matt in the backyard. "Man, this just does not add up."

"What doesn't?" Matt asked.

"Mrs. Marsh told me the Matthews' housekeeper didn't have a car. She always saw the woman coming on foot. This woman says that this Mary woman was driving a nice burgundy Concorde. The descriptions of the woman match. . ."

"But the names don't," JJ interjected. "Gerry, you go talk to the landlord. See what you can find out and see if he'll give you the keys. I'd like to take a look inside. Maybe she left something behind that will give us a clue as to where she went in such a hurry."

Nothing in the house told them where the woman had gone, and one envelope found in the bottom of the trash can muddied the waters even more. "It's addressed to a Nancy Darrington, but at a different address. That's three names now. Will the real name please stand up?" Gerry tossed the envelope into a plastic bag and marked it for evidence.

Matt walked into the room, disgust written all over his face. "Nothing in the bedrooms."

JJ leaned against the kitchen counter. Here was a woman who used three different names, had a key to the Matthews' home, quit a few days before the child disappeared from the home, and left no trace of evidence to say where she was headed. She was described by the neighbor as withdrawn, cautious, nervous, secretive. And she was seen with a child's car seat even though she didn't have a child. It all added up to one very strong suspect.

JJ pushed off the counter. "Find this woman."

"I'll get right on it," Matt assured him.

"And, Matt? Find her fast."

Matt nodded. "I hear ya."

Karen twisted the tissue in her hands, her head bowed, as Reverend Pollack continued to talk. His words flitted in and out of her mind, barely registering. It had been a mistake to come here and impose on his time. She should have realized that he was a busy man. But he'd been honest with her. He could give her twenty minutes just before choir practice.

Suddenly his words hit a chord and she lifted her head.

"They were already printed before we heard the tragic news, but we will have it in next week's bulletin."

Karen shook her head as if to clear it. "In the bulletin?"

"For prayer requests," he repeated slowly, as if he suddenly realized she wasn't "all there." He lifted his hands with a shrug. "I had hoped to get it in this week, but. . ."

"Next week," she parroted. "I can't let myself think that Jess might still be missing another week or more. I want her home now."

"I'm sure you do, Mrs. Matthews, but you have to understand the ways of the world. Most abducted children are never found. That's just the way it is."

The anger she'd been suppressing for days erupted. She jumped to her feet. "I don't want to hear about the way it is or statistics or anything except that Jessica will be returned to me. Alive and whole and in my arms. And I can't believe I've been attending this church all my life and not one person has bothered to call and offer help! It took a neighbor that I barely know to show up with prayers and support! Do you have any idea how sad that is?"

Reverend Pollack slapped his hands on his desk and used them to push himself to his feet, his round face turning a bright red that crept right across his bald head. "I'm sure you're just upset, but. . ."

Karen snatched up her purse and rushed out of the office, not stopping until she was out in the parking lot, ignoring the sideways glances of choir members making their way into the church. Leaning against the car, she let herself sob.

I'm sorry, God. I don't understand where You are in any of this. Where is my daughter? Why did You take her away?

"Like are you okay, Mrs. Matthews?"

Karen snapped her head up to find herself looking at one of the teens who sang in the choir. "I'm fine, Carolyn. Thanks."

"I heard about your little girl. I'm so sorry. I want you to know you're in my prayers."

The words pierced her heart with all the accuracy of a Bowie knife. "Thanks, Carolyn. That means more to me than you could know."

"I wanted to call, but. . .I just didn't know if you'd appreciate strangers calling at a time like this."

"You're not a stranger, sweetheart. But I appreciate your consideration."

"If there's anything I can do, like. . .will you let me know? I've been going to this youth group meeting over at that new church on Ridley Street, and we were talking about maybe putting together posters and hanging them up all over town."

"Jeff and Rene's church?"

Carolyn nodded then looked around cautiously. "Just don't tell anyone, okay? You know my family's been in this church for generations and my mom isn't thrilled that I like another church better. Considers it like treason or something."

Karen smiled as Carolyn shuffled her feet. "I won't say a word. I've been thinking about checking out that church myself. Maybe I'll see you there sometime."

Carolyn grinned, her braces flashing with red and black bands. "Great! I gotta go. Bye."

"Good-bye, Carolyn." Karen turned back to see a news van pull up next to her car. A few seconds later, a reporter jumped out of the van and ran over.

"Mrs. Matthews. Can I have a moment of your time?"

John Darrington was at the station less than two hours after Gerry called him. He was a big man, standing a shade over six feet and weighing at least 260 pounds. Wearing jeans, work boots, and a light flannel shirt over a T-shirt, he looked every inch a lumberjack. He said he was a trucker. *Close enough*, JJ figured.

"She'd been acting a little strange for awhile," he told JJ. "But I didn't figure she'd just up and run off like that. No telling what could happen to her. She ain't capable of taking care of herself."

She's been taking care of herself for the better part of a year, JJ thought. *And quite expertly, from the look of things.*

"Anyway, I'm just worried for her. You got any idea which way she went?"

JJ shook his head. "I'm sorry. She didn't leave any trail at all. We are trying to find her."

"You really think she took that woman's baby?"

"We don't know, but we do need to find her and talk to her."

"And you'll call me the minute you find her?"

JJ nodded. "Yes. Of course we will."

John Darrington was barely out of the building before Matt asked JJ, "Are you really going to let him know when we find her?"

"I doubt it. His story of a perfect little marriage doesn't ring true. And she seems awfully determined to make sure he doesn't find her."

"You thinking what I'm thinking?"

"If you're thinking abuse, yep."

"Where does that take us on the Matthews case?"

"She's still our prime suspect. The fact that she's hiding from her husband doesn't mean anything. She still may have taken Jessica."

"Miss Shefford said that the kidnappers were a man *and* a woman. So if this Darrington woman is our kidnapper, who's helping her?"

"I don't know. Maybe her new boyfriend. Maybe that's why she left her hubby."

Matt nodded. "Good thought."

JJ stood up and grabbed his jacket. "Then again, Miss Shefford doesn't know everything, does she?"

"Mommy! Can I have a toy?"

He stopped as the sweet, lilting voice curled through his mind. She was a tiny thing with light brown hair and big eyes. And those chubby cheeks! How precious she was.

The need, the hunger, crawled through him, digging into his soul. Not now. This wasn't a good place. Too many people.

The need argued back, arrogant against caution, taunting him with the promise of peace, contentment. She was so good. So precious. So perfect. To have her was to have that goodness. To hold that perfection in his hands. In his soul.

"Not today, Emily." The mother, pumping gas into her minivan one aisle over, smiled at the child leaning out the driver's window. "Saturday we can go to the toy store and buy you a doll. Okay?"

"How many days is that?" The child tilted her head up, her eyes narrowed, her face scrunched tight.

"Two days, honey. Today is Thursday. Tomorrow is Friday. And the day after that is Saturday."

The child dipped her head, staring at her tiny little hands gripping the edge of the window. Finally, she lifted her head with a wide smile. "Okay."

Perfection.

"Now, let's hurry, sweetheart. We need to stop at the grocery store on the way home."

Slowly he replaced the gas pump and pulled his receipt from the pump. With any luck, the sweet Emily would be his. The grocery store. He just remembered he needed a few things. What a coincidence. Obviously, she was meant to be his.

Forever.

Emily.

Can you hear me coming for you?

Zoe looked up from her needlework and stared out the front window of her living room. There was little to see—a neighbor clipping hedges along his front walk, a child racing down a driveway on his tricycle, a gray tabby cat stalking a squirrel in a nearby tree. But her eyes didn't see any of those things. They were turned inward. Inward where she could see Karen Matthews, nervous and distraught, telling her she couldn't accept Zoe's help because it was not of God.

Not of God? Of course it was. How utterly foolish of the woman. Desperate to find her child and slapping down the best chance she had of accomplishing that.

Not that Zoe considered herself infallible, but she knew in her heart that the baby was still alive, and she was confident that given the opportunity, she could have found little Jessica.

But she wasn't given the chance. Zoe sighed. Suddenly a cold shiver ran down her back. She stiffened as dark shadows began to swirl in her mind, blocking out all thoughts of Karen Matthews and her infant daughter. She saw another little girl, laughing at someone. The child showed no fear, but Zoe felt her heart lurch, desperately wanting to scream out. To warn the child. Run! Don't trust him!

Thrusting her needlework aside, Zoe jumped to her feet and began to pace. He was stalking another little girl! But this was impossible. She never knew of a child's abduction *before* it happened! What was going on? Why was she seeing this?

"I like cookies. Can I have cookies?"

He felt her sweet little voice roll through him like warm honey, touching all the black places in him and making them light. Need curled in his gut, hungry and demanding. An urge too strong to deny. Too forceful to ignore.

"Just hurry, Em." The mother gazed down at her shopping list and then back up at the shelves, distracted by her price comparisons. Emily skipped off with a wide smile, her doll tucked under her arm.

He glanced back at the mother. She was oblivious.

His eyes took in everything. Stock boy, one customer, two. Then he

found what he was looking for and smiled. So easy. It would be so easy.
And Emily would be his.

Nancy Darrington held her breath as a state trooper drove by on the opposite side of the highway. She kept glancing in her mirrors to make sure he didn't turn around and come after her, but he disappeared from sight.

A few miles later, she rolled her shoulders, easing the tension. The child in the car seat murmured softly. Nancy stole another look in the rearview mirror. The child was fast asleep.

The mirror revealed dark circles under her eyes, tight lines around her mouth, and the unfamiliar color of her hair. She'd dyed it again, of course. She couldn't even remember the color this time. It had been red, blond, and varying shades of brunette. This time it was almost black, making her green eyes look even more haunted than before.

She rolled her shoulders again as she spotted the Florida state line. Maybe she'd be safe here. Maybe no one would look here for her and the child.

Maybes were all she'd lived on for so very long. Maybe John wouldn't kill her. Maybe he wouldn't beat her today. Maybe he'd work late and give her a few more minutes of peace. Maybe she could get away. Maybe John wouldn't find her. Maybe no one would suspect that she wasn't Alice Denton or Mary Deere, or a host of other names she'd used to stay hidden.

Taking the child had been a mistake. She knew that. A woman on her own would attract far less attention.

One more mistake to add to the sum total of her life.

◆　　◆　　◆

"Emily?"

He turned away from the child as the mother came down the aisle. He flashed a quick but distracted smile in her direction and reached up to the top shelf to pull down a box of crackers.

"Emily? Did you find your cookies?"

"Here, Mommy."

He kept his back to them, trying to subdue his disappointment and frustration. He had been so close.

So close. He wanted that little girl. He wanted Emily.

And he was going to have her.

It was just going to take more planning, that's all. He'd watch. And wait. Another opportunity would arise soon enough.

Shoving the box of crackers back on the shelf, he wandered through the store, keeping an eye on his sweet little Emily. She skipped down aisles and made him smile. She giggled at something her mother said and his heart lifted with joy.

So sweet, his Emily. Look at her. That cute little pug nose and those chubby cheeks. Those bright eyes so full of innocence and love. Perfection. Goodness.

And it would be his. But not quite yet.

Jeff looked up from his paper and, tilting his head, stared over the rim of his glasses. "Rene? What has you pacing like a caged tiger?"

"I don't know," Rene said, blowing out a deep breath as she dropped down onto the sofa. "I can't get that psychic out of my mind." She looked over at Jeff. "The poor girl believes she's doing this for God. She has no clue she's been deceived."

"Do you think she's open to hearing truth?"

Rene shrugged lightly. "I don't know. She got real defensive when I told her that it wasn't God. I probably came on way too strong though. I do that sometimes, you know."

Jeff's lips twitched with amusement. "Do you?"

She laughed. "Like you haven't noticed." Her smile faded. "I didn't mean to come on that strong. Things were just starting to spin out of control. I had to stop her before she got Karen into trouble."

"And now you can't get the girl out of your mind."

"Yeah."

"And?"

Rene playfully glared at him. "I hate when you do that."

"I know." Jeff pushed his glasses back up his nose and turned his attention to his reading.

"Okay! Okay. I'll go pray for her."

"I never thought you'd do otherwise, my sweet."

Rene stuck out her tongue at him as she marched past him on her way to their bedroom. He reached out and smacked her bottom lightly. "I saw that."

Rene giggled like a little girl. "I meant for you to."

He picked up a box of rice and stared over the top of it as the mother pushed her cart up next to the meat counter. "Emily, come with me, honey."

"Where, Mommy?"

"I have to use the ladies' room."

"Awwww, Mommy. I want to stay here."

"You come with me, Emily." She took her daughter's hand and pulled her through the double doors into the back storage area where the

public restrooms were located.

He smiled. Oh, this couldn't get more perfect. It was a sign. Emily was definitely meant to be his. He put the box of rice back on the shelf and drifted toward the restrooms.

JJ looked at his watch and then at the men gathered around the conference table. He'd just finished forming two teams: one working on Gina's abduction and the other following up the Denton lead on the Matthews case. He knew he was spreading them thin, but he didn't have much choice.

The phone rang. Matt reached over and picked it up. Less than a minute later, he slammed it down and reached for his coat. "We have another missing little girl. Six years old."

JJ jumped up, sending his chair flying backwards to crash into the filing cabinet behind it. He didn't even bother picking it up. "Not again. Please, not another little girl. Gerry! Wayne! Forget Denton for now and come with us. I want this little girl back home with her family tonight!"

chapter 8

Zoe strolled through the mall, watching shoppers, eyeing bar-
gains, fingering soft fabrics, buying nothing—all in an attempt
to forget the haunting images of three little faces that had been
chasing her all morning. She saw it in the newspaper headlines,
then heard it on the radio, then watched it on the morning talk
show while she struggled through a light breakfast. Even in the
mall, televisions were tuned to some news show running the images
over and over and over.

Gina Sarentino. Jessica Matthews. Emily Terrance. Zoe felt helpless once again to stop the abductions. Or to find the children. She'd
"seen" him stalking Emily for hours and couldn't do a thing to stop
him. Now the child was gone. What good was this gift if she couldn't
save lives? Was it a gift or a curse condemning her to a life in the shadows of evil, always seeing the destruction and never able to stop it?

"Your gift is not from God."

Rene Taylor's words echoed through her mind. What could she
possibly have meant by that? Of course it was from God. Where
else could it have come from? The world had become enlightened
since the Middle Ages, but obviously Rene Taylor wasn't aware of that.

Psychics were acceptable in today's society. People didn't hunt them down, declare them witches, and burn them at the stake anymore.

Zoe stopped in front of a shoe store and eyed a pair of strappy sandals. They'd go perfectly with that blue skirt her mother had given her for her birthday.

Determined to buy them, she went inside the store and looked around for a salesperson. She found two over by the children's shoes, chatting away.

"And I'm telling you they're all fakes!" one said passionately as she straightened a display.

"They are not! I went to a psychic once and she told me all kinds of things she couldn't possibly have known. She wasn't a fake."

The first girl sniffed in derision. "Bull. She told you what you wanted to hear. They just give you generalizations that anyone could twist to match their own circumstances."

"Well, what about that psychic the police have called in to help them! She's supposed to be pretty good."

"Hah! She hasn't done squat, has she? You are so gullible some-times, Trish. Has she found any of those missing children? No. And has she been able to tell the police anything about the killer? No. And has she ever found a single child before they were killed? No. So what good is she? A cadaver dog could do what she does."

Zoe flushed hot as she backed away from the girls and slipped out of the store. The girl's words stung. *A cadaver dog could do what she does.*

She drove home with the words still ringing in her ears. A light changed from green to yellow and Zoe slowed, easing to a stop as it turned red. Drumming her fingers on the steering wheel, she glanced to her right.

It was a billboard. And the message sent a cold shiver down her back.

I'm talking to you. Love, God.

That night, Matt Casto chewed without tasting what he was eating. All he could think about was that poor mother collapsed on the grocery store floor, sobbing as she clung to JJ's shirt, begging them to find her little girl.

Emily Terrance.

The scumbag had taken her out of the grocery store without anyone noticing. He glanced at his watch. More than twenty-four hours had passed, and they still didn't have one clue as to the child's whereabouts.

"Matt?"

The security tapes had been no help at all. The cheap cameras were set too far away to get a clear look at anyone's face. They were clearly installed to intimidate shoplifters, not identify kidnappers. Once again, the kidnapper had been one step ahead of them. He'd gone out the back door with the child, making sure nothing would be caught on tape.

"Matt, are you listening to me?"

Matt started, nearly tipping over his glass and spilling his iced tea. He grabbed it, steadied it, and stared sheepishly at Paula. "I'm sorry. I was thinking about that little girl."

Paula tilted her head. "Maybe we should have just canceled tonight. Your mind is definitely *not* on dinner and a movie."

Shaking his head, he pushed his marinated chicken around on his plate. "I wanted to be here. Get my mind off the case for a few hours. Clear my head a little."

"But it's not working."

"I know." Matt looked up, frowning. "I'm sorry."

"Don't be." Paula reached across the table and stroked his hand. "What you do is important, Matt. Don't apologize for being good at it."

Tension flowed out of him as her fingers stroked, her eyes forgave, and her smile warmed. Yesterday he and JJ had gone up and down every aisle on what they knew was a fool's journey: to find evidence. They'd spent hours talking with store employees, customers, and the mother.

They had gone over security tapes and witness statements in between fielding calls from concerned or outraged citizens and the press.

By the time he'd pulled up in front of Paula's apartment, he felt as wired as a druggie on a bad high.

"Three little girls, Paula. And we don't have a single lead to go on."

"What about that psychic? Has she been any help?"

Matt shook his head as he toyed a little more with his food. "Not really. Besides, JJ doesn't believe in her or her so-called powers, so he's not giving her as much access to everything as Harris told him to."

"Won't Harris find out? He might talk to this woman and then JJ could be in trouble."

"Harris hasn't even met Miss Shefford. I think he's afraid to. No, he won't talk to her and find out anything. He's leaving it all to JJ to handle. In the meantime, we're getting nowhere on the Matthews case either."

"The missing baby?"

"Yeah." Matt speared a green bean and stared at it. "JJ still thinks the parents were involved, but we've got nothing so far to prove they were."

"Do you think they were? The parents? Do you really think they killed their own baby?"

He looked over at Paula. "Honestly? I'm not sure. The Matthews woman has me confused. On the surface, she appears to be devastated to have her child missing. On the other hand, something isn't quite right about her—like her circuits aren't all wired with solid connections."

"So you think she may be capable of. . .what. . .killing her baby by accident and then crying wolf?"

"Maybe." He rubbed his chin. "I can't quite get a handle on this one, Paula, and it's driving me a bit nuts."

"Hey! Look who's here!" Matt's cousin Pete Gribbon leaned down and kissed Paula on the cheek. She smiled up at him.

"Hey, Pete. How's Ginny?"

"She's fine. Took the boys to visit her mom for a few days, so I'm reduced to take-out or eat-out."

"Have a seat," Matt told him. "Eat with us."

"You sure?" Pete pulled out a chair but hesitated. "I don't want to intrude. You two looked pretty intense. I'm not interrupting something, am I? You know. . .wedding plans, stuff like that?"

Paula rolled her eyes and then pointed to the chair. "Sit, and bite your tongue. We were just talking about the little girls who are being kidnapped."

"Oh, yeah." The grin disappeared as he shook his head. "I've been hearing about that on the news." He pulled up a chair to the table and waved down a waiter. "There's two missing, right?"

"Three. We had another one disappear yesterday."

"Ouch. I didn't even realize you were on that case." Pete leaned back as the waiter appeared at his side. "I'll have whatever they're having and iced tea."

"Marinated chicken over wild rice with. . ."

Pete waved his hand, cutting the waiter off. "That's fine. I'm not hard to please."

"Yes, sir." The waiter moved away.

Pete propped his elbows on the table and looked over at Matt. "You're on this special task force they've been talking about?"

Matt nodded. In spite of JJ's intense dislike of Pete, Matt found that except for occasionally saying tactless things at the wrong time, he was a good man. He was a loving husband, a good father, and a good friend. When Matt moved into his new apartment, Pete was there that morning with a borrowed truck to help with the move. Pete loved to harass JJ though; that was certain. The two had never hit it off and probably never would.

"Matt? Pete asked you about the task force." Paula shrugged at Pete. "He's been like this all night. Don't mind him."

"I'm sorry," Matt replied sheepishly. "Just thinking. Uh, yeah, I'm on the task force."

"Any leads yet?"

Matt shook his head. "Nope."

Pete leaned over and placed his hand on Matt's shoulder. "Hang in there, pal. You're a good detective. You'll catch the guy."

"I hope so, and I hope we do it soon."

"I'm sure you will. In the meantime," Pete turned his attention to Paula, "how are you holding up with all this?"

"I'm used to it."

"Doesn't make it easy though."

"What are you talking about?" Matt sat there, empty fork in hand, and stared at his cousin.

"Oh, come on, Matt. We all know how you neglect Paula when you're chin-high in some case. It's gotta be lonely for her."

"I'm fine," Paula insisted.

"She's fine," Matt parroted. "And I don't neglect her."

"Right. Sorry."

"Do I neglect you?" Matt turned to Paula and watched as she dropped her eyes. "You think I neglect you?"

"Could we not discuss this here and now?" Paula whispered tightly across the table.

"I just want to know if you think I neglect you."

"No. I don't. Okay? Now, can we drop it?"

"Fine. Consider it dropped." He jabbed angrily at a piece of chicken and shoved it in his mouth. He didn't neglect her. Okay, maybe he only managed to squeeze in an hour or two a week to see her, but he called every couple of days, didn't he? He was on a case, for crying out loud. She knew how it was.

JJ unlocked the front door to the townhouse he rented and stepped inside. Tossing his jacket over a sofa chair, he immediately went into the kitchen, flipped on a light, and opened the back door. A large golden retriever came bounding in, jumping up on him. "Hey, Zip, miss me?"

The dog let out one sharp and very loud bark. JJ laughed and pushed the dog down. "Ready for dinner?" He reached out on the deck and brought in Zip's water bowl.

Zip stayed on JJ's heels while he changed the water in the water bowl and filled the food bowl. Then he settled down to eat while JJ went through his mail and fished through the refrigerator for something to make for dinner. He decided to broil a steak, throw together a salad, and toss a potato in the microwave.

While dinner was cooking, JJ changed into a pair of sweats. Treading barefoot through the house, he fed the fish in his aquarium, watered the plants in the living room, and checked on the steak.

It had been the day from hell. He'd thought it was rough after Gina Sarentino and Jessica Matthews had disappeared, but he'd found out that was nothing compared to the eruption after Emily

Terrance was taken. Harris could be heard screaming from one end of the station house to the other. The mayor was out to roll a few heads—and careers with them. The press was screaming. Civic-minded citizens were up in arms.

And he had nothing to tell any of them.

That thought had him pushing away his half-eaten plate in disgust and frustration. Zip was thrilled, of course. Half a sirloin steak ended up in his bowl.

After tossing the dishes in the dishwasher, JJ headed for his den. He turned on the radio to a classical station and settled down in front of his computer to do some work.

So far there had been no leads on the whereabouts of Nancy Darrington—or whatever name she was going by this week. Gerry Otis had obtained a photograph from John Darrington and sent it out to all the police stations not only in this state but in the four surrounding states as well.

They hadn't heard a word yet.

Then there were the three little girls. JJ looked down at the pictures again, although he didn't need to. He could see them in his dreams. The killer had been slick. And elusive. No fingerprints, no fluids, no trace of him at all. Nothing.

Leaning back, JJ rubbed his eyes with the heels of his hands. This was going nowhere fast. All he could hope was that his call to Quantico might provide some answers. Or at least some help. The profiler, a man by the name of Adam Zahn, had been with the Child Abduction Serial Killer Unit for over twelve years. He was supposed to be one of the best. CASKU had merged with Investigation Support at the FBI headquarters in Quantico and was now known as the National Center for the Analysis of Violent Crime. He didn't care what name they had on the door. He just needed someone who understood the mind of a kidnapper and could help find him. And bring him to justice.

He was certain the Matthews case was different. And he was sure Karen Matthews had something to do with the missing child. He no longer had any hope that Jessica Matthews was still alive. The way he figured it, Karen had killed the child—either intentionally or by accident—and was covering up the crime by screaming abduction. Was her husband in on it? Was he protecting his wife? Maybe.

JJ leaned back in his chair and propped his legs up on the corner of the desk. The man was obviously protective of her and had implied, ever so subtly, that she wasn't particularly stable. Yet was Ted Matthews protecting whom he believed was his innocent wife, or was he tossing out a smoke screen to deflect the investigation from looking at her too closely?

He didn't want to think of Zoe at all. There was no doubt that Harris was going to be all over him to call her again about Emily Terrance, but JJ was inclined to wait until he had no choice. The last thing he wanted was that little witch digging at him again.

His fist scraped across his chest as if he could still feel the pain of her words lashing out at him. *"Your father was right about you!"*

chapter 9

JJ woke up with a throbbing headache and temper to match. Rather than driving to the station after showering and dressing, he drove straight to the Matthews' house and caught Mrs. Matthews washing the breakfast dishes. Her husband, she explained, had already left to help some friends for the day. The conversation went downhill quickly. As soon as he started playing hardball, Karen withered into a worthless puddle of whining.

"But Alice wouldn't do such a thing." Karen wrung her hands, which only fueled JJ's temper. Why couldn't the woman just stand up and answer the questions without all these oh-poor-pitiful-me games?

"There is no Alice Denton! She didn't have children. And she uses at least three aliases that we've been able to come up with so far. If one of the aliases is her real name, she was married and left her husband almost a year ago. He's been looking for her."

"I didn't know. I swear. She seemed so nice, and she was so good with Jessica. I just didn't think to check her references."

"You place your child in the care of a woman you don't know just because you think she seems nice? No wonder your baby is missing."

"That's not fair!" Karen took a step backward.

It wasn't and he knew it, but this case was driving him crazy. He had never seen such ineptitude in his life. "You never thought it strange that she would only take her pay in cash? No checks?"

Karen shook her head. "She said she preferred cash. I didn't see any crime in that."

"What reason did she give you for leaving?"

"She said that she had a family problem and couldn't work for me anymore. She even cried when she told me. She was so upset to have to leave us."

"Right," JJ snapped caustically. "Well, what about her car? Did you ever see it?"

Karen shook her head again. "No. She said she didn't have one. I think she took the bus."

"She owns a fairly new burgundy Chrysler Concorde."

Karen stared down at her hands. "I can't believe she lied like that. I thought she was so nice."

JJ ignored her comment. He was afraid that if he responded she would sue him for attacking her. "What was she like with Jessica?"

"Oh, she adored Jessica."

JJ made a face as he continued to make notes. "Think back. Can you recall her ever talking about where she'd come from or some-place she always wanted to go? Anything that might give us a handle on where she might be headed?"

Karen thought for a moment. "No, I don't think so. She didn't talk about other places. I assumed she was local and always had been."

She wiped new tears. "I can't believe this. She was so good with Jessica. And she was always talking about her little boy. I think his name was Johnny."

Johnny. As in John Darrington. He hadn't thought to ask if they'd had a child together. Something else to check out. This water was getting muddier and muddier. In the meantime, he had to get back to the station. With any luck, he might hear from the profiler in Virginia. At least the aspirin had started to kick in and dissipate the headache.

◆　◆　◆

Most Saturday afternoons, Jan Alberry would be getting her hair cut or her nails done or cleaning her house and doing laundry—catching up on everything she didn't have time to do during the week while she was chasing the news.

But on this particular Saturday afternoon, she had her face buried in copies of old newspaper stories scattered across her desk. After nearly a week of research, she was finally hitting pay dirt. One old clipping in particular had her foot tapping beneath her desk.

LOCAL GIRL DISAPPEARS—COMMUNITY LOCKING THEIR DOORS

Ten-year-old Amy Marie Shefford disappeared yesterday after walking home from school with her twin sister, Zoe. "She was right behind me," cried the distraught blond-haired child. "When she didn't come in the house, I looked and looked for her but she was gone."

State police were called in by Police Commissioner Thomas Ryder when an extensive search of the neighborhood proved fruitless.

Jan flopped back in her chair, blowing out a heavy breath. "So the woman has a history after all."

"What did you say?" Lois Pollack looked up from her desk where she was working on recipes for the Sunday edition.

"Did you hear about that psychic the police brought in to help with the missing children?"

"Sure." Lois shrugged. "Who hasn't?"

"Well, I just found out that the woman had a twin sister, and when they were ten, the sister was kidnapped and killed."

"Whoa." Lois stared, her eyes wide with amazement. "No kidding?"

Jan picked up the clipping. "Her sister disappears and is never found, and now she's devoted her life to finding missing children. I wonder if she's still looking for Amy."

"Huh?"

Jan shook her head. "Nothing. Just thinking out loud."

She set the story aside and began searching through the rest, setting the articles in chronological order. She was on to something. She just knew it. Amy Shefford had disappeared in 1983. Then there was nothing more in the news for almost ten years. In 1992 Zoe Shefford made the news again when she found a missing boy down by the lake after he'd wandered off from his parents. He'd been seriously injured in a fall, and if Zoe hadn't found him when she did, he'd have died. The parents touted her as a hero. There was a picture of the mayor shaking her hand.

Quickly Jan gathered up all the copies and slipped them into a file folder. She'd only searched through the files for Zoe Shefford. She needed to go back and look at the files for missing children. More than likely she'd find a solitary blond girl somewhere in the background, trying to help.

"I thought you were working on the latest disappearance."

"Emily Terrance. I've already done all I can on the story and turned it in to Ed."

"I just can't believe we've got something like this going on in our town. Three little girls. Gone. It's enough to make you wonder. I mean, in a big city, sure. But not here."

"It's not just big cities anymore, Lois. Evil is everywhere."

Lois shuddered. "I'm glad right now that I don't have kids. It would drive me nuts constantly wondering if they were in danger. I'd have to lock them up in their rooms or something."

Janice felt a twinge of guilt. She'd been so caught up in the details of the kidnappings, she really hadn't thought about how the mothers and fathers must feel. She'd seen their tears, documented their impassioned pleas, but it was just news copy. At twenty-three, Janice felt that having children was something for the faraway future, not something she thought much of in the present. What would it be like to have a child and then have someone take that child? She couldn't relate. Couldn't imagine.

Grabbing her purse, she jumped up from her chair. "I have some more research to do."

Rene closed the car door and started up the front walk, groceries in hand, when a light blue convertible pulled up to the curb. She spotted the blond hair and knew immediately that it was Zoe Shefford. Halting at the bottom of the front steps, she waited while Zoe climbed out of her car and joined her.

"I hope I haven't stopped by at a bad time." Zoe sounded nervous.

"Not at all," Rene responded with a welcoming smile. "Come on in."

She settled Zoe at the kitchen table while she put on water for tea then quickly put away the groceries. A few minutes later, she placed a mug of tea in front of Zoe along with a small plate of shortbread and then settled into the chair across from the young woman.

"I gather you wanted to talk to me about something?"

Zoe nodded as she stirred sugar into the steaming tea. "I haven't been able to stop thinking about what you said. You know, about my gift not being from God. I guess I just need some clarification or something. None of it makes any sense to me."

"I know. And I'm sorry about what happened over at Karen's

that day. I didn't mean to come on so strong or so negatively. You had all the best intentions." She dipped a piece of shortbread in her tea and gathered her thoughts.

"I really wanted to find Mrs. Matthews's baby."

Rene nodded as she swallowed. "I know you did, sweetheart. But we couldn't let you get involved."

"Why not? I mean, if I could have found the child, wouldn't that have been a good thing?"

Rene watched as Zoe dropped her hands into her lap. She felt sorry for the young woman. "It might have been a good thing, Zoe, but it wouldn't have been a God thing. And there is a difference. Zoe, you're searching for answers, and they have nothing to do with Jessica Matthews."

Zoe's eyes met hers and held. Rene could easily read the questions and the confusion. Zoe's next words caught her off guard. "Did Karen Matthews hurt her baby?"

Unaware that her mental state was being discussed at that very moment by her neighbor, Karen Matthews entered her daughter's nursery. She knew she was only tormenting herself, but she couldn't help it. She moved past the crib, her fingers trailing over the smooth wood, before reaching out for the soft pink bear on the dresser. She folded it in her arms and held it close as she stood there in her daughter's room.

Was she dead? Was she alive? Was she gone forever? Would she be coming home someday?

Questions with no answers. Torment without relief. Grief without understanding, and loss without ending.

She wanted to hold Jessica one more time. No. That was a lie. She wanted to hold Jessica and never let her go. She wanted to bury her face in Jessica's soft skin and breathe her in. Listen to her little heartbeat. Smell the powder and shampoo and the very essence of her precious daughter. She wanted to see Jessica laugh and to hear her cry. To watch her sleep and stretch herself awake with that soft mewling cry for her mommy.

And she'd never let her out of her sight again.

What would she pay to get Jessica back? *Anything.*

Zoe Shefford?

The name rose up inside her, taunting her, teasing. Zoe had found other children. She could find Jessica. What real harm would it do?

Plenty.

Karen dropped down in the rocking chair, tears welling up in her eyes. The silence in the house seemed overwhelming. She glanced over to the blanket that Zoe Shefford had held in her hands.

Zoe might be able to find Jessica. Was it worth it? What would be her punishment for disobeying God? Wasn't her daughter's life worth anything?

What if Rene Taylor is wrong? What if she's just some fanatic?

"Karen?" Ted stood in the doorway. He had gone to help someone from work move into a new home and was a mess. He looked as though someone had dragged him behind the truck. His pullover and jeans were dusty and streaked with dirt. His dark brown hair was ruffled, as if he'd been dragging his fingers through it, and his dark eyes were solemn. He looked as bad as she felt.

Karen lifted her face and gazed through red-rimmed eyes at her husband. "Are you home already?"

"It's after four. Have you been in here long?"

After four? Where had the time gone? She shook her head, setting the bear down on the dresser as she moved over to him, lifting her face for a kiss. "No. Not long. How did the move go?"

"Not bad. Harry had enough people there to make it go fast. We were done a lot earlier than I thought we would be. He just overlooked pulling up the kids' swing set, so Jack and I were elected to pull it out of the ground and tear it down." He looked down at his shirt and frowned. "As you can see, the swing set won the tug of war."

Karen smiled wearily. "It was nice of you to help them."

"Harry's helped me out on more than one occasion." He pointedly eyed the bear on the dresser. "You're not making this any easier on yourself, coming in here and looking at all this. You know that, don't you?"

Karen gazed up at him. "Staying away doesn't make it any easier. Coming in here doesn't make it any easier. The truth is, until Jessica is home, nothing will be easier."

Ted turned and walked toward the bedroom. "And what if she never comes home, Karen? What then?"

Karen followed him to the door of their bedroom, watching as he pulled his shirt over his head and tossed it in the hamper by the bathroom door. "Never comes home? I can't even go there, Ted. This is our daughter we're talking about. How can you just write her off?"

Pulling a clean shirt out of the dresser, he used his hip to nudge the drawer closed and yanked the shirt over his head. "I'm *not* writing her off, Karen. I'm trying to face reality here. I can't bury myself in grief and stop living."

"And that's what you think I'm doing?"

"I don't know!" Ted hissed with frustration as he pulled the shirt back off and tossed it on the bed. "Yes! Maybe! You moon around with that sad face and cry at the drop of a hat. How long can you live like this?"

"I'm trying to deal with this, Ted. My daughter has been kidnapped. I don't know if she's dead or alive. I don't know if she's coming back or not, but I'm not ready to bury her yet."

"*Your* daughter?" Ted stepped into the bathroom and shoved back the shower curtain. He turned on the water before looking at her. "How about *our* daughter?"

"I didn't mean it that way."

Ted brushed past her. Karen rushed down the hall after him, following him into the kitchen. "You meant it exactly that way. Ever since Jessica was born, it's been Jess this and Jessica that. I've become incidental at best."

"That's not true!"

Opening the refrigerator, Ted stared at the shelves. "No? When was the last time you went shopping? Did it ever dawn on you that I might want to eat something?"

Karen nipped her bottom lip between her teeth. "I'm sorry."

"But," he muttered, slamming the refrigerator door shut, "you stepped into Jessica's room and that was that. Good old Ted was forgotten."

"Please, Ted."

"Please, what? Overlook this? Forget this? Or forgive this? Which is it, Karen? Just last month, you came home from church with Jessica and told me what a wonderful, inspiring message Reverend Pollack gave about trusting God. Now you act like God doesn't exist!"

"What?"

He started opening cabinet doors, pointing out the lack of food. "If you trust God with our daughter, then act like it. Get on with your life and trust God to bring her home!"

Karen took a step back, wanting to deny and defend but finding it impossible to do so. He was right. She hadn't been trusting God at all. She'd let everything go. It was a wonder Ted had clean clothes to wear. *The dry cleaners! She was supposed to pick up Ted's suits two days ago!*

Ted slammed one of the cabinet doors. "I'm going to take a

shower. Do you think you could manage to call out for food?"

Karen nodded meekly as he stormed out of the kitchen. With trembling hands, she reached for the take-out menus stacked near the phone. She would run by the dry cleaners on her way to pick up the food.

Ted didn't need to know she'd let him down again.

FBI profiler Adam Zahn's voice came across the line low and steady. JJ could almost picture him—suit and tie, dark hair, mustache, and broad shoulders to go with that steady personality. He had to give the guy credit. Zahn worked fast. JJ had called Thursday night after Emily Terrance's disappearance. It was now Saturday afternoon.

"It's hard to say if you have a serial killer on your hands with what little information you've given me, but if we go on the assumption that you do, I may be able to help."

JJ grabbed a legal pad and turned to a clean sheet. "Go ahead. I'm listening."

"It's hard to pinpoint the exact reason your unsub is going after children, but I suspect it's for their innocence or their purity or their goodness."

"I thought this was all about control."

"It is. You've got an unsub who strikes and then retreats. There could be months, even years, between killings. He is careful and organized, leaving few, if any, clues behind."

JJ snorted softly. "No kidding. We have no fingerprints, no DNA, no fibers."

"Exactly. He's a pro and the worst kind of killer there is. He can sit back patiently and watch you chase your tail. If my guess is right, he's probably been at this for years."

"Insane," JJ muttered darkly, seeing a long trail of unsolved murders in his future.

"Far from it. He probably appears perfectly normal to everyone around him. You could pass him in the grocery store, the mall. . . . He's the man who helps you buy a house or a car, or he could be your electrician. He's more than likely a white male between the ages of thirty-five and fifty. Neatly groomed, above-average intelligence, and probably has no traceable history of mental illness, although that's not a guarantee."

JJ sighed, shaking his head. This wasn't much. The profiler hadn't been exaggerating. "Okay, we have two little girls, both six years old, and an infant—"

"I don't think the infant is in this. Just my gut talking when I read over the reports. It's a different M.O. entirely. You've got two different things going on here."

JJ slapped his hand down on his desk. "Yes! Finally someone who agrees with me!"

"Been fighting the politics game, eh? How well I remember. Give you the job because they say you're the best man for it and then tell you how to do it every step of the way, even when you know they're wrong."

"Exactly."

"Well," Zahn said with a chuckle, "tell them I said you're right."

"I will. And then I'm going after Karen Matthews."

"If you're hunting a serial killer, do you really have time to worry about this case with the baby?"

"Probably not, but this has become somewhat personal for me. I want to nail that lady to the wall for killing her baby. And I will. I most definitely will."

chapter 10

Monday, April 17

Zoe was jerked out of sleep before her alarm went off by the sound of a lawn mower under her bedroom window. After another restless night tossing and turning, she'd finally drifted off to sleep just before dawn. Gina had come to her in her dreams, calling to Zoe through the swirling mists. Zoe had run to her, but each time she came close, the child would disappear in the shadows. And Rene Taylor would appear, shaking her head and saying, "This is not of God," over and over.

The dread that had been building all night was still with her as she slipped into her robe. It dragged at her limbs and shadowed her thoughts.

With a groan, she stumbled to the kitchen and started the coffee. Just once, she'd like to see Frank put her on the end of his route instead of the beginning. Every Monday morning, he started his day with her. He was dependable. Irritatingly so, sometimes.

She turned on the television and flipped through the channels to catch the news. When she saw a familiar newscaster's face appear, she tossed the remote down on the counter. It slid across the tile and went crashing to the floor.

Zoe dove for it and missed, watching it bounce off the little carpet in front of her sink. Picking it up, she turned it over and breathed a sigh of relief. It wasn't broken.

"And it came to pass, as we went to prayer, a certain damsel possessed with a spirit of divination met us."

Confused, Zoe looked over at the television. The bouncing remote had changed the channel. In place of the newscaster, there was a young man in a suit and wire-rimmed glasses.

"Today we would call them psychics," he said to his television congregation. "And Paul cast that evil spirit out of her."

Zoe changed the channel. *Evil spirit. Hogwash.*

By the time she was out of the shower and dressed, she'd forgotten about the TV sermon and Frank was mowing the backyard. With coffee in hand, she stepped out on the deck and watched him.

Frank Harrow was close to fifty years old with a shock of gray-streaked dark brown hair. He was a big man, although he only stood an inch less than six feet. Broad of girth, he had big hands and thick fingers that were uncharacteristically nimble around the delicate blooms he nurtured. His wife had cancer and the prognosis wasn't good. Frank mentioned that his daughter had come from California to help take care of her.

Hiring Frank to take care of her yard had not been her idea. It had been her father's. She frowned, remembering how Frank had shown up one morning with a copy of his contract.

"Your father hired me to take care of your lawn this summer. He tells me you travel a bit. It's all paid for, Miss. No need to worry about it."

As much as she wanted to call her father and tell him once again that she didn't want any favors from him, she just hadn't been able to resist Frank's forlorn expression when she said she didn't want the service. Five years later, he was still taking care of her yard. Besides, the man did a great job, even if he had remained aloof and cool toward her. He mowed the lawn, weeded the flowerbeds, and even planted flowers if she didn't get to it. He wasn't being paid to be friendly.

The engine on the mower suddenly died, and Zoe looked up to see Frank take a pair of pruning sheers out of his back pocket.

"Morning, Frank."

Frank tipped his head. "Morning."

"How's your wife, Frank? She feeling better?"

Frank frowned as he shook his head. "Chemo's taking its toll."

"I'm so sorry, Frank. You'll give her my best, won't you?"

The man nodded and went back to his pruning, and Zoe went back inside to make breakfast. The *whip-whir* of the weed whacker kept her company through a light breakfast of coffee and toast. Her thoughts kept pulling back to Gina Sarentino. It was a vague pull she knew well. As soon as she finished breakfast, Zoe called Mrs. Sarentino.

"Would you mind if I came by? I have a feeling I might be able to find Gina."

Gerry Otis scratched at the beard he was growing, now nearly two weeks old, and squinted at the fax he'd just picked up. A detective for nearly thirty years, he had been passed over for one promotion after another, but unlike most men, Gerry didn't take such things to heart. He was content exactly where he was. The way he figured, the more responsibility he took on at the station, the less time he had for his wife and four children, and he was nothing if not devoted to his family.

He'd let the younger, more ambitious men, like Johnson and Casto, burn out trying to make it to the top. They didn't have wives waiting for them at home or children who needed a father to guide them. He worked his forty to fifty hours at the station—except when it came to cases like these kidnappings—and gave one night a week to the church youth, but that was only because his four boys were all involved in the youth group.

"Anything? You're staring at that thing like it has four heads and a forked tail." Matt Casto walked up, coffee in hand.

"Close enough." Gerry handed the report to Matt. "Check this out. Our Mr. Ted Matthews seems to have no history before he turned twenty-one."

Matt glanced up at him and then down at the report, his lips moving silently as he read. "Strange. How do you figure this?"

"First guess? People change their names for a variety of reasons. Bad credit. . ."

"He was only twenty-one."

Gerry ignored the interruption. ". . .don't like the name they were born with, juvie problems. . ."

"We need to find out exactly who Matthews was before he became Edward Matthews." Matt handed the report back to Gerry.

"I'm on it."

Zoe pulled her car up to the curb in front of the Sarentino home and stopped. She stared with admiration at the rambling two-story brick home, the ivy winding its way up one side of the house, the neat flowerbeds, and the sweeping lawn. It was a beautiful home. Unfortunately, evil didn't care what kind of house you lived in.

At five minutes until one, Zoe walked up to the front door and rang the bell. The dark mists of knowing were already swirling through her mind, wrapping themselves around her senses. She stepped into the Sarentino house and felt the whispers of death.

JJ was pondering lunch prospects—call out for a sub or head across the street to the diner—when the door to his office suddenly swung open. Marsha Olsen stuck her head in the door. "You might want to check out channel five. Seems Mrs. Matthews is on the rampage."

While Marsha ducked back out, JJ flipped on the little TV set sitting on a file cabinet.

". . .and while Detective Johnson is trying to find some way to point the finger at us, no one is looking for my baby! And now a third child is missing. How many more little girls will be taken before Detective Johnson realizes we have a serial killer out there stalking our children! Please, if any of you have any information about my Jessica, please contact us."

Jessica's picture flashed on the screen along with head shots of Gina and Emily and a number scrolling below for people to call. JJ slammed his fist down on the desk. "What is that woman thinking?"

Matt lifted his coffee cup in a silent salute to Karen Matthews. "That the best way to get us off her back is to get the press on ours."

The office door swung open again. "JJ? Harris wants you in his office." Marsha rolled her eyes playfully. "Pronto," Marsha added in a fair imitation of Harris in full temper.

"And it worked," JJ grumbled under his breath.

JJ had barely walked through the door of Harris's office when the tirade started. For five minutes he sat and listened, gnawing on his impatience like a wolf on a deer bone.

Harris slammed his fist down on the desk, sending a pencil flying. No one paid it any attention. "And now I have the press breathing down my back! What have you been doing? Playing cards? We have three little girls missing, and you don't have one single lead! I want results, not excuses! Matthews doesn't like psychics? Tough!

Find some way of getting the Shefford woman what she needs! I want those children found, do you hear me?"

"But we're doing. . ."

"I don't want to hear it! Just find those little girls!"

JJ stood up, knowing the tirade had run its course and he had been dismissed. But he knew if he didn't come up with something solid soon, he might find himself dismissed all the way back down to a patrol car on third watch.

Coming out of the men's room, Matt fell into step with JJ but didn't say a word as he followed him back to his office. What was there to say?

JJ had his hand on the doorknob when Marsha looked up from her desk. "Phone message, JJ. The Shefford woman. Says she has to talk to you. It's important."

JJ took the pink slip of paper from Marsha. The last person in the world he wanted to talk to at that moment was Zoe Shefford. And she probably knew it. Which is why, he surmised, she was calling.

JJ sat down at his desk and counted to ten before dialing.

"Miss Shefford. Detective Johnson." He kept his voice cool and distant. "You called?"

"Yes. I went by the Sarentino home. I talked to her mother and she allowed me access to Gina's room. I think I know where she. . . where she is."

And pigs fly with blue wings. JJ ignored the emotional hitch in Zoe's voice as he counted to ten again. "I see. And just where would that be, Miss Shefford?"

There was a long moment of silence, long enough for JJ to start to wonder if she was still on the line. Or if she had suddenly disappeared in a mist of shadowy magic.

Rubbing his eyes, he wondered if he was losing his mind. "Miss Shefford?"

"I'm here. I think it would be best if you sent a detective over and I showed him."

JJ sighed impatiently. Then he saw Harris standing in the doorway, looking as curious as he was furious. "Fine, Miss Shefford. I'll be there at once."

He set the phone down and stood up, reaching for his jacket. "Miss Shefford thinks she may have a lead on the Sarentino child."

Harris grinned. "About time. Now we're getting somewhere."

That somewhere was ankle-deep in mud as JJ followed Zoe through the woods thirty miles east of Monroe, ten miles from the Taylor town limits. Two days of rain had brought the creeks to their limits. Some had overflowed their banks. The saturated ground sank beneath JJ's shoes as he and Zoe trudged up a slippery slope and into a grove of firs.

Dressed in jeans and boots, Zoe had obviously known what they were about to get into. She might have warned him—given him a little heads-up that his loafers were going to be ruined tracking in mud.

Zoe stopped and started to look around. She was silent.

JJ started to open his mouth, but Zoe lifted her hand to ask for his silence. He complied. Not that he had anything to say to her anyway. The last thing he wanted was to be on some wild-goose chase with this woman. They'd managed to maintain a tense silence throughout the drive and most of the trek across the mucky terrain.

Zoe slowly turned in a circle, stopping every few steps, as if waiting for something to speak to her. Or whatever it was that directed her to do whatever it was she was doing. JJ shoved his hands in his pockets and waited. Impatiently.

Finally, Zoe started moving again. A few steps to the left. Stopping again. A few more steps. Then a few more. Then every drop of color in her face disappeared in a flash, startling JJ.

"What?"

"She's here." Tears started streaming down Zoe's face. Slowly she knelt down, oblivious to the wet ground. She began to brush away the wet leaves and sticks.

JJ joined her. "What are you doing?"

She shook her head, frantic now, ignoring the tears as she tore at the ground. "Gina. Gina!"

JJ didn't know whether the woman had lost her mind or whether he had. He could only watch as she crawled around on the ground, her clothes getting muddy and wet, her hands covered in dirt.

Then she rocked back on her heels and lifted a tattered shirt. Closing her eyes, she bowed her head, handing the shirt to JJ.

JJ didn't need to see it twice. He grabbed his radio.

chapter 11

Monday, April 17

The area had a circus-like atmosphere within half an hour of JJ's call. Clowns with cameras and microphones ran around trying to get everyone's attention. Ringleaders shouted orders. Jugglers tried to do three things at once. Lions roared if something wasn't done fast enough to suit them.

And high above it all, JJ walked that tightrope—trying to keep order, get things done, and keep the crime scene clean and the press out of it.

Zoe and JJ had barely spoken since he'd called for additional detectives and the medical examiner. She'd followed him silently back to the car and gladly obeyed when he told her to stay put.

Zoe stood by JJ's car, her arms wrapped around her waist as she watched the body bag being carried out of the woods. There wasn't much to carry. One man had it cradled in his arms. What had once been a delightful little girl was now little more than forensic evidence.

It broke Zoe's heart.

And it reminded her of another. Another little girl who had once laughed and skipped and played. Another little girl who had woven dreams—dreams that would remain unfulfilled.

Oh, Amy. I will bring you home, sweet sister. I promise. Somehow I will bring you home.

Wiping at her tears, Zoe turned her head and stared over the top of the car, watching a maple tree swaying in the breeze. *Did you see it happen? Did you stand there, moving in the breeze when he took her out there into the woods? Did you wish you could talk or scream or stop him? Did it frustrate you to just stand there, leaves hanging as you watched? Did you feel helpless? Like I do?*

Feeling his presence, she turned and looked at JJ. She couldn't speak. Not yet. Closing her eyes, she swayed. *Here it comes*, she thought.

As it always does.

A second later, she collapsed in JJ's arms.

After passing Zoe off to another officer with instructions to take her home, JJ sat on the hood of his cruiser waiting for the crime scene investigators to arrive.

He turned his head as another cruiser pulled up, lights flashing. Groaning, JJ slid off the hood of the car and prepared himself for the worst.

"Heard you found one of the girls."

JJ took a deep breath. "Yes. The Sarentino girl."

The man rocked back on his heels, his hands resting on the belt weighed down by his gun, radio, handcuffs, and cell phone. "Heard they brought in a psychic."

There it was. Just what he'd been waiting for. Delivered on a silver platter with all the trimmings. "Wasn't my idea, Dad."

"Don't know what it is with detectives today. Used to be we

relied on good old-fashioned hard work, skill, and determination. Now, it's computers and psychics." He shook his head in disgust.

JJ wanted to remind his father that he'd never been a detective, but he knew such a remark would only make things worse. Or could they get worse? "Well, thank the mayor. He's the one who called this lady in."

"Just wanted to stop by and see what's what. Don't guess you need me though."

JJ shoved his hands in his pocket and bit down a nasty remark. "Nothing left to do now but wait for the CSIs."

"Nasty piece of work, this is." Josiah Johnson Sr.—Joe as he was called—took one last look around. "Well, it's best I get back to work. Crime isn't going to take a vacation while we stand here and do nothing."

No, Dad. You'd better go catch those speeding criminals on Marshall Highway. Heaven knows what crimes they're committing at this very moment in their sports cars.

But JJ held his tongue again.

Joe Johnson nodded and walked away, leaving JJ chewing on his tongue until he drew blood. Why? Why couldn't his father respect what he did? Why did he always try to humiliate him?

What did he ever do that was so bad?

Keyes Shefford shrugged out of the navy pinstriped suit coat and draped it over the back of a kitchen chair. Pulling at his tie, he opened the refrigerator and scanned the contents, looking for something to tantalize him into eating at home rather than calling out for food again.

At fifty-seven, Keyes might fairly have been described as

attractive, successful, and one of the most eligible bachelors in town. He would have laughed at such a description. Oh, he made good money as the owner of four real estate offices, but successful? Not in his eyes.

He once had an overwhelming desire for more. He hadn't been quite sure what *more* was, but he did learn its cost: everything near and dear to him. An affair with a coworker had sealed that fate.

At the time, he'd shrugged the desire off, thinking that *more* was going to replace her. And it wasn't as if he'd lost his children. He'd been given liberal visitation rights, even if he hadn't found much time to take advantage of them. Then Amy disappeared. Suddenly *more* seemed far less than what he'd had to start with.

His wife, his family, his dreams. Gone.

He'd never felt so alone. Everything became crystal clear that night as he sat listening to the police explain how sorry they were. He mourned for Amy, and he mourned not being able to reach out to his wife and hold her. They could not grieve together. He'd ruined all chances of that. She clung to Zoe. He clung to the emptiness in his own soul and cursed his foolishness.

Keyes turned his life around after that night. He stopped seeing Joan, spent more time with Zoe, and tried to get his wife back. Denise eventually forgave him but wouldn't take him back. He never managed to earn her trust again. Or Zoe's. It haunted him every day.

He didn't remarry, holding out some foolish hope that one day Denise would relent and take him back. Over the years, they'd regained some semblance of a friendship, although they never discussed Amy. Denise never allowed him too close, so he poured himself into his work. It made him a lot of money but did nothing to fill the gaping hole in his life.

Denise had refused any of his money, other than child support.

Zoe, on the other hand, still took his monthly checks without a word. He knew that she was, in her own way, trying to make him pay for his part in Amy's death by financing her work to find other missing children. Little did she know that he'd paid with far more than money. If only money could have somehow paid the debt and set him free.

Finding nothing in the refrigerator to interest him, Keyes pushed the door closed and reached for the phone. Intending to call his favorite deli, he was surprised to hear Denise's voice answer. For a moment, he couldn't speak, trying to accept that he'd called her number instead of Mario's.

"Hello?" she asked for the second time.

"Denise?"

"Keyes? Is something wrong?"

Taking a deep breath, Keyes leaned against the kitchen counter. "No. I'm sorry. I was hungry and meant to call a restaurant. I guess I had you and Zoe on my mind and called your number instead."

"Bad day?"

Keyes closed his eyes, letting her voice wash over him and sweep away some of the loneliness. "In some ways. How was yours?"

"It was okay. We were a little busy."

"How's Zoe?"

He heard the pause, the little intake of breath, and knew that something was bothering her. "Denise? Is she okay?"

"She's fine, Keyes. Wrapped up in another investigation. You know what it does to her."

Keyes closed his eyes, rubbing them with the tips of his fingers. "Yeah."

"Are you sure you're okay?"

"I'm fine." He reached for something to say. Anything. Just to keep her talking.

"Keyes?"

"What?"

"Why don't you come over? I made some pot roast and there's plenty. I figured Zoe might drop by, but I haven't heard from her, and I'd hate for it to go to waste."

"You sure?" Keyes hoped he didn't sound too anxious. Then again, whom was he fooling? Certainly not Denise. She knew him too well. "I'd appreciate it."

"I'll see you in a few minutes."

"Thanks, Denise." Keyes hung up the phone and grabbed his jacket, feeling a hundred percent better than he had just five minutes earlier. Snatching his car keys off the table near the front door, he glanced in the mirror and frowned. His curly brown hair was receding, his cheeks looked almost gaunt, and his gray eyes reminded him of an overcast sky just before a miserable, rainy day. He didn't want Denise to feel sorry for him. He just wanted her to love him again.

He just didn't have the foggiest idea how to win her back. He'd run out of ideas years ago. It was time to accept the way things were and move on.

JJ lay sprawled on the bench, pushing the bar of weights high enough to lock his elbows, hold it a few seconds, and then slowly lower it back down to the bar. Sweat was pouring off his face. He ignored it. He imagined that each time he strained against the weight, he was pushing out the anger and the frustration and the hurt. He was a grown man; still reduced to a child each time his father hit him with another slur.

"You aren't a man until your father says you're a man." He was eight years old and full of rage about the relationship he had—or didn't have—with his dad.

"Dad is never going to call me a man," he had confided to his grand-father. "Never! He hates me!"

"He doesn't hate you, Josiah. He just expects more of you than he does of himself, and that bothers him. Make some allowances—your dad is doing his best by you."

Make allowances. Oh, how JJ had tried. For years he'd tried. But it all came down to this: running to the gym every time he saw his father and abusing his body to the point of physical pain to erase the emotional scars.

"You know better, JJ. Never work this much weight without a spotter." Carl Fenlowe, the owner and manager of Weigh It Out, stood there with his hands on his hips and a scowl on his face. He was a small man in his late forties, but you'd never know it to look at him. His body was the envy of most thirty-year-olds. He had shaved his head, just for the fun of it, and wore a tiny diamond stud in his right ear. A tattoo of a wolf's head on his upper arm drew almost as much attention as his mischievous dark blue eyes. No humor was in those eyes this time. "I told you before, you keep this up, and I'm going to revoke your membership."

JJ dropped the bell on the bar and sat up, snatching the towel off the bench and wiping his face. "I didn't see anyone around."

Carl looked over to where three men were working out not ten feet from JJ, and then at two more who were on the treadmill. "Yes, I can see how empty this place is."

"They just came in."

"JJ," Carl sighed heavily, "you could have asked me."

"You were busy."

"I'm never too busy to make sure one of my customers doesn't kill himself. It's just a little quirk I have."

Carl leaned against the machine behind him. He was dressed as he always was in jogging pants and a sleeveless muscle shirt with the name of the gym on the front. "Just saw the news. Must have been bad."

JJ rolled his shoulders to ease the tension. "Bad enough."

"They say you have a psychic on the team."

JJ swung his leg over the bench and stood up. "That's a rumor. And the truth."

"You kidding?" Carl followed JJ to another machine and watched as JJ lay down on his stomach and hooked his feet under the bar. "You really using a psychic?"

JJ slowly lifted his feet, pulling his leg muscles so tight they strained visibly. "Not my idea, believe me. Some quack higher up got it in his head that she could actually help."

He slowly lowered his legs, his face tight.

Carl sat down on the machine next to JJ. "You think we have a serial killer on the loose?"

JJ stopped. He turned his head and stared up at Carl. "Honestly?"

"Wouldn't have asked if I didn't want an honest answer."

"Yeah. I think we do. He's already taken two little girls. I think there were others. And if we don't stop him, there will be more."

"Two? I thought there were three."

"Two. The baby is a different case. She doesn't fit the profile. The others were little girls, both over five years of age. Matthews was a baby. Just seven months old. My gut tells me it's different."

"What is this psychic woman like?"

JJ slowly started lifting leg weights again. "She faints at the sight of a body bag."

chapter 12

Fainting was embarrassing enough. Worse still, it had been captured on camera.

And now it was on the front page. Right there with the sensational story describing her discovery of Gina Sarentino. Or more accurately, Gina's body.

Zoe tossed the paper on the table and walked over to pour herself another cup of coffee. It was bad enough that she usually got lightheaded and passed out after finding a body, but to fall into the arms of a man who detested her, that was too much. She could imagine him smirking as he lifted her into the squad car.

At least he'd been considerate enough to have someone else drive her home so she could avoid the further embarrassment of facing him afterward.

Taking a deep breath, she sank into a chair and glanced at the paper again.

Psychic Falls for Detective after Finding Missing Child.

Zoe growled and swept the paper to the floor. She wasn't falling for anyone, least of all that arrogant. . .

That wasn't fair and she knew it. He was just a wounded soul, searching for some peace in his life. For a way to prove that he wasn't what he really thought he was.

The back door squeaked open. "Zoe?"

"In here, Daria."

Zoe's best friend stuck her head around the corner. "Hey, girl. Up for company?"

Zoe waved her over. "Come on in. Coffee's on if you want any."

Daria picked the paper off the floor and dropped down in the chair next to Zoe, tossing her handbag on the table. "I guess you aren't as crazy about the guy as they say." She grinned in that irrepressible way that usually brought a smile to Zoe's face. When it came to fun, Daria was first in line.

They had known each other since high school. Short and perky, Daria had dark hair in a spiky cut that made her appear fairy-like. Her flashing brown eyes never seemed to see the bad in anyone. She loved people, loved her salon, loved to talk, loved to laugh, and was the perfect friend for Zoe, whose life often crossed a line from which only Daria could bring her back.

"I think it's safe to say that he and I are not on the best of terms." Zoe wrapped her hands around her coffee mug. "Why aren't you at the shop?"

"I'm going to work eleven to closing. Should be a light day. I don't think I have more than a couple of cuts, a perm, and two frostings scheduled." She reached over and fingered the ends of Zoe's hair. "Speaking of which, aren't you due for a trim?"

Zoe shrugged with indifference. "I guess. I leave that stuff to you."

Daria frowned. "You have a few split ends. I'll drop over soon and trim it for you."

"Whatever's convenient for you." And convenient was not always easy to manage for Daria. In addition to running her own salon, she also dabbled in photography for salon magazines. When she wasn't at the shop, she was in her studio, managing temperamental models and stubborn lighting. She'd been begging Zoe for years to model her hair, but Zoe wasn't interested.

Daria dropped Zoe's hair and folded her arms on the table in front of her. "Now tell me how you really are."

"Angry at myself for picking that exact moment to pass out."

"Like you can control that."

"Upset about the little girl."

"As you should be."

"And ticked at myself for saying something to JJ that I shouldn't have said."

Daria tilted her head. "Who is JJ?"

Zoe nodded toward the paper. "The detective."

"You're on a first-name basis with the guy?" Daria's surprise lifted her eyebrows. "Since when do you get that close to the police?"

"I'm sure he doesn't think I'm on a first-name basis with him. He still calls me Miss Shefford in that icy voice of his. He has nothing but disdain for me, and I only made matters worse."

"How?" Daria reached over and picked up the paper, studying the man a little more critically.

"I saw something about his past and threw it in his face."

Daria dropped the paper as if it burned her fingers. "You? Since when do you use what you see against someone?"

"Since he made me angry."

"Since when can anyone make you *that* angry?"

Zoe made a face as she frowned. "He can."

"Wow. I'm impressed. I didn't think anyone could make you lose control." Daria squinted at the grainy photograph. "He looks like he might be attractive."

Zoe glanced over at the photograph and then pulled her eyes away. "He has some good qualities." She sipped from her mug. "Give me an hour and I might think of one."

Daria laughed lightly, her eyes sparkling with interest. "I absolutely must meet this man."

At that moment, the doorbell rang. Zoe sighed and stood up. "Be right back."

Zoe opened the door and groaned silently. Turning on her heel, she strode back into the kitchen with JJ following her.

Daria stood up and tilted her head back to look up at him. "I'm Daria Cicala. You must be the very nice man who helped my friend."

Zoe rolled her eyes and struggled not to laugh as her friend all but simpered.

JJ shook Daria's hand. "I don't know that I was much help."

"We're just having coffee. Would you care for some?"

JJ shook his head. "I just need to talk to Miss Shefford for a moment."

"Miss Shefford?" Daria laughed again, letting her fingertips slide across his arm ever so gently. "Honey, no one calls Zoe that."

"I do." Dismissively, JJ turned to Zoe, who was still struggling to keep her expression bland and unreadable. Leave it to Daria to put a little sunshine in her life. "Mrs. Terrance called. She was hoping you might be able to help."

"I can try." She walked over to the table and picked up her mug to keep her hands from shaking. Another child. How she dreaded this. "Have you been able to find out anything yet from Gina's. . ."

She let the word remain unsaid and took another sip of coffee that was too cool to enjoy.

"Not yet. Forensics is working overtime and the crime scene guys are out there again today."

Zoe nodded. "When did you want to go see the Terrances?"

"Now, if you can get away." He glanced over at Daria.

Daria picked up her purse. "I was on my way out anyway. Zoe,

I'll call you later. Mr. Detective, it was nice meeting you."

JJ closed his eyes for a second and then opened them again as a flicker of remorse shadowed his face. "I'm sorry. That was rude of me. I'm JJ Johnson."

Daria smiled again, a little more teeth showing. "Nice to meet you, JJ. And what does JJ stand for?"

JJ actually looked uncomfortable as he shifted his weight from one foot to the other. "Josiah. Josiah Johnson."

"Josiah. I like that. See ya." She waved airily and made her exit.

The moment the door closed behind Daria, Zoe felt the walls begin to close in on her. He was much too close and the tension was much too thick. She needed to get out. *Josiah.* She preferred it to JJ any day of the week. *No, kiddo, stick to Detective Sir. It's far safer.* "Let me get my purse and we'll go."

He followed her into the living room. "About yesterday?"

Zoe grabbed her purse and felt the tension slide down her spine as she locked the front door and pulled it closed behind them. "What about it?"

"Do you make a habit of fainting at the sight of maple trees?"

He had noticed the trees. Now, why did that surprise her?

"No," she admitted as she climbed into his car. Fastening her seat belt, she was dismayed to find herself inhaling his scent and finding it pleasant. She exhaled impatiently. "I usually pass out after finding a child. Sometimes within minutes; sometimes it's hours later."

She turned sideways in her seat. "And about. . ."

"What?"

"What I said to you. That was wrong of me. I want to apologize. I don't normally do things like that. I really don't. I lost my temper and there is no excuse. So I'm sorry."

JJ brushed her off as if it didn't matter in the least. She knew it did.

That aggravated her. The least he could do was accept her apology.

But he didn't reprieve her. Or give her absolution. He just ignored her on the drive to the Terrances' modest home twenty-five minutes away in Emmitt Falls. She figured it was about the most miserable twenty-five-minute drive she'd ever experienced.

By the time they pulled up in front of the split-level home, she was regretting her apology and ready to poke at him again. Even his hostile barbs were better than this cold silence.

"So, Josiah, when I get done solving this case for you, what else would you like me to do?" She followed him up the walk, barely noticing the pansies that lined the path to the front door.

JJ stopped and turned around to look at her. His green eyes went icy, like shards of glass that would leave a hundred slices in her skin. "Don't push me, Shefford."

"Should I conjure up some lightning bolts instead?" She tilted her head, cold stare meeting frosty glare. "Or perhaps you would prefer fire?" She raised her hands in a dramatic wave. "Oh, spirits of darkness. . ."

"I would prefer you back off."

"Then try being human." She marched past him and rang the doorbell. By the time JJ made it to the door, Mrs. Terrance had swung it open and was standing there wringing her hands.

Zoe graced the little woman with a gentle smile as she reached out and took the woman's hands in a gesture of compassion and understanding. "Hello. I'm Zoe."

He stared at the newspaper, panic welling up inside, encircling his throat like tentacles, squeezing slowly, cutting off his air.

They'd found Gina. His little wildflower, planted so carefully in the woods. They'd found her and dug her up. They'd disturbed his garden!

Anger, black anger, oozed through him, filling every part of his body until he felt he was drowning in it. They had dared to touch his garden!

No. . .that woman had. She was the one who had seen the beauty of his garden and destroyed it. She was the one who had taken away one of his wildflowers. She was the one who was a danger to him. She understood his garden.

The police were no threat. He was too smart for them.

But this woman. She was a problem. She wouldn't stop until she'd found all his wildflowers, and he couldn't allow that. No. He'd have to stop her. And then she would be part of his garden. A weed among the precious wildflowers.

He folded the newspaper carefully, set it on the table, and signaled the waitress for his check. She would have to be stopped soon.

Very soon.

Slowly he smiled and the anger abated.

Yes. It was only right that she join his wildflowers.

◆　◆　◆

JJ watched as Zoe spoke with Mrs. Terrance. She kept her voice soft and reassuring. Compassion dripped from her every word. JJ had to give the lady credit; she knew how to sell herself. After a few moments, Mrs. Terrance led Zoe back to her daughter's room. Zoe went from item to item; teddy bear to Barbie doll, hair ribbons to roller blades.

Tears glistening in her eyes, Zoe shook her head regretfully and took Mrs. Terrance's hand again. "I'm sorry. I'm not picking up anything right now. I can try again another time."

Obviously disappointed, Mrs. Terrance merely nodded as she clutched the teddy bear that Zoe had held a few minutes earlier. "I was hoping. Anything." She seemed to struggle just to speak. "It's the waiting."

"I know how you feel," Zoe said softly. "I know."

As soon as they got back outside, JJ went after her with both barrels. "Lady, I'll give you credit. You sure know how to play people, don't you? Telling that woman you can try again and you know how she feels. You are truly one of the best cons I think I've ever come across."

"Not now, Detective."

"I know how you feel," he said sarcastically, aping her words but not her tone. "As if you could ever understand what these women are going through. You're just using their moment of weakness to feed your own ego."

"You are so clueless. Can we drop this now?"

"Oh, yeah. We can drop this. Heaven forbid you actually answer a critic."

"You're not a critic, Detective. You're a bully."

Detective Gerry Otis could feel his instincts kicking like a frisky colt on a spring day. He found Matt Casto pouring over crime scene evidence at his desk.

"Matt." Gerry tossed down a file in front of Matt. "We were right. Matthews is an alias. He was born Theodore Matthew Bateman. His father, Thomas Bateman, was an electrician, killed in a car accident February 1960. The mother, Carol Bateman, married one Lou Jernigan in July of '61."

Matt blinked but said nothing.

"In June of '62, Carol Bateman Jernigan gave birth to a baby girl, Marsha Diane." Gerry tipped his head toward the file. "That's all I found so far."

"What about the sister? Half-sister. Marsha. Anything on her?"

"Nothing so far."

"The parents?"

"Both deceased in a fire in '78."

Matt tipped back his head. "Same year our Mr. Matthews turned twenty-one and changed his name."

"Yep."

"I'll let JJ know. In the meantime," Matt picked up the file and handed it back to Gerry, "find the sister. And see if you can find out why Matthews changed his name. There has to be something there. I can feel it. I'm going out to lunch."

"Where is JJ? He's been gone for hours."

Matt grinned as he stood up and stretched then grabbed his jacket off the back of his chair. "Out with our Miss Zoe."

"Oh, boy. He'll be in a fine temper when he gets back. She can get him on the bad side of a mood faster than anyone I ever met."

"I'm sure he has the same effect on her." Matt headed for the door. "I'm off to lunch. If JJ gets back before I do, let him know where I am."

❖   ❖   ❖

"Paula! Wait up!"

Paula stopped, half turning, her hand pausing on the handle of the glass door. "Hey, James."

James Parnell, one of the dispatchers at Heart-Care Medical Transport, walked quickly toward her. "Are you on your way to lunch?"

Paula nodded as she pushed open the door and stepped onto the sidewalk, James right behind her. "I was thinking about hitting the deli for a quick sub," she said.

"I got a better idea." He ran his fingers through his wavy blond hair, his blue eyes twinkling. "I'll treat you to lunch at Hunan Heaven. All you can eat buffet. Whattya say?"

"Chinese? Okay." Paula stepped sideways as a businessman hurried past her, his briefcase nearly clipping her leg. "But you don't have to treat."

"I insist." He held out his elbow. "Shall we?"

Paula laughed as she tucked her hand in the crook of his arm. Since the restaurant was less than two blocks away, they walked, talking business as they weaved in and out of the lunch crowd on the sidewalks.

"How's it going in your department? Ours seems busy enough."

Paula frowned. "Yeah, you schedule the runs and then we have to fight tooth and nail to get Medicare and Medicaid to pay us."

"I thought these people were covered for their medical transportation."

"They're supposed to be, but the Meds like to make us squirm for every dime, delaying as much as possible before paying. Last week they denied over five thousand, citing changes in the mileage codes. Thing is, they didn't tell us they were changing the codes."

James shook his head as he dropped Paula's arm and reached over to pull open the restaurant door. "The games they play."

Zoe felt anger swirling around inside like a violent storm. She wanted to get out of the car. Away from him. Away from his bitterness and those eyes that stripped her down to doubts.

JJ glared at her as they waited at a red light. "You prey on innocent people in their lowest moments. . ."

Zoe felt the insult like the snap of a whip lashing across her heart. He wanted to hurt her and he'd succeeded, but she'd die before she'd let him know just how much. He wanted revenge for what she'd said to him before, and she'd let him have his moment. But it would be the last time.

She turned and looked out the window. She *did* know how Mrs. Terrance felt—how every one of those women felt. But she wasn't going to let him know that.

Never in a million years.

They drove past a church, and Zoe read the message of the day on the sign out front. *God speaks in many ways. Are you listening?*

Zoe frowned. What was it with all these reminders of God lately? The billboard, the television station changing, the radio in her car set to a Christian station when she didn't even know there *was* a Christian station, and now a church sign.

She dismissed it all and forced herself to think of Gina Sarentino. The dark black hair, pulled back in a braid and tied with a ribbon. The little studs twinkling in her pierced ears. The missing front tooth.

Flowers.

Garden.

Wildflowers.

Zoe closed her eyes as the thoughts and images swamped her.

"He thinks of them as his flowers. His wildflowers. He wants them dark this time. Each time he goes through phases. Redheads, then blonds, now dark hair. Flowers in his garden."

"What in heaven's name are you spouting off about?"

Zoe hadn't even realized she was vocalizing her thoughts until he spoke, that frosty edge of hostility cutting through her thoughts.

"The man who is taking these little girls. He calls them his flowers. And after he kills them, he plants them in his garden."

"That was no garden we found Gina in," JJ reminded her.

"No. Not a garden. But wherever he places them becomes a garden to him. We dug up his garden. He's angry."

JJ pulled into her driveway and cut the engine. "What's this about redheads and blonds?"

"Each time he goes through the cycle. . . ." Another thought hit her. "He kills them and then buries them. He considers their graves his garden."

"How long has he been doing this?"

If she was surprised by his question, she didn't let on. "Years. Not always here, local. But he's been doing this for years. He's careful. Never more than two or three at a time."

"Because then the Feds would be called in."

Zoe turned to him, her brow creased. "You should call them anyway. I know it's procedure not to call them until it's obvious it's a serial killer. This is. Call them."

JJ scowled. "Trust me, I have. And he confirmed that the Matthews baby doesn't fit the pattern."

"You're right. So now what?"

"Now you get out of my car so I can dig and see what I can find out about any *other* missing children."

Zoe opened the car door. At least he appeared to be taking her seriously. She closed the door and leaned down to look at him. "He either lives near or works at a school."

JJ didn't answer her as she stood back. He just pulled out of the driveway and sped away.

Shaking her head, she moved quickly up the walk. She stopped at her front door and stared at the small bundle of wildflowers tied with a ribbon. A hair ribbon. She didn't need to pick it up. She understood.

Zoe unlocked the door, stepped over the flowers, and headed straight for the phone. "Detective Johnson just dropped me off at home, so I know he's still on the road, but you need to tell him that I just got a message from the killer."

Matt Casto's foot was tapping faster than eight cylinders at four thousand rpms. He had come to take her to lunch. A surprise. Just to make sure she didn't feel neglected. And what had he found? She was laughing at some smooth-looking jerk in chinos and a tie, her arm tucked ever so romantic-like in the crook of his arm. Going out to lunch with some guy!

Going out with someone else.

"Silly man, do you really think she'll wait forever? If you care at all, and you do, you'd better do something about it. Someone else is already trying to draw her attention away from you."

Zoe Shefford's words ploughed through his head, mocking him. She'd been right. Someone was trying to take Paula away from him. And he hadn't even seen it coming. Paula wasn't the flighty type. That's what he'd always loved about her. She was solid, dependable, always around when Matt called. Ready at a moment's notice if Matt suddenly found time off. Always anxious to spend time with him.

And now someone else was luring her away.

Slamming the steering wheel with the palm of his hand, Matt turned the key, revving the engine of his car. Fine. If that's what she wanted, he wasn't going to stand in her way. He had work to do.

Tires squealed as he spun out of the parking space and pulled into traffic. He ignored the blast of a horn when he cut someone off.

Nora McCaine lifted Kaitlyn from her crib. "Awake from your nap already, sweetheart?" She held her daughter close, breathing in the scent of baby shampoo and baby powder the way a starving man inhales the smell of food. Cradling Kaitlyn, she sat down in the rocking chair and brought the bottle to Kaitlyn's little mouth. Kaitlyn latched on to it.

Nora smiled softly. "We aren't too hungry, are we? After you eat, would you like to take a stroll in the park?"

Kaitlyn continued to suck on the bottle.

"And then by the time we get home it will be time to start dinner for Daddy."

Nora and Charles had spent nearly ten years trying to start a family, and with Kaitlyn's arrival they had finally found the happiness they'd wanted for so long. Both had wanted a large family, but if Kaitlyn was all they were to ever have, they would be satisfied.

Up until Kaitlyn's arrival, Nora had worked as a secretary for a law firm. Charles was a stockbroker. Even without Nora's salary, they continued to live comfortably.

By the time Nora had finished feeding Kaitlyn and dressing her for a trip to the park, Charles was coming in the front door. One look at his face and Nora knew something was wrong.

"Charles? Why are you home so early? Did something happen?"

"I just wanted to work at home this afternoon. Stay close to my two favorite girls." He kissed Nora and then took Kaitlyn from Nora's arms. "And how is my favorite daughter today?"

"Charles, what's wrong?"

Charles sighed as he kissed his daughter on the cheek and then handed her back to his wife. "Did you see the news?"

Nora shook her head. "No. Why?"

"There's a madman out there. He's snatching little girls. I'd rather you didn't take Kaitlyn to the park for a few days. Not until they catch this guy."

"I thought that was over in Monroe County." Just the thought of someone snatching her daughter away was enough to make Nora hold on to Kaitlyn a little bit tighter.

"Monroe County isn't that far away. Less than a half-hour drive. I just don't want to take any chances. One baby was snatched right from her crib."

"Oh, good heavens." Nora started unbuttoning Kaitlyn's sweater. "What kind of world do we live in?"

"It's out of control." Charles slipped out of his suit coat and arranged it neatly on the back of a chair. He picked up his briefcase. "I'm going to go work in the den for awhile."

"Charles?"

He turned around in the doorway. "Yes?"

"No one will take our baby, right?"

"I won't let them, Nora. Don't worry. I'll keep my two girls safe."

JJ headed straight for his boss. He knocked on Harris's door and quickly received a command to enter.

"I need additional help. We have more work than we can handle. Give me a few more men."

Harris looked up, peering over the top of his glasses, blinking furiously. "How many?"

"Three."

"Two. Take Cole and Chapman."

JJ shook his head. Chapman was okay, but Barone was better. Much better. "Cole and Barone."

Harris stared at him a long moment. Finally, he nodded. "Cole and Barone."

"Thanks."

JJ grabbed the door handle, looking to exit fast.

"And, Johnson?"

JJ half turned. "Yeah?"

"I want something solid and I want it fast."

"I'll have it. We're close to nailing this guy."

Harris nodded and dropped his head, dismissing JJ and returning his attention to the papers on his desk. Heaving a sigh of relief, JJ closed the door behind him. Close to nailing this guy. *And pigs fly with red wings.*

Fifteen minutes later, Chuck Barone stepped into JJ's office. Barone was Italian. He was on the backside of forty, slight of frame with a small paunch and a receding hairline. "You commandeered me?"

"Yeah. I need those most excellent research skills of yours. We have a serial killer on our hands." He nodded toward the stack of files on the corner of the small conference table. "That's everything we have. I need you to go back over the past few years and see if you can find a pattern."

Barone nodded as he reached for the stack of files. "How far back do you want me to go?"

"Find a pattern and keep going back until you don't see it anymore."

Barone blew out a heavy breath. "You don't ask much, do you?"

JJ smiled. "I heard you were the best—that you could find patterns where they don't even exist. Find me a pattern."

"You got it."

"And, Chuck?"

"Yeah?"

"Quickly."

"Yes, sir."

Chuck was barely out the door before Matt brushed past him, slamming down in the nearest chair.

"I thought you were having lunch with Paula." JJ leaned back in his chair. "From the look on your face, it didn't go well."

"She was on her way out to lunch with some GQ type in loafers."

JJ stared down at his loafers. "What's wrong with loafers?"

Matt glared at him. "On you, they're fine. On Mr. GQ, they're disgusting."

"I see. Because he was taking Paula out to lunch. Maybe he's just a coworker?"

"I don't care if he's her boss!" Matt stood up, walked over to the window, and drew the blinds. Sunlight spilled in. JJ blinked. "You should have seen her, with her arm all tucked in his, laughing so sweetly at something he was saying, batting her eyes at him. It was disgusting."

"Paula doesn't bat her eyelashes."

"She was flirting with him!"

JJ reached over and pulled the cord, dropping the blinds. "You flirt. How come it's okay for you and not for her?"

Matt began to pace, his agitation amusing JJ, who hid a smile behind his hand.

"I don't mean anything when I flirt."

"Maybe she didn't mean anything either."

Matt spun around. "Whose side are you on, anyway?"

JJ threw up his hands. "Hey! Truce! I'm just trying to calm you down!"

Barone stuck his head in the door. "How much of a radius do you want?"

"Go out a hundred miles to start."

Barone nodded assent and then, casting a quick glance at Matt's face, slipped quietly away. "Look at that, Matt," JJ said. "You scared off Barone. And he's Sicilian."

Matt dropped into the nearest chair and ran his hands through his hair. "I never thought she'd go out on me, ya know?"

"I'm sure it was just an innocent lunch with a coworker. You need to talk to her about it."

Matt shook his head then leaned back, stretching his legs out in front of him. "I can't, JJ. It would look like I was spying on her."

"You weren't spying, Matt. You showed up to take her out to lunch and saw her with some man. She'll tell you what happened, you'll kiss and make up, and all will be fine."

Matt's eyes narrowed. "Just you wait until you fall in love with someone. I'm going to enjoy watching you flop around on the end of her hook."

"Never happen, my man. Never happen. Ain't a woman born that can make me flop around on the end of any hook."

Matt choked out a laugh. "We'll see." Suddenly Matt sobered. "Oh, by the way, Gerry found out Ted Matthews isn't really Ted Matthews. He changed his name. Right after his parents died in a freak fire."

JJ squinted as he picked up a message left taped to his stapler. He jumped to his feet. "Let's go."

"What's going on?"

"Our serial killer just left a message on Shefford's doorstep."

When the bell over the door tinkled, Denise Shefford looked up and then smiled at the man coming through the door. "May I help you with anything?"

"Just looking. Thought I'd get this woman friend of mine something special."

Denise gave the sweaters she was folding a final pat and walked toward him. "Well, we have plenty of items that are special. Is there anything particular you had in mind?"

"Something in pink. She likes pink."

Nodding, Denise led him over to a display of scarves. He shook his head. "No, nothing like that. A sweater or shawl, maybe. Or maybe something like that." He pointed to a pink blouse hanging nearby with a bouquet of flowers embroidered on the front. "That's perfect."

Denise lifted one from the rack and looked at the tag. "It's pure linen, but it is a bit pricey. . .seventy dollars."

"Seventy?" He shoved his hands in his pockets and stared at it, as if having second thoughts.

"It's imported and of the highest quality."

He merely nodded and stared at it. Finally, he sighed. "I will take it."

"What size?"

"Size?"

Laughing, Denise leaned against the rack. This was not the first man to come in and have forgotten or overlooked something so essential. "If you could tell me about how tall she is, about how much she weighs."

"Oh. Yeah. Well. . ." He eyed Denise closely. "She's about your size but a bit taller."

Denise nodded and hung the shirt back on the rack before searching for another size. "Probably about an eight, then."

He shrugged as he looked around the shop. "Nice shop you have here. Are you Amy?"

Denise shook her head as she carried the blouse to the register. "Amy was my daughter. I named it after her."

"Was?"

"She died years ago."

"That's a shame. Was she your only child?"

Smiling wistfully, Denise removed the hanger and folded the blouse carefully in tissue. "No. I have one other daughter. She works here with me from time to time."

He leaned against the counter, invading her space just enough to make her fumble with the box. "That's nice. Must give you pleasure to have her around you."

Denise backed up a step, still smiling, and slid the box into a shopping bag. "It does. A great deal of pleasure."

"Tough losing a child."

"Yes, it is." Denise wrote out the receipt and handed it to him. "Have you lost a child?"

He shook his head as he counted out the money. "No. Can't say as I have. But I know others who have. Sad thing."

"Yes, it is."

"Seems like they just never forget."

"No, you never forget." Denise took the money from him and felt a shiver go down her back. Shaking it off, she smiled at him and counted out his change.

The man picked up the bag. "Guess it would hurt even more to lose the one daughter you have left."

Denise stared at him, stunned that anyone could make such a remark. "Yes."

"Guess we should just hope nothing bad ever happens to her, then, huh?" Smiling coldly, he walked out of the shop.

Denise ran her hands over her arms, trying to rid herself of the sudden chill. He was just. . .strange. Too strange.

But his words echoed in her head the rest of the day. *"Guess we should just hope nothing bad ever happens to her, then, huh?"*

chapter 13

Tuesday, April 18

Nancy Darrington looked furtively over her shoulder as she nudged open the motel room door and slipped inside. Quickly she locked the door and drew the faded drapes across the single small, dirty window. *The whole room is dirty,* she thought as she looked around the dismal accommodations. But what could she expect for twenty bucks a night and a hotel clerk who saw nothing and said nothing?

She spread a quilt on the bed before placing the child on it. "I'm sorry, sweetheart, but it's the best we can do for now."

The room was almost squalid with orange shag carpet, yellow striped wallpaper, and an orange and yellow plaid bedspread that she couldn't even be sure was reasonably clean.

Despair welled up as she sat down next to the sleeping child. She wanted to give up. She wanted to pull the covers over her head and never see daylight again. She couldn't do that. *Keep moving. Don't stop. Don't think about how close anyone might be. Don't think about what's waiting if they do catch up.*

No child should have to live in a house where the mother cringed every time the father spoke and the tension was thick enough to hang drapes on. That man didn't love his child. And he didn't love his wife. He was a control freak who just liked to see people jump when he opened his mouth to bluster.

And she wasn't going to let it continue. So she took the child and ran. But how long could she keep running?

Yawning, she reached over and ran her fingers gently over the child's soft hair. Forever, if she had to.

JJ walked into his office, flipped on the lights, and dropped into his chair. He was bone-weary tired and ready to pass out. He looked at Matt through drooping eyes that he was too exhausted to keep open. "Please put me out of my misery."

Matt draped his jacket over a chair and sat down. "This guy is threatening to kill her. Don't you think we should try to protect her?"

It took JJ's brain a few seconds to connect the dots and figure out what Matt was talking about. He shrugged. "I've asked Harris for some extra help. I'm waiting on him." He turned his attention to the fingerprint report on the note from the killer. Zoe had been smart enough not to touch the document and leave any fingerprints. So had the killer.

And there were no fingerprints on Gina Sarentino's hair ribbon. The wildflowers were also untraceable.

Bottom line? They had nothing. Frustrated, JJ shoved the fingerprint report into the Sarentino file and leaned back in his chair. He looked up, hope flaring as Gerry walked in. "What have we found out about our mysterious housekeeper?"

Gerry flipped open his notepad. "I've been trying to trace all three names. The landlord didn't bother to check up on her references because she seemed like such a nice lady. I did. No one has ever heard of her. She paid her deposit for the house in cash. Always paid the rent on time. In cash. I can't find any car registered to any of those three names in this state, and definitely not a Chrysler."

JJ stroked his chin. "Did you check surrounding states?"

"Working on that now."

JJ stood up. "Let me know when you have something."

Gerry nodded and went back to his work. JJ walked over to the window and stared across the parking lot. Zoe had guts; he had to give her that. When he got the call from dispatch, it had taken him nearly fifteen minutes to get back to her house. She hadn't touched the flowers or the attached note but had left them on the front porch for him to retrieve.

She hadn't cried, hadn't whimpered, and hadn't demanded protection.

Guts.

And a smile that sent shivers up his back. And, he was beginning to realize, these weren't bad shivers. They were the kind of shivers that made him want to bring out that smile every time he saw her. The kind that made him think of her when he didn't want to.

There was strength in her he didn't understand. And vulnerability she hid from everyone. She was part kitten and part pit bull terrier, and he couldn't figure out which one intrigued him the most.

Everything about her did.

Except for the fact that she claimed to be a psychic.

That drove him nuts. It ranked right up there with the fact that she knew how to push his buttons—did so whenever she felt like it. Which seemed to be pretty often.

No matter how much he tried to think of anything else, she would slip into his thoughts as quietly as a soft wind and blow everything out of his mind except her.

And the fact that there was a killer stalking her.

◆ ◆ ◆

"This guy is a killer." Daria combed out Zoe's hair and carefully snipped the ends. "Aren't you worried? He knows where you live. And he's obviously nuts."

"JJ has the note. They're going to test it for fingerprints."

"And that's it?" Daria paused, her scissors waving through the air. "What about protection for you?"

"I don't need protection."

"Bull. If this guy has it in his mind to kill you, you need protection." She lifted another strand of hair and began snipping again, but her movements were agitated now. "He could break in here at any time, and then what?"

"He's not going to get to me. I have an excellent alarm system."

"Alarm systems aren't perfect," Daria snapped as she combed out the hair. "Come stay with me."

"No, Daria." Zoe sighed. How could she possibly make anyone understand? "I'll be fine."

"You'll be dead! This guy is not someone to mess with!"

"I'm not taking this as a joke, Daria. Honest, I'm not."

Daria walked around Zoe's kitchen chair, scissors and comb in hand, and looked Zoe in the eye. "This guy wants you dead. Do you understand that?"

Zoe met Daria's eyes. "Yes."

"I don't think you do. Any sane person would be upset, worried, and at the very least, ready to hide until the police catch this guy."

"He just wants to scare me off the case. He's not into killing adults."

Daria's mouth dropped along with her hands. "You really believe that garbage, don't you?" She slammed the scissors down on the kitchen table. "You listen to me, girl. This is not a joke. This guy said that he was going to plant you as a weed among his flowers. He means it. Now, if you don't request some kind of protection, I'm going down to the police station and screaming my head off until someone is parked in a police car in your front yard!"

◆　◆　◆

Ted was just getting off the phone when his boss, Mr. O'Connell, stepped into view. He turned his chair and scooted back, giving Mr. O'Connell a little more room to fit his wide girth into the small cubicle.

"Mr. O'Connell." Ted swallowed hard. O'Connell didn't venture from his office unless it was an emergency.

"Ted, by any chance have you spoken to Miss Bubeck lately?"

"No, not in a couple of days. Passing in the hall sort of thing. Why?"

"She hasn't shown up for work the last two days. We've tried calling and her phone has been disconnected."

"Uh-oh." Ted didn't know what else to offer.

O'Connell hitched up his pants. "Yes, well, I was just wondering if perhaps you might have heard from her."

"No, sir, I'm afraid not. She hasn't called me."

"And you didn't notice that she hasn't been in?"

Ted lifted his chin. "We're in the last week of the budget crunch. I've got my hands full with Margaret out having a baby and Stephen in the hospital having knee surgery. I told Lana to handle any problems with the staff until I got this report down. Obviously, someone not showing up for work didn't rise high enough on Lana's priority list."

"Well, now you've been told."

Ted stood to his feet. "I'll go talk to Lana now and see if I can find out anything. I'll get back to you as soon as I have something."

O'Connell nodded and lumbered out of the cubical. Ted ran his fingers through his hair. As if he didn't have more important things on his mind. Not once had O'Connell said one word about Jessica. Not one word of sympathy. Anyone else would have taken time off to stay home with his wife. Not good ol' Ted. No, he had come in and done his work and then some. And what did he get for it?

Shafted.

chapter 14

Karen knew that if she stayed in the house one more minute, she'd go straight-jacket insane. Grabbing her gardening gloves from the closet shelf, she escaped into the yard, determined to pull weeds until she was too exhausted to think. To worry. To miss Jessie.

What had the kidnapper done to her precious daughter? Smothered her? Starved her? Taken her away to raise as his or her own?

A tear dripped off her nose and fell onto her arm, sliding inside her glove. She ignored it. "Why, God? Why did you give me such a precious child and then snatch her away from me? Why are you breaking my heart like this?"

"God isn't doing this to you, Karen."

Karen jumped, unaware that she had been speaking aloud and equally unaware that anyone had heard her. "Rene. You startled me."

Rene smiled, but it didn't quite reach her eyes. She knelt down next to Karen. "I'm sorry. How are you holding up?"

"How do you think?" Karen pulled at a weed. "It's Wednesday already. Another week is nearly gone by without any word on my daughter. I just don't know why this is happening."

"Bad things happen to good people. We do have an enemy, you know."

Karen tossed the weed into a pile on the sidewalk and smoothed mulch over the gaping hole. The last thing she needed was polite platitudes. She wanted action. "No one is taking Jessica's disappearance seriously. The press is more interested in covering the disappearance of the other little girls." Her head jerked up. "I don't mean that those girls aren't important!"

"I know," Rene assured her softly.

"I just want someone to look for Jess. I didn't do this. I would never hurt my baby."

"I know." Rene reached out and touched Karen's shoulder. "Karen, part of walking out our faith is handling the curve balls life throws at us. The Lord is there, every step of the way, whether we feel it or not. You need to hold on to your faith."

Karen shook her head. "I don't have any faith left, Rene. I keep asking God why and He doesn't seem to have an answer for me."

"He already gave you His answer, Karen. He told you He'd never leave you or forsake you."

"Well, He has forsaken me."

"No, He hasn't. We don't know what He's doing in all this, but He is working through it. I know He is."

"Is He going to bring my baby back to me?" Karen asked, her voice strained by desperation.

Rene's eyes filled with tears as she leaned forward and pulled Karen into her arms. "I don't know, Karen. I can't promise you that He will. But I know He's hurting, too, and that He's with you throughout this. Let Him comfort you. Let Him help you. He loves you so much."

◆　　◆　　◆

On Wednesday afternoon, Denise Shefford called her daughter and invited her to dinner. When Zoe tried to hedge out of it, Denise pushed. Zoe relented and arrived at her mom's house promptly at six.

Denise Shefford was, by anyone's standards, a handsome woman. At the age of fifty-four, she could still pass for forty. Her blond hair hid the gray well, her body was trim, and wrinkles weren't inclined to take up residence. If you looked closely, you would notice the slackness in the jaw or the looseness of the throat. But one was disposed to miss those things and notice the deep and sometimes penetrating sadness that dulled her gray-green eyes.

It wasn't that she fought age; she didn't think much of it, really. To her way of thinking, age was a mere slap in the face among life's many blows.

It was those other blows that she still struggled with—an unfaithful husband, a broken home, a daughter's death. A few lines on her face were hardly worth noticing. She had long since found a way to ignore the pain of Keyes' betrayal and desertion, but not the pain and horror of death.

At least she didn't have the one lingering question that most parents in her position had. She didn't wonder what Amy would have looked like had she lived. She had Zoe.

The question that haunted her now was what Zoe would have been like if Amy had lived.

Watching Zoe picking at her food, pushing her fork around, pouting just as she had as a child, it would be easy to believe she was the old Zoe. But she wasn't.

The child who was once exuberant, full of life and laughter, sparkle and shine, had been reduced to living in shadows and fogs of doubt. The child who once craved attention now hated it. The child who once saw nothing but the wonderful things life had to offer now saw only the tragic things life could bring.

Because of Amy. Because Zoe felt responsible for Amy.

Zoe blamed herself for not saving Amy.

Now she blamed herself for every child she couldn't save.

"I'm going to the cemetery tomorrow. Come with me?"

Zoe shook her head sadly as she looked over at her mother. "You know I won't, Mom. Why do you keep asking?"

"I keep hoping that one day you'll say yes. You need to face the fact that she's gone."

"I know she's gone, Mom. But she's not in that cemetery."

Denise leaned over and touched Zoe's hand. "It doesn't matter that her body isn't there, honey. It's a memorial to her life, that's all. A place where I can go and feel close to her."

"She isn't there for me."

"I understand." Denise removed her hand after patting Zoe's gently. She changed the subject. "I had the strangest customer yesterday. A man."

"You get men in the store all the time. What's strange about that?"

"It was the man himself. Creepy. And he mentioned you. Well, not by name. I mean he asked if I had children. We were just chatting. You know."

Zoe nodded, barely listening.

"And then he said something about how much it would hurt to lose the one daughter I have left and to hope nothing bad ever happens to her."

"That's all he said?"

"That's all."

"Just sounds like someone incredibly insensitive, Mom. I wouldn't worry about it."

Denise nodded and her face cleared. "I'm sure you're right. So what happened the other day with the Terrance family?"

"I picked up almost everything that child owned. Nothing."

Denise Shefford sighed heavily. "That poor woman."

"I know. She had such high hopes, and I wasn't able to do a thing." Zoe pushed the pork chop around on her plate, unable to provoke her appetite.

Denise reached over and took her daughter's hand, squeezing it gently. "You did your best, Zoe. You always do."

It broke Denise's heart to see her daughter suffer over every child she couldn't save. And it didn't matter how many times she told Zoe it wasn't her fault and she wasn't to blame. Denise would still see it haunt every aspect of Zoe's life.

"It's not enough, Mom. You know that." She reached for her iced tea, staring at the condensation that ran down the outside of the glass. "And of course my failure to help delighted Detective Josiah Johnson to no end. He was just waiting for me to fall flat on my face. I could almost hear him laughing at me."

"I'm sure he wasn't, dear. You just expect too much of yourself." She buttered a roll and offered it to Zoe.

Zoe shook her head. "You don't know this guy. He hates psychics. Do you know what he called me?"

"What?"

"A decked-out demagogue of deceit." Zoe stabbed at a piece of the pork chop and shoved it angrily in her mouth.

"Try saying that three times fast." Denise smiled as Zoe nearly choked on her piece of meat. "Sorry, dear. I couldn't resist."

Zoe swallowed. Hard. "Gee, Mom. A bastion of sympathy tonight, aren't you?"

Denise dabbed her lips with her napkin and then spread it back across her lap. "Honey, I think what you do is noble, but I also think you're human. You make mistakes. You can't always help. As for this detective, who cares what he thinks? He's probably just insecure."

Denise studied her daughter carefully. "You *do* care what he thinks, don't you?"

"No!" Zoe poked at the green beans, avoiding her mother's eagle eye. "I just don't like being insulted."

"Quit sulking and eat your dinner, Zoe."

Zoe glanced over at her mother. "Mom?"

"What, dear?"

"Do you believe in God?"

The question genuinely surprised Denise. Her brows arched. "Of course. What a silly question. My heavens, whatever brought that on?"

"A friend of the Matthews woman. She refused to let me help with her missing child because she said that she's a Christian and I'm not. That a psychic is like. . .working for the devil or something."

Denise laughed. "There are fanatics in every religion in the world, Zoe. Don't let her views bother you. God has given you a wonderful gift and you use it to help people. Focus on that, not on what some misguided woman says."

"I talked with this woman. She said that while my gift is from God, the way I use it is not."

Denise tilted her head as she studied her daughter. It wasn't like Zoe to question herself like this. "You use it the only way you know how. I don't understand what these people are trying to tell you."

Zoe laid down her fork. "She said that all gifts are from God and that I have a gift of being able to read or discern what is happening in the spirit realm easier than most people. But she said. . . because I don't ask *God* for the information—I ask the child—I'm doing something wrong."

"I have no idea what you're talking about, honey."

Zoe sighed heavily. "I'm not sure I do either. It made sense when Rene was explaining it to me, but the more time that passes, the less I understand. It's like if I want to use the gift for God, I have to ask God. And when I talk to these children, I'm talking to the dead.

Supposedly that is expressly forbidden in the Bible." Zoe threw up her hands. "I don't know. Maybe I need to look into this more."

"Well, why don't you talk with someone who understands this kind of thing? Perhaps our pastor or something."

Zoe's sigh released some of her tension. "That's a good idea." She picked up her fork. "So how are things at the shop?"

After Amy's disappearance, Denise had bought a little boutique and named it after her. Amy's stocked unusual clothing and accessories not found in the bigger department stores. It was a smashing success from the day it opened and was Denise's pride and joy. Zoe worked there when her mother needed a hand or when Zoe needed extra cash. The arrangement worked well for them both.

"The shop is fine. We just got in a wonderful assortment of fall sweaters from Ireland. Wait until you see the colors! They're just incredible." Every time Denise spoke of the shop or the clothes, her hands fluttered like a hummingbird approaching a flower. "And these darling silk shawls came in."

JJ almost felt like smiling. Almost. They were getting close on the Matthews case, and he was optimistic that something would break soon and they'd find the. . .what were the reporters calling him? *The Shadow Killer. Geeesh. You'd think they would have better things to do than come up with catchy phrases for a man who snatches innocent little girls off the street and disappears without a trace.*

He yawned at a red light. Yesterday had been grueling; he hadn't gotten to bed until after midnight. He was up and out of the house before seven. It was almost ten now. The light turned green, and JJ edged through the intersection and then turned into the Taco Bell drive-thru to pick up dinner. He was surprised to find a line. He drummed his fingers on the steering wheel.

In the course of tracking Ted Matthews's past, they'd hit a brick wall called a "sealed file." So Edward "Just Call Me Ted" Matthews, aka Theodore Bateman, had a juvie record. Well, it might be sealed, but that didn't mean it was inaccessible. He was going to get a copy of that file and find out what the man had done that was so bad he changed his name and moved halfway across the country.

His gut instincts had been right. These were two different cases. Someone in the Matthews' house had disposed of Jessica Matthews. Granted, JJ was shifting his focus from the flighty and unstable Karen Matthews to the secretive Ted Matthews, but he wasn't ready to dismiss the idea that they were both involved.

Then there was the serial killer. Though they'd found only one body, it was tragically likely they'd find at least one more.

He had been right on target again. Two different cases, just like he'd been telling Harris from the start.

While the Matthews case was progressing, the Emily Terrance case was going downhill faster than a seal on ice, and JJ felt hopeless to stop it. They had no leads, no clues, and no helpful evidence. The killer was slick. And he was toying with the police.

Who was this guy?

Worse yet, when and where would he strike again?

chapter 15

Thursday, April 20

He stood in the woods and watched her playing in the sandbox. He didn't know her name yet, but he knew she was going to be one of his precious flowers.

She didn't look to be more than five or six, with long, long dark hair, an impish grin, and the cutest dimples. He was particularly fond of dimples. He couldn't see the color of her eyes yet, but he would. He imagined they were hazel, or maybe green.

The mother came to the door and he shrank back against the tree trunk. She was wiping her hands on a dishtowel, looking a bit disheveled.

"Lisa!" She pushed open the screen door and stood there watching her daughter. "Your daddy will be here soon to pick you up; don't go getting dirty."

"I won't, Mommy." She lifted a shovel of sand and turned it, letting it slide through her fingers. She giggled.

He loved the sound of it. Lisa. Ah, sweet Lisa. What a perfect name for such a perfect flower.

The screen door slapped shut and he was left alone once again with the object of his desire.

Zoe had been awake since just after seven. She wasn't sure what it was that had woken her. The alarm hadn't gone off. The phone hadn't rung. Figuring she was already awake, she decided she might as well get up.

After working all morning with her mother at the store, she did some grocery shopping, browsed through the bookstore without buying anything, and then headed home.

The moment she walked into her house, she knew something was wrong. The hair on the back of her neck stood straight up. Warily, she slipped through the living room and into the kitchen, quietly putting the grocery bag on the counter. Then she slid a carving knife out of the block and set her purse down, carefully dropping her car keys into her pocket.

She went back into the living room, looking for any sign at all that someone was there—or had been there. Nothing. Slowly she made her way down the hall and peeked into the guest room. Nothing. She stepped into her bedroom and looked around. Nothing.

She was ready to laugh at herself as she slowly lowered the knife. *Idiot. Jumping at shadows.*

She turned.

And then something caught her eye.

She stopped. Frozen. And then screamed.

Stretched out in his chair, long legs propped up on the corner of his desk and crossed at the ankles, hands linked behind his head, JJ leaned back a little farther and eyed the clock. A few minutes after one. He'd expected a call from the D.A. by now.

He reached over and picked up Gina's autopsy file. In spite of the advanced decomposition, one thing had been glaringly obvious. The killer had taken the child's heart. JJ felt a cold shiver down his back. Why the heart? Love? Innocence? What did it represent to this sick mind? He'd sent a fax to Zahn at Quantico with an update but hadn't heard back yet.

The phone rang. Thinking it was someone from the D.A.'s office, JJ jumped for it. It was dispatch. Another missing child. This time a six-year-old by the name of Lisa Brandt had disappeared from her backyard.

"Page Casto for me," he told the dispatcher, slipping into his jacket and adjusting his shoulder holster. "Tell him to meet me at the scene."

Matt pulled up in his SUV just as JJ came down the front steps of the building. "That was quick."

"I was just blocks away. Climb in. I'll drive."

JJ circled the light blue Durango and jumped in. Knowing Matt, he quickly fastened his seat belt.

"Anything on Matthews?" Matt asked as he pulled away from the curb with a burst of speed that had JJ gripping the door handle.

"Nothing yet. I was waiting for the call when this came in."

The words were barely out of JJ's mouth when his cell phone rang. He flipped it open. "Johnson."

He listened, giving an occasional "Really" or "No kidding" before he finally smiled and disconnected the call.

"Anything interesting?" Matt asked.

"Yeah. Marsha Bateman, sister to our Ted Matthews, is deceased. Died at age five."

"Dead end there."

"Wrong. She died at the hands of her brother, Ted Bateman, aka Ted Matthews. As soon as we get back, I want you to place a call to

Ted Matthews. It will seem less threatening than if it comes from me. Ask him to come in and talk to us. Make it sound routine. Typical procedure. Want to ask him about his wife; we have a few questions, yadda, yadda."

"You got it." Matt turned the wheel sharply, nearly taking the corner on two wheels. A marked police car came into view in front of them, lights flashing. Matt started closing the distance between them while JJ's knuckles went white as he gripped the door handle.

"Matt?"

"Yeah?"

"It really won't help matters if we die before we get there."

Matt laughed and stomped on the gas, passing the police car. "Coward."

"Zoe! Slow down! I can't understand a word you're saying!"

Zoe, on her knees, rocked as her mother's voice snapped in her ears. Her grip on the phone tightened. "Amy's bracelet, Mom. Where is Amy's bracelet?"

"What bracelet? Zoe, what in the world is going on with you? You sound hysterical!"

"The bracelet!" Zoe screamed into the phone. "You and Dad bought us bracelets for our fifth birthdays—I.D. bracelets with a diamond in the corner. Where is Amy's bracelet?"

"I don't know, Zoe. I think she was wearing it when. . .she was taken. You two never took them off."

"Oh, God." Zoe folded as silent screams racked through her body. "Amy. Amy. Amy." The chanting didn't ease the pain that had her doubled over.

"Zoe, if you don't tell me what's wrong right now, I'm calling the police!"

"Call them. Mom, please call them. He's been here. Oh, God. He's been here. He killed Amy and now he's coming after me."

She lifted her head and stared at the I.D. bracelet lying on her pillow. A child's bracelet with a diamond in the corner. And a name engraved in script across the bar.

Amy.

Ted stormed into his home, startling Karen, who was folding clothes at the kitchen table. He tossed his briefcase on the counter and started pulling at his tie.

Karen set down one of the towels and picked up another. "What's going on? You're home so early. It's not even five."

"I heard from the kidnappers!"

Karen felt her heart lurch as she dropped the towel, staring at her husband. "Jess?"

"She's fine. At least that's what they told me. Said to bring the money but not to call the police or they'd kill her."

Karen reached out for Ted and clung to him, her emotions spinning out of control. She wanted to laugh and cry at the same time. "When? How soon? How much money? We can get more. I can. . ."

Ted shook his head as he stepped back out of her arms. "I cleaned out the account. It's enough." He reached out and gripped Karen's hand. "Karen, I need you to listen to me. No matter what happens, we can't let the police know what's going on. Do you understand?"

"Yes." Karen nodded, willing to agree to anything. Her baby was coming home! *Oh, Jess, my love. Just a few more hours.*

"I'm going to get Jess back." Ted looked around the kitchen, his fingers combing through his hair, his eyes darting from one thing to another. "Do you have dinner started yet?"

Karen shook her head. "No. I was going to make meatloaf. . ."

"I spent my lunch hour at the bank and didn't get to eat. I'm famished. Forget cooking. Just order something for me."

"Okay. But what time are you supposed to go get Jess?" Karen twisted an unfolded towel in her hands.

"I've got about an hour and a half before I have to leave."

"How long will you be gone?"

"I'm not sure. An hour. Maybe a little longer. As soon as I have her safe, I'll call you."

Karen put the towel down. "Why don't you go take a shower? I'll call Louie's and order some food. What do you want?"

"I don't know. I can't think straight. And my stomach is tied in knots. Just get me anything."

"I'll get you something light."

"Fine." Ted walked into the bathroom, unbuttoning his shirt.

"Ted, I want to go with you to pick up Jess."

He stopped and turned around. "You can't. They were very specific. Bring the money, don't call the police, and I'd better be alone or they'll kill her on the spot."

Karen sank down on the bed, feeling as though every drop of her blood had just turned to ice. "Please don't let them hurt our baby."

Ted knelt down in front of her, taking her hands in his and rubbing the chill from them. "I won't. I promise. Have I ever let you down, baby?"

Karen shook her head.

"A couple more hours, Karen. Just a couple more hours and you'll have Jess back in your arms. I just need you to hang in there a little bit longer."

"Okay."

"Good girl. Now, why don't you call Louie's. I'm starving."

He turned at the bathroom door and smiled at her. "It's going to be fine, Karen. You'll see."

◆　◆　◆

JJ eyed the coffee suspiciously as he poured some into his mug. There was no telling how old it was.

"I made it fresh half an hour ago," Gerry told him as he pulled out a chair at the conference table and dropped into it.

"Bless you, my son." JJ set his mug down on the table and looked around. "Where's Matt?"

"I'm here!" Matt breezed into the room and grabbed a chair. "I was just talking to the lab. Our guy may have gotten sloppy. They got a good cast mold from that shoe imprint."

"Finally, a break! And what about Ted Matthews?"

Matt nodded as he clicked his pen. "Talked to him. He said it was no problem. He had to work until about six and then he'd come straight over. Should be here by six-thirty or so. Sounded anxious to be of assistance."

"Let me know when he gets here."

Matt nodded and leaned back. JJ turned to Barone. "Next."

"You were right. There is a pattern." He tossed some papers on the table and started pointing to things so fast that JJ gave up trying to read anything and just listened.

"Every five years or so there are three to five unsolved abduction cases on the records. All are girls between five and twelve, and they've all occurred within a two-hundred-mile radius."

"How far back?"

"Long time," Barone said breathlessly. "Twenty years."

JJ whistled. "Twenty years this guy has been getting away with this?"

"Different counties, three different states, never too many to draw too much attention." Barone rocked back on his heels. "And here's another little thing I found interesting. One of the first children taken was. . ."

"Amy Shefford," Matt interjected, reaching over to pull a folded newspaper out of his coat pocket. He tossed it to JJ. "Twin sister of Zoe Shefford. It's in today's paper. I meant to show it to you earlier, but we got the call about Lisa Brandt and I forgot all about it."

JJ sank down in his chair, his gaze going first to Matt, then to Barone, then down to the paper. Page six, bottom of the page. *Psychic's Sister Starts It All...*

"She never told me. Why didn't she say anything?"

Matt shrugged. "Maybe she didn't think it was any of our business."

JJ glared at him and then went back to reading the article. "She was only ten. Dear Lord in heaven. And I called her a fake—telling people she knew how they felt. She *did* know. She knew all too well." Well, there was nothing he could do about it right now. He'd talk to her later. In the meantime, they had another missing little girl.

"Good work, Barone. Keep at it and let me know anything else you find as soon as you find it. Wayne, check in with Barone as often as you can and see if he needs you to help him run anything down."

Wayne nodded. "Sure, JJ."

"Okay, guys, listen up." JJ held up Lisa Brandt's photo. "This is our latest victim. She's five years old with dark brown hair, brown eyes, and distinct dimples in her cheeks. No tattoos, scars, or birthmarks. She was last seen wearing blue denim shorts, a red checkered top, white socks, and white sneakers with a Barbie logo on the side. Her ears are pierced, but the mother couldn't remember which earrings the child was wearing. Most likely just gold posts, but that's not confirmed yet."

Marsha poked her head in the door. "I'm sorry, JJ, but it's Mrs. Shefford on line two."

JJ's brows lifted and his face tightened. "Mrs. Shefford? As in Zoe Shefford's mother?"

Marsha nodded, her corkscrew curls bouncing around her ears. "She says the killer was at Zoe's and left her something. I couldn't make out what she was saying. She was just real upset and crying."

Matt stood up. "You want me to go handle it?"

JJ shook his head and tossed his notebook to Matt. "You take over here. I'll see what's going on over at the Shefford house."

Barone cleared his throat as JJ walked past him. "I think there's one more thing you should know."

"What's that?"

"He never abducts children beyond the end of April. If we don't catch him by May first, we won't get another chance for five years."

Karen headed down to the kitchen in search of her shoes. They were still under the kitchen table where she'd kicked them off earlier.

Jess was coming home. She wanted to laugh out loud with pure joy. Her baby. Safe and sound and coming home. She'd forgotten to ask how much the kidnappers had demanded, but it didn't matter. It was worth every dime they had. She would have paid anything. Any price.

Ted had promised her he'd get Jess back, and now Jess was coming home. She hadn't harmed her daughter! She'd tried to tell everyone, but no one would believe her. Well, they'd believe her now. And once she had Jess home, she was never going to let anyone tell her she was crazy ever again.

She grabbed her keys off the hook in the kitchen, picked up her purse, and headed out the door. She had the best husband in the world.

When JJ arrived at Zoe's townhouse, there were two cruisers sitting out front, a uniformed officer on the front porch, and nothing but chaos inside. Zoe was sitting on the sofa, her arms folded around her middle, and she was rocking back and forth, her face white with fear. Or hysteria. He couldn't quite determine which. The look in her eyes when she lifted them to meet his was frantic. She opened her mouth but no sound came out.

One of the uniformed officers, Jimmy Poole, handed JJ an evidence bag with a child's bracelet in it. "Says this was her sister's."

JJ took the bag and examined the bracelet through the plastic. *Amy.*

Denise stood, her fingers twisted and interlocked as she wrung her hands. "My husband and I gave both the girls I.D. bracelets when they turned five. They always wore them. I'm almost certain Amy had hers on when she was taken."

The full impact of what she said hit JJ like a sledgehammer between the eyes. He staggered back. "Amy was wearing this? When she was taken? You're sure?"

Denise nodded. "As sure as we can be. And there's something else I think you should know."

JJ stared at the bracelet in his hand. The killer had taken Amy Shefford nearly twenty years ago, and now he was coming after Zoe. *Dear God, could this get any worse?* He lifted his head. "What else?"

"Zoe has a matching bracelet—with her name on it, of course—and now it's missing." Her bottom lip trembled and her knees buckled as she sank down next to Zoe. She reached out and wrapped an arm around Zoe, but Zoe appeared oblivious.

JJ handed the bracelet back to Poole and dropped to his haunches in front of Zoe. "Zoe, listen to me."

She didn't look at him. Just kept rocking back and forth, back and forth. He reached out and placed a hand under her chin, lifting her face to his. "Listen to me, Zoe. You can't fall apart now. We almost have this guy. Do you hear me, Zoe? We're close. He messed up today. He got sloppy. He left evidence. We're going to get him now."

Zoe shook her head. "He didn't get sloppy. He didn't care. He knows he's smarter than you. He knows he has you running in circles. You don't scare him at all. He took another little girl today, didn't he?"

"Yes," JJ admitted with a heavy sigh.

"And now he'll come after me. At least now I'll find Amy. I'll be with her."

"No! Listen to me, Zoe. He's not that smart. We will catch this lunatic. I promise you!"

Zoe shook her head with a sad, resigned smile. "He's already miles ahead of you."

chapter 16

Karen pulled into Louie's parking lot. She sat there for a few minutes wiping away tears, taking deep breaths, trying to calm down before going into the restaurant.

In the short time it had taken to drive from the house to Louie's, she had started falling apart. Doubts crowded out all hope of Jessie's imminent return. What if the kidnappers had lied? What if they'd already killed Jess? What if Ted was late meeting them? What if they took the money but didn't give him Jess?

What if? What if? And all of them worst-case scenarios. She pulled down the visor mirror and checked her face. Her eyes were red and swollen, her cheeks splotchy. She looked exactly the way she felt—like a woman falling apart in the midst of a crisis. Well, it wasn't going to get any better sitting there. Taking a deep breath, she climbed out of the car and hurried into the restaurant to pick up the food.

Luckily the food was ready, and she wasted no time paying for it and getting out quickly, ignoring the sympathetic or curious glances she received along the way. Keeping her head down, she weaved through the small crowd waiting in line at the door, rushed back to her car, and drove straight home. When she pulled into the driveway, she was surprised to discover Ted's car was already gone.

She put the food on the table and searched the house, but there was no note. Had the kidnappers called and demanded he come right away? Had she taken too long and made Ted angry? Had she messed up—again?

She sank down in the nearest kitchen chair. She hadn't meant to fall apart. Now all she could do was worry. *God, please don't let the car break down. Don't let the kidnappers change their minds or lie to Ted. Please, just let them take the money and give Jess back.*

Zoe sat curled in a chair, her knees tucked up against her chest, her arms wrapped around them, her bare toes curled over the cushion. "I don't want you to call him."

Denise, pacing the room from end to end, waved her arms with as much impatience as frustration. "He's your father. He needs to know what's going on."

"I don't want him here."

Denise jammed her fisted hands to her hips. "When are you going to forgive him? He's been a good father to you."

"Have you forgiven him?"

"I never blamed him for Amy's death, Zoe. It wasn't his fault."

"Yes, it was!" Zoe's feet slammed to the floor as she jerked to her feet. "Yes, it was his fault. If he had been home where he was supposed to be, Amy wouldn't have been a target. She'd be here right now. Married with kids and happy."

"You don't know that, Zoe. Life holds no guarantees. And there was no way we could have known Amy was anyone's target. Believe me, if your father had known, he would have been there."

Zoe shook her head as she headed for the kitchen. "He was too wrapped up in that bimbo. You remember? The woman he left you for. The one he left all of us for."

"He made a mistake."

"And I don't see you rushing to take him back, Mom." Zoe yanked open a cabinet door and grabbed a glass. "He's been trying to reconcile with you ever since Amy was taken, and you've refused. So don't tell me how I need to forgive him."

Denise leaned her shoulder against the door. "It wasn't about Amy's death, Zoe. It was about trusting him in our marriage."

"Right." Zoe's sarcasm ripped through the kitchen as she filled her glass with soda. "He's been faithful to you for the past twenty years, and you still haven't taken him back."

"Why are you so angry at me, Zoe?"

"I'm not!" Zoe stormed past her mother and, after setting down her soda on a side table, flopped back down in her chair.

"Well, it sure seems like it from here. Did you *want* me to take your father back? Is that why you're angry at me?" Denise pushed off the doorway and walked over to stand in front of Zoe.

"No! I don't care whether you take him back or not."

Denise folded her arms. "Then what exactly is your problem all of a sudden?"

"Nothing!" Zoe went to stand up and Denise stepped forward, neatly trapping Zoe. She gently pushed Zoe back down in the chair.

"You're not getting up until you tell me what's going on inside that head of yours."

"Nothing!"

"Don't pull that on me, young lady. I know you far too well. Now talk to me."

Zoe glared at her mother and then dropped her eyes. "Do you remember how upset you were when Amy was taken?"

"Of course I do. It's not a moment I'm likely to forget."

Zoe lifted her face and stared at her mother with tears in her eyes. "Let me ask you something, Mom. Would you have been just as distraught if it had been me instead of Amy?"

◆   ◆   ◆

Karen knew she'd probably worn a hole in the living room carpet, but she didn't care. Ted had been gone for more than four hours and she hadn't heard a word. Surely he'd picked up Jess by now!

She lifted the corner of the drapes and peeked out once again. Nothing much had changed in the last five minutes. The streetlamps cast streaks of light throughout the neighborhood. Mr. Waltham was strolling down the street with his poodle. The lights were still off across the street at the Marshalls', but that wasn't unusual. They both worked late.

Suddenly the phone rang, jarring her to drop the drapes and spin around. She lunged for the phone.

"Hello?"

"Mrs. Matthews?"

"Yes?"

"This is Detective Casto again. Have you heard from your husband yet?"

"No, I'm sorry, I haven't."

"He promised to come in and answer some questions for us right after work. This doesn't look good for him, Mrs. Matthews."

"No! You don't understand! It's not like that! He's not trying to avoid you. I swear. As soon as he gets in, I'll have him call you. He's just out right now on an important errand."

"What kind of errand is more important than cooperating in the investigation into your daughter's disappearance?"

Karen bit her lip, wanting to tell him everything but too frightened to. "I. . .I can't say. Really, I can't. But I promise to have him call you."

She slammed down the phone before he dug out of her that Ted had gone to meet the kidnappers. She couldn't risk Jess's life. Or Ted's. She had to keep silent.

She began to pace again. *Oh, Ted. Where are you? And where's Jess?*

chapter 18

K aren stared at the clock. Seven-twenty. The sun was a thin shaft of light trying to penetrate the thick curtains drawn tight over the windows.

It had been a long night. Still dressed in the same clothes she'd been wearing the night before, Karen lay atop the navy blue comforter, curled in a fetal position. She hadn't closed her eyes all night.

Where were Ted and Jess?

Swinging her feet to the floor, she forced herself to get up. Anything could have happened. The car could have broken down, leaving them stranded. The kidnappers could have been very, very late. Ted might have taken Jess to the hospital.

No. He would have called.

She drew open the drapes; blinking at the bright light that instantly flooded the room. He shouldn't have been gone this long. *Oh, Ted, where are you?*

The phone rang, jolting her from her thoughts. She rushed to grab for it. "Ted?"

"No, Mrs. Matthews. This is Detective Casto again. I was hoping to talk to your husband."

"He's not here, Detective." She swallowed hard. "He didn't come home last night."

◆　　◆　　◆

Zoe pulled the door closed and fumbled with her car keys as she hurried down the sidewalk. Her mother—who had insisted on staying the night with Zoe after they'd cried together, clung together, and talked until the wee hours of the morning—was asleep in Zoe's guest-room. Zoe wanted to run down to the market and get some of those lemon Danish treats her mother loved.

Halfway down the sidewalk, Zoe passed the old park bench Frank had brought her. She intended to refinish it one of these days, but in the meantime, it added a warm touch to the front yard, even with its badly chipped paint.

She stopped and stared at what was lying on the bench. Then she reached into her purse and pulled out her cell phone.

"Could you find Detective Johnson for me?" She looked over her shoulder uneasily. *Was he watching her?*

"Yes. It's Zoe Shefford. The killer just left a doll in my front yard. I believe it belongs to one of the missing girls."

◆　　◆　　◆

"JJ, are you listening to me?"

JJ turned around. "What?"

Matt placed both hands on JJ's desk and leaned forward. "I just talked to Karen Matthews again. She swears her husband went out on some very important errand last night and hasn't returned."

"And pigs fly with green wings," JJ muttered darkly. "Put out an APB."

"You're charging him with the kid's disappearance?" Matt

asked with a trace of concern.

"It would get us twenty-four hours to hold and question him if he doesn't lawyer up. Right now, it looks like he's on the run, and I don't want him getting too far. If we're wrong and he's at the hospital with a dying friend, then we'll drop the charges and cut him loose, but I want him found."

JJ glanced up at the clock and frowned. Almost eight-thirty. He was supposed to brief Harris at ten. As if he had time for another meeting.

Gerry swung the door open, his face flushed with excitement. "Tripp from Homicide called. They found a car half submerged in the river out behind the Grove Shopping Center. There's blood but no sign of a body."

"And this is important to me how?"

"The car is registered to Ted Matthews."

JJ jerked to his feet. "Where is Ted Matthews?"

"They aren't sure, but it sure looks like he's dead."

JJ grabbed his jacket, checked his gun, and headed for the door. "Let's go, Matt. I knew there was something about those two that didn't feel right. You drive."

Marsha came running up just as JJ reached the top of the stairs. Breathlessly, she handed him a phone message. "Zoe Shefford just received another message from the killer."

JJ stared at the slip of paper then folded it and slipped it into his pocket. "Tell Gerry to get over there and hold the fort. I'll follow as quick as I can."

Marsha nodded. "Yes, sir."

JJ barely waited for Matt to bring the car to a stop behind the shopping center before he opened the door and climbed out. The entire area behind the shopping center had been marked off in yellow crime tape. At least six uniformed officers were walking around, making sure no one crossed the line. A small crowd had gathered to watch the action.

JJ flashed his badge, ducked under the tape, and headed over to the tow truck. It was pulling a recent model-year silver BMW out of the water. The doors gaped open. The open trunk lid bounced as the car hung by a chain. Muddy river water gushed out from the interior and underneath.

As soon as all four tires rested solidly on the ground, Vivian Amato took over, leaning into the car and gathering evidence.

JJ walked around the car slowly, looking for collision damage. There was none. He was leaning down, examining the rear under-carriage when Matt returned.

"A couple of teenagers saw the rear of the car just under the water and called it in. There's no trace of Mr. Matthews, but search and rescue said he could have been swept away by the current."

Nothing suspicious under the car. "Any skid marks on the road? Any indication that the brakes went out and he ran off the road? Maybe lost control and ended up in the river?"

Matt shook his head. "No skid marks, so I don't think he lost control. As for the brakes, can't say until someone gets under there to check."

"What do you have?" JJ asked Vivian as she backed out of the car, tucking a swab into a plastic bag.

"Blood on the seat and steering wheel. Luggage in the trunk. Appears he was going on a trip. Just didn't make it. Keys are still in the ignition. Offhand, I'd say he knew the killer—if indeed this was a homicide. No signs of a struggle."

Vivian pulled off one of her latex gloves and brushed a lock of dark hair back from her face, a light sheen of sweat on her coffee-toned complexion. "One of the officers called Mrs. Matthews. She said he was out on some errand."

JJ walked around the car, his eyes narrowed, his mind racing. "Did he tell her about the car?"

Vivian shook her head. "I don't think so. I think he just asked to speak to Mr. Matthews. Check with Tripp. He's the one who made the call."

JJ nodded. "I'll do that. Thanks, Viv. And I'd like the results as soon as you can get them to me."

"No prob, JJ."

JJ walked over to Matt, who was standing near the bright yellow tape talking to another officer. "Where's Tripp?"

"I think he and Walker went over to the Matthews' house to talk to the wife."

JJ touched Matt on the shoulder. "Let's go."

They arrived at the Matthews' house eighteen minutes later and were met at the door by a tall, thin uniformed officer with a military-style haircut. He jerked his head back toward the kitchen. "If you're looking for Tripp, he's back there. We found the knife and bloody clothes. Looks like the wife decided to get rid of her husband. Too bad she didn't think to get rid of the evidence."

Suddenly JJ heard Karen Matthews' voice, shrill enough to rake across his nerves. "I did *NOT* kill my husband! Do they only send imbeciles to this house?"

JJ smiled. That woman had really missed her calling. She was Hollywood all the way. She did outrage better than anyone he'd ever seen.

He walked into the kitchen to find Karen Matthews sitting at the table, gardening gloves in front of her, eyes flashing with annoyance. No. That was pure rage. Rage strong enough to kill.

Tripp nodded at JJ. "Johnson! I guess you heard."

JJ nodded. "I just came from the crime scene. What did you find?"

Tripp, a twenty-five-year veteran with heavy jowls and deep-set brown eyes, was well respected and had earned every accolade he'd received. With a scowl, he held up an evidence bag with a large butcher knife tucked inside. "Found this in the dishwasher. Still has blood on it. Whattya bet it matches the missing husband."

Karen's anger melted into panic. "This is all a mistake!"

Suddenly Rene came sweeping into the room. "Don't say another word, Karen. I've called an attorney. He's on his way. Until he gets here, say nothing."

"But Ted isn't dead, Rene!"

"Until this misunderstanding is cleared up, I was told you need to stay quiet. Wait for the lawyer. Let him handle this."

JJ didn't know whether to applaud or roll his eyes. He looked over at Tripp, who was now scowling at the woman in the doorway. JJ could relate. It wasn't the first time this woman had stalled an investigation.

JJ's cell phone rang. He stepped back out of the kitchen to answer it. "Johnson."

"Hey, boss." Gerry's voice rolled with inappropriate laughter. "Heard you're having fun at the Matthews' again."

"Just tell me what you have," JJ replied dryly.

"A possible lead on our housekeeper. We got a hit from law enforcement in Orlando. Physical description of a car parked at an out-of-the-way motel matches our suspect. They talked to the motel manager. At first he wasn't too cooperative. When he was asked if he wanted to be an accessory to kidnapping and a few other felons, he buckled. Says the lady checked in last night with an infant."

"Gerry?" JJ turned and stared out the front window.

"Yes, sir?"

"I thought I sent you to the Shefford house."

"Wayne went. I was in the middle of a call from the Orlando police."

JJ snapped his phone closed and then marched back into the

kitchen. "Mrs. Matthews?"

She looked up at him with tears streaking down her cheeks.

"What errand did your husband go on last night? And just in case you don't realize it, this is no time to hide anything."

She wrung her hands nervously before she finally spoke in a soft voice. "He said he was going to meet the kidnappers."

JJ raised one eyebrow skeptically. Tripp looked from the woman to JJ. "What's going on here?"

"They found the housekeeper and the baby."

Karen sprang to her feet. "Where?"

"Is that why you killed him, Mrs. Matthews? Because he was having an affair with Nancy Darrington?"

Confusion crossed Karen's face, but JJ had his theory all lined up and her act wasn't cutting it any more now than it had when all this started. "Nancy Darrington. Aka Alice Denton."

"Our housekeeper? That's ridiculous! He wasn't having an affair with her, and I didn't kill him! He's fine. He went after Jess. He'll be back soon."

"I doubt it. Nancy Darrington is being picked up as we speak. In Orlando, Florida."

◆　　◆　　◆

JJ pulled into Zoe's driveway just after eleven. Wayne was standing on the porch with a uniformed officer. He handed JJ the evidence bag with the doll inside.

JJ held up the bag. "My guess is that it belongs to Lisa Brandt."

"You'd be guessing right," Zoe replied softly.

JJ looked up to find her standing in the doorway. She was pale, trembling, and as far as JJ was concerned, barely holding it together.

"He wants to shake you up, Zoe."

"He already did that," she replied. "This is nothing but overkill."

Turning on her heel, she disappeared inside the house, leaving JJ to follow or leave.

"Wait here," JJ instructed Wayne. He stepped inside the house and closed the door. He found Zoe in the living room, pacing.

"You can't stay here until we catch this guy. Do you have a place to go?"

Zoe nodded. "Daria asked me to stay with her."

"Good." Thinking the subject dealt with, JJ turned and headed for the door. "I'm going to take this down to the station. I doubt we'll find anything, but it's worth trying."

"Okay." She followed him, her sandals barely whispering across the carpet.

At the door, JJ looked back at her, taking in the dark shadows in those pretty eyes. It was fear. For the first time since this had all begun, he realized just how afraid she truly was. In that moment, he didn't think about his motives, his intentions, or even his actions. He reached over and pulled her into his arms.

She was stiff and unyielding as he held her. "It's going to be okay, Zoe. We're not going to let this guy get to you."

She placed her hands lightly on his shoulders. "You won't be able to stop him, Josiah. I've invaded his garden. He wants me dead."

"I don't care what he wants. He's not going to touch you."

Later, he would say it was the scent of jasmine and roses. Or the look in her eyes—the incredible need that could turn any man into a mindless idiot with visions of white horses and slaying dragons.

But at that moment, all he could think of was how well she seemed to fit in his arms.

His lips came down on hers as soft as a whispered promise. There was a moment of hesitation before he felt her yield. Her arms slid around his neck and her fingers curled in his hair. And he was lost.

He tasted her mouth, his lips moving over hers in a ritual as old as breathing and just as instinctive. And if he felt those fingers wrapping around his heart, he didn't notice. He was far too consumed with the way she felt, tasted, breathed.

When he broke the contact, he was breathing hard. She opened her eyes slowly, and while the look of fear had abated, the look that had replaced the fear was far more potent.

He dropped his arms and stepped back reluctantly, trying to break those tiny threads that seemed to bind him to her.

"That was a mistake. I'm sorry."

Zoe turned her face away. "Don't sweat it, cowboy. A moment of insanity, right?"

"Right." He held up the doll. "I'd better go."

Zoe merely nodded. "You have a good day."

"Yeah. Uh, you, too."

It wasn't until she heard the front door close that she sat down and let the tears well up in her eyes. *A mistake!*

For the first time in her life, she felt a connection with a man that didn't involve seeing his every dark secret or the motive of his heart or the lust in his soul. For once, all she felt was wonderful. And he called it a mistake.

Arrogant, self-centered, judgmental, self-righteous. . .

And this was the man she was depending on to protect her from a killer? She'd lost her mind. The sight of her sister's bracelet glittering on her pillow still shimmered in her mind. The killer had left two messages for her with that bracelet. *I killed your sister and I can kill you. And I can get to you anytime, anywhere. You are not safe from me.*

Suddenly Zoe snapped to attention. What was it? Something her mother had told her about a man coming into the store. She jumped to her feet and ran down the hall. "Mom?" She tapped on the guest room door.

"Come on in, honey."

Zoe pushed open the door. Her mother was sitting on the freshly made bed, brushing her hair. She smiled up at Zoe. "You know what I was just thinking about? Belgian waffles. The kind with strawberries and whipped cream all over the top. You always loved those. How about we go down to that waffle. . ."

Zoe cut her off. "Mom. The other day. You called me and you told me a man had come into the shop. A weird man. Do you remember?"

Denise shoved her brush into her purse. "Well, of course I remember. He was way beyond weird. He said something about what a shame it would be if I lost both daughters. That's what sent those creepy crawlers up my spine."

Zoe spun on her heel and ran back into the living room. She grabbed the phone and stared at it a moment before she realized that she didn't know the phone number.

"Who are you calling? What's wrong, Zoe? Did that man come back again?"

"Mom, what's Dad's number?"

Denise lifted a finely arched brow as she rattled off the number to Zoe. Zoe dialed it without answering the questions in her mother's eyes.

"Dad? I'm sorry if I woke you."

"Zoe? Uh. . .no, you didn't wake me. I was just about to make some coffee."

"Mom is here. I need you to come here now. Now, Dad. Do you understand?"

"Well, yes, of course I understand. I can be there in ten minutes."

"Make it eight." Zoe slammed down the phone and started pacing again.

"Zoe, what is going on?"

"I'll tell you as soon as Dad gets here."

Denise frowned in that delicate way she had and folded her arms across her chest. Zoe could see so much of herself in her mother. They were both as stubborn as twenty-year-old mules. This wasn't going to be easy.

Keyes Shefford arrived a shade under ten minutes. Zoe opened the door and waved him in before he even had a chance to knock. She was stunned to see how he'd aged. Gray threaded through the thick, curly brown hair that had begun to recede from the corners of his forehead. He'd always been slim, but now he was almost too thin. The way his shoulders slumped, it was as if life had finally succeeded in wearing him out.

Only those gray eyes of his snapped with energy, and most of that was curiosity and bewilderment. "What's going on?"

Zoe took a deep breath and waved him over to the sofa. "The man that killed Amy is now after me."

She watched the color drain from his face and, for the first time in years, felt her heart ache for her dad. And for the relationship she'd once had with him. She longed for him to hold her tight and keep her safe. But she knew he couldn't keep her safe. He hadn't been able to keep Amy safe.

"It gets worse," she continued as her mother sidled over and sat down next to her father. "He's been leaving me messages, letting me know that I have nowhere to run and nowhere to hide. But that's not what I'm worried about right now. It dawned on me this morning that he left another message for me and I almost overlooked it."

"What message, Zoe?" Denise reached for Keyes' hand and held it tightly.

"He was in your shop, Mom. Remember? He was right there in your shop telling you that it would be a shame to lose me."

Keyes' head jerked back as he stared first at Zoe and then at

Denise. "He was letting you know he could get to your mother."

"Yes. Dad, I need you to take Mom away. Someplace safe until this is over. Mom said you bought a cabin somewhere in Ohio—on one of the Great Lakes, isn't it?"

"Yes, I. . ."

Zoe cut him off. This was no time for specifics. "Just take her there. Stay there. Fish, swim, picnic, explore, buy her all the antiques she wants. I don't care what you have to do, but keep her away until I let you know it's safe to come back."

Denise shook her head. "Not unless you come, too. It's you he's after, not me."

"He'll follow me. He won't follow you. The police and I can handle this. I just need to know you're safe." She wasn't so sure the police could handle this situation. Nor was she certain she could. The lie was necessary, however, to get her mother to cooperate.

"I don't know, honey." Denise shook her head. "I don't like this. I don't like it at all. I'll be worrying the whole time."

"I can handle this, Mom. I've been handling this world for a long, long time. Trust me. Trust the police. We'll catch this guy."

"You're going to set yourself up as bait, aren't you?" Her father's voice cut right to the heart. She could only hope he believed she wasn't alone in this.

"We have it all worked out, Dad. I'll be safe the entire time. We have to stop this guy before he takes another little child. It's the only way."

Keyes wrapped his arms around Denise. "I'll keep her safe, Zoe, but I want your promise that you'll do exactly what the police say and nothing else. No rash heroic moves. Don't take any unnecessary chances. I've already lost too much in my life. I won't lose you, too."

Zoe stood there and stared at her father. Didn't he realize that he'd already lost her? He'd lost her twenty years ago.

chapter 18

Sitting at the kitchen table, Karen tried to ignore the incessant ringing of the doorbell. "Go away," she kept whispering as she buried her head in her arms.

The ringing finally stopped and silence fell around her like a warm mist. Images kept swimming through her head. The police searching her house, asking her questions, insisting that Ted's car had been found in the river, his body swept away.

Impossible. He couldn't be dead. God couldn't be so cruel as to take her baby and her husband.

A bloody knife in the dishwasher? She couldn't remember using it. Couldn't remember the last time she'd even seen that knife. It wasn't one of her regular cooking knives. It had been one of her mother's and was usually left unused in a kitchen drawer. Karen didn't like the way it cut.

How did it get there? Whose blood was it? It couldn't be Ted's. It was absurd for anyone to think she had killed him. She loved him. Respected him. Needed him. She loved Ted. Sure, he could be overbearing sometimes, but. . . She pressed her knuckles against her mouth to keep from crying out in despair. Her head hurt and she felt sick to her stomach.

She knew Ted was only hard on her because she needed someone to keep her focused. But to kill Ted? Ridiculous! Beyond belief! She couldn't even stand the sight of blood!

Idiots! That's what they were. Complete idiots! This was all a major misunderstanding. The kidnappers dumped Ted's car. He probably had to go with them in their car somewhere, and now he was trying to hitch a ride home with Jess.

Karen sat up in a rush. *Of course! That had to be it!*

Footsteps in the hallway penetrated her thoughts, and she jumped to her feet. "Karen?"

Her father's voice echoed through the house. Karen slapped a hand to her chest. "You scared the daylights out of me, Dad."

"Why didn't you answer the door? I had a heck of a time finding my key."

She sank back down in her chair. "I didn't answer the door because I didn't want company."

The hint was ignored as he pulled out a chair and joined her at the table, his eyes hard and condemning. "Why didn't you call me? I had to hear it on the news?"

Karen shrugged. She had no desire to answer his questions any more than she wanted to be pounded on by the police. There was very little difference in the impact on her heart and mind.

"You've finally snapped, haven't you?" His voice slapped at her, stinging. "Gone around the bend."

Karen looked over at him, still saying nothing.

"Why did you do it, Karen? Did you just get tired of being a wife and mother? Is that it?"

"Don't be ridiculous, Dad. I didn't *do* anything."

"Of course not. Ted and Jessica are just missing, right? Someone took them, right?"

"Yes," she whispered. What else could she say?

"Just like someone took Kipsey, right?"

Karen felt the words hit her like a fist, knocking the breath out of her. "What?"

"You killed that kitten and refused to admit it."

"I was a child! Give me a break, Dad! It was an accident!" A terrible accident. The little tabby had been climbing on her mother's curtains, and her mother had threatened to give him away if Karen didn't control him. Desperate, Karen had put the kitten in a box and lined it with blankets so he would be comfortable. She'd sealed it shut to keep him from escaping.

She hadn't realized that between the blankets and the sealed box, the cat had been smothered.

"You could never own up to it, could you? No. You had to tell everyone that someone had taken that kitten, that it had been stolen. That's what you kept saying, because you couldn't admit that you'd killed it. Are you doing it again, girl? Refusing to admit the truth?"

"Leave her alone, Dad."

Karen jumped up out of her chair at the sound of the familiar voice. "Ray!"

He held out his arms and she didn't hesitate. She flew into them and let him wrap her up in comfort. "Thank goodness you came."

Walter lumbered to his feet. "And here *you* finally are. You don't bother with any of us until there's trouble, then the first thing you do is coddle that girl."

"And as always, you have to beat her up rather than admit that you may have judged Ted wrong. You're never wrong, are you, Dad? Heaven forbid. No, it's always someone else's fault—usually Mom's or Karen's."

"You don't know what you're talking about. You don't know what's been going on here." He pointed to his daughter, his voice tight with anger. "First her daughter and now her husband."

"And Karen is innocent. End of story."

"So say you. You don't have all the facts."

"I have enough facts to know that my sister would never kill her child. Or her husband. She isn't built that way."

"You have no idea, Ray. You aren't here to see her. Forgetting things, shifting blame, always shuffling around with her head in the clouds, neglecting the baby, not doing right by her husband."

Ray gently extracted Karen from his arms. He looked down at her, and she felt a tremor run down her spine.

"Did you kill Jessica? Did you kill Ted? Tell me, Karen. Tell me the truth. Did you do this?"

He smoothed the ground with his hands and then rose, clapping his hands together to knock off the surface dirt. With a critical eye, he examined every aspect of the area. Nothing looked disturbed. Nothing to indicate that anything was amiss.

Of course, he wasn't concerned at the moment. His superior thinking had the cops running in fifteen different directions and getting nowhere fast. He laughed out loud, picturing the police scratching their heads as they tried to figure out what was going on.

Oh, he was good. Smart. Far too smart for Johnson. It was utterly presumptuous of Detective Johnson to think that he could actually catch him.

No, Johnson would be chasing his tail for years to come. In the meantime, there was more work to be done. A few more warnings to that nosy Shefford woman and then he'd take her out of the equation completely. And of course, he would lay so many rabbit trails the good detective wouldn't know which way to look. The bracelet was a stroke of genius. He laughed to himself. *She probably still hadn't noticed that he had taken something of hers. A little trinket to send the police running in the wrong direction again.*

Fools. That's what they all were. They didn't understand him and they never could. None of them. He'd learned how to play the game, letting them think he was like them. But he wasn't. Oh, no. Not even close. He was far superior. They looked him in the eye and never knew he was laughing at them behind that bland stare he'd perfected in front of his mirror.

And he would keep on laughing.

It had been a long morning, and the tension was still lingering on the edge of fear. Zoe's father had called her from somewhere outside Columbus, Ohio, with an update on their travel. They had stopped for breakfast before hitting the road again.

He sounded upbeat. She could only imagine that the time alone together was giving them a much-needed opportunity to sort through relational issues.

Licking the mayo off her fingertips, she stacked the ham on the bread. At least her mother was safe. Carrying her sandwich to the table, she sat down and stared at it. Being relieved of one set of worries had only given her more time and inclination to dwell on another worrisome situation: her attraction to JJ.

Zoe shook her head. What was she thinking? Nothing was ever going to develop between them. He'd made that perfectly clear after kissing her.

She pulled the newspaper closer and perused the top stories. They had fished Ted Matthews's car out of the river and he was presumed dead.

Karen Matthews must be at the end of her rope.

You use the devil's powers and I can't allow that. I'm sorry, but Karen is a Christian. Karen's friend's words echoed in her mind. Taunting her. *Your gift is not from God.*

Enough!

She was going to settle this once and for all! It took her almost fifteen minutes, but she finally found her old Bible—the white one her parents had given her as a child—tucked in the back of a closet with her old Nancy Drew books and a copy of *Grimm's Fairy Tales*.

Wiping off the dust, she carried it back into the living room. She flipped randomly through the pages.

Your gift is not from God.

You use the devil's powers.

Zoe slammed the Bible closed. She didn't know where to look—where to find answers to her questions. She hadn't been able to find one word about psychics.

"Who do you call to, Zoe? Do you call on God?"

Zoe shook her head as if to dislodge Rene's voice. *"Is your life submitted to Him? Is your gift submitted to Him? All gifts come from God and are given without repentance. He has given mankind free will. How you choose to use your gifts, whether for Him or for His enemy, is up to you."*

"Stop it!" Zoe whispered forcefully. "Just stop it! I'm not using my gift for evil. I'm using it for good!"

"There is a difference between good things and God things."

Zoe reached for her purse and dumped the contents out on the table. She fished through everything—brush, lipstick, tissues, bottle of aspirin, two pens, checkbook, wallet, receipt from the drugstore—and finally found the card Rene had given her.

Reaching for the phone, Zoe read off the number. Then she noticed the scribble at the bottom of the card. *Read Acts 16:16.*

Huh? What is Acts? Oh, the Bible. Duh.

Zoe reached over and slid the Bible closer as she slowly sat down. Acts. Acts. She flipped through the pages and finally resorted to the table of contents in the front. It took her another minute or so to locate Acts and then chapter sixteen.

With her chin resting in one fist, she started to read. *Once when we were going to the place of prayer, we were met by a slave girl who had a spirit by which she predicted the future. She earned a great deal of money for her owners by fortune-telling.*

Zoe winced.

This girl followed Paul and the rest of us, shouting, "These men are servants of the Most High God, who are telling you the way to be saved." She kept this up for many days. Finally Paul became so troubled that he turned around and said to the spirit, "In the name of Jesus Christ I command you to come out of her!" At that moment the spirit left her.

When the owners of the slave girl realized that their hope of making money was gone, they seized Paul and Silas and dragged them into the marketplace to face the authorities.

Zoe made a face as she went back and read it again. This was what that guy on television had been preaching about. Then she noticed the little mark by the word *fortune-telling*. She went to the bottom of the page and found the corresponding mark. *Fortune-telling, Soothsaying. Greek* manteuomai—*to divine, utter spells under pretense of foretelling; divination. See Deut. 18:10; Jer. 14:14.*

Under pretense? Zoe felt her temper rise. *This is such bunk. I'll show you pretense!*

But as much as she wanted to slam the book shut and walk away, she grabbed her pen and the receipt from the drugstore instead and wrote down the two Scriptures on the back of it. Then she started searching for the first one.

She found Deuteronomy 18:10: *Let no one be found among you who sacrifices his son or daughter in the fire, who practices divination or sorcery, interprets omens, engages in witchcraft, or casts spells, or who is a medium or spiritist or who consults the dead. Anyone who does these things is detestable to the LORD.*

Zoe felt like someone had just punched her in the heart. *Anyone who does these things is detestable to the Lord?* Detestable? Did He really think of her that way? As a detestable thing?

She searched for Jeremiah 14:14. *Then the Lord said to me, "The prophets are prophesying lies in my name. I have not sent them or appointed them or spoken to them. They are prophesying to you false visions, divinations, idolatries and the delusions of their own minds."*

Zoe leaned back in her chair. *The delusions of their own minds.* Stunned, she reached over, picked up the phone, and dialed Rene's number.

"Rene, this is Zoe." She propped her elbow on the table and brought her forehead down to rest on her clenched fist. "I was just reading those Scriptures you wrote down. I have a question. Does God really think I'm detestable?"

"Oh, Zoe. He loves you so very much. What you are doing grieves Him, but that's why He's gone to such lengths to get the truth to you. He's always loved you."

Zoe stared down at the Bible, and suddenly a shiver of fear ran down her back. "Rene. You said the last time we talked that I would have to renounce my gift in the way it's being used right now."

"Correct."

"And if I do, then I wouldn't have it, right? I mean, being able to sense the killer and stuff, that would all stop, right?"

"I don't know. It's likely, Zoe."

Oh, no. There was no way she could stop the killer if she couldn't use every ounce of her psychic ability to do it. She had to be able to use it or she'd be a sitting duck.

"Zoe?"

"I can't, Rene. I think I understand all this, and I believe I want to do this God's way, but not yet."

"Zoe, don't fall for this. It's a lie. You don't need to be a psychic anymore."

"Yes, I do. One last time, Rene. I have to."

"No!" Rene almost sounded as if she was crying. "Please, listen to me, Zoe. God will help you. He will. You don't need the gift."

"I'm sorry, Rene. I have to do this. It's important."

JJ stopped at Zoe's on his way home from the station. He refused to believe he was just looking for an excuse to talk to her when he went down to Evidence and signed out the blanket they'd confiscated from Jessica Matthews's crib the morning she was taken. He just needed to apologize. He wanted to make sure she was okay. And he was forty different kinds of a fool while he knocked on her door, baby blanket in hand.

She swung open the door and stood there looking at him without saying a word. Her hair was tied back with a blue ribbon, almost the same shade of blue as the cotton drawstring pants and short-sleeve shirt she wore. He looked at her bare feet. "Did I catch you at a bad time?"

"Yes."

Her response was terse. Her voice harsh. He paused. "Don't you think you should at least ask who it is before you open the door?"

"I looked through the peephole. I knew it was you."

He shifted his weight from one foot to the other. "I brought this. . ." He thrust the blanket at her. "From the Matthews' baby crib."

"I see," she replied coolly. She stepped back from the door and waved him in.

The tension was a thick fog, but JJ tried to ignore it.

Zoe took the blanket and sat down on the sofa, ignoring JJ. She closed her eyes, fingering the fabric.

"That's odd."

JJ, who was looking around the room, turned back to her. "What is?"

"I can usually pick up something, even if it's just a sense of the person. But there's nothing on this blanket at all. It might as well have come straight from a store. I can't pick up anything."

"We took it out of the child's crib. Karen Matthews said Jessica was sleeping on it when she was taken."

Zoe shook her head. "I can't pick up anything." She folded the blanket, stood up stiffly, and handed it back to him. "Will there be anything else?"

JJ took his time standing up. "I'm sorry, but am I missing something here? What's with the attitude?"

"You'll have to excuse me, but I see no reason to pretend that yesterday morning didn't happen."

"Hey, I haven't forgotten what happened yesterday morning. I just don't think it was very smart."

Zoe jammed her fists on her hips, the fire in her eyes nearly incinerating him on the spot. "I'm not the one who started it, so don't make me out to be the bad guy."

"Did I say you started it?" he snapped.

"You're doing a great job of implying it!"

JJ raised his voice to match hers. "All I said was that it shouldn't have happened!"

"And it won't happen again!"

"Not in this lifetime!"

"Then I see no reason to continue this discussion!" She marched over to the front door and yanked it open. "I think this is the way out."

"Fine!"

He started for the door, but something in her face stopped him. His gaze followed hers down to the threshold. "Oh!"

Dropping the blanket, JJ ran forward as Zoe backed away. She closed her eyes and leaned against the wall.

He knelt down. Without touching the bloody garment, he determined it was the same color and pattern shirt that Lisa Brandt was supposed to have been wearing.

The killer was taunting them—daring to come up to the house while she was home. Not only at home but in the company of the police. He was thumbing his nose at all of them. Anger surged as JJ pulled out his cell phone and called Matt.

"We're talking within the last ten or fifteen minutes. If there's anyone patrolling nearby, have them sweep. I doubt they'll find anything, but do it anyway. And I need an evidence bag."

He glanced at Zoe. Her pale, bloodless face pulled at him even as he fought it. "Go sit down," he told her, trying not to snap at her.

She disappeared into the kitchen, where she made herself a cup of tea. He joined her there half an hour later. "Go pack a bag. You're not staying here."

She raised one eyebrow. "I beg your pardon."

"This guy is not kidding around, Zoe. I can't leave you here alone. He may come back."

"I don't think that's your problem, Detective Johnson. Now, if you don't mind, I had some reading I wanted to do this evening."

He pulled out a chair and propped one foot up on it. "Look, I can't leave you here. Now, be a good girl, pack a bag, grab your book, and let's go."

"I'd appreciate it very much if you would leave."

"Do you have a death wish or something? This guy wants you dead. Do you understand that?"

"I understand quite well, Detective. I'm not a child and I'm not stupid."

"But you are one of the most obstinate women I've ever known."

"I feel sad for you."

"Yeah, I can tell you're just bleeding all over the place for me. Come on, pack some things."

Zoe stood up and carried her cup to the sink. "I will say this one more time. Please leave. If you don't, I will call your boss and tell him that you have attacked me, kissed me, and now refuse to leave my home."

There was something in her tone of voice that let him know she wasn't kidding. But he still couldn't keep himself from saying, "You wouldn't."

She turned around at the sink and leaned back against it, folding her arms across her chest. "Oh, I would. No one is running me out of my home."

"Then we'll carry you out in a body bag."

She stood there, staring him down. He quickly realized that pushing wasn't getting anywhere. "Fine. Have it your way."

Zoe waited then curled up in a chair with a book until she heard the last car pull away from the curb. Everything fell silent again. It had taken hours for JJ to leave, but at least he had stayed outside, directing the investigation and sending Matt in if there were questions. It rankled her, but she did her best to ignore the fact that he was still out there.

It didn't matter that the words ran together on the pages or that she had been staring at the same page for nearly an hour. What mattered was that she told JJ she was going to read, and by golly, she was going to read.

Slowly she began to hear every little noise. The house creaked. A dog barked. A car backfired. Something scraped across the window.

She jumped at every sound. Even after turning on every light in the house, she wondered if her pride hadn't made her foolish. She could be someplace safe. Instead, she was holed up in her home, skittish and afraid.

Trust me.

Zoe closed her eyes. Trust who? Her father? He'd already proven that he couldn't be trusted. Good old Detective Josiah Johnson with the penetrating eyes and devastating kiss? Right. The killer had JJ running around in circles. She had no one to depend on but herself. She had a knife tucked under her thigh, although she didn't expect the killer to show up tonight. He wasn't done playing with her yet. She knew that. Just as she knew she would face him.

He'd taken her innocent little sister away from her, and she was going to make him pay dearly for it. She was going to make him suffer. He was going to feel every inch of pain he'd ever inflicted on a child. He was going to beg to die. And then, maybe, she'd let him. Let him go straight to hell where he'd suffer for all eternity. And that wasn't even long enough.

"He's going to pay, Amy. I promise you, he's going to pay."

Trust me. I will never leave you nor forsake you.

Zoe picked up her book. There was no one she could trust. Not now. Not with this. She had been born for this: to confront a man who had nothing but evil in his heart. She would succeed. Alone. She could do this. *She could.*

In the meantime, it was going to be a long night.

Karen closed her eyes and willed herself to go to sleep. Ray was snoring softly across the hall in the guest room, and her father had finally left.

When Ray asked if she'd killed Jess or Ted, she'd felt the floor tilt under her feet. Her answer was an almost inaudible "No."

Then Ray had turned to their father. "Good enough for me."

Why Ray had come was still a mystery. She hadn't expected him. But he was here, and she felt nothing but gratitude and relief.

They had retreated to the living room after their father stormed out of the house. There, curled up on opposite sides of the sofa, they had discussed Ted's disappearance. Ray was convinced Ted had met with foul play after messing around with someone's wife.

"Ted wouldn't do that," she'd claimed, but Ray had only snorted in disbelief.

"I never trusted him, Sis. Trust me, he isn't worth defending."

But she'd tried to defend him, finding it more difficult with each passing minute as Ray pointed out the obvious. Suitcases had been found in Ted's car. He had packed his clothes and lied about going off to meet with the kidnappers. Karen remembered how the police had been anxious to talk to him, claiming he'd agreed to answer some questions. But he disappeared instead. This, as Ray had emphasized, was the behavior of a man with something to hide. Karen's faith in Ted had slowly begun to crumble, until finally she'd retreated to bed with a headache.

She vacillated between confusion, pain, and numbness. She was no longer sure what she believed or why. Ray accused her of avoiding the truth because it was easier to pretend. She was starting to believe he was right. She'd been so miserable for so long that pretending had become her escape.

It was time to see truth for what it was and deal with it. But was she strong enough to handle it?

She stared at the ceiling with more questions than answers. Had Ted been avoiding the police? Why? Had he lied? Had someone killed him?

Her heart jumped with pain as she twisted her fingers into the blanket and fought back hysteria. *He just couldn't be dead.*

JJ couldn't shake the feeling he'd made a mistake with Zoe. Stretched out on his bed, he went over the entire scene with her again in his mind. He'd strong-armed her and he shouldn't have.

With arms folded under his head, he stared at the ceiling and wondered how to protect Zoe without getting her all riled up. If he hadn't called her onto the case, she wouldn't even be a target. But she *had* become a target, so he was honor bound to protect her.

His fingers itched to pick up the phone and call her—to see if she was okay.

But the phone rang before he could gather the courage to call. He glanced at the clock. It was just after 2:00 A.M. He reached over and picked up the receiver. "Johnson."

"JJ? It's Matt. We have another missing child."

JJ zipped up his sweatshirt against the cool spring night as he stood outside the apartment building and talked to a police officer. He couldn't begin to describe the relief when he arrived on the scene and learned that the killer hadn't struck again after all. It was a case of parental abduction. The mother had called in a panic sometime after midnight when she woke on the sofa to find that her husband hadn't returned their son at nine the way he was supposed to. After calling his apartment and finding the phone number disconnected, she'd called the police.

Someone at the station heard that a child was missing and turned it over to Matt Casto, who was on call. Matt had called JJ.

Now they could both go home.

JJ climbed into his Cherokee and took a deep breath. He hadn't realized how tense he was until that moment. With one hand on the wheel and one elbow propped up on the window's edge with fingers buried in his hair, JJ drove down empty streets through quiet neighborhoods. Except for the occasional flicker of a television through someone's curtains, houses were dark. Until he reached Jasper Drive.

He pulled up to the curb in front of her house and stared. The house was ablaze with light.

She had to be scared out of her mind.

Climbing out of his vehicle, he walked up to the house and knocked on the door. Zoe opened the door, looking much the same as she had a few hours earlier, but this time there were dark circles under her eyes and tightness around her mouth.

"I was responding to another call and drove by. I saw the lights."

She stepped back, silently inviting him in. "I just made some coffee. Would you like some?"

He noticed the tension in her voice and wondered if it was because he was there or because she was frightened. Following her into the kitchen, he spotted the book on the arm of the sofa. She should have finished it by now.

He waited until they were back in the living room with their coffee before he asked, "Having a problem sleeping?"

"I guess you could say that." She tucked her feet under her.

"You have good enough reason. If I had a killer stalking me, I don't think I'd be sleeping."

"I didn't think it would bother me."

"Then you're crazy."

She shrugged, a little smile tugging at the corner of her mouth. "You've been implying that all along."

"I didn't mean to." He sipped his coffee, struggling to break the tension between them.

He set down his coffee cup on the table next to his chair, clasped his hands between his knees, and leaned forward. "Look, we've been at each other's throats since this began. I've made no secret of the fact that I don't think much of this psychic business. But I don't want you dead."

"So you're concerned for my life," she said dryly.

"Look, Zoe. Miss Shefford. I can't deny that I find you attractive, but I'm not looking to get involved with anyone."

"That makes two of us." She lifted her cup and took another sip, her eyes downcast.

"Then you understand that my interest is purely in the line of duty. This man is serious about wanting you dead. I'm serious about making sure he doesn't get what he wants."

"I understand completely."

"And I want it to stay purely business. My. . .I stepped over the line. It won't happen again."

"Of course not."

"Good. Then why don't you go get some sleep while I keep watch."

Her head jerked up. "I beg your pardon?"

"You need to get some sleep. I'm going to sit here and read this. . ." He picked up the novel she was reading. *"Wild Hearts in Paradise?* No, I don't think so." He dropped it as if it were a snake ready to bite him. "I'll find something to do. Go get some sleep."

She stood up. "Thanks."

"Somehow I didn't take you for the type."

"What type?"

He nodded toward the book she was picking up. "Romance, love novels, whatever they call those things."

"Who do you think reads them?"

"Housewives with five kids looking for a little escapism."

"Everyone needs to escape once in awhile."

Before he could reply, she padded off down the hall with her book. As soon as he heard her bedroom door click shut, he shut off most of the lights. Then he perused her book collection and found a mystery novel that looked promising.

Kicking off his shoes, he stretched out on the sofa with the novel and prepared for a long night.

Zoe curled up under the covers and switched off the lamp next to her bed. It was the first time all evening she felt safe in the dark.

And it was because JJ was in her living room, keeping watch.

She closed her eyes and yawned. If he weren't such a jerk, he would be someone she'd want to know better. She knew what made him act that way though. His relationship issues were not insignificant. Like Macy.

Someday he'd resolve that situation in his mind and in his heart, but until he did, he wasn't any good for any woman.

And certainly not for her. He'd be nothing but a heartache. And she'd be left with the scars on her heart.

No thanks.

She had enough of her own issues to deal with.

She yawned again, snuggling deeper into her pillow.

But he sure could kiss.

chapter 19

Sunday, April 23

Yawning, Karen shuffled into the kitchen, flipped on the television, and started the coffee. She had barely slept for the third night in a row. And then when she did manage to drift off, nightmares of Ted drowning in a river, Jess trapped in the car, and a bloody knife on the dashboard jerked her awake in a cold sweat.

". . .Here's a follow-up to Friday's story about a car discovered in the river and the fate of its driver. Police are saying that the apparent victim is forty-six-year-old Ted Matthews, who had left home, according to his wife, to meet with the alleged kidnappers of their infant daughter."

Karen whirled around, spilling grounds across the counter and onto the floor.

"The police have been dredging the river since early Friday in hopes of recovering the body, but so far the search has been fruitless. One police officer admitted that they are focusing their investigation on Karen Matthews, who they claim has been extremely uncooperative."

With a scream of outrage, Karen threw the coffee can at the television. "I didn't *do* anything!"

The can hit the television and bounced off, scattering black coffee grounds all over the television, counter, and floor.

The phone rang, causing her to jump. She stared at it, debating, but the prospect that it might be her attorney drove her to it.

"Hello?"

"Mrs. Matthews?"

The voice was decidedly female, driving out every hope that it was Benson. "Yes?"

"This is Alicia DeSimone from WRRS News. Do you have. . ."

Karen slammed down the phone and backed away from it. It started ringing again. She put her hands over her ears. "Go away. Just go away and leave me alone!"

"Karen?" Ray was still buttoning his shirt as he hurried into the room. "What in heaven's name is going on?"

She looked down at the coffee grounds strewn all over the kitchen and then up at Ray, who was still trying to wake up. "Nothing. I'm sorry I woke you."

"You call this nothing? It looks like the Boston Tea Party but with coffee grounds."

"It was the news. They were blaming me, saying I killed Ted." It was a nightmare she couldn't wake up from.

Ray opened his arms and swept her into a hug. "Don't listen to the news, Sis. You know they're just trying to beef up ratings any way they can."

"I didn't kill him, Ray. I didn't."

Zoe awoke to find JJ sprawled on the sofa with a novel across his chest. He had one foot propped up on the arm of the sofa, the other rested on the floor. His hair was sticking up in every direction possible.

Traces of a beard shadowed his face.

And he snored.

She wrinkled her nose, covering her mouth with her hand, trying not to laugh as he choked on a snore and shifted positions. Tiptoeing into the kitchen, she quietly emptied the coffeepot from the night before and made a fresh pot.

While the coffee was brewing, she padded softly to the front door and retrieved the morning paper. She wondered if she would find something besides the paper on the front porch but was relieved to see that the killer had given her a night off.

She sipped her coffee while skimming through the paper.

"Anything interesting?" JJ scratched his stomach as he made his way groggily to the coffeepot.

She smiled and pulled her eyes back to the paper. "Not much. The mayor wants to enlarge the playground at the park; the fire at the old warehouse was determined to be arson; and there's a sale at Carson's hardware."

"A sale on what?"

"Power tools."

"I'll have to check it out."

Zoe slanted him a glance and a smile. "Hey, thirty percent off—you'd better hurry."

"I'll buy two of everything." He pulled out a chair and dropped into it. "Sleep well?"

"Yes, thank you. Like a rock. You?"

"Good enough, all things considered."

"I thought you'd be up all night keeping watch."

"I dozed off." He glared over at her. "You were safe enough."

"I wasn't implying otherwise. Would you like some breakfast?"

He stood up. "No. Thanks anyway."

"Here we go again," she muttered as he stalked out of the

kitchen. "Have a nice day," she yelled out seconds before she heard the front door slam shut.

After setting her coffee cup in the sink, the phone rang. "Hello?"

Zoe stood swaying as harshly whispered words echoed in her head.

"Weeds in the garden, so you must die. Will today be the day?"

"No," Zoe replied as her heart lurched in her chest. She could feel the sweat break out on her forehead, and her hands went icy cold.

"Did you think you were safe with that nice policeman on your sofa all night?"

"It made *him* feel better."

"I notice your mother didn't come home again last night. Now, I wonder why."

"This is between you and me. It doesn't involve her."

"You really are a smart woman, Zoe Shefford. How unusual. I'm going to take such delight in killing you."

"Like you killed Amy?"

"Now, there was a true delight."

Zoe felt the tears spring to her eyes. *Not now. Not now. Fall apart later. Don't let him see it bothers you.* "Amy was one of a kind."

"No. There is one just like her. And I can't wait to have you join her."

chapter 20

J J shrugged out of his jacket just as the phone started ringing. Matt stood. Barone came skipping in with a smile. JJ threw up his hand, stalling the two men, and grabbed the phone. "Johnson."

"Hey, Johnson. It's Tripp. Just wanted to give you the heads-up. The blood on the knife was confirmed as the same type as Ted Matthews. We're bringing the wife in for questioning."

"Keep me posted."

"You bet."

Barone leaned forward. "I did a little checking on the locations of the missing girls over the years. Get this. Nearly twenty percent of the missing children came from homes that were, or are, owned or managed by Keyes Realty."

JJ shook his head, shrugging. "So?"

Barone smiled smugly. "Keyes Realty. As in Keyes Shefford, father of Zoe Shefford."

JJ felt as if the ground beneath him had just shifted. He grabbed the edge of the desk. "Zoe's father?"

Barone nodded. "Do you think it's possible that Shefford, or someone who works for him, is involved in this?"

Matt whistled now as he pulled up a chair. "This is not good."

JJ continued gripping the edge of the desk, afraid his hands would start shaking if he let go. Had she conned him? Could he have been so blind?

He managed to look up at Barone, who was eyeing him with anticipation. "See what else you can find while we check out Keyes Realty." He turned to Matt. "Matt, see. . ."

"Hold on, JJ. You don't really think this man could be a viable suspect, do you? One of the kids that was killed was his own daughter."

"We don't know what happened to the Shefford girl."

"Amy," Matt supplied tersely.

JJ ignored him. "The Sheffords were going through a nasty separation at the time. Suppose the father took the child as leverage and something went wrong."

"I don't buy it."

"I didn't ask you to. I didn't ask you to arrest him either. But a connection like this deserves a closer look."

"Yeah, Keyes Shefford. I'm on it." Matt turned on his heel and sprinted for the door.

He was back less than five minutes later looking very grim. "Keyes Shefford has disappeared. His secretary says he called in yesterday afternoon. Said he had to go out of town for a few days and would call in for his messages. He wouldn't tell her where he went."

JJ slammed his fist down on the desk.

Karen sat quietly, her hands clasped in her lap as her attorney jotted notes on his yellow legal pad.

"We talked to his boss, who confirmed that Ted was *not* sent out of town on a business trip. We checked the company phone records, and Mr. Matthews did not receive any calls from outside the office any time during that day. We spoke to the cashier at the restaurant, who confirmed that you were in there Friday evening, picking up food."

Tripp lowered his reading glasses and peered over the top of them. "So we know that your husband was not scheduled to leave town, did not get a call from the kidnappers, and is now missing."

Karen looked over at her attorney, Lawrence Benson, a rail-thin man in his fifties with thick gray hair, bright blue eyes, and a thousand-watt smile.

He patted her hand gently as he kept his eyes on Tripp. "As we explained, Mr. Matthews informed my client that he was going to meet with the kidnappers, pay the ransom, and bring their child home. If he lied to my client, that is not my client's fault."

"Perhaps she can explain how a knife with her husband's blood on it was found in her sink?"

Benson smiled slowly, deliberately. "This is his house, too. Perhaps he was cutting something prior to leaving and nicked his finger."

"And the shirt with Mr. Matthews's blood on it?"

"Perhaps he grabbed it out of the laundry basket and wiped his blood on it, thinking it was a rag."

Tripp frowned, tapping his fingers on the desk. Benson tossed his legal pad back into his briefcase and closed it, snapping the locks with quiet deliberation. "You have nothing, Lieutenant Tripp. If and when you feel you have something convicting my client of a crime—you know, like a body or something—call me."

He stood up, taking Karen's elbow and guiding her to her feet. "We're leaving now, Karen. They don't have anything to hold you."

Tripp stood up, glaring. "We have a missing husband, an abandoned car, a bloody knife, and blood on the wife's clothes. I'd say we have something."

"You have nothing, Tripp. You know it and I know it."

"The cashier at the restaurant said that Mrs. Matthews was quite upset when she came in, obviously crying."

Benson narrowed his eyes, leaning forward, forcing Tripp to move back. "Her child is missing. She believes her husband has gone to meet with kidnappers. She is facing hours of sitting around wringing her hands waiting for her husband to return safe and sound with their child. In the meantime, the police haven't done squat to find her daughter. Don't you think the woman has something to be upset about?"

Tripp growled.

"Let's go, Karen."

Karen let Benson guide her from the interview room, her heart pounding. Ted was missing, presumed dead, and they thought she'd done it. Her daughter was missing, and they thought she was responsible for that, too. How much worse could things get?

Suddenly she gasped. "What if he *was* killed, Mr. Benson? What if he was taking the money to someone? Maybe the people who have Jessica *did* call Friday. Maybe they contacted him while he was out to lunch or something. Maybe they followed him, contacted him there so there was no record of a call into his office. Maybe when he met them with the money, they took it all and killed him. Oh, no. Oh, my God. They've killed my husband and my daughter. Oh, God. What am I going to do?"

"Calm down."

"Maybe he's still okay. Maybe the kidnappers just want more money. Maybe they'll contact me."

Benson looked skeptical as he glanced over at her. "Maybe. We'll see."

Karen leaned against the seat as he shut her door. His skepticism was palpable. Definite. There would be no ransom. He believed Ted was dead. She just wasn't ready to accept that. Her whole life had collapsed in two weeks. Two weeks ago today, Jessica was taken. Fourteen days later her husband was also missing and the police thought she was guilty of murder.

"God, what have you done to me?" she whispered.

Benson opened his door and climbed in. "Did you say something?"

Karen shook her head and turned to stare out the window, fighting back the tears.

Business was slow at her mother's boutique and Zoe was bored. She wandered around the store, straightening the same racks over and over, mindlessly fingering the silks and cashmeres.

She had promised her mother to open the store for a few hours every day, and it had seemed like a small concession at the time. Now she wished she'd convinced her mother to close for a few days.

Zoe glanced at her watch. One forty-five. She'd sold $225 worth of clothes. Barely enough to cover payroll, taxes, rent, and electricity.

Hanging the closed sign, she locked the door, grabbed her purse, and set the alarm before slipping out the back exit.

When she got home, Zoe put a load of wash in the machine, straightened the kitchen, swept the deck, and stretched out on a deck lounge to read. Minutes later, she was fast asleep.

Zoe clawed at the weight pressing down on her face, suffocating her. She tried to move. Tried to fight. Panic ripped through her. She struggled to open her eyes. To see death. To face it.

He'd managed to get to her. But how? She hadn't suspected he'd come during the day. Darkness swirled in her like dancers in a macabre death march.

Forcing her mind to slow down, she lurched forward.

Gasping for air, Zoe stared at the long shadows stretching across the deck. Whirling around, she searched for her attacker.

Her book lay on the deck, its pages fluttering. The wind chimes stirred softly, tinkling as the soft scent of roses drifted on the breeze. Somewhere in the yard, a bird whistled to its mate.

A dream. It had only been a dream. Sweat ran down her face and neck. Her shirt was drenched. Burying her face in her hands, she concentrated on breathing. On letting her lungs fill and empty without fear. No one was suffocating her. She wasn't going to die. She wasn't. . .

Pictures flickered through her mind like a slide show gone crazy. She closed her eyes and took a deep breath, trying to capture one of the images and hold it. Stone wall. *Hold it.* Ivy. *Hold it.* Emily. *Where are you, Emily?* Her mind and thoughts reached out like a hand, stretching out to touch, to hold. The images slipped through her fingers like water, flowing out and away.

But it was enough. Zoe jumped up and ran inside, grabbing the phone off the wall. Quickly she dialed. Then waited.

"Detective. . ."

"I need Johnson," she sputtered, cutting the woman off. "This is Zoe Shefford. I need to talk to Detective Johnson right away."

"Hold on."

Zoe's knees rocked beneath her as she waited impatiently to hear his familiar voice.

"Detective John—"

"This is Zoe. I know where Emily is!"

"I'll be right there."

Zoe slammed down the phone and scrambled into the bedroom. She rushed to change into jeans and sneakers, exchanging her sweat-drenched shirt for a pullover. Grabbing her hair, she tied it back quickly with a scrunchie and rushed to the front door. JJ wasn't there yet.

She began to pace. Another five minutes passed. She grabbed her purse and stepped outside, locking the door behind her. She paced up and down her driveway. She had made one full trip up and back when JJ whipped his Cherokee into the driveway and screeched to a halt.

Zoe ran over and jumped in. "The park near the college."

JJ nodded and backed out of the driveway. Zoe took a deep breath, letting her head drop back against the headrest. "Where's your regular car?"

"This is mine. The department car is in for maintenance. I didn't feel like taking time to check out a loaner."

She nodded as she noted the CDs scattered on the floor at her feet. Reaching down, she picked them up. Garth Brooks, Mark Chestnut, Reba, Tim McGraw. "You're into country music."

"Yeah."

Zoe noticed it then, the cool distance, the icy remoteness. "Is something wrong?"

"I'm a cop. Something is always wrong."

"I see." Zoe turned and stared out the window.

"I doubt it," he muttered softly.

Zoe whirled her head and stared hard at him. "What's going on? This isn't just about you and me this time, is it?"

"Let's just do this. We can talk later."

"You have something specific you want to talk to me about?"

Ignoring her, he slowed down and made a sharp right into the park. "Now where?"

Zoe closed her eyes. "Go left. All the way around to the back-side of the park. Where it meets the college property. There's a stone wall there."

"I know the place."

When they reached the stone wall, JJ pulled up on the grass and parked. Zoe climbed out, dreading what she knew was coming. With reluctance, she began to walk along the wall, her eyes barely noting how the ivy draped or the way birds sprung up from the grass, disturbed that she was interrupting their dinner.

She stopped midway along the length of the wall and walked over to it. She placed her hands on top of the wall. Then she pushed up and scrambled over it.

"Where are you. . ."

Zoe tossed a hand up in the air, silencing him as she closed her eyes again. She waited a few seconds and then opened her eyes and began to move again. A few feet to the left. *Stop.* Close her eyes. Another few feet. *Stop again.* Another few feet.

She turned and looked at JJ who had climbed over the wall and was following her quietly. "She's here."

JJ nodded and pulled the radio off his belt. "This is two-four-seven. Code Two. I have a 10-55. Going to need CSI and backup at. . ."

Zoe tuned him out, kneeling down and running her hands over the rough ivy ground cover. A few minutes of digging and she uncovered the hand of a little girl. Bowing her head, she let the tears flow for a little girl who would never cry again.

Karen stumbled blindly into the house, dropping her keys on the small cherry table near the door. Her nose picked up the scent of savory beef and something else a little subtler. Bread?

"Ray?"

"In the kitchen."

She walked into the room and stopped short in the doorway. Counters gleamed, the floor sparkled. A pot on the stove bubbled softly, filling the room with aromas that made her think of her mother. But what surprised her even more was the sight of her brother sprawled in a kitchen chair. His stocking feet were propped up on the table and crossed at the ankle. He wore a kitchen apron around his waist, and his fingers were busily snapping beans. He grinned up at her as he tossed bean ends into the trash can.

"Ray?"

"What?"

"You cooked?"

"Sure. You have enough on your mind. It's the least I could do to help out."

"You cooked," she repeated softly as she pulled out a chair and dropped into it, slipping out of her shoes.

"Don't look so shocked. I know how to cook." He pitched a snip of green bean at her.

She ducked, smiling. "Obviously. I just. . . Thanks, Ray. I really appreciate it. It smells divine." And it was turning her stomach in knots. No, her stomach was already in knots and had been for days. The smell of food was just making it worse.

"How did it go?"

The smile fled quickly as she sighed heavily, every trace of delight that someone had done something for her vanishing like the steam rising from the stew. "The police are convinced I killed him, but they don't have enough evidence to arrest me. *Yet*. My attorney thinks Ted took the money and ran to avoid the police, which would imply that he knew what happened to Jess, and I can't believe that."

"Wouldn't surprise me," Ray muttered darkly. "Now you understand why I couldn't let Ted control your trust fund."

"Don't, Ray." Her stomach twisted tighter. "We don't know

what happened. Maybe Jessica's kidnappers *did* call Friday and he took them the money."

Ray swung his feet off the table, his feet hitting the floor with a thud as he stood up. He snatched the bowl of green beans. "Right."

She watched him cross over to the sink, frustration shimmering around him. "Ted is a good husband, Ray. Why can't you see that?"

He spun around, his face tight. "Good husband? Are you nuts? The man talked to you like you were a dog! He spoke and you jumped. He put you down, he ridiculed you, he ignored you. You call that a good husband?"

The knot in her stomach jumped from uncomfortable to painful. "I have a good life, Ray. Can't you see that? He gives me a nice home; he takes good care of me."

"And there were men who took good care of their slaves, so what's your point?"

Karen twisted her hands in her lap. Why did everything always have to end in a fight? Why couldn't the men in her life get along with each other? "Ray, you don't know him. You never gave him a chance."

"That's where you're wrong, my dear sister. I did know him and give him a chance. Before you married him. He and I had a nice long chat, and I got his number real quick." Ray turned his back to her, rinsing the beans with quick, jerking movements.

"He's my husband, Ray."

Ray turned around slowly, the fierce expression on his face in direct contrast with the frilly apron around his waist and the dishtowel he tossed over his shoulder. "And where is your beloved husband, Karen? Where is he?"

JJ moved closer, the radio in his hand. "You gonna pass out now?"

"I don't think so," she replied with a sniffle.

Reaching into his pocket, JJ pulled out a handkerchief and handed it to her. "It should be clean."

"Thanks." She sniffed back another rush of tears. "You never fail to surprise me."

"Oh, I bet I could," he whispered cryptically.

She stared hard at him, trying to get some feel for his mood. It eluded her as deftly as peace of mind always had. "You going to tell me what's on your mind?"

"I have a lot on my mind, Miss Shefford, not the least of which is finding the sicko who is hurting these little girls. And when I get my hands on him, he's going to wish his mother had been sterile."

The harshness in his tone slapped at her. She'd never seen him speak so emotionally. React so harshly. "What happened, JJ? Is another girl missing?"

"No," he said abruptly. "I'm sure you'd tell me if one was."

His terse answer confused her. He was making no sense at all. "I've never seen you act like this."

"You don't know me."

"True." Zoe climbed to her feet and handed JJ his handkerchief. Enough was enough. If the man wanted to be a jerk again, let him. *Heaven knows he's had enough practice at it.*

❖   ❖   ❖

When backup arrived, JJ walked Zoe over to his Cherokee and gave her the keys. "Stay here. As soon as we get some extra help out here, I'll have someone drive you home."

Zoe nodded.

Turning, JJ tried to push the image of her big green eyes, full of tears, out of his mind. He had a job to do, and this was no time to be getting tangled up with a woman who mourned a child she didn't even know. And who didn't run at death threats. *Or perhaps didn't have any reason to take them seriously.*

The cop in him knew that Keyes Shefford wasn't a suspect. But the man in him dearly wanted Keyes to be guilty so that he could justify all that Zoe had seen and done. It couldn't be supernatural. He longed for an explanation that suited him.

The simple fact was that Zoe Shefford was getting to him and he didn't like it. Worse, he resented it. He didn't need someone to complicate his already complicated life. JJ walked over to a patrolman stretching the bright orange crime scene tape. "Do me a favor. Drive Miss Shefford home, will you? And then get back here fast."

◆　◆　◆

Karen clasped her hands in her lap. She hated fighting with Ray. They hadn't fought often as children. Ray had taken on the role of protector.

Big brother Ray hadn't liked it when Ted took away his baby sister. Ted knew it. "I don't blame him, sweetheart," he'd said. "He's been looking out for you for a long time, but it's my turn now. Don't worry about Ray. I'm not taking his attitude personally. I'd probably be the same way if I had a little sister as sweet as you."

She hadn't taken Ray's objections seriously, figuring Ted was right and her brother would come around eventually. But he hadn't. If anything, things only grew worse after Ray was designated executor of their grandparents' estate and Ray refused to hand over her inheritance. Ted was furious, and the relationship between Ted and Ray had nosedived, fueled by Walter's outrage that he'd been overlooked in his own mother's will. When faced with both his father and his sister's husband anxious to do battle, Ray had retreated to his home in Richmond. Karen had lost all hope that the two would ever become friends.

"I'm sorry, Sis."

Karen looked up at her brother, staring at him for a moment. The bleak look in his eyes made her heart twist.

"No need, Ray. I just can't seem to think straight right now."

Ray pushed off from the counter and pulled out a chair across the table from her. He spun it backwards on one leg and straddled it. "No small wonder. I think you're entitled."

"I just don't understand any of this, Ray. Did Ted take the money to the kidnappers? Or was he really lying to me? And where is he? What if he's really dead like the police say?" Her head began to throb. "I just can't accept that he's dead. Maybe I just don't want to." She choked out a laugh full of bitter self-condemnation. "Good old Karen. Never could accept reality."

"You accept reality just fine. Don't listen to Dad. You saw what it did to Mom." He folded his arms over the back of the chair and set his chin on his arms. "As for Ted, there's no telling what he was up to. And that makes it difficult for me, because you know I never trusted him. If I say he lied to you, you'll get defensive again."

It wasn't hard to tell they were related. Both had inherited their mother's dark brown hair that leaned toward auburn and the brown eyes that could seem anywhere from burnished gold to pale green depending on the color of their clothing. While Karen had the same petite figure as her mother and Ray was much taller and broader, they had the same long face, straight eyebrows, and full lips.

And both could be as stubborn as their father when it suited them.

But Karen wasn't feeling the least bit stubborn on this particular evening. She was feeling lost and confused, and if Ray could make any sense at all out of the situation, she was willing to listen.

"How about if I promise not to disagree with anything you say?"

Ray's smile was more of a crooked grin, but it was enough to make her heart feel lighter than it had all day. "Okay, but the minute

I see that pout, I'm running for the guest room."

Karen rolled her eyes. "Deal."

Suddenly, as if a switch were flipped, Ray turned very serious. "My take is this: Ted has his own agenda, and after clearing out the bank accounts, he told you he had to go meet the kidnappers. He made you promise not to call the police so that he would have more time to get far away."

"Okay. Let's say you're right. If he wanted to leave me, why not just say so and leave? Why pretend to be going to meet the kidnappers? He had me sufficiently cowed that he could walk out with minimum fuss."

Ray stared at her. "Don't ever let anyone tell you that you aren't one very smart broad."

Karen laughed, feeling the compliment down to her toes. "But why would he be avoiding the police? Unless he had something to do with Jessica's disappearance. See, that's where I have a problem. He couldn't have planned all this."

"Okay," Ray continued. "If he didn't plan all this, how did that knife get in your dishwasher? And how did his blood get on your blouse? And how did it get in the laundry room? And why is his car in the river?"

Pursing her lips, Karen's fingers played with the fringe on the pillow she'd been hugging. "That I can't explain. And it's driving me crazy."

"So do we agree that Ted had to have planned all this?"

"I don't know. What if. . .I don't know, let me ramble here. Let's say that maybe Ted has been gambling or something—something he wouldn't tell me about—and the people were getting antsy for their money and pressuring him, so he cleaned out the bank and went to pay them, and they killed him and then planted evidence here to throw the police off."

Now Ray was pursing his lips as his fingers tapped out a beat on the arm of the chair. "Maybe. But why risk coming back here and running into you?"

"They knew I wouldn't be here."

"How?"

"I don't know." Karen felt the cold fingers of fear and uncertainty crawling up her spine. "I don't *know*. I don't know where my baby is. I don't know what happened to Ted. I don't know why God is doing this to me."

Ray lifted his head. "God isn't doing this to you, Sis. Why would you think He is?"

"Then why is this happening?"

"Because of free will."

"What do you mean?"

"Free will, Karen. The only way God could have stopped all this was to prevent Ted from having a free will. He wouldn't do that." Ray seemed to shift gears. "So Ted tells you he's going to meet the kidnappers, stages his own death, frames you for murder, and vanishes with all your money."

Karen opened her mouth to object, but Ray threw up a hand. "Regardless of what he did or did not do, just follow me here."

"Okay."

"So Ted had a free will to make his own choices and he did. And he didn't care how those choices would affect you. But God does care. He's with you in this. He'll see you through this and bring you out on the other side."

"Can I ask a question?"

"Sure."

"The police brought a psychic here to help. My neighbor Rene wouldn't let them use her. She said that it's against God's Word."

"Hmm." Ray closed his eyes as if to collect his thoughts. "I believe she's right," Ray replied.

"So did God bring her here or the devil?"

"If the enemy can get you to participate in something that God has forbidden, he can effectively cut God out of the situation."

"Then did God bring Rene here?"

"I believe He did. God knew you didn't know His Word well enough, so He brought in someone who did to help protect you."

Karen leaned back in her chair. "I didn't realize God worked that closely in our everyday lives."

"All the time, little sister. All the time."

"Ray, what will I do if Ted really is dead?" She lifted her tear-filled eyes to his. "Do you understand what I'm feeling?"

"Not entirely. But I'm sure it's not easy to have your life ripped apart at the seams. But don't believe the lie that you're weak. You're not. Not by a long shot. Somewhere deep inside you is the strength to face all this. To grieve if you have to grieve and to let go of what you only *thought* was real."

"I want my daughter back safe and sound, Ray."

He reached over and took her hand. "I know you do. I'm praying for that to happen. But in the meantime, you're going to have to face this. You'll hit emotional bottom and that's where you'll find Karen waiting for you."

"I *am* Karen," she said with a trace of exasperation.

Ray shook his head. "No. You're the shadow of who Karen used to be. You're the creature that Ted and Dad have molded you into. They've pounded you down until you don't know who you are anymore. You don't know your strengths. You don't know your capabilities. And you don't know how to be anything but miserable."

Zoe looked through the peephole in the door and then unlocked it. She tilted her head and stared at JJ. "What happened?"

"Got any coffee?"

Zoe stepped back and let him in. "Sure."

In the kitchen, she poured him coffee, not bothering to announce that it was left from breakfast. He didn't seem to notice as he leaned against the counter and drank it.

"What happened?" Zoe repeated.

He sighed and set the cup down. "Emily wasn't alone."

"Another little girl?"

"Yeah." Pushing off from the counter, he walked into the living room. "She was buried right next to Emily. You were right; he's been at this awhile."

"I'm sorry."

JJ shook his head as he moved around the room, his fingers trailing over shelves, books, pictures. "Tell me about your father."

Zoe looked up at him, confused by his quick change of topic. "My father? What about my father?"

"I'm just curious." JJ shoved his hands in his pockets.

It made her suspicious. She gave him a long, considering look. "What's going on, Detective? Why this sudden interest in my family?"

"Just your dad. Are you and he close?"

"Not particularly," she replied dryly.

"So you don't share little secrets together?"

"No."

"He owns a lot of real estate, doesn't he?" He picked up a glass butterfly, examined it, set it back down.

"I suppose he does. I think he has four offices."

"Within what? Two hundred miles of here?"

"I guess. What are you doing, Detective?"

"Just asking. Curious. That's all."

"And. . .what is it you always say—pigs fly with pink wings?"

JJ smiled and shrugged. "Do I say that a lot?"

"Well, you tend to change the color from time to time, but

yeah, you say that a lot."

"Where's your father, Zoe?" He stared at her.

She returned the stare, ice for ice. "He took my mother out of town to protect her."

"Where?"

"Why do you want to know?"

His eyes narrowed a little. "How did you know where Emily was?"

"I just knew."

"Uh-huh, you just knew. No one clued you in?"

"No."

"Maybe gave you a quick call and told you where to find her?"

With cool deliberation, she stood to her feet. "Why don't you just come out and ask me straight, JJ? You want to know if I know the killer?"

The look in his eyes all but took her breath away. She saw more than questions without answers. She saw pain curling there, whipping him forward. The glare intensified. "Do you?"

"No." Regardless of why JJ was acting like this, she'd had enough. "And now I think you'd better go."

"Does this bother you?"

"Yes, it does. You play nice, make me think you trust me, respect me for who and what I am, and then come in here and accuse me of collaborating with a child killer?" She pointed at the door. "Get out—now!"

JJ swung the front door open and then looked back over his shoulder at her. "By any chance, do you know where your father was when Amy disappeared?"

Zoe felt the words slam into her, stealing her breath even as her mind fought what she knew he was implying. She reached out and picked up the nearest thing she could find—a book—and threw it at him. He ducked and slammed the door closed.

chapter 21

Monday, April 24

Collapsing to the floor, she folded like an accordion, emitting a sound closer to mourning than music. The pain, buried for so many years, rose like a specter from a cemetery of memories. It mocked her for thinking she had vanquished it.

"By any chance, do you know where your father was when Amy disappeared?"

JJ's words echoed across mists of time and distance. She was, once again, a child in pain, listening to the police explain that a killer had taken two other little girls, both from single-parent homes. *"We figure he's looking for unprotected targets."*

Understanding had come to her, quick and crystal clear. She'd flung herself at her father then, fists flailing, tears streaming. *"Where were you when that bad man took Amy? Where were you, Daddy? You should have been here!"*

The police officer had gently pulled her back, holding her clenched fists. Her mother had held her close, offering reassurance that it wasn't her daddy's fault. But she knew better. She looked into her father's eyes and saw the guilt lodged there. She saw it in the way his shoulders hunched forward in defeat. He was guilty. He had failed as a father. And now Amy was dead.

From that day forward, she'd shunned her father, refusing his attention, putting up a wall of silence, and denying him access to her heart. She was determined to punish him. As an adult, she could reason that it had been a tragic incident. That her father wasn't truly at fault. But her heart still hadn't let go of the judgment lodged there as a child.

But this was a new feeling. Did the police actually believe that her father was capable of. . .

It was unthinkable. Despicable. JJ was grasping at straws, looking for something, anything, that would discredit her. He'd blamed the Matthews for their own child's disappearance, and now it seemed he was blaming her father for the other missing children.

Zoe Shefford knows where the children are; therefore, she must be getting the information from the killer. Her own sister was taken; therefore, Zoe's father must be the one who killed her.

Zoe wondered if JJ could actually be capable of that kind of reasoning.

Zoe sat up, brushing away tears with the heel of her hand. Poor Mrs. Matthews. Her child had been kidnapped, and before she even had time to deal with her grief, Josiah Johnson began pointing his finger at her.

And now he was aiming his missiles of guilt at her father.

Or was he? Zoe grabbed the doorknob and pulled herself up to her feet. Something just hadn't felt right—his accusations didn't ring true. It was as if he was trying to convince himself.

Of what? That she wasn't a psychic? That she wasn't worth his attention? Or was it his affection he was worried about?

◆ ◆ ◆

Paula Horne hesitated before climbing out of her car and locking it behind her. It had been nearly a week since she'd heard from Matt.

Squaring her shoulders, she marched up the steps and through the police station door. Barely acknowledging a greeting from Sergeant Colmes at the front desk, she jogged up the metal stairs to the second floor. She wove through the desks in the bullpen like a copperhead on the hunt.

She spotted Matt before he saw her. He was bending over a dispatcher's desk, laughing at something the woman was saying. *Keep laughing, Matt Casto.*

He caught a glimpse of her and straightened, his lips going tight with disapproval. *Tough.*

"I need to talk to you. Now." Without waiting to see if he followed, she went into one of the empty offices and turned on the lights. She heard the door close behind her and whirled around.

"Care to tell me what's on your mind?" Matt leaned against the closed door, his arms folded across his chest, belligerence oozing from every pore.

"I haven't heard from you for awhile. Thought I'd find out why before I said what I came here to say."

"Didn't think you'd notice."

"Really? And what would give you that idea?"

Matt shrugged evasively. "I'm sure you've been busy."

"Actually, I haven't, but that's not the point. You're not going to tell me what's on your mind, so I'll tell you what's on mine. I've had enough, Matt. I love you. I've always loved you, but I can't play second fiddle to your flirting anymore. I've had enough. It's over. I'm out of here."

She started to move past him. He reached out and grabbed her arm. "Off to your new boyfriend?"

"I don't have a new boyfriend. Unlike you, I don't feel the need to be validated by every man I meet. I've never gone out on you, Matt. Never."

"I *saw* you. On Tuesday. You and some GQ in loafers."

It took a minute before Paula could figure out what Matt was talking about, but finally the fog cleared. She almost laughed. "That was a coworker. It was the first and only time I'd ever had lunch with him, and he asked me as we were leaving the building. Had you bothered to walk over and join us, rather than sulking from wherever you were spying, you would have known that and we could have had lunch together."

She pushed him aside and stormed out of the office, feeling the hot sting of tears behind her lids. She wasn't about to let him see her cry. That could come later. She'd go home, curl up on her bed, and cry her eyes out, but not yet. Not here. Not now.

Janice Alberry looked stunned as she walked in and found Zoe waiting for her. Zoe stood up, smoothing her skirt. "I probably should have called first, but I thought you might like an exclusive interview."

"Uh. . .yeah. . .I'd love to talk to you." She took a deep breath. "Come on back. We can talk in one of the conference rooms."

Zoe followed Janice out of the reception area, weaving down one hall after another before entering a small conference room. She hoped she didn't have to storm out in a huff, because she was positive she'd never find her way out of the building.

"Please, have a seat. I just need to get a notepad and my tape recorder." Janice stopped at the door. "I can tape-record this, can't I?"

"Sure," Zoe waved a hand airily.

While the reporter was gone, Zoe started to have second thoughts. Standing up to a killer's threats was one thing. Deliberately taunting him was a much more serious matter. She had no choice.

He had to be stopped. The thought that he had been so close to her mother was enough to send chills down her spine.

The door opened. In a rush of breathy apologies for taking so long, Janice set up the recorder and started the interview.

"I'm so glad you came in. I thought about calling you. But I'm no star in the news business. I figured you wouldn't want to talk to me."

"That's precisely why I chose you."

"Oh. Well. That's great. My anonymity finally works to my advantage." With a nervous laugh, she picked up her pencil. "Okay, let me ask you a few questions."

Zoe reached out her hand and covered Janice's. "Let me tell you what I want you to say."

"But," Janice's eyes went wide, "I'm not supposed to do that. I mean, I'm supposed to direct this. . ."

Zoe's smile was polite but firm. "I'm going to give you the article. I guarantee it will be picked up by papers all over the country."

Janice didn't look convinced, but she slowly nodded. "Well, okay."

"Good. The killer has taken and murdered dozens of little girls over the past twenty years. . ."

"Dozens?!" Janice squealed with shock.

"Yes. Now write. He's a coward who picks on children because they can't fight back. He's afraid of the police and afraid of adults. He preys on helpless things like children, puppies, and kittens. He doesn't have the nerve to face—"

"You're taunting him." Janice stopped jotting notes, her face reflecting the horror of the sudden realization. "You're trying to make him come after you."

"Honey, he's already after me. I just want him to come after me *now*."

JJ looked at the list of suspects and frowned. At the top of the list was Keyes Shefford, age fifty-seven, owner of Keyes Realty. *Whereabouts currently unknown.* Not so much as a parking ticket to pin on him. Keyes Shefford was a squeaky-clean, upstanding citizen.

He drew a line through Keyes's name. This was no time to let personal feelings get in the way of an investigation. He'd tried to hurt Zoe. He'd wanted to put some distance between them. He'd accomplished that in spades. She'd never speak to him again, of that he was sure.

Then they had Frank Harrow. Age forty-eight. Married with two children. Landscaper with unlimited access to Keyes's properties. One arrest for being drunk and disorderly when he was nineteen, a couple of parking tickets, and that was it. He had opportunity. He *could* fit the profile. And he lived only two blocks from an elementary school.

Zoe. Pushing thoughts of her aside, he kept going down the list.

Robert Maysonet. Keyes Shefford's right-hand man. Age fifty-two, single, never married, a loner. Has access to properties. Lives a mile from an elementary school. Wayne's interview notes indicated that Maysonet was arrogant and disdainful of the police. A profiler would flag that.

Was one of these men the killer, or were they chasing shadows? If he really had to narrow in on someone, he'd go with Maysonet or Harrow.

In the meantime, Alice Denton, aka Nancy Darrington, was on the run again. By the time the police had closed in, she was gone. Ted Matthews's body was still missing, and Tripp said they were having trouble tying his disappearance to Karen Matthews.

It made JJ long for the days when he worked Homicide. He'd have pressed charges and locked her up before she had time to lawyer-up. Too late now. And it wasn't his case. His worry was the child, not the husband. He had increasingly less hope that the child would be found alive.

If Zoe was surprised to find Rene sitting on the park bench in her front yard when she got home, she didn't show it. "Come on in."

Rene waited until Zoe offered her a seat before she said, "I had to try again."

"I figured you would." Zoe sank down in a chair and stretched out her legs. "I'm sorry, Rene. I wish I could explain it to you, but I can't. Not yet. Let's just say that I need my gift one more time before I give it up."

"If you don't give it up now when you know the truth, what makes you think you'll be able to give it up later?"

Zoe flipped back her hair, more to buy time than because it was annoying her. She didn't want to be having this conversation. "I can't explain what's going on, Rene. I wish I could."

"You don't have to." Rene leaned forward. "You're convinced that you need to be a psychic a little while longer, probably to do one last act of good, and then you'll be able to set it aside forever. It doesn't work that way."

The woman's words hit too close for comfort, and Zoe oddly felt like squirming. Instead, she stared at Rene and concentrated on keeping her hands steady. "I won't deny what you're saying is truth, but you don't have all the facts. You don't understand what's at risk here."

"I don't have to, Zoe. I understand the battle that's going on for your soul, and that's all that's important to me. Everything else is illusion, meant to deceive you and draw you away from the truth."

"And what truth is that, Rene? That God finds me detestable?"

"Not you, child. Not at all."

Zoe sighed and closed her eyes. She wasn't sure she had the strength to go through with this. Her plan was starting to look foolhardy and downright stupid and incredibly dangerous. "I know, Rene. It's the psychic bit, not me. He loves me. He died for me. I understand all that. You explained it all very well. I just. . ."

"What are you going to do, child? Take him on alone? Draw him out and defeat him? Do you honestly think you can?"

Zoe's eyes flew open and she sat up straight. "I have to try, Rene. Do you understand? He went into my mother's shop and taunted her. He was letting me know that no one I care about is safe from him."

Rene shook her head. There was obvious compassion in her eyes. "I'm sorry. That's despicable."

"The killer is targeting me. He wants me. I can get to him. I'm the only one who can."

"No," Rene replied. "You're the last one who should even try." She stood and gathered her purse and keys. "I can see that I can't talk you out of anything right now. I'll let you think about some of what I've said. In the meantime, Karen's brother is in town. We had a nice long talk this morning. He and Karen are coming over tonight for prayer and fellowship. I'd like you to come. I'd like you to see what we're talking about."

"I'll think about it," Zoe replied, slowly standing to her feet. "I can't promise any more than that."

"It's enough."

As Zoe escorted Rene to the front door, another thought occurred to her. "Rene? Does God—I don't know how to explain this—but does He like, chase you down? Leave messages for you everywhere? Things like that?"

Rene laughed and squeezed Zoe's hand. "Oh, my, yes. And He won't stop until you start paying attention."

Frank Harrow was close to tears as his eyes shifted from Matt to Wayne and back again. "I wouldn't hurt a child. You can't think I would. I just mow lawns and trim shrubs."

"And you had a whole bag of candy in the front seat of your truck."

"I have it there for the children. I give them treats, you know, when I go to a house that has children. I love children. I wouldn't hurt them." His eyes begged for someone to believe him. His hunched shoulders marked his fear. This was not a man who thought he was smarter than the police.

Matt tapped his pencil on the table, his instincts screaming to apologize to the man for hauling him in for questioning. A few more minutes of this and he might give in to those instincts. "What can you tell us about Keyes Shefford?"

The landscaper looked confused at the change in questioning and tilted his head. "Mr. Shefford? He's a nice man. Sad man. Has had some rough times in his life. Loves his wife and daughter. Would do anything for them."

"Anything? Maybe kill for them?"

"Well, I wouldn't say that. Maybe to protect them or something. He's not a violent man. Can't rightly say he's even got much of a temper. He's good to people. Once, a single woman with three kids rented one of his properties. Now usually when someone rents a house, I don't take care of it unless they hire me on their own. But this time he told me to keep on caring for the place 'cause he knew she couldn't afford to hire me on. That's the kind of man he is."

This was going nowhere. Matt wanted to spit with frustration. "What about Robert Maysonet?"

Frank almost curled his lip in distaste, and it was comical

enough to make Matt smile.

"Mr. Maysonet, huh? Don't know that I have anything good to say about the man."

"Why not?"

Frank leaned back in his chair, warming to the discussion. "He's one of them stuck-up types. Thinks he's too good for common folk, you know. Looks down his nose at just about everybody, including Mr. Shefford sometimes. Saw him nearly smack a little boy once for accidentally hitting him with a ball when he was showing a house to some couple. Got real nasty with the kid 'cause it left a streak of dirt on those fancy clothes he wears."

"So he doesn't like kids?"

Frank shook his head. "Calls 'em rug rats or animals." He wrinkled his nose. "And what was it he said once? Oh, yes, he said kids are 'worthless vile creatures that prove abortion is a good thing.'"

Matt felt his blood run cold. "Oh, *did* he now?"

chapter 22

Monday, April 24

Nancy Darrington stared helplessly as the police came through the door with guns drawn. She didn't move a muscle, afraid they might shoot and hit the child in her arms.

"Nice and easy now, Mrs. Darrington. I'm going to ask you to hand over the child to my partner and then slowly raise your hands and put them behind your head."

"I didn't do anything wrong," she whispered huskily, trying to speak through her dry throat and fear.

"Well, time will prove you right or wrong. In the meantime, there's a detective who would like to talk to you."

One of the officers lifted the child from her arms and backed away. She slowly lifted her hands and turned around. Immediately she felt the small pinch of a handcuff as it circled her wrist and slapped shut. Then her arm was yanked down and around to the small of her back.

It was over. No more running. No more safety. It was over. They would take the child away. She'd go to jail for kidnapping and she'd never be free again.

Tears streamed down her cheeks as the officer snapped the handcuff around her other wrist and turned her around. She hadn't been able to save the child after all. And she hadn't been able to save herself.

"I don't know about this, Ray." Karen pulled the front door closed and followed her brother down the front steps and across the lawn. The night air hinted at a warm summer, and she barely needed the sweater she was wearing and clutching closed.

"It'll be fine. I like Rene. And we need to get together and pray about Jessica. And for you."

"But Ted doesn't like me to be around Rene."

"Ted isn't here, and he doesn't run your life. He probably doesn't like Rene because he knows she sees right through him and he didn't want her cluing you in."

"He said she would be a bad influence on me." She jogged up Rene's front steps behind Ray.

"In his mind she would be."

Rene opened the front door at Ray's knock. Ray smiled. "Hey, Rene."

She stepped back and held the door wide. "Come on in. I think just about everyone is here."

Karen expected to see a small group. She was wrong. At least fifteen people were milling around the living room. Rene introduced everyone. Karen didn't bother trying to remember names. As they were about to get started, the doorbell rang.

"Excuse me a minute." Rene went to answer the door and returned a few minutes later with the last person Karen ever expected to see at a prayer meeting.

"Excuse me," Rene said loud enough to get everyone's attention. "This is Zoe Shefford."

Karen leaned into Ray and whispered, "That's the psychic

I was telling you about."

"Really?" Ray stepped forward and offered his hand to Zoe. "Hi. I'm Ray Timms. It's nice of you to join us."

◆　　◆　　◆

JJ was fuming. No, he was more than fuming; he was ready to explode into a fireball of white-hot rage. "The woman went too far this time! She practically begged the killer to take her on! Has she lost her ever-loving mind?"

"Not if the killer is her father," Matt reminded him from his chair across the room.

JJ glared at him. "Keyes Shefford was never a viable suspect and you know it. Do you think this is just a ploy to make me look at someone besides her father?"

Matt shook his head. "No. I think it's exactly what you said it is: a deliberate and calculated attempt to get the killer to come after her.

"And I talked to him, by the way. Keyes Shefford. He and Mrs. Shefford are at his summer house up on Lake Erie. I have to get to know this man. His house is in Marblehead. Best walleye and perch fishing in the country. And there's a lighthouse there that's over a hundred years old, and—"

"Matt. Shut up."

Matt raised his eyebrows a notch. "Touchy."

"Zoe Shefford is deliberately taunting a cold-blooded killer, and you want to talk about fishing?"

"Well, no. I was just trying to tell you that he called to let me know where he was and would happily answer any questions I might have. He said he went there because the killer came into Mrs. Shefford's store, and he and Zoe thought it best to get her out of town. For her own safety."

JJ felt his temper rise another notch. "The killer was in Mrs. Shefford's store and no one told us? Did anyone stop to think that she could give us a *description of the man?*"

Matt flinched.

People out in the bullpen stopped, turned, and looked, but JJ didn't care. He couldn't believe this had slipped through the cracks. "Call him back. Talk to Mrs. Shefford. Find out what the man looks like!"

"JJ?" Matt spoke in a soft, even voice. "It's done. As soon as he told me she could ID our man, I arranged for her to meet with the state police up there and work with a sketch artist. It's being done even as we speak."

Standing up, Matt looked down at JJ with disappointment in his eyes. "I'm not stupid. I know my job. I thought you always believed I was good at it." He turned and walked away.

JJ slumped behind his desk and ran his fingers through his hair. He was losing it. Yelling at Matt like that. And Matt was right. He'd never questioned Matt's ability before. He was jumping out of his skin and it was unacceptable.

He stared at the newspaper again. Taunting the killer. Was she out of her mind?

He picked up the phone and called her. There was no answer. Grabbing his jacket, he ran out of the building.

chapter 23

Monday, April 24

Zoe sat on the edge of the sofa, bent over, with her forehead resting on her knees.

Sobbing.

She couldn't help it and couldn't have explained why in a million years.

At first, when everyone started praying for the police to find Jessica and Ted and for the families of the little girls to have peace in His arms and for Karen to have faith, she merely sat there, eyes closed, and listened to them pray, one after another. But then Ray started praying for her, and suddenly she felt like everything raw in her had been touched.

Caressed.

It felt wonderful. Warm and loving. And it brought tears to her eyes that quickly turned to uncontrollable sobs. She couldn't stop. Someone came over and put an arm around her. She didn't even look up to see whom. She didn't care.

Oh, God. This is You, isn't it?

"*Trust Me.*"

I want to. Oh, how I want to. But someone has to stop him.

"Trust Me."

Why do you keep saying that?

"Because you trust no one. Trust Me."

Gerry Otis stared at the fax in his hand as he talked on the phone with the police officer in Altamonte Springs. "Say that one more time?"

"We have the woman in custody."

"No. The other part." Gerry closed his eyes and wished for a miracle.

"And we have the little boy."

So much for a miracle. "That's what I thought you said. Are you sure it's a boy? We're looking for a little girl. Jessica Matthews."

"No. This is definitely a little boy. I changed his diaper myself a few minutes ago in the lounge."

Gerry sat down, his mind spinning. "Could you put the woman on the phone? I think we may be able to clear this up in less than five minutes."

"Hold on."

Gerry waved Matt over while he waited. He put his hand over the mouthpiece of the phone. "I think the Darrington woman is a dead end."

"Why?" Matt pulled up a chair and sat down.

"They have the woman in custody. There is a child with her, but it's a boy."

Just then, a woman's voice came on the other end of the phone. She sounded defeated.

"Mrs. Darrington? This is Detective Gerry Otis. The child you have with you. Can you tell me whose child that is?"

"Mine. My son. John, Junior."

"When you were living here and helping Mrs. Matthews, where was your child?"

He heard her sniff. "With friends. Friends I had in college that my husband didn't know about. They kept him while I got some money together."

Gerry leaned back and nodded at Matt, indicating that his suspicions had been true. She hadn't kidnapped Jessica Matthews.

"Mrs. Darrington, would you like me to keep your whereabouts a secret from your husband?"

Suddenly hope seemed to alight in her voice. "Would you? Could you do that for me, please?"

"I can and will. As far as he is concerned, we never found you. I just have one more question for you. Do you have any idea who might have taken Jessica Matthews?"

There was silence for a long moment, and it started to make Gerry a little nervous, but then she spoke up. "No. I can't say that I do. Karen loved that child. She must be going out of her mind."

"What about Ted Matthews? Did he seem the loving father to you?"

"I can't say that he did. He was aloof. Indifferent. I wasn't around him all that much. He usually didn't get home from work until after I left for the day, so it could be that I was just catching him on bad days or something."

"Is there anything you can tell me about Ted Matthews that might help us?"

Again there was a moment of silence. "I don't know if it would help you find Jessica, but I do know that Ted Matthews was having an affair with a woman from his work."

Gerry grabbed a notepad and wrote quickly. Matt read as Gerry wrote; then his eyebrows shot up. He grabbed the pencil from Gerry and wrote, "Any idea who the woman was?"

"Mrs. Darrington. Do you have any idea who the woman was? Her name? Anything?"

"I saw them just that once at the mall at lunch. It was my day off, and Mr. Matthews didn't see me. He was buying her perfume and he called her Mary Anne. Or Marion. Something like that. That's all I know."

Gerry jotted down the information. "Thanks. You've been a big help. I'm really sorry about the mix-up. If you can put the detective back on the phone, I'll see about having you released to go on your way."

Gerry spoke to the detective and then got off the phone. "Whattya think?" he asked Matt.

"Maryanne Bubeck. The woman who disappeared just before Ted Matthews did. Coincidence?"

"Want me to check her out?"

Matt stood up. "Yeah. Her address is in the file. See if you can find out where she is."

◆   ◆   ◆

JJ sat in Zoe's driveway, drumming his fingers on the steering wheel. The house was dark except for the light on the front porch, and Zoe's car was gone. He hoped she hadn't gone to meet the killer.

Suddenly old memories washed over him. And they weren't warm and fuzzy.

"The psychic says no one is stalking me, Josiah. I've been imagining it, you see. I have nothing to fear." Macy smiled up at him, her eyes shining like blue diamonds in the candlelight.

"Macy, I never believed anyone was stalking you. You have nothing to prove to me." He reached up and ran his fingers lightly

down her cheek. *Oh, how he loved this woman. His soul mate. No. His soul. She was the essence that brought him life.*

"You thought I was being foolish. Weak. A typical woman who faints at the sight of blood or something. Admit it."

"I did not."

Macy laughed, a high, tinkling laugh that always made him smile. "Yes, you did. I could see it in your eyes. I was simpering, cowering. Wasn't I?"

JJ shrugged. "Okay, maybe a little, but I didn't love you any less for it."

Macy crawled over the sofa cushion and into his lap, wrapping her arms around his neck. "My big, tough macho man. Going to be a cop and save the world."

"Come on, Macy."

"I love you, Josiah. Everything about you. Including the fact that you fear nothing."

"I fear losing you."

"I'll never leave you, Josiah. We'll get married as soon as you're out of the academy and we'll have lots of babies."

"Whoa. Not more than four, okay? Cops don't make tons of money."

Macy laughed again and laid her head on his shoulder. "Okay, no more than four babies that all look like you."

"Please, anything but that." JJ pulled her close. "The psychic was certain no one is stalking you?"

"That's what she said. She said it was just my imagination. That I had a secret admirer, but that he wasn't a danger to me or anything like that. Everything is fine."

"Well, if the psychic says everything is fine, then everything is fine."

But it hadn't been fine. Macy had disappeared less than forty-eight hours later, and it was three days before her body was found in the basement of a student who had been writing her anonymous love letters. His obsession had led to stalking Macy and then murdering her.

The psychic had been wrong.

Dead wrong.

JJ bent his head, his forehead resting on his hands on the steering wheel. Macy had been snatched out of his life because some voodoo psychic didn't know her crystal ball from her tarot card. She was a fake. A phony. A real con artist. And he had been a fool for believing her.

Oh, Macy. I wish you were here.

Zoe groaned when she pulled into her driveway and found JJ parked there, waiting for her. He was in quite a temper from the dark looks he was shooting her.

"What were you thinking? Have you lost what was left of your mind? Or did you just decide to commit suicide and figured this was a heroic way of going about it?"

Zoe brushed past him. "I have nothing to say to you."

"Well, I have plenty to say to you! That was the most asinine thing I've ever seen! Do you have any idea what that man wants to do to you?"

"Kill me," Zoe said quietly as she unlocked her front door, flipped on the lights, and walked in. JJ remained on her heels.

"And I suppose that's just fine with you?"

She tossed her purse and keys on the coffee table. "No, it's not."

"All right. I'm sorry I said what I did about your father. That was out of line. We know he isn't a suspect."

"Bully for you." She glared at him with a look sharp enough to cut gems. "Could you leave now?"

"And let you sit here to wait for the killer?"

Zoe slipped off her jacket and hung it in the coat closet. "He isn't ready to kill me yet, Detective, but when he is, not even you will be able to stop him."

JJ shoved his hands in his pockets. "You don't have much faith in me, do you?"

She brushed past him and walked into the kitchen. He had no choice but to follow her. He watched while she opened the refrigerator and pulled out the orange juice.

"Are you going to answer my question?"

Zoe poured herself a glass of juice without bothering to offer him any. "I didn't realize something so obvious needed to be stated."

"I *said* I'm sorry about your father, okay?"

"I heard you the first time. You're forgiven. Will there be anything else?"

"Why are you doing this, Zoe?"

"Because someone needs to, and I ended up with the job by default." She finished her juice and set the glass in the sink. "Now, if you'll excuse me, it's been a long night and I need to get some sleep."

"Do you honestly think you'll get one minute of sleep tonight?"

Blast him for seeing past her wall of indifference. "If you're going to sleep on the sofa, be my guest, but I'm going to bed. Don't forget to turn out the lights."

"I want a blanket this time!" he yelled as she started down the hall.

"Then take the guest room and leave me alone!"

Keyes stared out the window. The clouds, obscuring the moonlight, left the lake a dark, eerie black. Only the most turbulent of whitecaps could be seen. His boat, *The House Keyes*, rocked gently against the dock.

"What are you staring at?" Denise walked up behind him, slipping her arms around his waist and leaning into him.

"I'm worried about Zoe," he said in a rough voice. He rubbed his temple with his fingertips. His anxiety manifested as a dull throb. "I don't like leaving her at the mercy of a killer. I need to be there, Dee."

"I know."

He turned and pulled her close again. "I don't want you in danger. I won't lose you again."

"I'm not going anywhere, Keyes. I'll stay here. I'll be fine. Go. Protect our daughter."

He took a deep breath and rested his forehead against hers. "I love you both so much. These years have been hell. I don't deny I deserved them, but I can't tell you what it means to me that you've forgiven me and are taking me back."

"It just means you have to pay for another big wedding."

Keyes laughed as he leaned down to kiss her. His heart was so full it almost hurt. "I'll give you the biggest, grandest wedding you ever saw. Anything you want, Dee. Anything. And anywhere you want to go on a second honeymoon. Just name it."

"I never stopped loving you, Keyes. You know that, don't you?"

"You just couldn't trust me. I know."

"But I trust you now. Go take care of Zoe. She needs you more than I do right now."

Keyes held on to her for another minute and then, with great difficulty, backed out of the embrace. He'd waited twenty years to hold her again. Most of that time he had been sure he would never have the chance again. It had been hard to believe that somehow, some way. . .

"I'll call and charter a plane. It'll be faster and that way you can keep the car."

"Leave a credit card and I'll go back to that little market we passed today. The one with all those antiques that you wouldn't stop at."

Keyes laughed.

In the bedroom, Keyes repacked his clothes. While Denise was in the shower, he sat down and wrote her a quick note. He tucked a credit card in the envelope. Along with the simple words of love, he wrote, "And the Visa is a gold card. Go as crazy as you want."

chapter 24

Tuesday, April 25

K aren gave up trying to sleep when she heard Ray in the kitchen and smelled the coffee. Sliding off the bed, she grabbed a robe and joined him.

"Did you sleep?" he asked, cracking eggs into a bowl.

Karen shrugged. "I keep thinking about Ted."

"What about him?" Ray started whisking the eggs.

"I don't think he's dead."

Ray looked at her, studied her, then turned his attention back to the eggs. "What do you think is going on?"

"I think he ran."

Ray set the whisk down and turned around. He leaned back against the counter. "I'm listening."

"You know how last night at the prayer meeting Rene said something about trusting what God put inside me? You know, when she was praying."

"I remember."

"All night, thoughts kept going through my head, and instead of tossing them out the way I usually do, you know, discounting them as foolishness, I paid attention."

Ray nodded.

"You were right. Ted *did* try to make me feel stupid. So does Dad. And I'm *not* really stupid. I just felt like they were smarter and I should listen to them because they probably knew what was best for me. But it wasn't right for them to make me feel stupid."

"Hallelujah!" Ray threw both hands in the air and laughed out loud. "She got it, Lord! By Jove, she got it."

Karen stared at her hands, her lips quivering. "I'm a little slow—what can I tell you."

Ray grabbed a chair and flopped down on it. "No, listen to me. Between you and me, who always got the better grades in school?"

Karen thought a moment before answering. "I did."

He just stared at her, his eyes begging her to think it out and take it one step further. Finally, she smiled. "That makes me smarter than you."

Grinning, he jumped out of his chair and threw his arms around her. "You always were, Sis. You just let Dad and Ted convince you otherwise."

While it felt good to smile and laugh with Ray, she could feel her smile drifting away. "Ted ran because. . .I think he did something to Jessica."

That wiped the smile off Ray's face. He pulled away from her and dropped back down into his chair. "I have a bad feeling you're right. Maybe he was jealous of the attention you gave her."

"That's stupid."

"Yes, it is."

Tears trickled down her face. She didn't bother to wipe them away. "The police began to suspect him, so he had to run."

"I think so, Karen. I'm sorry."

Karen shook her head. "I've done enough grieving over the past couple of weeks. There's nothing left for Ted. But Jess. . ."

"Don't give up hope, Sis."

Karen continued as if she hadn't heard him. "I never thought him capable of. . .murder, you know? He could be mean and nasty, and he'd put me down and make me feel stupid and ugly, but I never thought in a million years he'd kill someone. And especially not. . ." She couldn't say it. *No God, please don't let it be true.* She closed her eyes to the image, her hands twisting in her lap.

"Jess could be alive. The police said someone was outside that window. He passed Jessica to someone."

Hope grew once again. "You think that person has Jess?"

Ray nodded. "Yeah, I do."

"I can hope for that."

He squeezed her hand. "You do that, Sis. You hold on to Jess. The police will find Ted, and they'll find out who he gave Jess to and they'll bring her home."

Karen felt more tears welling up and swallowed them. This wasn't the time to fall apart. She'd done enough of that, too. Now she had to be strong. She had to find Jess. She had to find out what her husband had done with their baby. And then she would make sure Ted went to jail for it.

Lord, help me to be strong. Help me to see that You're right here with me.

Matt spent most of the day trying to track down Maryanne Bubeck. He talked to her boss again. He talked to coworkers. No one could tell him anything. They went through her desk but found nothing personal. He called the family references on her employment form. The numbers were bogus.

After four, her landlady returned. She wasn't even aware that Maryanne Bubeck was missing and probably wouldn't have noticed until her rent was due. But the woman let Matt into the apartment. *Just in case something bad had happened.*

The apartment had been cleaned out. There wasn't even any dust in the corners. The landlady was livid that Maryanne Bubeck had moved without notice and huffed and puffed about how she'd better not be expecting any of her security deposit. Matt didn't think Miss Bubeck would bother to ask for it.

The landlady allowed him to see photocopies of Miss Bubeck's rent checks. He then went to the bank. Miss Bubeck had closed her account.

Another dead end.

Matt dragged himself back to the station to talk to JJ.

JJ took one look at him and narrowed his eyes. "What's wrong with you?"

"Dead ends on Bubeck. She's gone. Cleaned out her apartment and her checking account."

"That's not the reason for those dark circles under your eyes. Are you and Paula still fighting?"

Matt sank down in a chair. "You could say that. She broke up with me."

"You didn't tell me that part."

"I didn't think she meant it at the time, you know?"

"And she broke up with you because. . ."

"Because I didn't call her for a week and when she came here, I accused her of cheating on me with that GQ from her work."

"Let me guess: She explained it was innocent, and you didn't believe her."

Matt shuffled his feet. "Something like that."

"Figures."

Matt glared at JJ. "Look who's talking. You're head over heels for Zoe Shefford, and I don't see you asking her to the prom."

"I'm not head over heels. And this isn't about me; it's about you and the woman you love. Don't be an idiot. Call her. Beg her to take you back. Send her roses. Take her to Hawaii. Something. Anything. But don't lose her. She's the best thing that ever happened to you."

Matt folded his arms across his chest. "I am not begging anyone for anything."

"Go ahead; be an idiot. It's your own life you're messing up. Have you found out anything more on Ted Matthews?"

Matt shook his head, grateful to be off the subject of Paula. "Gerry is handling that. But we did talk to Nancy Darrington last night after you left. Did Gerry tell you?"

"He left me a note. She was with her son."

"Yeah. So that's a dead end, too."

"Where do we stand with Maysonet?"

Matt rolled his head, trying to work the stiffness out of his neck. "Wayne is talking to him today."

JJ drummed his fingers on his desk. Matt stood up. "I'm going to go get some food. Wanna come along?"

"Call Paula."

Matt didn't respond. Instead, he turned and walked briskly out of the office. He didn't need JJ managing his love life. JJ—the man who couldn't keep a woman for more than two dates if he tried; the man who couldn't see where his heart was with a microscope and a map.

If Paula wanted to dump him, that was her prerogative. He didn't need her.

"Hey, Suzie-Q. How about dinner?"

Patrol officer Susan Meredith looked up at him from her report. "Can't, sugar. I'm on tonight. Gotta get back out there."

"Another time."

He punched the button to the elevator, heard it whine and creak, and opted for the stairs. On the way down, he saw Michele going off duty. "Michele, baby. How about some dinner?"

"Sorry, Matt. Got a hot date."

He flopped an open hand over his heart. "I'm crushed."

"Right." She smiled and shook her head. "That'll be the day. Go home to your wife."

"Wife? *Wife?* I don't have a wife!"

"Well, if Paula isn't, she should be. Or is she too smart to take you on for life?" Michele flashed him another smile and disappeared into the women's locker room.

"Another comedian." Matt shoved his hands in his pockets. *Too smart to take him on for life. Hah! Paula would have married him in a heartbeat. She was crazy about him. She. . .*

Was gone.

Matt pushed open the front door and stepped out. Zoe had warned him, but he hadn't listened. And now Paula was gone.

Zoe was putting away her dust cloth when the doorbell rang. She looked through the peephole, half expecting JJ to be standing there with a sneering expression on his face and his hands in his pockets.

She flung the door open. "Dad?"

Keyes strode past her and dropped his suitcase on the floor. "Your mother is safe at the house in Marblehead. And I'm not leaving here until this is over."

"Dad, you don't have to do this."

"Yes, I do." He folded his arms across his chest and gave her a look she hadn't seen since she was five. "You are my daughter, and regardless of how you feel about me, I happen to love you with all my heart. Now, maybe you can't find it in yourself to forgive me for a mistake I made twenty years ago, but your mother has and we're getting married again. In the meantime, someone is threatening my daughter, and no one, no one, threatens my daughter and gets away with it."

Zoe stood there gaping. *Mom and Dad are getting married*

again? "You and Mom. Well, that's. . .great."

"I think so. She seems to think so, too. I believe she's out making me pay for past transgressions with my gold card as we speak."

Zoe laughed. "Nah, not Mom. If I know her, she's using *her* gold card."

Keyes smiled widely. "You're probably right, just to prove to me that she can." He opened his arms wide. "Do you think you could handle giving me a hug?"

Zoe hesitated for a moment. Then she found herself launching into his arms. His embrace felt safe. Just like she was a child. Suddenly she was crying again. What in the world was happening to her?

"I've missed you, Zoe," he whispered in her ear.

"I've missed you, too, Dad. And I'm sorry for treating you the way I have. I was just so hurt."

"I know. I know, baby."

The phone rang and her father slowly released her. She backed away from him and picked up the phone. "Hello?"

"That wasn't smart at all, calling me a coward. I was going to let you live a little longer, you know. Now I can't."

"You don't scare me—"

"I'll give you one gift before you die."

Zoe turned her back to her father. "And what's that?"

"Want to know where Amy is?"

Before she could respond, he hung up. She closed her eyes and set the phone on the table in slow motion.

"Who was that, Zoe?"

Zoe shook her head, unable to answer. The killer knew exactly which card to play. Amy. What would she pay for such a thing? What would she risk? Everything. To bring Amy home.

The killer was very smart indeed. And now she would be forced to play this game his way.

chapter 25

JJ knocked firmly on Karen Matthews's front door. He was surprised to find a barefoot man standing there in jeans.

"Yes?"

"Detective Johnson. I need to talk to Mrs. Matthews if she's home."

"Come on in. I'm her brother, Ray." He held out his hand and JJ shook it, liking the man immediately.

He followed Ray into the living room, where Karen was going through an old photo album. "I'm sorry to disturb you, Mrs. Matthews, but I need to speak to you if I could."

"Have a seat, please. You've met my brother, Ray?"

"Yes. Would you prefer we do this alone?"

Karen shook her head. "Not at all. Ray can be here."

JJ took the nearest chair. "Have you ever heard the name Theodore Matthew Bateman?"

Karen tilted her head and shook it. "I don't think so, why?"

"Because that's your husband's real name."

"I knew the man was up to something!" Ray exclaimed.

Karen looked from Ray back to JJ. "I don't understand."

JJ scratched one eyebrow, searching for the right words. "What, if anything, has he told you about his family?"

Karen shrugged. For once, her hands were calmly in her lap, her eyes meeting his without wavering or shifting. JJ made a mental note of the changes to ponder later.

"Not a great deal. He was an only child. His father died when he was young. His mother passed away in a fire when he was in his early twenties. That's about it."

"Well, some of that is true." JJ leaned back in his chair, glancing from brother to sister. "Ted's father died in a car accident when Ted was three. His mother remarried and had another child—a girl, Marsha. When Ted was ten, he murdered his half sister in a rage because he felt she was getting all his mother's attention."

Karen's hands flew to her mouth, and her eyes widened in horror as the color drained from her face. Ray shook his head as if none of this surprised him.

"Ted was tried as a child and remanded to juvenile detention until he was twenty-one. Two weeks after he got out, his parents' house was torched and they died in the fire. No one was able to prove Ted did it, but the police had their suspicions. Ted collected the insurance money, changed his name, and moved."

Karen sank back, tears streaming from her eyes. "I married a monster. How could I marry a man and live with him all these years and not know? How could he seem so normal?"

"That's the way these people are, Mrs. Matthews. They fool everyone. Jeffrey Dahmer's neighbors thought he was a wonderful man. These psychopaths make a science out of blending in with society to appear just like everyone else."

Karen's voice shook. "Do you think. . . Do you think he killed my baby?"

"I don't think so, Mrs. Matthews. We believe he has her though. Of course, there are any number of scenarios, and we plan to examine them all."

JJ hesitated a moment, gathering his thoughts. "We know he was involved with someone else. She's missing now, too."

Karen closed her eyes for a moment. "I suppose I should be upset about another woman, but at this moment, I'm more concerned about my child."

"Mrs. Matthews. . ." JJ took a deep breath. "I want to apologize for being so hard on you. Your husband fooled me, too. And that isn't easy for me to admit. He had me believing you were the one behind your child's disappearance."

She nodded and attempted something close to a smile, but he knew the pain she was feeling made it difficult to smile.

JJ stood up. "I'd like to ask a favor. I can get a search warrant if you prefer, but I'm hoping you'll give me permission to go through your husband's desk, computer, and personal papers."

"If it will help you find him and my child, please do. You have my permission. His office is down the hall, second door on the right."

"Zoe? Who was that? Was that him?"

Zoe turned and walked into her father's arms. "Yes. He was just taunting me. I don't think it's time to worry yet."

"I'm already worried. I've *been* worried."

"Everything is okay." She stepped back and tried to smile. "I was just about to make some dinner. Are you hungry?"

"I could eat. But don't cook. Let's go out."

"Okay. That sounds good. Let me just change my shoes."

◆ ◆ ◆

All the way to the restaurant, Zoe fretted over the haunting words: *Want to know where Amy is?*

When they were seated in a booth at the back of a nearby steak-house, her father shook out his napkin, placed it in his lap, folded his arms on the table, and looked at her. "Tell me what he said to you, Zoe."

Her father looked so much different than when he'd rushed into her house with slumped shoulders and dark shadows under his eyes. There was still worry in those eyes of his, but there was also a sparkle. Something her mother had put there, no doubt. Today he walked with shoulders squared, chin up, and determination streaking across his face the way the gray streaked his hair.

Zoe busied her hands playing with her napkin, picking up and setting down her water glass, moving silverware. After a few moments, her father reached over and placed one of his hands over hers. Stilling her. Calming her.

She took a deep breath. "He asked me if I wanted to know where Amy is."

He hissed an audible confession of shock. "He knows your weak spot."

"Yes."

"She's not there. You know that, don't you, sweetheart? Those are just bones. They don't mean anything. Amy is with the Lord."

"I know, Dad."

His eyebrows rose and she knew she'd managed to surprise him once again. "You do?" he asked.

"Last night I went to a prayer meeting. I can't explain what happened there; I just know I couldn't get enough of whatever God was doing to me." She lifted her eyes to his. "I know now that Amy is with Him. She has been for a long time."

"Thank You, Father," her dad murmured softly.

Now it was her turn to raise an eyebrow. "You, too?"

"Who do you think gave me the strength to wait for your mother all these years? To keep believing that someday I'd have my family back?"

"I didn't know." Zoe reached over and took his hand. It was warm and comforting. Not unlike what she'd felt the night before. Suddenly it dawned on her. "But then you knew my being a psychic was not a good thing."

"Yes," he admitted in a voice so low she could barely hear him.

"Then why didn't you say something?"

He tilted his head. "I had the distinct impression that if I would have come to you and told you what I thought, you would have shown me the door."

Zoe couldn't argue with that. She definitely would have shown him the door—and thrown in a few choice comments to accompany a door slamming. "Okay, fair enough. When did all this happen to you? Becoming a Christian, I mean."

"After Amy died. I was so completely. . .done in. I was lost. You and your mother had each other. I was grieving. I felt guilty for not being there, but I knew you didn't want me there. I was forced to go through it alone.

"No," he said quickly, cutting off anything she might have been on the verge of saying. "Don't feel sorry for me. Granted, it was the worst time of my life. I'd lost everything important to me and I was wallowing in my grief. But at some point I realized the Lord was holding out His hand to me, so I grabbed on and haven't let go since."

"Dad?"

"Yes?" He handed her a menu and opened his to peruse the offerings of the day.

"I'm scared."

Matt sat in his truck and stared out the windshield. This was stupid. Not only was it stupid, he was absolutely sure he'd lost his mind. There were plenty of fish in the sea. Yeah, she loved him. *Big deal.* A lot of women loved him.

Okay, maybe they didn't love him the way Paula did, but she wasn't exactly the last woman on earth.

Just the last person he wanted to lose.

Turn the key, Casto. Start the engine. Drive away. Don't look back. She bailed on you. A light tap on his window startled him. He caught his breath and then slowly rolled down the window.

"You going to sit out here all night, hot shot?"

"Maybe," he said belligerently.

Paula shook her head. "Guess you need some more time growing up."

She turned and headed back into the house. Matt hesitated about a half second before jumping out of his truck and running after her. "Wait a minute! I came here to talk to you!"

Paula sat down on the front step. "So talk." She propped her elbows on her knees, resting her chin on her fists, and stared up at the evening sky. The sun was sinking low in a blaze of orange and blue. It was spectacular.

"I have never cheated on you, Paula Horne."

"I never said you did," she countered.

"I saw you with another man," he parried.

"I've seen you with a lot of other women."

"They never meant anything. Lunches and dinners with coworkers because I hate eating alone."

She smiled knowingly. "Exactly."

"Stop it, Paula! You have me so twisted up I can't think straight."

"Good."

"Why are you doing this to me?"

She stood up and brushed off the seat of her pants. "Because you needed to know one way or the other."

"Know what, one way or the other?"

"That you love me."

Matt opened his mouth but couldn't find words. She opened the front door, slipped inside, and shut it firmly behind her.

JJ was summoned to Harris's office with little fanfare. Stepping into the office, he was surprised to find two men standing there in dark suits. He knew immediately what was up. One man was tall and thin with blond hair and blue eyes. He was probably in his late twenties to early thirties and had the kind of charming good looks that would draw women like flies. JJ dismissed him as an FBI "FIT"—Feebie In Training.

The other man was older, perhaps late fifties, with the neck of a bull, the shoulders of a gorilla, and the paunch of a beer lover. He had deep-set eyes that brimmed with good humor and acute intelligence. This was a man to be reckoned with.

JJ turned to Harris. "You called in the FBI."

"Have a seat, Johnson. And I didn't call them in. That news story saying this guy has killed dozens of little girls brought them running. They're not here to take over."

"And pigs fly with blue wings," he muttered under his breath.

The bull stepped forward and held out a beefy hand. "Jack Fleming." He nodded his head toward the heartthrob. "This is my partner, Don Bevere. Adam Zahn filled us in on some of the particulars. We'd like to be of assistance."

JJ's lips twisted in a mock smile. "That's a polite way of saying this is now your case."

Fleming shook his head as he unbuttoned his jacket and shoved one hand into his pants pocket. "Not at all. I could push, if you prefer it that way, but I'd rather we blend into the team you already have, get caught up on the files, and help out wherever we can."

JJ would have liked to tell the men to hit the road, but he knew he needed their help. He stood up and waved a hand through the air. "Welcome to the team."

Harris beamed.

JJ looked at him. "We're going to need more space."

The smile vanished and was replaced by a scowl. "I'll see what I can do."

JJ hid his smile as he motioned for Fleming and Bevere to follow him. Once he was out in the hall, the smile broke out across his face. Bevere was the first to notice.

"Like jerking his chain, don't you?"

"The highlight of my day," JJ admitted.

Fleming laughed.

"I don't see it as a laughing matter," Bevere said grimly. "One should respect authority. This is exactly why—"

"Put a lid on it, Bevere," Fleming retorted and then turned to JJ. "The kid really has to lighten up."

chapter 26

For the next twenty-four hours, JJ didn't budge from the newly assigned third-floor conference room. Boxes and files were stacked everywhere. Bulletin boards were covered with pictures, notes, scenarios, suspects, and profiles.

He and Fleming poured over autopsy reports, crime scene photos, evidence, interviews, and investigation notes. Matt—with his white-knuckle grip on a surly attitude that everyone ignored—came and went with Gerry, Wayne, and Barone. Harris poked his head in once and disappeared. He, too, was ignored.

Bevere became fascinated with Zoe Shefford. "She's a looker," he commented when he saw her picture in the file. "Is she single?"

"Yes," JJ snapped.

"So that's the way the wind is blowing. Sorry."

"Did you assign someone to watch her place?" Fleming asked over the top of a file folder.

Bevere looked bored. "Yeah. Vince is watching the house. And I ordered her phones tapped. Maybe I should go over there and make sure everything is okay."

"Sit down," Fleming ordered. "You've got more important

things to think about than your love life."

"What love life?" Bevere lifted an eyebrow as if insulted, but his eyes were twinkling.

"Keep it up and you won't have to worry about it."

Smiling to himself, Bevere went back to work, but JJ had the distinct impression that the entire conversation had been intended to bait him.

They ordered lunch in and hit a nearby diner for supper before returning to the conference room. Around 4:00 A.M., Bevere fell asleep in a chair while Fleming and JJ continued to discuss theories.

"If he's after Miss Shefford," Fleming continued while stirring another cup of coffee, "then we could use that."

"You mean use her as bait."

Fleming drummed his fingers on the table. "It's been done. Not my first choice, but it could work."

"And it could get her killed," JJ replied dryly.

Fleming looked around the table and picked up one piece of paper after another. "Where is the composite sketch of the killer? The one Mrs. Shefford worked on with the sketch artist?"

JJ thumbed through one stack of files and then moved to another stack. He pulled out a paper and handed it to Fleming.

"You asked Miss Shefford if she recognized the man?"

JJ nodded. "Casto took a copy over and showed it to her. She said she'd never seen him."

Fleming stroked his chin as he studied the picture. Thick dark hair, bushy eyebrows, close-cropped beard, thin lips. The notations at the bottom read: "Approx. 5.10–6.0, dark brown hair, no visible scars or tattoos, approx. 140–160 lbs., average build."

"What about running this in the paper? Maybe someone around town will recognize him."

"It'll hit the papers tomorrow morning." JJ glanced up at the clock. "*This* morning's papers."

Fleming rubbed the back of his neck. "How many bodies have you found so far?"

JJ blew out a deep breath. "Five. We got a positive ID on Gina Sarentino, Emily Brandt, and Theresa Cooper, a seven-year-old who disappeared five years ago. The medical examiner is still working on the others."

"Any chance there are more bodies in either of the two areas where these were found?"

"We've ripped the area around the college apart and found just four bodies. They're still working on the field out in Emmitts Falls where we located the Sarentino girl. So far, nothing."

"I can't see him leaving one child out there all alone. The area where the Brandt girl was found indicates that he groups them, even if he doesn't do it all at once."

"I know." JJ stood up and stretched. "I'm fairly certain we'll find more out in Emmitts Falls. It's just a big area."

"I can order more cadaver dogs."

"Fine by me."

"I'd like to talk to this psychic of yours, if I can."

JJ shot him a dark look. "She's not *my* psychic. Just for the record, I don't believe in psychics. But you're free to talk to her anytime you want."

Fleming leaned back and stretched his legs out in front of him. "You don't believe in the supernatural?"

"Nope."

"Let me guess. Your parents never indoctrinated you with Santa Claus, the Easter Bunny, and the Tooth Fairy. Hence, you grew up a pragmatic soul with little color in your life and kept your experiences to what you could taste, touch, and see."

"No wonder he's so droll," murmured Bevere from his slouched position in a chair across the room.

"I am not droll," JJ shot back.

Bevere lifted his head, squinting at JJ. "Really? When was the last time you laughed? My partner here is the king of comedy, and he had me rolling twice in the last. . ." He flipped his wrist and grimaced at it. "Dear heavens, have we been here this long? Anyway, he's cracked some mighty fine jokes, and you barely cracked a smile. You, sir, are droll."

"Are you up from your beauty sleep?" Fleming asked.

"Am I beautiful yet?"

Fleming's mouth twisted in an attempt to hide a smile. "Oh, yes. Beyond belief."

"Then I'm up." Bevere climbed to his feet and stretched, his arms wide as he groaned. "Chairs were not meant to sleep in."

"He's a smart one, isn't he?" Fleming shot a grin at JJ, who returned it. "Figured that out in no time. And they said he was just another dumb blond."

Ignoring Fleming's sarcasm, Bevere leaned over the table, obviously not eager to make company with another chair anytime soon. "Okay, where are we?"

"Autopsy reports."

"Five victims ranging in age from five to seven years. Ligature marks around the neck indicate death by strangulation. The markings on the ligature signature indicate common household clothesline rope. None of the vics showed any sign of mutilation or torture. The heart was removed from each vic postmortem. No foreign body fluids, so we have no DNA sample. There was one strand of hair on one of the vics—I don't recall which one—and it was determined to be medium brown and belonging to a male. Duh. News to us. No help there."

Bevere stood up and began to pace around the room. "Blood

work showed no traces of drugs or chemicals, so the vics were not tranquilized prior to death. All vics were unusually clean, suggesting that the unsub washed the bodies before burial to prevent transference of evidence. Even the fingernails were clean, so we don't know if they scratched him in an attempt to save themselves."

He stopped at the coffeepot, picked it up, smelled it, and wrinkled his nose before setting it back down and resuming his pacing. "None of the vics showed any trace of rape, so the crimes are not sexual in nature. It's personal to him. He wants something they have, and the taking of the heart is an indication that it has something to do with their love, innocence, or purity."

JJ leaned back against the conference table and watched Bevere summarize all the information he'd read over the past twenty-some hours like a computer. He was impressed. The pretty boy had a brain.

"One of the unknown vics, approximately age six, showed indications of leukemia. This might help with identification if the leukemia had been caught and diagnosed by her pediatrician. The unknown vic with blond hair had apparently had her tonsils removed—another possible help in identification."

Bevere turned around and looked at JJ. "And that's it in a nutshell." He grinned, as if he knew he'd just impressed the daylights out of JJ.

Fleming looked up at JJ with an apologetic shrug. "Now you know why I keep him around."

chapter 27

Wednesday, April 26

Ray stood at the window and watched as his father marched up the front walk like a man heading into battle. A smile flitted across his face. If the old man thought he was going to show up and bring Karen to heel, he had another thing coming. Karen wasn't the same mouse she'd been a few weeks earlier. Slowly she was learning her worth, and her confidence was growing. Yesterday morning he'd found her pouring over the employment classifieds.

"You don't have to get a job, Karen. I'll release some of your trust to you."

She shook her head firmly. "This isn't about money. I know that's there if I need it. This is about having something for myself. Doing something with my life. Even if it's just part time."

She'd found a recent color photo of Jessica and made big color posters and fliers at the local copy shop. She'd called people and teamed up with Rene to distribute the posters and fliers. She'd called reporters and television stations. She'd talked to radio stations.

And she'd collapsed exhausted and smiling on the sofa at the end of the day.

Ray's sister was definitely finding herself. She'd even come out of her bedroom with several bulging trash bags and hauled them to the street. "*His* things," she'd announced with a touch of disdain.

Ray opened the front door before his father could knock.

"You still here?" Walter Timms eyed him with scorn. "Don't you have a job?"

"I'm on vacation."

Walter sniffed loudly. "Where's your sister?"

"I believe she's outside burning Ted's clothes."

Walter's eyes flew wide. "What? Has she lost her mind? He'll kill her for doing that!"

"He won't do squat," Ray replied. "He's gone. He'll never hurt my sister again."

"He never laid a hand on your sister!"

"It doesn't always take a fist to hurt someone."

His father stalked out of the room, ignoring the direct hit. Ray shut the front door and followed him through the house to the back patio. Sure enough, Karen was pouring lighter fluid on clothes she'd tossed into the barbecue pit.

"Karen!"

She jumped, throwing a hand to her chest. Ray started forward, afraid she was going to cower. But she just frowned. "You startled me, Dad. You shouldn't sneak up on people like that."

"What do you think you're doing?" he demanded.

"I don't *think* anything. I know exactly what I'm doing. Why? Did you want some of this garbage to wear?"

"Don't you get smart with me, young lady. Ted will have a fit when he finds out what you've done to his clothes."

She defiantly poured more lighter fluid. "Ted doesn't need these anymore."

The old man's eyes narrowed. "What has happened to you? Your brother has corrupted you."

Karen laughed lightly as she set down the can of fluid and picked up two more shirts and a sweater. "My brother has been a gift from God. What has happened to me is that I finally woke up and smelled the coffee. Not only that, I *tasted* it and realized just what's been wrong with my life for far too long."

She threw the shirts onto the grate and tossed a match on them, watching with delight as they caught fire with an audible *whoosh*.

Walter stepped forward. "I can't allow you to do this! These are Ted's personal belongings. You have no right."

Karen whirled on him, her eyes narrowed with determined intent. "Don't you touch those things! You don't allow or disallow anything I do. I am a grown woman. This is *my* house and these belonged to *my* husband. I'll burn them if I want to. I have every right."

Ray smiled as he perched on the edge of the brick wall surrounding the patio. *Go, Sis.*

"I can't believe you're talking to me like this!" Walter bellowed. "I won't allow it!"

"*Allow?* This is *my* house, Dad. You abide by *my* rules here. If you don't like it, you can go home."

Walter spun around and glared at Ray. "This is your doing!"

"I wish it was, but I can't take the credit for this. Karen has always been bright and talented and delightful all on her own. I'm pretty sure God made her that way and should get all the credit." Ray grinned. *This is so much fun.*

There was another *whoosh* as flames shot up into the air. Karen jumped back and let out a laugh that was pure music to Ray's ears.

Show the world what you're made of, Sis.

Nora McCaine pushed her grocery cart up to the conveyor belt and began unloading her groceries. Kaitlyn lay quietly in her carrier, belted in at the front of the cart. She held a soft plush puppy in her hands and alternately stared at it and chewed on it. She looked like a perfect angel in her pink and white overalls and matching hat.

Nora checked the straps to make sure Kaitlyn was secure. She wasn't afraid of Kaitlyn falling out. She was afraid of someone walking by and snatching her away.

Every mother she knew was keeping an eagle eye on her children. You rarely saw a lone child playing on the quiet streets anymore. Not like before. Before the abduction stories hit the airwaves. Now if you saw children on bicycles, skateboards, or roller skates, you were certain to find a parent or two nearby.

No one sent a child across the street to borrow a cup of sugar or to see if Johnny could come over and play. Play dates were arranged by phone and carried out with adult supervision.

Even the malls were strangely void of little feet and giggles. Mothers left their children with trusted friends while they ran to the mall.

The world had changed.

Nora pulled her cart up to the register and smiled at the cashier. While the cashier scanned the groceries, Nora noticed a poster taped to the front of the nearby ATM unit.

Missing. Jessica Matthews. Born October 15. Brown hair. Small birthmark on cheek.

Below the contact information was a full-page color photograph of the missing baby. Nora stared at it, wondering how in the world this child's mother was coping. She couldn't begin to imagine. She reached out and traced a finger over the picture, something stirring in her heart.

"Sad, isn't it?"

Nora looked up at the cashier with a nod. "Yes, it is. I can't believe how bad this world has gotten."

"I know. When we were kids, we roamed the streets. No one worried. There was no danger."

"I remember. Days of innocence."

"Yeah."

Nora studied the picture again and then felt her heart lurch. She knew where she had seen this child before!

"Do you have an extra one of these fliers?"

The cashier nodded. "Stack of them at the customer service desk on your way out. That'll be $64.83."

Nora paid the cashier then pushed her cart to the customer service desk. She grabbed a couple of fliers, folded them, and shoved them in her purse.

Every time she'd seen a picture of Jessica Matthews, something seemed familiar. But it wasn't until she saw the big color photo that it had come to her. She knew where Jessica Matthews was.

Nora hurried out of the store. She had to talk to her husband right away. Kaitlyn tossed her plush puppy into the air and watched it land inside the grocery cart. Nora stopped and retrieved it, handing it back to the child. "Let's go, sweetheart. It's time to go home."

"Paula?"

Paula looked up from her computer to see the receptionist standing in front of her with a huge vase of roses. At least two dozen red and pink roses. "For me?"

"That's what the card says."

"Wow." Paula took the vase and lowered it to her desk.

"Wish someone loved *me* that much," the receptionist said wistfully before walking away.

Paula pulled the card out of its holder and opened the envelope.

Okay. I'm a jerk. I'm sorrier than I can say. I love you. Will you marry me?

Matt

Paula felt tears spring to her eyes. "Yeah," she whispered softly. "But I can't let you know that yet. You'll have to do better than this."

Zoe stood at the window, staring across the front yard, while behind her, her father and FBI agent Vince Larson hooted and cheered at a football game on television.

It had been almost three days since she'd heard from the killer. He was playing with her and she knew it. He wanted to keep her on edge, never knowing when or where he might strike. And it was working. Her nerves were as tight as violin strings.

She was surprised, and perhaps a little disappointed, when the FBI descended. She had gotten used to having JJ as her defender. Maybe he *was* a reluctant defender, but she had begun to trust him. She should have realized that once the FBI moved in, JJ would be shuffled to an assisting role. This was their area of expertise. It was logical for them to head up the investigation. Still, she missed taunting JJ and watching him do a slow burn.

Eyeing the men who were engrossed in the game, Zoe slipped out the front door. She hadn't been outside in almost twenty-four hours and needed to feel the sun on her face. Needed to feel the breeze through her hair.

Needed to feel. . .

"Excuse me. Miss Shefford, isn't it?"

Zoe jumped.

"I didn't mean to startle you. I'm Jack Fleming. FBI. I'd like to talk to you."

That's when she saw JJ climb out of the car. He appeared tired. There were dark circles under his eyes, and his mouth was tight with fatigue. Zoe looked back at the agent and smiled. "Of course. Come on in."

As soon as they came through the door, Special Agent Larson sprang to his feet, his face white. "Sir."

"Is this how we protect someone, Larson? Watching football while the protectee saunters outside in plain sight? Last time I checked, there was a direct threat against this young lady's life. Or has that been resolved and someone forgot to inform me?"

"No, sir. I mean, I'm sorry, sir. She was just standing right here."

"No, she was just standing out front when I got here."

Zoe stepped forward, feeling sorry for Larson. "I'm sorry, Agent Fleming. This was my fault. I was feeling cooped up and slipped out when no one was watching."

Fleming lifted an eyebrow in her direction. "That is entirely my point, Miss Shefford. You slipped out while no one was watching. And watching is the only reason Agent Larson is here."

"Yes, sir." Zoe almost laughed when she realized how she'd answered him. Instead, she just smiled. "Would you care for anything to drink?"

Fleming's mouth twitched. "I'm fine, thank you." He turned to JJ. "Detective Johnson?"

JJ shook his head as he stared at Zoe with an unfathomable expression. He could have been staring at a brick wall for all the emotion he showed.

Zoe looked up at Fleming. "Won't you have a seat?" She reached out her hand to her father. "This is my father, Keyes Shefford. Dad, this is Agent Fleming and that," she waved dismissively at JJ, "is Detective Johnson."

Agent Fleming took the lead. "I'm here because I wanted to talk to you not only about your impressions of our unsub but also—"

"I'm sorry. Your what?"

"Unsub. Sorry. Unknown suspect. It's just lingo for the man we're trying to catch."

"Ah," Zoe nodded. "The serial killer."

"Yes." Fleming cleared his throat. "Anyway, I wanted to discuss the possibility of you working with us on this."

Zoe shook her head. "I'm sorry. I can't. I don't have any psychic ability to help you anymore. I've renounced it. . .and it's gone."

Fleming looked confused. So did JJ, but she tried to keep her eyes on Fleming. "You see, I became a Christian recently and—"

"Oh, great." JJ stood up, rolling his eyes.

Zoe lifted her chin. "I beg your pardon. Are you talking to me?"

"I thought you were smarter than that! 'God forgives all.' 'God loves.' 'God will send you to hell if you don't do it His way!' " He jammed one hand in his pocket and cocked his knee as he leaned forward a little. "First you're this superpsychic; now you're going to be some super-Christian. Ever think of just being yourself instead of exchanging one phony crutch for another?"

With calm deliberation, Zoe came to her feet. She saw her father start to open his mouth, and she waved him to silence. "He's mine," she told her dad in a quiet but firm voice.

She stepped toward JJ, her eyes focusing in on what almost looked like fear in his eyes. She didn't need her old abilities to know what was tormenting him. "I don't need crutches and I don't need someone to feel responsible for protecting me. I'm not Macy, Josiah. I'm nothing like her and I never was."

"I never said you were! And this isn't about Macy! You don't know anything about her."

"You loved her. More than anything in this life, you loved her and someone killed her. And it tore you up because you felt you should have protected her. You felt you had failed because you didn't keep her safe—because you didn't take her fears seriously."

"That blasted psychic told her that no one was stalking her!" His voice trembled with rage. "Macy threw caution to the wind after that con artist lied to her."

They were both heaving with anger, but neither was willing to let it go. It was time for JJ to let it out.

"Macy threw caution to the wind because she wanted you to think that she was as brave as you were—that she was worthy of your love!" Zoe reached out with both hands and shoved against his chest. He barely moved. "You never let her see your weaknesses, so she didn't think you had any."

"So it's *my* fault she was killed? Is that what you're saying?"

"No! It was never your fault. She built you up in her mind until you were perfect and strong and capable and Superman. Only a very special woman would be worthy of such a man."

As sweat began to glisten on his forehead, JJ yanked off his jacket and tossed it angrily to a nearby chair. It slid to the floor. He ignored it as he narrowed in on Zoe. "I never tried to be Superman."

"You didn't have to try, Josiah. You *were*," Zoe said, evening her tone. "You simply were. You worked so hard trying to prove you were wonderful because you didn't believe you were. You didn't believe your parents loved you. You didn't believe anyone cared about you."

JJ took a step closer to her, his fists clenching and unclenching. "Shut. . .up."

"Not this time, JJ." Zoe straightened and looked into his eyes. "Your father loves you. He thinks you walk on water, just like Macy did. He's so proud of you that he brags everywhere he goes. But he can't let you see that because he's terrified someone as special as you would see him as unworthy. He's so afraid of losing respect that it's driven him to blustering arrogance. He hates it. You both hate it.

But you have the power to turn it around. It's enough, Josiah."

JJ's glare was hot enough to make the sun envious. He spun on his heel without another word and stormed out of the house, slamming the door behind him. Zoe flinched. Then sighed. "Well, that was fun."

Linda Foxwell slid open the glass door and stepped onto her patio. "Pogo! Here, boy!" She whistled loudly and then looked around for her dog. "If you've jumped the fence again, I'm going to tie you to a rope!"

She stepped out to the edge of the patio. "Pogo! Come!"

Suddenly the black lab came sailing over the back fence from the yard behind. He bounded toward her, tail wagging. "You are so bad! You're not supposed to go in other people's yards!"

Pogo stopped a few feet away, wagging his tail harder, then dropped something from his mouth. Plopping down on his haunches, he stared up at her.

"What in heaven's name is that?" Linda stepped closer, bent down, and looked more closely. Then she stiffened.

And screamed.

And fainted.

Patrolwoman Rachael Carstairs and Kevin Kirkwood answered the emergency call on Nebel Street at 3:27. At 3:29, Kirkwood notified dispatch of the need for backup and the medical examiner's van. He also notified Tripp in Homicide that he would be needed at the crime scene.

Lieutenant Tripp was, at that moment, on his way back to the station. He turned his car around and arrived on the scene at 3:51. He found Carstairs at the curb; she looked white, and from the smell of things, she had been sick to her stomach. She lifted her blanched face and pointed to the backyard.

Stepping over a red plastic Big Wheel, Tripp opened the gate to the backyard and quickly took in the scene. Two patrolmen stood at the rear of the yard talking to the medical examiner. A third officer was on the patio talking to a young couple. A dog was tied up on the patio and looking extremely unhappy about it.

"Someone called for me?"

One of the patrolman nodded and pointed to an area on the other side of the fence. Tripp leaned on the fence and looked over. He felt the blood rush to his feet.

It was a corpse—or what was left of one, anyway—buried in a shallow grave.

One hand rested on his gun as the other rubbed one of his heavy jowls. He was pretty sure he already knew the answer to the question he had to ask, but he asked anyway. "Whose property is that?"

"Matthews'."

"That's what I thought." He looked over the fence again. "I think we have probable cause to enter the property, folks. Let's get this done. I want this whole area taped off back here. No one goes over this fence. We're going in through the Matthews' gate."

He returned to his car and radioed dispatch while he drove around the block and pulled into the Matthews' driveway. It took that long for dispatch to patch him through to JJ. "Yeah, Johnson. I'm at the Matthews' house. We've discovered a body behind the shed in the Matthews' backyard. Any bets it's our missing husband?"

Vivian Amato pulled up in her van. Tripp leaned against the front fender while she pulled out her evidence kit and locked the van. "This is going to be a nightmare, Roger. I'm going to have neighbors leaning over that fence down there."

Tripp shook his head. "I'm going to have them tape off everything for at least fifty yards in every direction. You'll have your privacy."

"Thanks."

The front door of the house opened, and a man stepped out. Tripp eyed him suspiciously. *Has the woman replaced her husband already? Or did she already have this one in the wings?*

"What's going on?" the man asked.

Tripp strode up the front walk, pulled out his badge, and held it out to Ray. "Tripp. Homicide. Who are you?"

"Ray Timms. This is my sister's house."

Then Tripp noticed the family resemblance and eased up a little. "Is your sister home, Mr. Timms?"

"Yes."

"A neighbor found something suspicious back behind the shed at the rear of your sister's property. We need to check it out, if you have no objections."

He didn't really care if Timms objected, but just in case a lawyer decided to try to suppress evidence on an illegal search and seizure, he'd have his backside covered.

"No. No objections."

"Then I'm going to have to ask you and your sister to remain in the house until we figure out exactly what we have. I'll post an officer on the front porch to ensure no one bothers you."

"Bothers us or prevents us from leaving? What is it, exactly, that was supposedly found back there?"

The man wasn't stupid. "I can't say anything more until we check it out more closely. I'm just asking that you remain indoors so as not to contaminate any evidence while we're working."

"Look, maybe this isn't such a good idea. I think I need to call my sister's lawyer first."

Tripp took a step forward. Time to play hardball. "You can call anyone you like. We have probable cause to enter the property and we are going to enter the property. Please don't make things worse for your sister by getting arrested for obstruction of justice or interfering with an investigation in process."

Vivian knelt carefully at the edge of the shallow grave and shook her head as she pulled her gloves out of her evidence bag. Nasty piece of work. Time of death was going to be tricky. The body had been burned beyond recognition and looked to have been in the ground anywhere from three to six days. Animals hadn't helped matters any. She pulled out a small whiskbroom and began to carefully brush away dirt still piled on the body. It was going to a long, tedious process to extract the body and save any evidence.

"Anything I can help you with, Vivian?"

Vivian looked up at Tripp and jerked her head back toward the patio. "On my way down, I passed that barbecue pit. It looks like someone has been burning something besides hamburgers. Have someone tape it off. There might be evidence."

"You got it."

Two hours later, Vivian and two seasoned officers carefully lifted the body out of the grave and rolled it onto a pristine white sheet. Most of the burn damage had been done to the front of the body, as if someone had laid the body down on the ground, applied an unknown accelerant, and then tossed a match.

"What's that?" Tripp asked sharply, pointing to the back of the body.

Vivian reached down and gently pulled a wallet out of the

singed back pants pocket. Carefully she held the wallet with two fingers and let it fall open. "Some of the credit cards appeared to have melted from the heat, but there is a driver's license."

"Name? As if I didn't already know."

Vivian looked up at him. "Edward Matthews."

Tripp walked back to the house. He didn't bother to knock as he entered through the glass sliding doors off the patio. The brother jumped to his feet. His sister was standing at the sink. She turned and looked at Tripp, surprising him with the curiosity he saw in her expression. No fear. Just questions. Somehow that wasn't what he was expecting.

"Mrs. Matthews?"

"Lieutenant."

"Do you know what we found back there?"

She shook her head.

"Your husband."

"My. . ." Her face went white and she looked like she was about to faint. Johnson was right. She'd missed her calling. Hollywood would have loved her. "Ted?"

"Ma'am, if you'd be kind enough to turn around."

"Turn around? Why?"

"Karen Matthews, I'm arresting you for the murder of Edward Matthews." He pulled out his handcuffs. "You have the right to remain silent. Anything you say can, and will, be used against you in a court of law. You have the right to an attorney. . ."

chapter 28

Thursday, April 27

Matt strolled into the conference room with his hands in his pockets. Disappointment washed over him when he saw that JJ was deep in conversation with Agent Fleming. He wanted to drop into a chair, prop his feet up, and tell JJ all about his failure to get Paula back.

He'd sent roses and cards. He'd sent her favorite candy. He'd apologized until he was out of breath. He'd left messages on her answering machine. And she hadn't returned a single call or acknowledged his efforts in any way. He was certain he'd lost her.

But JJ didn't have time to talk to him about anything other than the case. He felt a pair of eyes on him and looked around to find Don Bevere staring at him.

"Hey, Matt."

"Donnie."

"Has she called?"

Matt shook his head. "Nah."

"Time to get serious now. If you are really serious about her."

"I am," Matt confessed in a low voice. He was miserable. Of course he was serious.

Donnie grabbed his jacket off the back of the chair, swung it around his shoulders, and slipped his arms in as he strode forward. "Let's go, buddy. We got some work to do."

Matt followed him out into the hall. "What work?"

"Operation Paula."

"What are we going to do?" Matt had to step up his pace as Donnie jogged down the stairs.

"You want her back; she wants to know you're serious. Simple."

"Nothing has worked so far."

Donnie flashed him a devious smile. "Trust me, pal. I was raised with six sisters. They taught me well. You drive. We're looking for a jewelry store."

Matt climbed in behind the wheel. "I tried that. A bracelet."

Donnie curled his lip. "Small potatoes. Good if you're saying sorry for being late for dinner. Worthless when you're saying that you totally screwed up and can't live without her."

Karen sat on her cot, her back to the concrete wall, her knees drawn up to her chest. *Murder.* They'd arrested her for murder. How could they do that? She hadn't murdered anyone! *Couldn't they see that?*

Somewhere down the hall, a cell slammed closed and Karen flinched. She was going to go to prison. She'd heard horror stories of innocent people declared guilty.

She dropped her head to her knees. *Oh, God, don't let this happen to me. You can get me out of this; I know you can! Just make them see the truth. Please. I don't deserve this. You know that. You know I didn't kill anyone.*

Get me out of this, okay, God?

◆   ◆   ◆

"I don't like it." JJ folded his arms stubbornly across his chest and stared at the locket and ankle bracelet on the conference table. Fleming had convinced Zoe to wear the jewelry in an attempt to catch the killer. The anklet had a homing device in it. The necklace would transmit conversations back to a recorder monitored by the FBI. Still, she'd be a sitting duck hoping to get rescued before she got killed.

He didn't like it one bit.

"I'm not thrilled either, JJ, but we've got two things to think about. One is that we know his killing spree ends May first, which gives us only days to catch him. And second, we already know he's coming after her anyway. We might as well try to catch the guy while he's at it." Fleming picked up the two items, recently delivered from Quantico, and set them back in the box.

"She's better off in a safe house," JJ argued. "You guys do that stuff. Don't tell me you don't."

"We do."

"But not this time. Not if you can use an innocent woman as bait. Never mind that you could get her killed." JJ knew he was being difficult and annoying Fleming, but he didn't care. The notion that Zoe could get hurt or killed didn't sit well with him.

Never mind that he hadn't spoken to her since the day she'd stuck her nose into business that wasn't hers. Never mind that he still didn't *want* to speak to her.

Fleming buttoned his jacket. "We're not going to let her get hurt, JJ."

"And pigs fly with green wings." JJ shook his head and turned to the window. "You can't guarantee that, Fleming. You know it and so do I."

"You going to change your mind and come with me?"

"No." JJ continued to stare out the window. "I have too much to do here. Karen Matthews has been arrested for the murder of her husband. I got a call from some attorney who thinks he knows where Jessica is, and Tripp is playing hardball, refusing to let Matthews go with me to identify the child."

"Have the child brought here."

JJ heard the door click shut; then the room went silent. Fleming wasn't fooled for a second. He knew JJ didn't want to see Zoe after the way he'd childishly stormed out of her house like a two-year-old on a tantrum.

How else was he supposed to react when confronted by someone who knew his deepest and most painful memory and threw it in his face like confetti? In the moment, all he had felt was the pain. Later, much of the truth she'd tossed at him surfaced, but it was too late.

There was no simple way to ease back into seeing her without dealing with what she'd said—and the way he'd acted.

If she lives long enough for me to ease back into seeing her.

Fleming was experienced and dedicated. Bevere, for all his fancy ways and Hollywood charm, was sharp and astute. Both were determined to catch this guy before he killed again, and they were equally determined that Zoe would come through it without so much as a scratch.

JJ wasn't that optimistic.

In the meantime, the need to follow this case to the end was like hunger at two in the morning. He had to acknowledge the hunger but didn't have the wherewithal to satisfy it. He didn't know if the need was just the detective in him wanting to finish what he'd started or the man in him needing to make sure Zoe didn't end up like Macy.

Until he resolved that issue, he wasn't sure he'd be any good to anyone.

A light tap on the door caused JJ to turn. Matt was standing there with that same haunted look in his eyes that he'd been wearing for over a week now. "Paula still won't talk to you?"

Matt shook his head. "I'm working on it. Donnie came up with a plan."

"Donnie?" JJ couldn't help being surprised. He hadn't realized the two men had become friends. Then again, he'd been so consumed with this case that he hadn't realized a lot of things lately.

"I hope it works." He meant to put more enthusiasm into his comment but couldn't seem to drum up enough emotion to pull it off. He reached out and patted Matt's shoulder instead. "I really hope she gives you another chance."

"Yeah, you sound it."

"Sorry, Matt. Just have a lot on my mind."

"I know. Speaking of which, there's a lawyer here by the name of Whitlow with a Mr. and Mrs. McCaine to see you. They said you knew they were coming."

JJ draped his arm over Matt's shoulder. "Come on. You should be in on this."

"In on what?" Matt fell into step next to him.

"Jessica Matthews may be coming home."

The minute they entered the conference room, the woman came to her feet, clutching the infant close.

"I'm Detective Johnson. Please, Mrs. McCaine, have a seat. I just wanted to talk to you a few minutes before we bring Mrs. Matthews in to make a positive identification."

Nora McCaine eased back into her chair looking distraught and nervous. JJ figured she'd calm down as soon as she realized that she and her husband were not going to be charged with anything. None of this had been their fault.

JJ sat down across from Whitlow. "Let me run through this again.

A man came into your office with a woman he said was his wife and told you they wanted to give their daughter up for adoption."

Cameron Whitlow nodded. He was a heavyset man with small eyes that blinked behind tiny wire-rimmed glasses. "I had no idea that it was fraudulent in any way, I assure you. They showed identification; they had the baby's birth certificate. It all seemed entirely legitimate."

JJ opened the file folder in front of him and passed a photo to Whitlow. "Was this the man?"

Whitlow squinted at the picture and then nodded. "That's him. Edward Matthews."

"And this was the woman?" Another picture slid across the table.

Whitlow shook his head. "No. That isn't Mrs. Matthews."

"Actually," JJ responded, "it is." He pulled out another picture. "How about this woman?"

Whitlow nodded. "That's her. That's the woman who said she was Karen Matthews."

JJ looked over at Matt. Whitlow had just identified Maryanne Bubeck.

JJ rubbed the back of his neck. Had they found Karen Matthews's motive for killing her husband? Karen must have found out that Ted and Miss Bubeck were having an affair. Perhaps she knew they were conspiring to give the child up for adoption, and she'd killed him for it. It sounded logical enough.

"I don't buy it," Matt said quietly, as if reading JJ's mind.

"Buy what?"

"If Karen Matthews didn't hurt her child and she didn't give the child away, then she was telling the truth all along. And if she was telling the truth about that, why should we think she's lying now?"

"They found the body in her backyard!" JJ winced as he heard Nora McCaine gasp. He jerked his head toward the door. "We'll figure this out later. Bring Karen Matthews in."

Matt nodded and hurried out of the room.

Charles McCaine cleared his throat. "If Mrs. Matthews goes to jail for murder, is there any chance that we might be able to keep Kaitlyn? I mean, Jessica? I mean, she's going to need a home. . . ."

"I wish I could tell you one way or the other, but the truth is, Karen Matthews has family: a brother who is married with two little girls. He would probably take custody of Jessica."

"Oh."

The man sounded so forlorn and his wife looked so miserable that JJ's heart went out to them. They'd gone to an attorney in hopes of adopting a child of their own. After paying over twenty-five thousand dollars in fees, they'd taken home whom they thought was going to be their daughter.

The door opened again and Karen Matthews entered, led by Matt and Tripp. Nora McCaine rose to her feet and slowly, with great hesitation, pulled back the blanket so Karen could see the child's face.

Karen stared at the child, tears streaming down her face. She looked up at Nora, who was also crying, and then over at Charles McCaine, who looked like he'd just lost his best friend.

"That's not Jessica. Could you take me back to my cell now?"

JJ looked from her to the child. "Mrs. Matthews, are. . ."

"I said I want to go back to my cell!" She turned her back on him and walked stiffly to the door.

He crept closer to the house, staying in the shadows as he moved silently through the yard. He saw her move past the window in the dining room and stopped. Watched. He smiled. She didn't know he was there.

Zoe Shefford thought she'd outwitted him, but she was so very wrong. He knew all about the taps on the phone. Expected it, really. He knew about the FBI. Knew about the bodyguard. Knew she felt relatively safe as long as she stayed in her house.

She thought he couldn't get to her.

She was wrong.

He eased along the side of the house until he came to the power lines. Then he pulled a pair of cutters from under his black sweater and deftly cut the power to the house.

Instantly the house plunged into darkness.

He smiled again.

Fools. They were all fools. They thought they could outsmart him. They were about to find out how wrong they were.

◆　◆　◆

"Excuse me." JJ jumped up from his chair and strode purposefully toward the door. He looked over his shoulder at the McCaines. "Stay here just a minute, please."

He pulled the door closed behind him and rushed down the hall, catching up to Karen Matthews as she was being escorted back to her holding cell. He grabbed her arm and spun her around. "What do you think you're doing?" he demanded.

The misery in her eyes was palpable. And it nearly stole JJ's breath. "I should think it's obvious."

"Well, it's not obvious to me. That was your daughter in there, and you just handed your child over to strangers and walked away."

"They're not strangers to Jessica."

Her shoulders slumped, and he realized she'd given up.

"I'm about to go to prison for a murder I didn't commit. I have no idea how long I'll be in prison, but I imagine it will be a long time. What will happen to my daughter, Detective?"

"There's no guarantee that you're going to prison. And even if you did, what about your brother? Why give her to the first people that come along?"

"Those people love Jessica. They're good people; bringing Jessica back must have been incredibly difficult for them, but they did the right thing. That tells me something about them. Jessica has bonded with them. Should I rip her from the second family she's bonded with and shove her into a third?"

JJ didn't know why it mattered. He'd just spent weeks looking forward to putting her in jail, and now that the time was here, he was trying to make her fight back. "I never thought of you as a quitter."

Karen's laugh was brittle and raspy with emotion. "You thought I killed my baby, and then you thought I killed my husband. No, you didn't think of me as a quitter. You thought of me as a murderer and a liar and a despicable human being."

She turned to Tripp. "Can we go now?"

JJ stared at her retreating figure. Then he strode back into the interview room. The three people sitting around the table lifted their heads and stared at him as he shut the door.

"For the record, Mrs. Matthews has confirmed that the child in question is her daughter, Jessica. While she's straightening out this mess her husband has gotten her into, she'd like to know if you would be willing to continue caring for Jessica. She trusts you and believes it would be best for the child not to be taken away from you at this time."

Nora closed her eyes and began crying as she nodded. Her husband stumbled to his feet. "That would not be a problem. We love Kait. . .Jessica. Anyway, tell Mrs. Matthews that it won't be a problem."

Whitlow stood up and began to gather his papers and shove them back in his briefcase. "On the off chance that Mrs. Matthews is convicted of this crime, does she intend to stay with this arrangement?"

"I believe she does."

Nora looked up at JJ. "A woman who cares more for the well-being of her child than she does for her own is not the type of woman who would do the things you've accused her of."

JJ frowned. "I know. And for the record, I have my doubts about her guilt."

◆　　◆　　◆

"She did what?" Ray stumbled backwards and dropped into one of the vinyl chairs in the police station's reception area. He stared at his sister's attorney. "Why would she do that? Jess is her life!"

"She said it would be best for the child not to be moved to another family until all this is settled."

Suddenly Ray understood. "She's given up. She thinks she's lost and Ted has won."

Benson nodded, his blue eyes unusually dim.

"I want to see her. I need to talk to her."

The attorney shook his head. "It's too late to see her today. I'll arrange for you to see her tomorrow. Go home, and if you're a praying man, pray for her. First thing tomorrow morning, I'm going to go talk to the forensic pathologist. I know they're backed up down at the morgue because of the serial killer, but maybe we can push for a positive ID before Karen is formally charged and arraigned."

"And then she won't be. They'll find out that's not Ted."

"*If* that's not Ted, then you're right. The charges will be dropped unless they have some reason to believe she killed our John Doe."

Ray slapped his thighs and came to his feet. Fatigue cloaked him like a wool blanket, heavy and thick. "I can't thank you enough, Mr. Benson."

"That's because you haven't seen my bill yet." He winked, and the twinkle returned briefly in those deep blue eyes. He placed a hand on Ray's shoulder. "Go home, have dinner, get some sleep. Tomorrow is going to be a long day."

On the way home, JJ decided to drive by his parents' house. He had an overwhelming desire to see them, even if they did drive him crazy. It was almost dinnertime, and no one could cook like his mother. If he was lucky, she'd be making pot roast with those little onions and baby carrots.

His mouth started to water.

He wasn't stopping by for that reason though. It was something Zoe had said to him about his father actually caring, actually loving him. JJ found it hard to believe or accept. But he had begun to realize that Zoe was right more than she was wrong. He was learning to take her seriously.

He parked in the driveway behind his father's sedan and got out. Music was blaring from a radio somewhere behind the house, and the front door was wide open.

JJ stepped into the living room. He could smell chicken baking in the oven, and mixed with that warm aroma was the distinct scent of cinnamon and apples. *She made apple dumplings.*

"Mom?"

There was no response, but he could hear the sound of the vacuum from somewhere down the hall. He passed his old bedroom and stopped to look in. It hadn't changed a bit since he'd moved out years ago except that it looked a shade cleaner. His old posters still hung on the wall, his baseball still sat on the dresser, and his comic books were still stacked on the bookshelf in the corner. He'd have to go through those one day. *Might be something of value in that stack.*

He continued down the hall and glanced into his parents' room. It was empty. He passed the bathroom and the linen closet, stopping in the doorway of the third bedroom, which had been his parents' TV room for as long as he could remember.

This is where they all came to relax after dinner. His father would watch the news and then *Bonanza* or *Marcus Welby, M.D.,* while his mother darned socks, embroidered pillows, or crocheted afghans for every room in the house. JJ would stretch out on that carpet and do his homework, page through his comics, or read a mystery novel.

"I didn't hear you come in, dear." His mother lifted her cheek for a kiss as she dragged the vacuum out of the room. A dust cloth was stuffed in the front pocket of her apron. He wondered if anyone else in the world still wore those bibbed aprons like his mother.

"Just dropping by. Where's Dad?"

"Up on the roof of the garage. Replacing shingles or something."

"He should have called me."

She whipped out her dust rag and wiped off the top of the television. "Oh, you know he won't bother you with such things. He doesn't like to take you away from your work."

"Or doesn't want my help."

She stopped wiping and lifted her face to stare at him. "What in heaven's name would make you think such a thing, Josiah?"

"He never. . . Oh, never mind."

"No, don't give me that never mind hogwash. You tell me what has crawled into your mind and taken root."

He started to slip out of the room, only to feel the playful snap of his mother's dust rag. "Don't you go thinking you can ignore me when I'm talking to you. Get in here and sit down."

JJ groaned inwardly as he stepped back into the room. But he didn't sit down. "Do you realize Dad has never told me that he loves me?"

"Oh, for goodness' sake. Is that all that's got you tied in knots?" His mother resumed dusting. "Heavens, he hasn't told me he loves me since our wedding day. That's just the way he is. Emotions don't come easy to him. He shows his love. Like when you wanted that bike. Timmy Osborn got one, and after that, you just had to have one, too."

She stopped and looked up at him, hands on her hips. "Your daddy had been saving up for a new fishing rig. Had his heart set on this fancy rod and reel set. Then one day he comes home with that bike for you. He never mentioned the rod and reel again. Do you understand what I'm saying here, Josiah?"

"Yes, ma'am. I think I do."

She nodded with satisfaction. "He's a good man. A kind man. And he loves you more than himself. You are his pride and joy, Josiah. Don't ever doubt that. He busted two buttons on his shirt the day you made Detective. Pride, Josiah. He's got pride in you."

"I got it, Mom." He leaned down and kissed her cheek again.

"Roast chicken for dinner. And I made apple dumplings. You staying?"

JJ laughed. "Have you ever known me to turn down your cooking?"

He was almost out of the room when the dust rag snapped him on the back. He laughed and continued through the kitchen door to the backyard. A ladder was propped up against the rear of the garage. JJ shrugged off his suit coat and climbed it.

He found his father hammering shingles while the radio blasted jazz. His father looked up, squinting. "Didn't expect to see you. Got that big case going, don't you?"

JJ held his tongue, trying to see beyond the words. "I do and it's a tough one. Needed a break. Came by for some of Mom's cooking."

His father nodded and set the hammer down. He reached over to lower the volume on the radio. "Can't say as I blame you on your momma's cooking." He leaned back, one hand draped over his raised knee. "How's the case going?"

"Not good. This guy is slick."

"You'll get him, Son. He'll make a mistake and you'll get him. They all do."

JJ wasn't sure what made him decide to test the waters, but he figured it couldn't make things worse. "I don't know, Dad. This is a real hard one. The guy seems to be playing with us."

Josiah Sr., nodded as he fingered a tear in his old work pants. "Some are right smart, but don't underestimate yourself, Josiah. I know what you got in here." He tapped his finger on the side of his head. "You'll figure him out and you'll get him."

JJ felt the words seep into him like warm oil.

"Well, Dad, if I do catch him, it's because you taught me well."

JJ could have sworn his old man blushed. His dad turned his head and reached for a shingle. "I gotta get this done. Gonna get dark soon."

"I'll give you a hand."

"Not in that fancy suit, you're not. You go help your momma. I'll be down shortly."

JJ was going to ask what in the world he was supposed to help his mother do but decided to let it slide. *One step at a time.*

chapter 29

Paula didn't normally read the paper before she went to work. She seldom had time. It wouldn't have mattered. No fewer than four different people accosted her as she made her way from the front door to her desk, anxious to show her the ad in the paper.

Someone else, determined to be first, had set the ad on her desk in full view so she couldn't possibly miss it.

The ad had roses along its border and a large heart at the bottom of the page. The words, in bold script, were simple and to the point.

Paula Horne, you are the love of my life. I can't imagine living my life without you at my side. I want to be your husband, your best friend, your confidant, and your soul mate. Marry me and make me the happiest man on earth. All my love forever, Matt.

An hour later, at precisely ten o'clock, a dozen long-stemmed red roses were delivered in a white box. There was no note. None was necessary.

"Marry the guy and put him out of his misery," one of the older women in the department told her. "If *you* don't, I will."

"I'll fight you for him," the receptionist interjected.

At noon, a white stretch limo pulled up in front of her office.

Work stopped. Keyboards went silent. Phones rang unanswered. Everyone watched as a chauffeur opened the back door of the limo and a man climbed out dressed in a tuxedo with tails and a top hat. His hands wore white gloves and firmly held a silver tray covered with a white cloth.

"Paula! This has got to be for you."

"Paula! Please tell him no and give me a shot!"

"If you don't want him, Paula, I do."

Curious and fascinated, Paula ignored all comments as she watched the chauffeur rush up and open the front door of the building. The man in the tuxedo strutted in and asked for Miss Paula Horne. The receptionist, struck dumb, merely pointed in Paula's direction.

Paula stood there as the man walked up to her and set the silver tray on her desk. He whipped off the white linen napkin to reveal a white rose, a rolled scroll tied with a red ribbon, and a ring box. Then he leaned forward and handed her the rose. She took it, still stunned.

All her coworkers sidled over, trying to get a firsthand look at what was happening. There were giggles, a groan (purely masculine), whispering, and audible sighs.

The man lifted the scroll and made a great production of untying and setting aside the ribbon. He opened the scroll.

"Master Owen Paul Horne, in accordance with the traditions of marriage, does hereby formally grant his permission to Master Matthew Jonathon Casto to present a proposal of marriage to his daughter, Paula Marie Horne, and enter into a covenant of love and honor to last no less than one hundred years. So signed by Master Owen Horne and Master Matthew Jonathon Casto and duly notarized."

The scroll was rerolled and handed to Paula. She couldn't help shaking her head and smiling. Matt had actually gone to her father and asked for her hand in marriage. And her father had said yes! Her father had never approved of Matt, calling him flighty and undependable. Matt must have pulled out all the stops to get her unyielding dad to go along with this.

The ring box was lifted in white gloved hands as if it were a fragile piece of crystal. He opened the ring box and she gasped.

"Master Matthew Jonathon Casto requests the honor of your hand in marriage."

Stunned, Paula felt her heart flip. She'd wanted a gesture. She'd wanted him to show some effort.

She'd never expected anything like this.

With trembling hands, she reached out and lifted the ring from the box. It was gorgeous. It was huge. It must have cost him a fortune. She started to cry as she slid the ring on her finger.

She lifted her head and stared at the stranger. "Yes."

He nodded without so much as a smile, but Paula could have sworn she saw a twinkle in his eyes. He turned on his heel and strode out of the building, disappearing inside the limo.

"So much for Matt," breathed one of the secretaries. "But what about that gorgeous blond in the tuxedo?"

Paula stared at the ring on her hand, twisting it from one side to the other, watching it catch and magnify the light, shimmering like fire.

She looked up in time to see Matt tumbling out of the limo. He tugged at his jacket and then practically ran into the building. He skidded to a halt a few feet from her desk. Paula circled her desk and stopped. "I didn't expect this."

"Me either," he said breathlessly.

"I love you."

"I love you, too."

"Yeah," Paula replied, choking out a giggle. "I can see that you do." And then she jumped into his arms.

Her mind barely registered all the applause, wolf whistles, and cheers.

Inside the limo, Donnie pulled off the white gloves and tossed them on the seat. "Another job well done, Donnie Bevere. Once again, you have outdone yourself."

"Facts are facts and the facts don't lie."

Justus Gallagher, one of the top forensic pathologists in the state, frowned as he studied the body stretched out on the stainless-steel autopsy table. He spun his stool around and scooted it back over to the microscope on the counter behind him. Squinting, he looked again. Frowned again.

It didn't add up.

Vivian Amato, humming something that sounded vaguely familiar, was across the room working on one of the unidentified bodies of a child uncovered in Emmitt Falls. "Aha. So, you're Kimberly Fields. Hello, Kimberly."

Justus looked over at her, eager to take his mind off his problems for a minute. "ID one?"

"Yeah. Medical records indicate that Kimberly Fields had surgery on her leg when she was eight months old. And guess what this little bone just told me?"

"Surgery."

"Bingo. So unless there are two little girls who had surgery on their left tibia, we've found Kimberly." She made a notation on a chart and then looked over at him again. "Problem on your end?"

"You could say that."

She set her clipboard on the counter and walked over, her scrubs rustling as she walked. "What have you got?"

"Discrepancy."

"In what way?"

"Well, according to the police, Ted Matthews disappeared on the night of the twentieth. He was seen at work that day. He was seen by his wife that night."

Vivian tilted her head impatiently. "Get to the point."

"This body," he pointed to the autopsy table, "was dead a good three days before that."

"Impossible." Vivian drew closer, keeping her hands aloft to prevent any contamination from one body to another, and looked into the microscope. "Well, phooey."

She backed up, her gaze moving from the microscope to the body and then back to Justus. "We've got us an anomaly."

"We've got us a John Doe. Not only was this man dead while Ted Matthews was still walking and talking, this man shows deterioration in the liver that indicates extensive alcohol consumption. According to these medical records, Edward Matthews was a nondrinker."

"A little nip on the side, perhaps?" Now she was frowning.

Justus shook his head. "We're talking severe alcoholic. And over a long period of time. No way to hide the kind of drinking this man did."

"Okay, I hate to ask the obvious, but what about blood work?"

"I was just about to call and see if it's ready."

She nodded and headed back across the room. "If you're right, we're going to have one very unhappy homicide cop on our case."

"Facts are facts and the facts don't lie."

chapter 30

Friday, April 28

He watched dispassionately as she struggled against the ropes that held her in the ladder-back chair. Every once in awhile, she would look at him and glare daggers, but they didn't faze him. She wasn't going anywhere. He would have disposed of her already, but he wasn't done with her yet.

"You might as well give up. You won't get loose."

She turned a tear-streaked face in his direction and then spit at him, her eyes overflowing with venom.

"I'm impressed," he said dryly. "A few feet more and you might have hit my shoes."

"You won't get away with this!"

He smiled, amused with her persistence. "Dear woman, I've already gotten away with it."

"They will catch you!"

He shrugged, letting the comment roll off easily. "They aren't smart enough."

"They're smarter than you think! They're just luring you in!"

This time he was amused enough to laugh. "Of course they are. How silly of me not to realize that. And you were the bait? Is that it? I

suppose those smart FBI agents are surrounding this building as we
speak. I am so afraid."

He shook his head in disgust. "Please don't insult my intelligence."

The cell phone on the table rang, and his lips twitched in anticipa-
tion. It was time for the next round of the game to begin. He picked up
the phone.

"Hello?"

"Who is this?"

"Mr. Shefford! How delightful to hear from you. I do suppose you
called to talk to your ex-wife, but I'm afraid she's a little tied up at the
moment."

"Tied up? Who is this? Where is she?"

"Scream for him, Mrs. Shefford. Let him know how frightened you
truly are at this moment."

Karen stared emotionless at the featureless interview room, ignoring her brother as he waved his hands, talked, pleaded, and cajoled.
She studied the dull gray walls, cracked floor tiles of gray and white,
metal table, metal chairs, barred window.

Her brother was upset about her decision to leave Jessica with the
McCaines. How could she make him understand? She was going to
prison! It didn't matter that she hadn't killed anyone. No one believed
her. And if the police didn't believe her, why would a jury?

Between the time she was arrested and the time she was locked
into her cell, the truth had set in. Ted had set her up. No one else
could have done it. He said he was going to meet with the kidnappers. He told her not to call the police. Then he didn't come back.
Their money was gone, a bloody knife appeared conveniently in her
kitchen, and a dead body showed up in the backyard.

That's when she'd lost all hope. God had abandoned her. Fate had conspired against her. Her life was over. Nothing would ever be the same.

Ray's hand slapped the table hard and she jumped.

"If you don't listen to me, Karen, I swear I'm. . ." He sputtered.

"Ray, you don't understand."

"I understand all too well. You've given up!"

She leaned forward, her hands clasped in front of her. "Ray, listen to me. It's over. Ted won. I'm going to prison."

"No! God is *not* going to abandon you."

Frustrated, Karen flopped back in her chair, throwing her hands up in the air. "He's already abandoned me! Don't you see that?"

"No, I don't. He may be testing your faith, but—"

"Testing my faith?" Karen snapped. "You call this testing my faith? I've been arrested for premeditated murder, Ray. Murder. No bail, do not pass go, do not collect two hundred dollars."

Ray slapped the table again. "We prayed to get Jessica back and God brought her back to you! Do you think that was just chance? Do you know how easy it would have been for those people just to turn a blind eye to the fliers? They love that baby. They thought that baby was theirs. God intervened and they came forward with her. That was God talking to you, Karen! Is this over? No. But being the loving God that He is, He gave you a sign. He's still here and it's going to work out. He's given you something to hold on to through the rest of this."

"Well, He hasn't given me enough."

Karen looked over at Detective Johnson, who was still leaning against the wall, arms folded across his chest, listening to the entire conversation with a curious expression on his face. "Can I go back to my cell now?"

JJ pushed off from the wall. "If that's what you want."

She stood up. "It's what I want." Turning, she placed her hands behind her back so he could snap the handcuffs back on.

"Can I ask you a question, Mrs. Matthews?"

She shrugged silently.

"I admit that I don't know what I believe about God, but answer me this. If you call yourself a Christian, what good is it if when things go wrong, you blame God and turn your back on Him?"

Zoe brushed at the tears that ran freely down her cheeks. He had her mother! A half-hour earlier, her father's knees had buckled and he'd slid to the floor. He'd stared at the phone in disbelief and then dropped it as if it had suddenly burned his hand.

"He has your mother," he'd said. Then he'd looked up at her with horror still framing his eyes. *"He said you were the next one to join Gina in the garden of death."*

Vince had immediately called Fleming. Any minute now they would descend like scavengers, picking at every nuance and word in the message, considering possibilities and scenarios, ripping apart objections to their authority.

Zoe chewed on her thumbnail as she looked at her father, his arms wrapped around his midsection. He was pale and shaken. She watched him struggle with fear and wished there were some way to ease his pain. He buried his head in his hands, his shoulders shaking.

When they'd asked her to help, she'd agreed without a second thought. Now that she knew her mother's life was at risk, she had more than a fair share of doubts. One wrong move on her part and her mother could die.

Suddenly Fleming bolted through the front door with JJ and Matt. Zoe had no more time to guess, second-guess, or question anything.

JJ never looked in her direction. The only sign that he was uncomfortable with the situation was the way he kept fidgeting. His hands would go in his pockets, only to reappear a few seconds later and be folded across his chest. He'd rest his fists on his hips, then run his fingers through his hair, then stuff his hands back into his pants pockets.

She turned away and sat silently while the men discussed options, argued over methods, and eventually agreed on a plan. Meanwhile, her mother—her gentle, sweet mother—was in the hands of a madman.

Five minutes passed. Then ten. Then fifteen. Police officers came and went. Agents checked in with Fleming and disappeared out the door. Still no one said a word to Zoe or her father.

Jumping to her feet, she clenched her fists. "Enough!"

Sudden silence. Everyone in the room turned and stared at her as if she'd lost her mind. Well, maybe she had. She didn't care much what they thought. "While you all stand around talking, my mother is being terrorized!"

Her father turned pale, and Zoe immediately regretted her words. "I'm sorry. I can't just sit here and do nothing."

Donnie Bevere took a step toward her. "I know this is hard for you, Miss Shefford, but you have to trust us. We're going to get your mother back safe and sound."

"Don't give me that routine, Agent Bevere. I've worked with law enforcement for years. You can't guarantee anything. You need me to calm down to make things easier for you. The last thing you want is a hysterical female in the mix. For all you know, my mother could be dead right now while you're making promises."

Keyes released a keening sound that made Zoe's blood run cold. She ran to him, dropping to her knees in front of him, grabbing his hands in hers. "I didn't mean it, Dad. She's alive. You know she is."

He stared at her with unfocused eyes. "Is she?"

Dropping her head to his knees, she struggled to gather her strength. She lifted her head again. "Can't you tell? Don't you think you would know if something happened to her?"

"I don't know, Zoe. I just don't know. I keep praying for God to keep her safe, but I know God won't interfere with free will. If that lunatic wants to kill her—"

"Dad! He won't. He wants me. Mom is only bait to get to me. Don't you see? He needs her."

She saw it then. A subtle shift in his eyes, a tightening around his mouth. He was struggling with something more than the fact that the woman he loved was in the hands of a madman.

"Dad? What is it?"

He started to shake his head. Stopped. Stared at her again. "Can you *feel* anything?"

The question rocked her back on her heels. It was the last thing she expected from him. And yet, in an odd way, she couldn't blame him. She'd been wrestling with the same question herself.

"I don't know. I haven't. . . I don't think I should. . . I don't know what to do."

She felt her soul being ripped in half. She had renounced her psychic abilities. If she used them now to try to find her mother, she'd be renouncing God. Could she even sense anything now that she'd renounced the gift? It might not work, and then she'd have turned her back on God for nothing. But what if she *could* sense where her mother was?

A cold sweat formed and trickled down her sides.

What was it Rene had told her? She rubbed her forehead with her fingertips, trying to remember. Something about gifts being given without repentance. *What mattered was how they were used.*

But she didn't know how to use her gift the way God intended.

She crawled over to the phone and yanked it off its receiver.

"Zoe, I didn't mean to ask. I'm sorry. Don't do it."

She glanced at her father and saw the misery pooling in his eyes. This was torturing him, and she was the only one who could stop it.

Pulling her eyes away, she punched in Rene's phone number. It rang three times. Then four. "Come on, Rene. Where are you when I need you?"

It rang again. And again. She slammed down the phone. There would be no help this time. She would have to make this decision on her own. Could she live with herself if her mother died and she hadn't even tried to find her?

Her father reached out with a shaking hand. "I can't ask you to do this. We have to trust God."

"Can you?" she asked in a rough whisper.

"We have to try." He took a deep breath as tears streamed down his face again. "We have to try."

"I don't know if I can, Dad."

Justus Gallagher ran long, thin fingers through his red hair as his foot rocked back and forth under the tall stool.

"What does it say?" Vivian stepped into the autopsy room, tying her scrubs.

"Edward Matthews was O negative."

"And the body?"

"B."

"Ouch." Vivian reached for a pair of latex gloves. "Well, call Johnson or Tripp and let them know."

Zoe paced. Then stopped. She glanced at her watch. Nearly two hours had passed since her last attempt to reach Rene. She'd left a message, but Rene hadn't called back.

The late afternoon sun streamed down through the trees, highlighting some areas, shadowing others. A squirrel appeared in the front yard, sniffed the air, turned, and quickly darted off.

Zoe turned away from the window and started pacing again.

JJ, Fleming, Matt, Bevere, Vince, and a host of other police officers and FBI agents were scattered all over the house and yard. Fleming had commandeered her rarely used family room downstairs as a command post. Occasionally someone would come up and get coffee or water and then disappear again. No one told her anything. It was driving her crazy. Her only consolation—small thing though it was—was that Vince, sitting near her father, was probably getting dizzy watching her pace.

She took a deep breath and looked in the hall mirror. There were circles under her eyes and worry lines around her mouth. She was pale and her hair was mussed from constantly running her hands through it. She was a mess.

And she felt worse than she looked.

She spun on her heel and headed for the kitchen. Where was he? What was taking so long? Why hadn't he called back? What was he doing to her mother? The thought hit her mind and pain washed over her with the intensity of ice water on a hot day. *Please, God. I don't care about me, but don't let anything happen to my mom.*

Heavy footsteps thundered up the basement steps. She glanced over, expecting to see Matt with an empty coffeepot. But it was JJ who came through the door this time. His eyes met hers then darted away as he headed for the back door. With his hand on the knob, he turned his head and stared at her. He licked his lips nervously. "Why don't you try to relax? He's not going to call again today. It's part of his game to make you suffer."

She shook her head. "He's going to call again. I know he is."

"Not today. Maybe not even tomorrow."

He reached out and touched her shoulder. She flinched, backing away from him. "We're going to get him, Zoe. I promise you, we're going to get him."

"Before or after he kills my mother?"

"He's not going to hurt your mother until he's sure he doesn't need her to get to you."

The words had the effect of a blow, causing her to stagger back a step or two.

"I'm sorry, Zoe. That was insensitive of me."

"Nothing new," Zoe whispered to herself as JJ stepped outside and pulled the door closed. *Insensitive, but also the cold, hard truth.* As long as this maniac needed Denise Shefford, she was safe. The trouble would come when he had Zoe. Then what was to stop him from killing her mother?

Karen followed the officer down the long hall. She had no idea what she was about to face. No one had told her a thing. She'd asked, of course, but the officer had said he didn't know.

He stopped, opened the door to Lieutenant Tripp's office, and then stepped aside to allow her to enter.

She stepped inside to find Ray, her attorney, and Tripp waiting for her. Tripp didn't look the least bit happy. Ray looked ecstatic.

Tripp nodded to the officer at the door. "Uncuff her."

The cuffs fell away and Karen rubbed her wrists. "Now what? Rubber hoses?"

Ray swept her up in a hug. "It wasn't Ted. The autopsy proved it."

Ted was alive. She didn't know how that made her feel.

Suddenly she frowned. "Then who was that man?"

Tripp sat on the edge of his desk, folding his arms across his chest. "We were hoping you might know."

"I have no idea."

Benson picked up his briefcase. "I believe that takes care of everything. You know where to reach my client if you have any further questions." He turned to Karen. "Let's go home, Mrs. Matthews."

"Home? You mean. . .I'm free?"

"The man they found had been strangled. You aren't tall enough or strong enough to have pulled it off. They arrested you for the murder of your husband. That man is not your husband. Therefore, all charges have been dropped and you are free to go."

"Just don't leave town," Tripp added gruffly.

◆　　◆　　◆

Just after seven, Matt came through the front door with a stack of pizzas and a case of sodas. While the men downstairs ate, Vince and another agent relieved the two men posted outside so they could take a short break.

Neither Zoe nor Keyes ate a bite. They sat in the living room staring at a sitcom on TV and never cracking a smile.

At 11:00 P.M., Fleming came upstairs and told Zoe he was sending everyone home except two agents who would be staying at the house. The rest planned to return in the morning.

Zoe nodded, too exhausted, both mentally and emotionally, to ask him what they'd been doing in her basement for the past six or seven hours.

A little while later, she convinced her father to lie down in the guest room. After taking off his shoes, she covered him with a blanket.

Clutching at the blanket, he started to tear up again. "I can smell your mother's perfume. Am I going crazy?"

Zoe shook her head as she reached out and stroked his cheek. "No. Mom stayed here the other night."

He tugged the blanket closer to his chin and closed his eyes.

As she stepped out of the room and started to pull the door closed, she heard her father. "Zoe?"

"Yeah, Dad?"

"I love her. I've always loved her. Do you know how I met her?"

Zoe stood in the doorway, leaning against the doorjamb. "Tell me again. I don't remember."

"It was a frat party. She came with a friend of hers and she hated it. Hated every minute of it. You could tell. She stood in a corner and just watched everyone drinking and dancing all around her. It was like she was above it all. None of it could touch her. That fascinated me. It took me twenty minutes before I could even get her to talk to me."

"And she fell in love with you."

"Not right away." His voice drifted across to her as if coming from a deep tunnel. "I kept asking her out and she kept turning me down. She said she didn't have anything in common with a boy who was more involved with frat parties than he was with his studies."

Zoe smiled to herself. Her mom had been no fool, even back then. "What did you do?"

"I lied. Told her that I had only been there at the party because I promised a friend I'd go."

"And she believed you?"

"No. But she went out with me anyway." There was the sound of a husky chuckle. "I think I just wore her down."

"She did fall in love with you though."

"Yes. Yes, she did. And she married me. Then I blew it. I knew how seriously she took things, and I blew it anyway."

"That was then, Dad. She's forgiven you. You can get married again and—"

"We were never divorced, Zoe."

That shocked her. She'd always assumed they had divorced right after Amy disappeared. "I thought she filed for divorce. I could swear I remember her talking about meeting with an attorney."

"She threatened to. But she didn't. She said that if I wanted to divorce her, then I could sue her for divorce. She said she'd taken a vow for life and was going to stay married to me for life, even if we never lived in the same house again."

"I didn't know."

She heard him sigh heavily and waited to see if he was going to say anything else. When he didn't, she whispered goodnight and quietly closed the door.

The despair in her father's voice stayed with Zoe as she took a shower and changed into a pair of light blue cotton drawstring pants and a T-shirt. Her stomach wanted food, but her breaking heart trumped the hunger. She stretched out on her bed in the dark and stared at the ceiling. Was her mother asleep? Or was this lunatic keeping her awake? Was she alone but too frightened to sleep?

God, please. I don't know You all that well. I know it's going to take time for me to understand You and trust You the way people like Rene do, but I don't know where else to turn. You're the only one who can protect my mom. And help my dad through this. Please.

She must have fallen asleep, because suddenly she choked awake. It was still pitch dark, so she knew it was the middle of the night. Gasping for air, she turned and looked at the clock. It was blank.

Did the electricity go off?

Why is it so hard to breathe?

It was then she heard the screams. She tried to sit up, but her limbs felt weighed down. Suddenly she jolted awake. Smoke. Acrid, thick, black smoke. It was obliterating everything.

Sirens wailed in the distance as she rolled off the bed and started crawling toward the bedroom door. Confused and panicked, she went in the wrong direction and slammed headfirst into her dresser. She turned and headed for the door.

She groped in the dark for the door handle and found it. Voices shouted in the distance. The sirens were growing louder.

"Dad!"

She staggered to her feet and rushed into the guest room. Her father was groping in the dark and their hands met. "Zoe! What's going on?"

"Fire. Maybe next door. I don't know. Come on! We have to get out!"

They made their way down the hall to the living room, trying to stay as close to the floor as possible. Zoe could hear Vince coughing violently. She let go of her father. "Vince?"

He'd been asleep on the sofa. She ran her hands across the cushions but couldn't find him.

"He's over here," her father yelled.

The sirens were blaring just outside, the strobe lights on the trucks alternately flashing red and white. They lit an eerie path to the front door.

Zoe helped her dad get Vince to his feet. "Take him out. I'm right behind you. I need to grab the photo album."

"Forget the photo album!"

She shoved her father out the door and turned to make her way back into the living room. Coughing as the smoke thickened, she frantically ran her hands over the bookshelf until her fingers closed around the leather-bound book. She lifted it from the shelf and pressed it against her chest.

"I've got you," a disembodied voice said. She felt a blanket sweep around her. A flash of white light from the truck outside illuminated the fireman's neon stripes on his turnout coat. He lifted her into his arms.

A few seconds later, her lungs caught a touch of fresh air and erupted into a spasm of coughing.

"Just breathe nice and easy. I'll get you oxygen in just one second."

"Zoe!"

She heard her father's voice and tried to turn her head.

"She's fine, sir. Stand back. I need to get her an oxygen mask. Stay right there. Someone will help you in just a moment."

Then they were moving again. She looked over the fireman's shoulder to see her townhouse and the one next to it engulfed in flames. Nothing would survive that. For a brief second, she wanted to mourn all that she would lose. The moment passed and she felt thankful everyone got out alive.

The fireman set her down. "You're going to be just fine." She felt a slight prick on her thigh. "I've got you, Zoe."

Her mind started to go fuzzy and her limbs grew heavy. One thought penetrated the fog in her brain.

How does he know my name?

chapter 31

Saturday, April 29

JJ could see the flames shooting into the air from two blocks away. His heart jumped, racing as fast as the engine of his vehicle. He took a left turn, squealing the tires and fishtailing erratically before he brought the vehicle under control.

He'd been at the office, stretched out in his chair, his feet on his desk. He was sound asleep when the call came through. He, Fleming, and Bevere had raced down the stairs and out the station door.

Now Fleming screamed into his cell phone, trying to reach the agent stationed outside Zoe's house. He shut the phone. "Fire chief says they got everyone out alive. Shefford's home and the connecting townhouse are fully engulfed. From the looks of it, he thinks it started next door to Miss Shefford and spread. That's not yet confirmed."

JJ sighed with relief as he skidded the car to a stop behind one of the fire engines. Fleming and Bevere were right behind him as he wove through ambulances and fire trucks, stepping over water hoses and dodging firefighters.

He stopped at the curb and stared at the destruction. Most of the flames were succumbing to the walls of water being showered down on them, and smoke billowed into the night sky, a light gray against the black.

Both townhouses would be a total loss.

JJ spotted Keyes sitting on the rear bumper of an ambulance, a blanket around his shoulders. An EMT held an oxygen mask to his mouth.

He walked over and nodded to the EMT, flashing his badge. "Keyes? Where's Zoe?"

Keyes gave him a blank stare that slowly cleared. "Zoe? She was with one of the firefighters."

"Where?"

Keyes pointed somewhere behind him. "He took her that way."

JJ nodded and walked where Keyes had pointed. No Zoe. He walked around every truck, stopped at every ambulance, talking to one firefighter after another. No one had seen Zoe.

Bevere showed up at his side a few minutes later. "Find Zoe?"

JJ shook his head as he stopped and looked around. He should have been able to find her by now.

"We got another problem."

"What's that?"

Donnie edged JJ away from a group of neighbors clustered on the sidewalk watching the action. "Linc. The agent posted outside. He's dead."

JJ's brows raised. "What?"

Bevere shook his head. "One shot to the temple. He never saw it coming."

Realization came fast and hard. "This was a diversion. He has her!"

"Looks that way."

"He got Zoe." JJ slammed his open hand against the side of the fire truck. "I want a roadblock set up now!"

"It's in the works."

He grabbed his cell phone and dialed the station for backup. "I want them here on the double! And call Casto!"

JJ spied Fleming walking toward them, talking furiously into his cell phone, a stormy look on his face. He stopped when he reached them.

"No, I do not want to hear excuses. I want it done now!" He lifted his eyes to the power lines above their heads. "Let me put it this way: If it's not done within the next fifteen minutes, there are going to be some very abrupt ends to some careers. Do you copy that?"

JJ's gaze drifted over Fleming's shoulder as the first pale ribbons of dawn began to appear on the horizon. The day was off to a real bad start.

No sirens. No shouts. No engines. It seemed as if the world had been swallowed up in silence. Zoe tried to open her eyes but found it difficult. Her body felt heavy, as if the blood that ran though her veins had turned to lead. She didn't know where she was. She didn't know what time it was, or even what day. Time came to a sudden halt and she drifted in a cloud of nothingness.

She had a vague recollection of flames and smoke, but it was more a dream than a memory. A photograph album. A fireman. Her father's voice. Had it been real, or was she on the edge of a nightmare?

A voice drifted through the silence and into her thoughts. *Familiar. Male.* She reached for it with her mind and recoiled.

"Ah, my dear Zoe. How foolish of you to think you could beat me at my own game."

◆ ◆ ◆

Justus leaned against the counter, his powdered donut dusting his chin and shirt as he ate. He watched the antiquated fax machine send his request slower than an old tortoise on his way to the soup pot. He glanced at the clock. It wasn't six yet, but he was still hoping to receive a response within the hour. He was hanging his hopes on the off chance that someone would come in early on a Saturday.

He was close to identifying the John Doe found in the Matthews' backyard. An examination of the victim's teeth revealed dental work infamous in the military. A piece of shrapnel in the man's hip confirmed Justus's suspicions.

Finishing his poor excuse for a breakfast, Justus brushed off the powdered sugar and reached for his coffee. He'd been up for almost thirty-six hours straight and felt every minute of it. A glance in the mirror would confirm he looked horrible, so he avoided looking.

It didn't matter anyway. Solving this mystery was far more important than his looks.

◆ ◆ ◆

Zoe heard herself whimper, but the sound was distant and detached. Her head hurt, her body ached, and she couldn't feel her legs. She tried to lift a hand to her face, but it refused to move.

Slowly, painfully, she opened her eyes and blinked, trying to see through blurred vision and dark shadows. She smelled dirt, decay, and dust. The air was dank and heavy with mold. Little by little her vision cleared and she could make out the cellar—the dirt floor, the concrete walls, the spider webs, the narrow staircase, a door.

"Mom?"

There was no answer.

She wiggled her fingers and felt the rough fibers of the blanket below her and the cold metal frame of a cot. She was tied down.

Lifting her head a little, she glanced at the ropes binding her arms and feet. She let her head fall gently back to the cot.

"Where is my mother, you filthy piece of human trash!" she screamed as loud as she could.

A door hinge creaked and she knew he was there, somewhere in the shadows. She could feel the evil as sure as if the devil himself had entered the room.

"Ah, so you're awake. How delightful." He remained in the shadows. Watching.

"Where is my mother?"

"Alive. And that's all you need concern yourself with at the moment. How long she remains that way depends entirely on you."

"Why don't I believe you?"

He laughed. "Because you don't trust me. I can't imagine why. But then again, you're a woman. One can't expect you to understand everything."

She narrowed her eyes, trying to see the murky silhouette. "I understand enough to know that you are sick."

Then he moved.

A sliver of light from the room behind him illuminated his face.

She gasped. "You! How. . .but. . ."

The look in his eyes sent a shiver down her back.

"My dear Zoe, now you understand why I couldn't allow you to live."

chapter 32

Karen placed a hand on Ray's arm. "Stay here." She didn't wait for acknowledgment as she slowly made her way to the front of the church. She stared up at the cross on the wall behind the pulpit, trying to formulate the words in her heart.

Dropping to her knees on the velvet-padded altar, she bowed her head. "Thank You. You were faithful even when I wasn't. You were there even when I didn't believe You were. And in spite of all my faults and all my doubts and all my inadequacies, You stayed in control. Help me to never doubt You again."

She heard the door open behind her and the whisper of additional voices. With one last word of thanks, she stood to her feet and turned around.

Nora McCaine stood next to Ray with Jessica in her arms. Benson had called Nora from the police station to arrange Jessica's return. Karen insisted that the meeting take place at the church. The Lord had brought her baby back to her. What better place for her happy reunion than in His house.

She walked briskly to the rear of the church and, with a flood of tears, reached for her daughter. She couldn't see Jessica's face through the blur of emotion, but she didn't need to. She could smell her familiar baby smell. She could feel Jessica in her arms. She could hear Jessica's familiar whimper.

"Hey, baby. Mommy has you now. Everything's okay now."

She knew even as she said the words that they weren't entirely true. Ted was still unaccounted for and would remain a constant threat. And she wouldn't be blind anymore to the fact that evil was out there, ready to pounce on innocent lives. It would take every bit of her will to keep Jessica safe without smothering her with overzealous protection.

Lifting her eyes, she blinked and smiled at Nora McCaine—a woman with a heart as big as Karen's love. "I can't even begin to thank you for all you've done."

"You don't have to. She was the delight of our lives. We're going to miss her so much."

Karen reached out as Nora's voice began to shake. "Don't. Don't walk out of her life. You're an important part of it for her and for me. I want us to be friends. I never gave Jessica godparents. I'd be honored if you and your husband would consider taking the job."

Nora choked out a laugh and a crooked smile as she leaned into her husband. "I'd love that."

Karen squeezed Nora's hand. "Good."

After a few more minutes, Karen walked out of the church with Ray at her side and Jessica in her arms. She looked back. "Why aren't Nora and Charles coming?"

"They're talking to Rene." Ray grinned down at her. "It seems a young girl came to Rene and Jeff a few days ago. She got pregnant and she's just sixteen. She wants to give her baby up for adoption to someone special."

Karen smiled. "They don't come much more special than Nora and Charles McCaine. I hope it works out for them."

"Somehow I think the Lord has this all worked out."

Karen laughed as he opened the car door for her. "For once, I am not going to disagree with you."

"Good. Now I'm going to take you and my niece out for breakfast."

◆ ◆ ◆

JJ was leaning so far over the seat that he was almost in Donnie's lap as Fleming drove and Donnie studied the screen. "Take a right here."

Donnie glared over his shoulder at JJ. "Do you mind?"

"No." Ignoring Donnie's hint, JJ studied the screen for himself. It wasn't all that hard to figure out. The little dot that was stationary, and had been for the past fifteen minutes, was Zoe. That the little point of light kept blinking was no indication, however, that her heart was still beating or that her lungs were still drawing air.

And it was driving him crazy.

Thirty minutes after the discovery of the murdered agent, Fleming and his forces were already tracking Zoe. They figured the killer had about an hour's lead on them. Every minute counted.

They had wasted almost five minutes trying to calm Keyes and convince him to stay behind.

"Left! Left!" Donnie jumped in his seat and JJ jumped with him, startled by the sudden high-pitched emotion in the agent's voice.

JJ was thrown sideways against the door as Fleming hit the brakes and turned the wheel sharply. The car bounced as it slid onto a dirt road with more ruts than a railroad crossing.

They were heading south-southwest, deeper into land covered with dairy farms, soybean fields, and trees.

The dirt road curled and wove through thick patches of foliage that nearly obliterated any sunlight. JJ had no idea where they were, and sweat trickled down his back. They could, at any moment, break out of the trees and be right on top of where Zoe was, losing all element of surprise. They could, even now, be close enough for the killer to hear the car engines.

JJ turned and looked out the back window. It was hard to see clearly through the dust kicked up by the tires, but the other cars were still behind them.

"Slow down," Donnie instructed Fleming. "We're close."

JJ felt his lungs empty in a sudden rush of adrenalin. He reached down and pulled his weapon out of its holster. With one practiced movement, he dropped the clip, checked to make sure it was full, and then popped it back into the handle. He pulled back the slide and felt the nervous anticipation that always came with the sound of a bullet being chambered.

Fleming slowed the car to a stop. JJ tugged the blue cap he'd been given lower over his eyes and climbed out of the car. White FBI letters were emblazoned on the front of the cap for immediate identification in the heat of battle.

JJ wouldn't be keeping the hat as a souvenir. The FBI weren't earning any brownie points with him.

Within moments, a crowd of blue uniforms, black suits, and Kevlar vests congregated around Donnie. He spoke quietly, making eye contact with as many as he could as his gaze swept the group. "Directly west, maybe a hundred and fifty to two hundred yards. We have no idea what we're facing, so be cautious, keep your eyes open, and be ready for anything. We have two women in danger, and we want them both coming out of this alive."

JJ tuned him out as Donnie formed groups and fanned them out in a sweep to surround the target area. His mind was already tuning into the path he was assigned. Anything could be waiting for them. One wrong move and this whole thing could go wrong. Terribly wrong.

Donnie nodded at him. "Let's go."

Somewhere along the way, JJ had learned to trust Bevere. When the rubber hit the road, Donnie was a solid, no-nonsense, confident FBI agent with more sense than age and enough training to make him dangerous to the wrong people.

And in less than three minutes, JJ found out something else about Donnie Bevere: The man was no stranger to moving through the woods like a hunter. He was an expert. JJ suspected Bevere had spent years learning to move silently upon his prey, blending in with the brush and all but disappearing into the foliage.

"You were raised in the country," JJ whispered.

Donnie smiled. "Shh. Don't tell anyone. You'll ruin my big-city image."

They continued in silence for another few minutes—Donnie leading with JJ just behind and to his right. Suddenly Donnie stopped, held up two fingers, and then pointed to his left. JJ nodded, palmed his weapon, and slipped away to Donnie's left.

Zoe stumbled and nearly fell as he pushed her from behind. He grabbed her arm and yanked her around. "Don't play with me! I'll kill her right now in front of you!"

Zoe's eyes flashed with rage as she straightened, jerking her arm away from him. "You may have already killed her for all I know! Where is she?"

He shoved her through the door. Bare light bulbs hung from the ceiling. The light blinded her for a second. She blinked. There was another cot, another chair, but her mother wasn't in either of them.

She was sitting on the cold concrete floor, chained to the wall.

"Mom!" Her mother didn't move—didn't appear to hear her.

Zoe tried to run forward, but he yanked her back. "You animal! How could you do that to her?"

"You wanted to see her; now you've seen her." He shoved her down on the bed, picked up a roll of duct tape from under the cot, and tore a piece off, sticking it across her mouth.

"That should keep you quiet."

JJ eased his head around the tree and studied the small cabin. It was small—maybe two or three rooms—and in desperate need of attention. Windows were boarded up, the porch sagged precariously, and the roof looked like one good wind could send it toppling.

He felt his heart lurch. Then he shook off the fear. He had a job to do. *Stay focused. Breathe. In. Out. Steady. Pay attention.*

A soft whistle to his right brought his attention to Donnie. The agent nodded and then waved JJ toward the front porch. JJ acknowledged him with a quick nod of his own and then held up three fingers.

On three. One. Two. Three.

JJ spun out from behind the tree and ran, zigzagging, tucked low, toward the porch. He dived behind the woodpile and took another deep breath. Then he cautiously raised his head toward Donnie and nodded. Seconds later, Donnie came darting across the same way JJ had. He disappeared on the other side of the porch.

Then he stuck his head up. JJ watched Donnie as he keyed the microphone to his headset and quietly checked in with the rest of the team surrounding the house.

Donnie looked at JJ and pointed to the front door. JJ nodded and slowly moved out from behind the woodpile in a low crouch.

He stepped carefully onto the porch, wincing when a board creaked softly. He backed up against the building and moved sideways toward the door.

Donnie came up on the other side. He nodded and, with one swift kick, knocked down the door. JJ went in low—Donnie high. Their guns swept the room as fast as their eyes did.

JJ saw it first. He slowly straightened, feeling the blood rush to his feet.

"Donnie?"

Donnie looked at JJ and then followed JJ's gaze. "That smart son of a swamp rat." Donnie reached out and picked up the ankle bracelet Zoe had been wearing.

JJ picked up the note that lay next to it.

"You lose."

Zoe watched as he tied her to the cot. He pulled the knot tight. She winced.

He gazed down at her, smiling with confidence or arrogance or perhaps both. "If you're depending on that little tracking device they put around your ankle, forget it. It came in handy though. Gives me more time while they chase their tails."

Rocking back on his haunches, he laughed. "Did you really expect those Feds to come running to your rescue? Or maybe you were expecting Detective Josiah Johnson to be your hero." He spit on the ground between his feet in disdain. "The man couldn't find a criminal if he was locked in the same room with him."

Furious, JJ stalked out of the cabin.

"We're going to get him."

"And pigs fly. . ." JJ whirled around and glared at Donnie. "When? After he kills her or before?"

"He has to be close by."

"How do you figure that? Did he leave you some obscure message I missed?"

"There was no time." Donnie explained in a quiet voice.

"He has all the time in the world! He could be anywhere. He could be over the state border. He could be holed up on the other side of the county."

"Vince found tire tracks out back. The ground was soft. He left us a trail, and I don't think he knows it."

JJ rolled his eyes. "How long do you think that trail is going to last? Let me give you a hint. Until he hits pavement—and then you're chasing your tails again."

"It's an old logging road," Vince explained. "It's on the map. It goes deeper into the woods and then up into the mountains."

JJ knew his temper was reaching the boiling point. He clenched his fists. "Do you really think he's stupid enough to leave us a trail?"

"We can stand here and argue about it or we can follow his trail and see where it takes us." Donnie tossed the anklet at Fleming, demonstrating his own form of disgust.

JJ climbed into the back seat of the sedan, his temper still simmering just below the boiling point. "Where's that map?"

Donnie tossed it to him. Fleming drove, not saying a word.

JJ spread the map out on his lap and looked at it. His finger followed the logging trail as it wound its way up the mountain. *Zoe, I swear, if we can get you out alive, I will never yell at you again.*

He stared at the map. *Come on. Come on.* There had to be something. Anything. *God, if You're real, I could really use Your help right about now. Show me where she is and I'll never deny You again.*

Desperation clung to his mind. Fear held on to his heart. Dread slid up his spine.

◆ ◆ ◆

Zoe held her breath as he came back into the room with a rope in one hand and a glistening knife in the other. How long had he been gone? Twenty minutes? Thirty?

After cutting the ropes around her hands and feet, he pulled her up off the cot. "We're going for a walk."

"What about my mom?"

"Someone will find her eventually."

Zoe stopped. He pushed. She stumbled. "You can't just leave her here."

"Well, I could take her with us and let her watch you die. Do you want her to watch, Zoe? Is that it? Or are you afraid of dying alone?"

"You're sick."

"I've been called worse. But you're wrong. I'm just very clever."

"It isn't cleverness that drives you to kill innocent children."

"No. That's hunger. You people don't understand. You think life and death are something special. Something to be grieved over and coveted like precious jewels. You build monuments to a pile of bones. You spend fortunes to engrave names in marble and granite. Why? To ease your troubled little minds that you weren't as nice to them while they were alive as you should have been? And you call me sick? You hide behind elaborate funerals and line the pockets of greedy funeral homes and florists, and for what?"

He shook his head as if pitying her. "Death is death. People live, people die—so what. Hearts stop and they're gone."

"People who die leave behind people who loved them!"

"Loved them!" He spat the words with distaste. "Don't give me that mindless garbage! A father loves his children, but he has no problem leaving them when a pretty woman crosses his path. So much for love when lust comes calling."

"What about the mothers you leave grieving for their children?"

"Mothers?" His eyes narrowed with a violent hatred, and she could only wonder what his own mother had done to him to make him hate them so much. "Don't talk to me about those feckless creatures."

Denise Shefford moaned and Zoe started to move toward her. He yanked her back. "Oh, no, you don't."

"Mom!"

Her mom moved her head a fraction of an inch and moaned softly again.

He pulled Zoe out of the room and slammed the door shut.

JJ stared at the map. Something nagged at him. He squinted, staring harder at the area all around the logging road. *And there! Son of a swamp rat! The guy had led them in circles!*

He shoved the map over the seat at Donnie. "Look. Right there. That's where we found Gina." He pointed and then dragged his finger across the squiggly lines. "And that's where we found Lisa Brandt. And this is where we are now."

Donnie's eyes darted from one point to another. He looked up at JJ and then at the map. "Do you think it could have been that simple?"

"Yes."

"So do I." He looked over at Fleming. "Turn around."

Fleming shot him a look. "Are you nuts?"

"No. This is another rabbit trail. Up ahead, we're going to find that he cut off the road and went through the woods. By the time we follow it all the way around, it may be too late. Turn around."

Fleming shrugged and grabbed the radio. "Everyone stop and turn around. Go back out the way we came."

◆　◆　◆

Cliff Maren pulled his fishing rod and tackle box out of the bed of his pickup and slammed the tailgate. Carrying them, along with a small folding stool and a thermos, he made his way down the bank to the river.

When he got to his favorite fishing spot, he set everything down and popped open his stool. He sat, poured himself a cup of coffee, and opened his tackle box. He fingered through his favorite lures and settled on the one he wanted.

Attaching lures was a delicate art. He took his time, taking pleasure in every step of the process. His fishing rod was state-of-the-art, a birthday gift from his wife, who knew he'd been coveting it. It felt like an extension of his own arm as he swung back and then let the line fly out over the water.

He picked up his coffee and took a sip. He was a patient man and didn't mind studying the trees, the bushes, the birds, and the river itself. He knew this piece of land almost better than he knew his own backyard.

As his steady gaze drifted, following a squirrel, he noticed a strange blue object on the ground near the base of a tree. Something wasn't right.

He set down his coffee, carefully propped his rod against the stool, and walked over to see what it was. Stooping down, he reached for it. *A suit coat.*

With a furrowed brow, he stood up. Out of the corner of his

eye, he noticed something else. All the color drained from his face.

A hand, pale blue and lifeless, was sticking up out of the water.

◆　◆　◆

He pushed Zoe again, this time up the narrow wooden staircase. When she saw the double doors above her, she realized she was in a storm cellar. They went through the doors and emerged in a small clearing at the edge of the woods. She saw a small cabin not far away.

It looked deserted. *Of course it was. He wasn't stupid enough to bring them to a place where anyone could hear her scream.*

With a shove, he flipped the wooden doors closed. One slammed shut, but the other jammed on its rusty hinges. He shoved at it. Cursed.

The sound of distant car engines broke into the quiet. He grabbed some loose brush and tried to cover the opening. Then he pushed her forward again, this time toward the woods. "Where are we going?"

"For a walk. Move!"

Zoe felt her heart racing. Her mouth was dry. *This was it. No cavalry. No second chance. No fairy tale hero in a white hat to ride to her rescue.* Death had never been more real to Zoe than at this moment. She was going to die. He was going to strangle her, just as he had all those little girls, and then he was going to toss her in a grave and walk away.

Oh, God, please don't let this happen. I don't want to die. And help my mom. God, where are You?

◆　◆　◆

The caravan of law enforcement vehicles drove back the way they'd come. One by one, the cars passed the cabin and headed back toward the main road.

As Fleming drove, JJ glanced out the window—then whipped his head and stared. "Stop!"

Before the car came to a full stop, JJ flung open the door and leaped out.

The cellar door! It had been closed. Now it was sitting wide open. He had been there the whole time. Right under their noses and they'd walked right past him.

Son of a swamp rat.

"What is it, JJ?"

He pointed at the cellar door. "That wasn't open when we drove away."

"How did we miss this?" Fleming snarled.

"It was covered with branches and vines." Donnie picked up a vine and tossed it aside in disgust. "Blended right in."

Fleming called everyone back to the cabin. JJ took his gun out of the holster. Donnie followed suit. The two men quickly entered the cellar.

"She's been here," JJ said as he picked up a trace of her perfume in the musty air.

Donnie pointed to an empty cot. "I think he's taken her out of here."

JJ nodded and then jerked his head in the direction of a closed door. Donnie nodded. It would be just like the guy to be hiding right under their noses. This time, they weren't going to overlook anything.

JJ turned the knob slowly and then shoved the door open. Donnie jumped through, gun drawn. Denise Shefford stared at him with wide eyes, her face white with fear.

"Mrs. Shefford?"

Donnie knelt down and pulled the duct tape carefully off her mouth. "You okay?"

She nodded, swallowing hard. "Zoe. He took her."

"Where?"

She shook her head.

"How long?" JJ asked.

She tried to shrug, looking despondent. "I don't know. Five minutes. Maybe longer."

JJ stood up. "I'll send someone down here to take care of you. I'm going after Zoe."

"I'm right behind you."

JJ grabbed Matt as he climbed out of one of the cars. "Mrs. Shefford is in the cellar. Get an ambulance. And take her some water."

"On it."

JJ started frantically searching for footprints, scraps of clothing—anything that would tell him which direction he'd taken Zoe.

Donnie emerged from the cellar a moment later. JJ waved him over to the edge of the woods. "Do these look fresh to you?"

Donnie knelt down. "Hard to tell with the tracks, but this broken branch is recent." He stood and drew his weapon. "Hold on one second."

Donnie jogged over to Fleming, and JJ saw him talking, pointing toward JJ; Fleming nodded. Then Donnie ran back over. "They'll be right behind us. Fleming's going to set up a sweep. Let's go."

JJ led the way, following tracks, broken branches, and bent grass as best he could. They traveled deeper into the woods. Three minutes stretched to five. JJ could feel the sands of Zoe's hourglass running out. Suddenly Donnie reached out and grabbed his arm, stopping him in midstride.

Then JJ heard it.

Voices.

One male. One female.

Zoe!

He started to move forward, but Donnie shook his head. He pointed to the left and indicated that he'd swing to the right. JJ acknowledged the instruction and then moved quietly to the left.

◆ ◆ ◆

"Don't do this," Zoe pleaded as he untied her wrists.

"Are you going to beg now? Oh, good. I love it when they beg. Makes me feel all warm and fuzzy." The dry tone in his voice was dispassionate as he wrapped the rope around her neck.

He tightened the rope and she went up on her toes to ease the pressure. "Don't," she gasped.

"Oh, but I have to. We mustn't leave Amy out here alone. You do want to be with her, don't you?"

"She's. . .not. . .here," Zoe whispered roughly, trying to breathe and talk at the same time. It was difficult. It was almost impossible. She felt her head begin to spin.

"Oh, but she is. Don't you recognize this place?" He pointed to the far end of the field, barely visible to her. "Way over there is where you found Gina. And here, right here, is where Amy is."

Amy. She'd been so close. Her precious psychic gift. It was to bring Amy home. Amy had been right here while Zoe hadn't been able to pick up a single trace of her. What good had the gift been after all? It had brought nothing but heartache and misery to all it touched.

Zoe felt the tears slip through her lids and run down her cheeks.

"Aw, now, don't cry. Amy can't see your tears, and," his voice grew harsh, "I really don't care."

She clawed at the rope, but it was too tight. There were no more words now. Spots danced before her eyes, and she grew light-headed. There was a roaring in her ears, and she could no longer hear anything he was saying to her.

This was it.

She was dying.

There was no more air.

No more life.

Okay, God. Take me, then, but save my mom. Somehow, save my mom.

The spots in front of her eyes faded as blackness settled over her. She knew her hands had dropped, too heavy now for her to hold up. The weight bore down on her and she felt herself sinking. . . sinking. . .deeper into the inky black. . . .

JJ couldn't get a clear shot. His heart was in his throat as he watched the man tighten the rope and then watched Zoe's struggles cease. He raced forward and nearly screamed aloud when her knees went out from under her.

A shot cracked through the silence, and the man whipped around. Donnie had missed, but the man had turned, giving JJ all he needed. Now JJ had him. He stopped, lifted his weapon, and pulled the trigger.

The gun jumped in his hand.

The man jerked as the shot hit him in the back.

JJ fired again, hitting him in the thigh.

The man spun, releasing Zoe. She dropped to the ground. And then everything seemed to move in slow motion. The man staggered and turned toward JJ. The rope in his hands slowly slid through his fingers and fell silently across Zoe's arm.

JJ's eyes widened as he continued to approach cautiously.

It couldn't be!

The man went to his knees, still staring at JJ. A smile began to curl up on his face. "You. . .weren't as dumb. . .as you looked."

"Why? My God, man, why?"

"It is. . .as the scorpion. . .told the frog. . .my nature."

And with a heaved sigh, Ted Matthews collapsed at JJ's feet.

chapter 33

Tripp knelt down beside the body as Vivian started to zip the body bag closed. "Any identification?"

Vivian handed him the black leather purse. Water still dripped from it. He reached inside and pulled out the wallet.

Looking from the picture on the wallet to the body stiff in death, he frowned. "You know how many people have been searching for you, Miss Bubeck?"

But Maryanne Bubeck was in no condition to answer him. Or anyone else ever again.

◆　◆　◆

JJ knelt down and cradled Zoe's upper body in his arms. Her head lolled lifelessly against him. She was deathly pale, contrasting sharply with the violent red burn around her throat.

"Don't you dare go and die on me, Zoe Shefford. I need you around to annoy me."

Donnie skidded to a halt next to them. He knelt down and placed two fingers on her neck. "She's alive, but her pulse is weak."

He keyed his mic. "I need an ambulance, and I need it now! No, wait. Get a medivac chopper in here."

JJ aimlessly brushed Zoe's hair from her face as he looked at the man who had nearly killed her. *Ted Matthews.* How in the world had he missed that?

He reached up with his free hand and wiped sweat from his face. It was one big case after all. Harris had been right for all the wrong reasons. And JJ had been wrong.

He'd been wrong. And it could cost Zoe Shefford her life.

Matt jogged across the field. Fleming followed, trying without success to keep up.

Donnie reached over and checked Ted Matthews' pulse. "He's alive. Nice shooting there, partner." Donnie slowly stood up.

Matt came to a stop. "JJ? You okay?"

"Ted Matthews," he whispered, then raised his eyes to look at Matt. "It was Ted Matthews."

"The infant baby kidnapping?" Fleming asked, huffing and puffing from running.

JJ nodded. "The baby's father. It was all a smoke screen. Part of the game. To keep me guessing and running in the wrong direction."

Donnie placed his hand on JJ's shoulder. "He fooled us all. You're not to blame for any of this."

"We were too late."

Matt knelt, resting on his haunches, one hand on the ground to keep his balance as he caught JJ's eyes and held them. "We weren't too late, JJ. Zoe is alive. She's going to be fine. Everyone's going to be fine."

"Except for Gina and Lisa and. . ."

Matt shook his head, his face dark with emotion. "Don't go there, JJ. We can't afford to. We stopped the monster from touching another child. We did our job."

◆　　◆　　◆

Carlton Lyle Livingston. Former Vietnam Veteran. Fifty-five years old. Former resident of the V.A. Hospital in Richmond, Virginia. Carlton had walked away one day and for four years lived as a homeless drunk, wandering from city to city, trying to outrun his demons.

Instead of outrunning them, he'd fallen victim to one.

Justus shook his head in pity. "Sorry, pal. What did he do? Promise you a bottle? Some easy cash if you went with him?"

Vivian signed off on the chart and set it down. "The only family we could find was a sister in Youngstown, Ohio. She's going to come for the body and take it back for burial."

"Shame."

"Yes, it is."

Justus slowly covered the face with a sheet. "Well, that mystery is solved. Now they just have to find out who killed him and why."

"In the meantime, we just had another body come in. Looks like a drowning."

◆　　◆　　◆

She wanted to lift her face to the warm light and bask in it. It was the most amazingly wonderful thing she'd ever felt in her life. Electrifying. Comforting. Loving. All-encompassing. Pure.

Her heart seemed to beat in rhythm to it—as if it pulsed with a life force that was connected to her. Part of her.

Love.

It was love. The most unbelievable love she'd ever sensed in her life. It overwhelmed anything she'd ever felt or known. It swelled and moved in and around and through her.

She wanted to embrace it but didn't know how. And suddenly it responded to her desire and swelled within her. It continued to grow, increase, and enlarge.

Intense. More and more intense until she almost felt too over-whelmed by it.

She felt it withdrawing and cried out.

It's not yet time, My child.

Time for what?

Time for you to be with Me.

"Zoe, don't you dare die on me."

JJ?

The light began to dim and the sensations eased away. No, don't go! I want to know You.

You will. Each day you will grow closer until the day you are once again this close to Me.

"Start an IV drip."

"Do we need to intubate?"

"Pulse?"

"Ninety over sixty."

She tried to reach back for the light, but it faded to little more than a soft glow.

Please, come back.

I am always with you.

JJ pushed the car door closed and reluctantly headed up the sidewalk to the front porch. Matt followed close on his heels. For a moment JJ wrestled with what he had to say and how in the world he was going to say it. He looked at Matt and then at the front door.

"You could have let me or Gerry handle this," Matt told him.

"No, I couldn't." Lifting his hand, he knocked briskly.

A minute or so later, Ray Timms opened the front door. His smile faded when he saw their faces. "It's not good news, is it?"

JJ shook his head. "Can we come in?"

"Are you going to arrest my sister again?"

"No. Please, we just need to talk to her."

Ray thought about it a moment before he stepped back and waved them in.

Karen Matthews was sitting in the living room, holding Jessica in her arms. Rene Taylor was seated in a chair across from her. Both women looked up with suspicion in their eyes as JJ and Matt walked into the room and sat down.

JJ fiddled with his car keys, summoning the words that seemed so hard to speak. Finally, he lifted his head and looked at Karen. "I wanted you to know that we found your husband."

She went white. He saw emotion in her eyes, but he wasn't sure what emotion it was. Fear? Hostility? Confusion?

"Is he. . .?"

JJ shook his head. "He's alive. He's in the hospital. We just came from there."

"Alive." Karen seemed to be testing the word to see how it felt.

"I want you to know that I'm the one who shot him."

Karen's eyes went wide, and Rene reached over to take her hand. "You shot Ted?"

JJ nodded. "He was trying to kill Zoe Shefford."

She gasped and nearly dropped the baby's bottle. "Why—"

Matt rescued him. "Mrs. Matthews. Your husband is the serial killer we've been trying to catch. He's killed many children. Miss Shefford was getting too close to him."

Karen seemed to sway, and Ray rushed forward, lifting Jessica from her arms. Rene jumped up and rushed to sit next to Karen, wrapping her arms around her.

"That's. . .that's just not possible. He wouldn't. . .couldn't have. . ."

"He did," Matt said firmly. "There is no doubt. No question."

"I see," she said softly.

"Karen?" Rene rubbed Karen's arm. "Are you okay?"

Karen gave her a blank stare. "He was a serial killer? He killed children? How could I not have seen such evil?"

"Evil hides behind many masks, Karen. It's not always so easy to see."

Karen stood up, swaying a little. Her face was drained of all color, unnaturally pale and translucent. "Excuse me."

JJ stood to his feet as she walked stiffly out of the room. Matt also stood.

"I'm sorry, but we had to let her know. It's going to hit the papers, and that's not the best way to find out something like this."

"I know," Ray replied, cradling Jess in his arms. "Thanks for telling us."

Rene continued to look down the hallway after Karen. "We'll take care of her, Detective."

Rene looked at her watch. "Karen has been in the shower for almost thirty-five minutes, Ray. I'd better check on her. I don't like the feel of this."

"You don't think she'd do something crazy, do you?"

"I don't know. She just got some horrific news. Just let me check and put my mind at ease."

She hurried down the hall and into the master bedroom. At the bathroom door, she tapped. She could hear the water running. "Karen?"

Still no response.

She turned the handle, relieved to find the door unlocked. Steam hit her in the face as she stepped in. It rolled and tumbled toward the open door. Through the shower curtain, Rene could see Karen's silhouette. She looked like she was scrubbing her arms. Hard.

Rene pulled back the shower curtain. Karen's arms looked an angry red, as if Karen had been trying to scrub the skin clear off.

"Karen, honey. What are you doing?"

Karen continued to scrape the bath brush across her skin with furious intensity. "Gotta get *him* off. I have to get clean of it."

Rene flinched and reached back for a towel. She shut the water off. Karen looked stunned, as if she had only at that moment realized that Rene was there. Rene wrapped a big bath towel around Karen and helped her from the shower.

"There's nothing to scrub off, honey."

Karen's bottom lip trembled as she stood there shaking. "He touched me. So many times, he touched me. Evil. I didn't know."

Rene put her arms around Karen as Karen's knees buckled and the two women sank to the floor. "It's okay, sweetheart. You're okay."

"I lived with him. Had his child. Cooked his meals and did his. . ." She sniffed back tears. "Did his laundry. And all that time, he was. . .he was. . ."

Karen wailed and began crying hard, her shoulders shaking at the onslaught of heart-wrenching sobs.

Rene pulled her close and began to rock her like a child. "Shh, baby, it's okay. Shh. He's never going to touch you again."

"I have to wash the evil away," Karen cried out in a panicked voice.

"No, honey. Jesus already did that for you." She rocked her closer, letting Karen collapse in her arms. "You're all clean. Jesus made you all clean."

About the Author

Wanda L. Dyson is a Christian counselor and author residing in Maryland's horse country with her daughter, two Australian Shepherds, and twelve horses. Her writing has appeared in various Christian and general publications. She is currently working on the sequel to *Abduction*.

chapter 34

Monday, May 1

K aren rocked back and forth, ever so gently, as Jessica slept in her arms. She stared down into the baby's face, unable to get enough of seeing her. Holding her.

"Sis?" Ray set his suitcase down at the door and leaned against the doorframe. "I'm ready to go. Cab will be here any minute."

Karen lifted her face. "Are you sure you don't want me to drive you to the airport?"

Ray shook his head. "No. You need to stay home. Unwind. Relax. Regroup."

Moving carefully, Karen stood up and laid Jessica in her playpen. She walked over and put her arms around her brother. "I can't thank you enough for being here."

He hugged her tight and then released her, setting her back at arm's length. "You're going to be okay, Sis. You've found out who you are."

"I called the hospital this morning."

"Karen—"

She cut him off, knowing he was going to disapprove. "I had to find out."

"And?"

"He's going to live. They said he's paralyzed from the waist down, but he's going to live. Do you think it will make a difference? That they won't send him to prison because he'll be in a wheelchair?"

"No. He will be lucky if they don't sentence him to death." Ray reached out and touched her cheek. "If you need anything, call me."

"I know. And as long as we're on the subject, I want my inheritance. I see no reason why I can't take control of it myself." She folded her arms across her chest, lifted her chin, and prepared to do battle for what was hers.

"I'll take care of it first thing when I get back."

Karen's jaw dropped. "That's it? No argument?"

"That's it. It's yours. You can take care of it now. I'll go over everything with you."

A car horn sounded. Ray picked up his suitcase. "My cab is here. I gotta go. Love you, Sis." He wrapped one arm around her and squeezed her.

"Love you, too, Ray."

She opened the front door and followed him outside, watching from the porch as he jogged down the stairs. Halfway down the sidewalk, he turned around toward her, walking backwards. "I forgot to tell you! Dad called."

Karen groaned.

"He said he'd like to come over and see Jessica if it's okay with you. Call him and let him know." He turned and handed his bag to the cab driver. Then he lifted a hand to wave and disappeared inside the cab. Karen waited until the cab was gone before she turned to head back inside the house. Her dad wanted her permission to come over and see his granddaughter. Permission! Well, would wonders never cease.

As she started to turn, she caught sight of Rene.

"Hey there."

"Hi, Rene."

"You look great," Rene told her as she stepped up onto Karen's porch.

Karen sighed heavily and then smiled. "It's been a horrible path to get here, but. . . I've never felt better."

"Tea?" Karen pointed to the door.

"Love some."

"I heard you're helping the McCaines." Karen shut the front door and then led Rene into the kitchen.

"What a wonderful couple they are." Rene sat at the table, her hands running over the quilted placemats. "One of the young men in our church's youth group came to us, oh, must have been a month or more ago. His younger sister was in trouble—you know, pregnant— and didn't know what to do. They come from a broken home, poor things. We talked to her, prayed with her, and her brother started bringing her to the youth group with him. Two weeks ago she accepted the Lord."

Rene smiled at the memory and at Karen as Karen placed the sugar in front of her. "A couple days later, she called me and said she felt the right thing to do was to give the baby up for adoption and would I please help her find a nice couple. She didn't want to go through an agency."

"They were so good to Jessica." Karen pulled two teacups down from the cabinet and reached for the tea. "I'd love to see them have a child of their own. They've been through so much."

"Well, everyone signed the papers yesterday, so unless something happens and Leeza changes her mind, the McCaines will have a little boy in about four months."

"That's wonderful!" Karen exclaimed. The teakettle started whistling, and Karen pulled it off the stove. She reflected on the simple pleasure of enjoying a cup of tea with a friend in the middle of the day. No need to worry that her husband was going to get angry. No guilt that she might have forgotten to do something.

"Why the sudden frown?"

Karen's face cleared, and she laughed. "Sorry. I was just thinking how wonderful this feels."

"And frowning?"

"No. Frowning that I once lived in such fear of doing these pleasurable little things."

"I understand."

Karen set the teacups on the table and pulled out a chair.

"Do you?"

Rene spooned sugar into her cup and stirred. "I never told you, did I? My first husband abused me. Physically as well as emotionally."

"Then you really do understand."

Rene lifted her cup and looked at Karen over the rim. "More than you can imagine, my friend. Which is why I'm so overjoyed to see you so happy now."

Karen toyed with her spoon. "I want to thank you for what you did." She lifted her head. "You'll never know what that meant. To have someone care like that."

"I was just worried about you. I don't normally go barging in on people when they're in the shower."

Karen laughed and reached for Rene's hand. "Well, we'll let it slide this time."

◆　◆　◆

Zoe opened her eyes slowly, blinked, and then gently smiled up at her dad. "Hi," she whispered in a raspy voice that sounded strange to her own ears.

The hospital room smelled of flowers and disinfectant. Sunlight streamed into the room between open drapes. To her left, monitors beeped and chirped, keeping an electrical watch over her vital signs.

"Hi, yourself. Feeling better?" He sat down on the edge of her bed, stroking her hand.

"Little."

He nodded. "You had us worried there for awhile. I kept running from your room to your mother's. Between the two of you, I think I've aged twenty years."

A worried expression formed on Zoe's face. "Mom? She okay?"

"She's fine. A little dehydrated, a few bruises, but nothing to worry about at all. She was released last night and I took her home. Today she's complaining because I won't let her do anything but rest. She probably got up the minute I pulled out of the driveway."

Zoe nodded, finding it easier than trying to talk. Her throat still felt raw, and it hurt even to think about speaking. It was worse when she tried to swallow.

"I just wanted to check in on you. Every time I've been in to see you, you've been asleep. I brought you some flowers."

Zoe squeezed his hand in acknowledgment. "Go, Mom . . . needs you."

Keyes nodded and stood up. "She wants to come in today and see for herself that you're on the mend." He reached over and kissed her on the forehead. "I love you, kiddo."

She nodded, swallowing gently and flinching at the pain. Closing her eyes, she heard her father slip out of the room and the door click shut. Her mom was safe. Unharmed. That news made everything else worthwhile. So what if she couldn't swallow without flinching? So what if she sounded like a frog when she talked? Her mom was alive. That was all that mattered.

Zoe couldn't remember anything after the rope had tightened around her neck except for a few faint echoes of voices around her, urgent and authoritative.

There was a light . . .

Suddenly it was a vibrant memory. Her heart soared as she recalled the sensation. He'd been there with her. God had been right there, holding her through the whole thing. And oh, how He loved her! Even as Ted Matthews was trying to kill her, God had been right there holding her in His arms.

Ted Matthews. The name sent shivers down her back. She couldn't believe it when she saw his face. He looked nothing like the police sketch her mother had helped with. Either he'd been wearing a disguise, or he hadn't been the man who was in the store that day, spooking her mother.

She'd met him just once as she was leaving René's house. He was coming back from work and René had introduced them. Her only impression of him had been that of an arrogant, rude man. She'd never suspected the evil that lurked beneath the surface.

Did he get away? Did they kill him? Will he live to terrorize again?

"You're supposed to be resting, but from the look on your face, you're too busy worrying about something."

Zoe's eyes opened as JJ walked over to her bed. He shoved his hands in his pockets and looked at everything but her. "Matthews?" she rasped harshly.

He glanced at her quickly and then away. "He's alive. Paralyzed. He'll spend the rest of his life in a wheelchair. In prison."

Relief came cool and sweet. "Thank . . . you."

"You don't have to thank me," he replied. "If I'd been any kind of detective, he never would have gotten that close to you."

She shook her head, reaching for his hand. He ignored her attempt, keeping his hands safely in his pockets. Her hand dropped and she frowned. "Not. . your. . fault."

"And pigs fly with purple wings." He snorted with derision.

"He played me like a child, running me all over creation, chasing one lead after another, and he was right there under my nose the whole time, laughing at me."

"Mom. . me. . alive. You did. . that. You won."

JJ yanked his hand out of his pocket, grabbed a chair, and slid it over close to the bed. He dropped down in it like a sack of flour.

"I didn't find Jessica Matthews. I didn't figure out the truth about Ted Matthews. What kind of cop does that make me?"

"Human." She reached out again. He was too close to avoid her touch this time. Her fingers curled around his wrist. "You didn't. . . give up."

"No. I couldn't do that."

"How. . did you. . find me?"

JJ rolled his eyes. "Of all the questions in the world, why that one?"

The corners of her mouth lifted in a smile as she waited for his answer.

"Okay. Believe it or not, God. I know—sounds crazy. But I was at the end of my rope. I told Him if He'd help me find you, then I would never deny Him again. He kept His promise, so I'm keeping mine, even though it sounds about as wacky as it can get."

"Not. . wacky." She swallowed carefully. "How?"

JJ gazed at his hands. "I was looking at a map and thinking about what Matthews told you. About where Gina was buried. I made everyone turn around. On the way back past the cabin, I saw the storm cellar door open. I knew it wasn't that way earlier."

Zoe closed her eyes. *Thank You, Lord.*

"It wasn't like with Macy. I mean, you weren't."

She opened her eyes and gazed at him, watching the emotions war in his eyes.

"You were right. Macy did look at me like I was some super-hero. I needed her to. You said something to Matt that first day I met you—about how he needed women to stroke his ego. Macy did that for me.

"I didn't take her instincts seriously. She kept telling me that she felt like she was being stalked, and I blew off her fears as nonsense."

"Because a superhero. . .would have known. . .before she did."

JJ glanced over at her, a wry smile twisting his lips. "Something like that." He took a deep breath. "And then there you were, defy-ing me at every turn, turning my ego inside out and upside down, and laughing at me all at the same time."

"Not. . .at you."

"*At* me. I was making a fool out of myself with all that macho garbage and you knew it. Then suddenly you were being stalked and it wasn't your imagination and I couldn't blow it off. And you wouldn't look at me like a superhero. You turned around and taunted Matthews and I wanted to strangle you."

"Because you. . .didn't know. . .if you could. . .protect me."

He nodded. "Yeah."

"But. . .you did. You're a. . .good cop, JJ. Just have to. . .be you."

"I'm not sure I know who I am."

"When you figure it. . .out, let me know."

He smiled again. "Somehow I think you already know and I'm the only one who doesn't."

Zoe closed her eyes as his voice drifted over her. Her throat hurt worse. She'd talked too much.

The sound of chair legs scraping against the floor made her open her eyes again. JJ was standing up.

"I've stayed too long. You need your rest. I just wanted to check in and see that you were okay."

"I'm. . .okay. Thanks to. . .you."

348

He frowned at her again and she smiled up at him. *Typical male. If he doesn't control the situation, he pouts like a child. Get used to it, JJ. I think God's getting ready to take over your life.*

"I'd best be going. I'll. . .um. . .check in on you again."

She nodded. "You'd. . .better."

She saw it then—just a glimmer of a smile in his eyes as he turned and walked toward the door. He pulled the door open, stopped, and looked at her. "I think I like you this way."

Rather than asking, she tilted her head and let her eyes ask. He grinned at her. "Unable to talk." Then he hurried out the door, letting it close behind him before she could retort. Or find something to throw at him.

◆　◆　◆

Donnie Bevere stepped off the plane at Dulles International Airport and walked with Fleming to the baggage claim. After picking up their bags, they separated with few words and grabbed their respective cabs home.

Donnie didn't talk much about his private life with Fleming or anyone else at work. He preferred not to bring his work home, and his home wasn't something he wanted to share at work. Keeping them separate kept him sane.

Somewhere along the line, he had given his coworkers the impression that he dated a different woman every night and never took any of them seriously. He didn't know how or why they'd gotten that impression, but they had him tagged as a womanizer. He never bothered to dispel that notion. It amused him.

The cab pulled up in front of the little cookie-cutter house, and he climbed out after paying the driver. Lugging his suitcase up the front walk, Donnie Bevere smiled. The grass needed to be mowed, the hedges needed to be trimmed, and the kid next door had left his football in the front yard again.

Donnie set down his suitcase, picked up the football, and tossed it back over the fence. It was good to be home.

He pulled out his keys and opened the front door.

"Daddy!"

A blond dervish came at him full bore. He dropped his suitcase, grabbed the whirlwind, and tossed her high into the air. "Hey, darlin'. Miss me?"

"Yep!" She nodded vigorously, her blond curls bobbing around her face.

"Where's your mom?"

"Right here." Her voice was soft and warm and wrapped itself around him. He turned, setting his daughter on his hip while reaching for his wife.

"I missed you like crazy." He wrapped an arm around her and pulled her close. "And how is my son?"

She rubbed a hand over her swollen belly and laughed. "Kicking up a storm. Mandy was never this active."

"She waited until she was here to raise a ruckus."

"Truth."

He set Mandy down and the three-year-old went running off. He wrapped both arms around Lisbeth and brought his nose down to hers. "Guess what I did."

"Uh-oh," she replied with a cautious laugh. "There's no telling when it comes to you. What did you do?"

"Helped a guy get engaged."

Lisbeth tossed back her head and laughed brightly. "Oh, no. Don't tell me there's another woman out there who got the full-page ad and silver platter routine!"

chapter 35

Monday, May 15

Karen hesitated at the polished oak door, wanting to be anywhere but here. Cold sweat trickled down her sides as she clutched her purse in her hands and tried to take deep, calming breaths.

"It'll be okay," Rene assured her, reaching out to squeeze Karen's hand.

"I'm not so sure, Rene. How do I look him in the face?"

"You don't have to. Look at the judge. At the district attorney. At me. You don't have to look at him. Karen, you don't even have to be here."

"Yes, I do."

Someone brushed past them, opening the door and hurrying inside. Rene pushed her forward. "Come on. It's almost time."

Karen felt like she was dragging concrete blocks by her ankles as she entered the courtroom and followed Rene to a front-row seat. She wanted to scream at Rene to take her to the back row. Or back home.

Suddenly she was sitting and a guard was rolling Ted into the courtroom. She slowly lifted her eyes to look at him, holding her breath. His hands were cuffed and lying in his lap. He was thinner, almost gaunt, his hair curling wildly. He wore an orange county prison jumpsuit but held his head high, as if he were entering the courtroom wearing one of his Brooks Brothers' suits.

His eyes caught hers, and she felt her breath leave her in a rush, as if he'd reached out and punched her in the chest. His lips curled in a sneer, and then he looked back at the guard.

"All stand."

All but Ted came to their feet in a rustle of movement and hushed whispers. "The Honorable Willard T. Hooper, now presiding."

Out of the corner of her eye, Karen studied Ted sitting next to his attorney. He seemed so confident. So assured. A condescending smile on his face, he seemed amused to be playing yet another round of his sick game.

Suddenly the district attorney was standing and addressing the judge. Karen pulled her eyes away to listen to him.

"Yes, your Honor. An agreement was reached."

Agreement? Karen felt a cold chill. She reached for Rene's hand.

The judge fiddled with his glasses as he shuffled the papers in front of him. Then he looked down at Ted. "Does your client understand the terms of this plea bargain, Mr. Trump?"

Ted's attorney stood up. "He does, your Honor."

"And he's in total agreement?"

"Yes, your Honor."

Karen's eyes darted from one man to another, trying to understand what was happening. He was supposed to go to trial. He was supposed to be found guilty. He was supposed to be sent to prison for the rest of his life. What was going on?

The judge nodded to the district attorney. "Let's get on with it, then."

The district attorney lifted a document in his hands. "The County of Monroe hereby charges the defendant, Theodore Matthew

Bateman, also known as Edward Matthews, with twenty-seven counts of the kidnapping of a minor and premeditated murder."

"How does your client plead?" The judge turned to Ted's attorney.

"Guilty, your Honor."

Karen felt her heart lurch in her throat. He was pleading guilty? He was admitting it? What had she expected? That he would somehow manage to convince everyone that it was a big mistake? That he hadn't really done all those terrible things? Maybe that's exactly what she wanted him to say. Perhaps, somewhere deep in her heart, she wanted to hear him say that he hadn't done all those things. Hadn't killed. Hadn't lied.

"Mr. Matthews, in exchange for a life sentence with no chance of parole, you have agreed to plead guilty and to answer certain questions put to you by this court. Do you understand this?"

Ted looked almost bored as he replied, "Yes, your Honor."

"You may proceed, Counselor."

The district attorney turned to Ted. "Did you conspire with one Maryanne Bubeck to kidnap and sell your daughter, Jessica Matthews, to an adoption attorney for the purpose of putting the child up for adoption without the knowledge or consent of the mother of said child, Karen Matthews?"

"Yes."

"Why?" The district attorney glanced only briefly at Karen before turning his hard gaze back on Ted.

"Because getting rid of the brat served my purposes. The company was catching on to the money Maryanne and I were stealing, and the police had put together a task force to investigate the kidnapping of those kids. I had to confuse them."

Karen sank down in her seat as Rene wrapped an arm around her shoulder. He really did do it! Dear God, he really did. And all because he'd wanted to confuse the police and cover his tracks? He'd put her through hell to cover his tracks?

Rage shot through her, hot and reverberant. She wanted to pound into him with her fists until he begged for mercy! Until he knew what it felt like to be betrayed!

"Did you then kill Maryanne Bubeck, disposing of her body in the river?"

"Yes."

"Why?"

"Because I didn't need her anymore. She would do anything I asked her, but she started feeling guilty for helping me get rid of the brat. I had to kill her before she did something dumb."

"Like tell the police."

"Yes."

"Did you conspire to fake your own death, framing your wife, Karen Matthews, for the alleged murder?"

"Yes."

"Why?"

Ted rolled his eyes. "Because she was a ditz and I was tired of her whining. Thought prison might toughen her up." He smirked over at her. "I hated her and just wanted to make her as miserable as she'd made me."

"Who was the man in the grave?"

"Some old drunk I picked up off the streets. A nobody."

The district attorney began to go down the list of missing children, but Karen tuned him out. Her husband had framed her for murder just to make her miserable. He'd killed for the pure pleasure of it. Lied to cover his tracks. Destroyed people's lives without an ounce of remorse.

Evil.

Rene leaned in close. "I heard that his attorney tried to get him to plead insanity and he refused."

"I can't believe it, Rene. He's just sitting there with that grin on his face like this is all a big joke."

"He has no soul, Karen. Can't you see that? To him, this is nothing. He's still thinking he can walk away from this."

"How? He's getting life in prison. He's going to *die* in prison."

"Who knows—maybe in his sick mind he thinks he can escape."

Escape. Karen swallowed the word. It almost made her sick to her stomach. That a man like him should ever get the opportunity to walk the streets again was inconceivable.

She glanced over her shoulder and saw Zoe Shefford sitting with the mother of one of the murdered children. Zoe had her arm around the crying woman, trying to console her. She lifted her eyes, as if sensing Karen was looking at her, and smiled a sad yet warm smile. Karen returned the smile. How was Zoe dealing with this? Her own sister had been one of Ted's first victims. She had walked in the path of his chaos all her life. Who could ever make that right for her? Or for any of the parents?

Quietly Karen turned and looked up at the judge. Then at Ted. Someone had to make this right.

And maybe, just maybe, she knew how.

epilogue

Monday, June 15

I've been told many times that all things work for the good of those who love God." Zoe took a deep breath, looked at the woman standing next to her, and smiled. Then she looked back over the people gathered in front of her.

"Many of you today are here with heavy hearts. This memorial has your child's name on it along with the names of eighty-four other children who died far too soon. Among them is my sister, Amy. In spite of what we feel, God has worked something good out of this terrible tragedy.

"I need to say something that I hope you will take to heart. Your children aren't here. This place is merely a testament to the life and love they experienced on this earth. They are all in heaven now."

Zoe turned and looked at the white marble monument that stood nearly six feet tall behind her, topped with an angel looking down as if reading the names. She wiped tears from her eyes. When she turned, she noticed that many other people were crying as well.

She smiled at them. "Now for the awesome thing God has done."

Zoe turned and held out her hand. Karen Matthews, looking

nervous, took her hand and stepped up to the podium. Flashbulbs went off in a flurry, and Karen ducked her head.

"You go, girl," Zoe whispered as she stepped back.

Karen took a deep breath and licked her dry lips. "I wish with all my heart that I could return each of these children back to their families. I wish I had known what my husband had been doing. I wish I could have done something to stop *all* of the murderers before they took your children from you. But wishes don't make anything different. People do."

She took another deep breath. "According to the Department of Justice, over half a million children disappear in this country every year. Over sixty thousand of them are never found. Six is too many. Sixty thousand is unacceptable.

"Of those sixty thousand abducted children, over one hundred are taken with the intent to kill. An overtaxed police force with limited resources is trying to find a needle in a haystack. We want to change that. And we can.

"Several businesses have joined with me in raising funds for a foundation that will help parents with missing children. We will provide resources to help them: detectives who specialize in child abductions; counseling services; information packets that include police procedures; Internet resources; and access to other agencies and churches. I don't want these children to have died in vain. I want their lives to reach beyond death—to help keep other children safe."

She took a deep breath, infused with a strength she didn't expect, and spoke for fifteen more minutes, then calling to the podium Keyes and Denise Shefford and the other business owners who were donating time and money to the foundation.

While Keyes Shefford spoke, Karen turned and hugged Zoe.

"Thank you," she whispered in Zoe's ear.

◆　◆　◆

Zoe knelt and carefully placed flowers next to the growing garden of color. She'd brought yellow roses. They stood out like sunshine among mostly red and orange blossoms left by other visitors.

"Hey, Amy. Sorry it took so long. But you're home now, I mean, not really, but you know what I mean. I just want you to know that I still miss you."

Slowly Zoe stood up and turned to walk back to her car. She saw him standing there and felt the aggravation surge again. "De-tective," she acknowledged in a cool voice. She stepped around him, pushing the keyless entry remote in her hand. Her car chirped as the door lock popped up.

She hadn't seen or heard from him since his brief hospital visit. That stung a little bit. Maybe more than a little bit.

"You have every reason to be miffed at me," he said, as if reading her mind.

"Do I?" She yanked open her car door.

"You were right."

"Was I?"

"I've been bitter and angry and taking it out on everyone instead of dealing with the reason."

Curious, Zoe turned and looked over her shoulder at him, noticing for the first time the dark circles under his eyes and the tight lines of tension around his mouth. She almost felt sorry for him. "And?"

"And I owe you an apology."

"Accepted." She slid into the car and reached for the door.

JJ stepped forward, blocking her effort. He leaned down, one hand braced on the roof of her car. "That day we first met, you brought up Macy and my dad."

"Yes?"

"My dad was the officer on the scene. Did you know that he was in on the investigation?"

Zoe stared out the windshield, trying to ignore the pain in his voice and her own need to make it better for him. She wasn't his savior. He'd have to find his own way, just like everyone else. "I knew."

"I blamed him. They never caught the guy who did it. I blamed my dad for that."

"I know."

"Zoe, I need some time to work through all this."

"You don't need my permission, JJ."

He lifted his head, stared at the sky, and exhaled sharply. "I'm not asking for your permission. I'm trying to apologize here."

"You apologized and I accepted. Done deal. What do you want from me, JJ?"

"I want to see you again."

Zoe shoved her key into the ignition and turned it. The engine roared. "We fight like cats and dogs, JJ. Why in heaven's name would you want to see me?"

He moved in a little closer, and a hint of smile danced at the corners of his mouth. *"Because* we fight like cats and dogs. Because you don't take any garbage from me and you're not afraid to tell me when I'm wrong. Because you have the most wonderful smile and you intrigue the daylights out of me."

"JJ, find your answers. Find peace with it all. And when you do, *if* you do, you have my number. That's all I can say right now."

"You're not going to make this easy for me, are you?"

Zoe couldn't help smiling. "Not on your life, Detective."

A Word from the Author

Nothing is more heart-wrenching to a mother than suddenly realizing a child is missing. For three hours one day, I experienced just a touch of what these parents go through. In my case, the state police search and rescue team found my seven-year-old autistic daughter safe and sound a little more than a mile from my home. But for many parents, the ending isn't a happy one.

While writing this novel, the ten-year-old daughter of a friend asked me what I was writing about. I told her I was writing about children being kidnapped. She said, "Oh," nonchalantly and proceeded to tell me that a friend of hers had been kidnapped. She then went on to tell me in graphic detail about her friend's abduction, torture, and murder. After researching many such cases, the details didn't strike me nearly as much as her calm acceptance of the event. To her, it was part of life. Such things were to be expected.

And that broke my heart.

Our children are being raised in a society in which such events are commonplace. They are losing friends and siblings to drive-by shootings, abductions, and worse, with little more than a shrug of their tiny shoulders. Innocence is lost and their senses barraged by violence. We have the power to change that. It begins with prayer. And for some of you, it means getting involved. I hope you will feel led to do something, even if it's just writing a check to help someone else bring a child home safe and sound.

For more information on how you can help bring our children home, please contact any of the following organizations:

Klass Kids Foundation: www.KlaasKids.org; (415) 331-6867
National Center for Missing and Exploited Children:
  www.missingkids.org; 1-800-The-Lost
Amber Alert Foundation: www.AmberAlertNow.org
Safe Kids International: www.SafeKidsInternational.com
Child Find: 1-800-I-Am-Lost

acknowledgments

With love to all those wonderful people that the Lord placed in my life to help make this book possible: Marlene Bagnull, Christi Horowitz, Tracie Peterson, Karen King, Joanie Barineau, Gary Mascelli, and all the prayer warriors who kept me undergirded. Gratitude and thanks to Mike Nappa, Shannon Hill, Tracie Peterson, and the people at Barbour.

Special thanks to the people at the U.S. Department of Justice, the KlaasKids Foundation, and the National Center for Missing and Exploited Children for their research assistance. And to law enforcement officers across this nation who work so hard to bring our children home—and especially the Maryland State Police for bringing my little girl back to me safe and sound.

Would you like to offer feedback on this novel?

Interested in starting a book discussion group?

Check out www.barbourpublishing.com
for a Reader Survey and Book Club Questions.